THE CHILDREN'S HOUR

From Many Lands

A BOOK TO GROW ON

THE CHILDREN'S HOUR

MARJORIE BARROWS, *Editor*

From
Many Lands

MATHILDA SCHIRMER
Associate Editor

DOROTHY SHORT
Art Editor

Grolier
INCORPORATED
NEW YORK

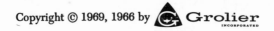
Standard Book Number 7172–1350–1
Library of Congress Catalog Card Number: 74–76542

PRINTED IN THE UNITED STATES OF AMERICA

Acknowledgments

The editor and publishers wish to thank the following publishers, agents, authors, and artists for permission to use and reprint stories, poems, and illustrations included in this book:

CONSOLIDATED BOOK PUBLISHERS for illustrations by Fiore Mastri for Louise De La Ramée's "The Nurenberg Stove."

MRS. CARYL MOON COREY for "The Silver Belt" by Carl Moon.

COWARD-McCANN, INC., for "Desert Adventure" from *Boy of the Desert* by Eunice Tietjens, copyright, 1928, by Eunice Tietjens.

THE ESTATE OF HENRY CREW for "The Baedeker Boy," "That Boy," and "The Macdonald Plaid" from *Saturday's Children* by Helen Coale Crew, published by Little, Brown & Company.

DOUBLEDAY & COMPANY, INC., for "The Desirable Shawl" from *Chee-Wee* by Grace Moon, copyright, 1925, by Doubleday & Company, Inc.

E. P. DUTTON & CO., INC., for the first stanza of "America the Beautiful" from *Poems* by Katharine Lee Bates.

HARCOURT, BRACE AND COMPANY, INC., for "How Birgit Danced in Her Red Shoes" from *The Seven Crowns* by Eleanor Frances Lattimore, copyright, 1933, by Harcourt, Brace and Company, Inc.

HOUGHTON MIFFLIN COMPANY for story and illustrations for "The Eskimo Twins Go Coasting" from *The Eskimo Twins* by Lucy Fitch Perkins.

J. B. LIPPINCOTT COMPANY for "The First Lamb" from *Children of North Africa* by Louise A. Stinetorf, copyright, 1943, by Louise A. Stinetorf.

LONGMANS, GREEN & CO., INC., for "The Skeleton Windmill" from *Racing the Red Sail* by Alice Geer Kelsey, copyright, 1947, by Alice Geer Kelsey; "Bim's Gift from the Forest" from *Gift of the Forest* by R. Lal Singh and Eloise Lownsbery, Chapters I and II, "Off to the Jungle" and "Gift of the Forest," with illustrations by Anne Vaughn, copyright, 1942, by R. Lal Singh and Eloise Lownsbery.

THE MACMILLAN COMPANY for story and illustrations for "The Forbidden Island" from *Call It Courage* by Armstrong Sperry; and "The Singing Saucepan" from *The Saucepan Journey* by Edith Unnerstad.

RANDOM HOUSE, INC., for "Who Is Who?" from *Mouseknees* by William C. White, copyright, 1939, by Random House, Inc.

RINEHART & COMPANY, INC., for "Boiling the Billy" by Faith Baldwin, and "Cake at Midnight" by Norma Bicknell Mansfield, from *Picnic Adventures*, copyright, 1940, by Rinehart & Company, Inc., Publishers.

STORY PARADE, INC., for "The Secret Staircase" by Melicent Humason Lee, copyright, 1942, by Story Parade, Inc.; "The Silver Llama" by Alida Malkus, copyright, 1938, by Story Parade, Inc.; and "The Monkey Spirit" by Martha Lee Poston, copyright, 1943, by Story Parade, Inc.

THE VIKING PRESS, INC., New York, for story and illustrations for "Easter Eggs" from *The Good Master* by Kate Seredy, copyright, 1935, by Kate Seredy; "Dobry's New Year" from *Dobry* by Monica Shannon, copyright, 1934, by Monica Shannon; and story and illustrations for "A Visit with Pierre" from *Canadian Summer* by Hilda van Stockum, copyright, 1948, by Hilda van Stockum Marlin.

CAROL RYRIE BRINK for "Farmer of Paimpol" first published in *Junior Red Cross Magazine*.

FLEMING H. CREW for "Tungwa" by Alice Crew Gall and Fleming H. Crew, first published in *Child Life Magazine*.

PHILLIS GARRARD for "The Fern Tiki" from *Hilda's Adventures* by Phillis Garrard, published by Blackie and Son, Ltd.

NAN GILBERT for "House of the Singing Windows" first published by Association for Childhood Education International.

HELEN TRAIN HILLES for "Going Up."

ELIZABETH FOREMAN LEWIS for "Hok-Hwa of the Waterfront."

WILLIS LINDQUIST for "The Curse of Kaing," first published by *Boys' Life*.

HARRY H. A. BURNE for illustrations for Willis Lindquist's "The Curse of Kaing," first appearing in *Boys' Life*.

MARGUERITE DAVIS for illustrations for Helen Train Hilles' "Going Up."

HAZEL FRAZEE for illustrations for Eunice Tietjens' "Desert Adventure."

JANET LAURA SCOTT for illustrations for Elizabeth Foreman Lewis' "Hok-Hwa of the Waterfront."

KEITH WARD for illustrations for Alice Crew Gall and Fleming H. Crew's "Tungwa."

Contents

WHAT happened on a holiday in Denmark.

Eleanor F. Lattimore

HOW BIRGIT DANCED IN HER RED SHOES

ILLUSTRATED BY *Esther Friend*

NEW things were happening every day, since it was spring. More and more flowers were growing in all the parks in Copenhagen, and more and more birds were singing in all the trees. Then there came a day that was more exciting than all the rest. This was Children's Day.

All that morning in school everyone felt restless. None of the little girls seemed to be able to keep her mind on her studies at all. Usually they worked very hard until the recess bell rang. Not a laugh would be heard, hardly a whisper.

Today, though, their minds were on something quite different from their studies. From where the teacher stood could be seen five rows of excited faces, with round excited eyes.

Birgit had on her best dress, which was white trimmed with red cross-stitching. She had on her best shoes, which were red too. Lisbet beside her kept whispering, "Children's Day, it's Children's Day!" But of course Birgit knew that already. That was why they were all so excited.

All the time Birgit was doing her sums and adding them all up wrong, she kept thinking of the afternoon. For then as soon as school was over, she was going down to the shops with Lisbet and Lisbet's sister.

There would be lots of fine sights to see there, she knew. There would be things to buy, too. In the pocket of Birgit's best dress there was a crown to spend. She had left her purse at home for fear she might lose it in the crowd.

1

As soon as the last bell had rung and school was over for the day, Birgit and Lisbet and all the rest went up as usual to the teacher to shake her hand and to say good-bye. But almost before they had left the classroom they were running.

In the hall outside were mothers and nurses and older sisters waiting for them. There, among the rest, was Lisbet's sister. She was four years older than Birgit and Lisbet, and big enough to take care of anyone.

Soon the three of them were hurrying along down the street, the big sister in the middle, with Lisbet and Birgit on either side of her. They were going to the center of the city, where things would be happening.

The city was so different today from the way it was on ordinary days that you could hardly recognize it. In all the many squares were little shops called booths where people sold things. They had not been there the day before. They were filled with toys and balloons, and ice cream in pasteboard cups.

All the money that was paid for these things was to be given to poor children and children in hospitals. That was why this was called Children's Day.

Lisbet and Lisbet's sister and Birgit all stopped in front of the first booth they came to. They were selling ice cream here.

Lisbet and Lisbet's sister and Birgit all remembered how much they liked ice cream and thought how thirsty they were. "I have just enough money to buy three cups of ice cream," said Lisbet's sister.

So she bought the ice cream. After it was eaten, she and Lisbet and Birgit all went to the next booth.

This was a very fancy booth. They were selling balloons here. The balloons were tied in bunches, purple ones and yellow ones and red ones. Birgit and Lisbet each wanted one, though the big sister said that *she* was too old for balloons.

However, Lisbet had a small silver coin of her own, so she said, "I will buy one for myself and one for Birgit."

When they left that booth Birgit and Lisbet each held a balloon by the string. The balloons bobbed above their heads as though they were talking to each other.

2

Then they came to the third booth. This one was filled with toys of all sorts, dolls and balls and tiny automobiles. "It's my turn to buy something now," said Birgit. She fished in her pocket for the crown she had brought.

"Can I buy three toys with one crown?" she asked anxiously, and the man in the booth said, "Yes."

So when they left that booth Lisbet had a doll, and her sister had a ball, and Birgit had a tiny car that she thought her smallest doll might like to ride in. But her crown was gone.

"We can't possibly buy anything more now," said Lisbet's sister. "We've got all that we can carry, and besides we have no more money." So they left the square where the booths were and wandered off down a street.

Everyone in Copenhagen seemed to be around the shops today, and everyone seemed gay. Bands were playing here and there. At all the street corners people dressed in fancy costumes were shaking boxes and holding out hats, collecting money for the poor children.

Birgit and Lisbet and Lisbet's sister began to feel sorry that they had spent all their money. They had nothing left to give.

Suddenly along the street a huge car came driving. Inside were children. The best part of the day had begun!

The children in the car were all dressed up. They were dressed to look like the people told about in Hans Andersen's stories. Birgit knew who they were all meant to be, because her grandmother had told her the stories many times, while she was knitting.

"Look, Lisbet!" she cried. "There's the Snow Queen!" And, "Look, Birgit!" said Lisbet, "there are Kay and Gerda."

The children in the car were all waving to the crowd of people on the sidewalk. They held out their hands as they went by, and the people in the crowd threw them coins. All the money that was thrown was to be given to poor children and children in hospitals.

Behind the first car came other cars. There were fairy-story people in them, too. There was The Little Mermaid beside her prince. And there was the witch who lived at the bottom of the

4

sea. There were Thumbelina, and The Brave Tin Soldier, and the soldier with the tinderbox. And there was even the dog with eyes as big as cartwheels.

Birgit as she watched them go by could hardly believe her eyes. They all looked just the way she had imagined they would look when her grandmother told her the stories.

"Oh, Lisbet," she said, "I wish I could be in a fairy tale, and drive around and collect money for poor children!"

"I wish I could too," said Lisbet. "But the trouble is we haven't any costumes."

Lisbet's sister looked down at Birgit's feet. "Birgit has red shoes," she said. "There is a story about a girl with red shoes."

Birgit looked down at her best shoes and then she looked at Lisbet's sister to see if she was joking. But she wasn't joking. Her face was perfectly serious.

"Good-bye," said Birgit quickly, handing her balloon to Lisbet and her toy automobile to her sister. Then she turned and hurried off after the cars filled with children!

But even though the cars were driving slowly they went more quickly then Birgit could run. This might not have been the case if there had not been so many people blocking the way, for Birgit was quite a fast runner. But as it was, she could not catch up with the cars. The last car finally passed out of sight. Birgit stopped on the sidewalk, wondering what to do.

Lisbet and her sister were nowhere to be seen. All around

her were tall grown-up people that she didn't know.

"Are you lost?" someone asked her.

"No," replied Birgit. "I was just trying to catch up with the children. I am the Girl with the Red Shoes."

"Oh, yes," said another person. "Of course you are. But the Girl with the Red Shoes danced, in the story. Can you dance?"

Birgit didn't answer, because she began to feel very shy. Everyone around her was looking at her now. But when a band near by began to play a tune she knew, she forgot that she was shy and danced a few steps.

The people gathered around her in a circle. They began to clap and to throw her money. She danced some more, and the people clapped still harder and threw her more money.

Everybody said, "This is a Hans Andersen child too. Don't you see? This is the Girl with the Red Shoes."

Birgit had never felt so proud and excited before. Her cheeks were nearly as red as her shoes now. Her hair flew about her head because both her bobby pins were lost. Her hat was on the sidewalk. Silver coins and copper coins were tossed into it as she danced. Some of them missed and rolled into the street. And all this money was for the poor children.

The band went on playing, and Birgit went on dancing, till suddenly an interruption came. "Birgit!" cried a voice.

Birgit stopped short and looked up. There, looking at her in astonishment, was her grandmother!

"Birgit," she said again, "what are you doing? Where are Lisbet and her sister? What have you done to your hat?"

Then before Birgit could answer she took her by the hand and started to lead her away. But, "Wait!" cried Birgit. "I must pick up my money!"

Then everybody who was there helped Birgit to collect the scattered coins. When the last one had been picked up there was a whole hatful of them.

"They're all for the poor children," Birgit explained, and her grandmother looked pleased.

"But you must not run away like that again," she said as she and Birgit went off to look for Lisbet and her sister.

Birgit had never felt so proud and excited before.

How a young French boy learns one
can be a hero on land as well as on sea.

Carol Ryrie Brink

FARMER OF PAIMPOL

ILLUSTRATED BY *Helen Prickett*

THE masts of a dozen ships pricked through
the mists of a damp February morning in Paimpol. The fishing
fleet was ready for the voyage to Iceland, and nearly two hundred of the stoutest men of the little town were sailing away
to be gone for six months. Six months of rough seas, of ice-
coated masts, of sudden gales and blinding snows, of decks
reeking with the smell of cod, and hands and garments stiff
with salt! There would be nights when the two-masted *goëlettes*
would toss and groan in laboring seas, and days when the
monotony of living a half year in one little boat would almost
drive men mad, and always there was the danger of sudden,
icy death.

Yet Perrik wanted to go. He wanted to go more than he had
ever wanted to do anything else. Yann was going this year for
the first time on *La Paimpolaise*. It was also the first time that
Perrik and Yann had not done everything together. They had
been like brothers ever since their fathers had gone down with
the *Ste. Anne* on the coast of Iceland many years ago. Little
Madame Guélou had lost her husband on the *Ste. Anne*, too,
and, having no one left, she had taken the two orphan boys
and reared them as her own. The pain of those far-off days had
long been forgotten, and Madame Guélou and her two boys
had been happy together.

Madame Guélou was silent now as she stood beside Perrik
on the quay and saw Yann make ready to depart. Yann had

grown into a great, broad-shouldered lad this year, and he looked very fine in his new blue jersey and oilskins.

"But I am almost as old as he," Perrik said bitterly. "If I had grown faster, they would have taken me, too. It is not right. I could be as useful about a boat as Yann. But instead of that I must be a farmer! A farmer of Paimpol!" All of the bitterness of a race of seafaring men was in Perrik's voice, when he said "farmer." Madame Guélou said nothing, but one of the young men on the boat called out: "Perrik will be raising artichokes," and everybody laughed.

One by one the ships went out of the basin on the full tide and were lost in the gray mist on their long journey to the coast of Iceland.

Madame Guélou touched Perrik's arm, and they turned away from the empty port. They had a long walk out toward the open sea before they reached home.

"I am not needed here," Perrik said. "If there were something here for me to do, there would be some sense in my staying. I am old enough to be a fisherman as my father was."

"There are many things to do here, Perrik," said Madame Guélou. "With two hundred men gone, there should be more than enough for the few who are left."

They walked on in silence, but, before they reached the cottage, Madame Guélou turned aside to a little churchyard which they had not visited for a long time. There were not many graves, but on the walls were many tablets. The tablets bore the names of men who had been lost at sea, in the *Ste. Anne, St. Liboubane,* and other ships. The names of Perrik's and Yann's fathers were there, along with that of Monsieur Guélou. The inscriptions on the tablets read: *Perdu en Islande—disparu en mer—qu'ils reposent en paix.*

The words echoed in Perrik's ears as he walked on: "Lost in Iceland—disappeared at sea—may they rest in peace." But it was a brave life all the same—better than staying home. Perhaps next year he could go. There were other words which rang more bitterly in his ears: "Perrik will be raising artichokes," and the laughter at his expense.

Madame Guélou had a little plot of ground about her cottage, and on it she raised flowers and a few vegetables which she carried in to market in the summer. She had a cow, too, which Perrik milked for her. It was a very frugal life which they led, and Perrik knew that it had often been difficult for the little woman to feed and clothe her two big boys. Now Yann would be able to contribute to her support, for he would have a percentage of his catch of codfish, but Perrik was still considered too young to help. The thought was sharp and bitter in his heart.

The cold mists of February drifted away, and March came in with keen, strong winds from the sea. Perrik thought of Yann's ship tossing somewhere in dark, foam-laced waters. There would be no news of her until August when the Iceland fishers began to return.

One March night Madame Guélou's cow was taken sick. Perrik noticed at milking time that her head drooped and her hay stood untouched. In the night her mournful bawling reached the cottage, and Perrik and Madame Guélou left their beds and hurried to look at her. Madame heated water and applied what simple remedies she knew, but the cow was no better. The little widow and her boy looked at each other in the yellow lantern light. If the cow died, their living would be poor indeed.

"If only Monsieur Yffiniac were here! He would know what to do. By morning it will be too late."

"I will fetch him," said Perrik. He took the lantern and set off along the dark, long path to Paimpol. It was not an easy walk by day, and on a stormy March night it would have been impossible for Madame Guélou. Perrik made use of his seaman's sense of direction, using the lighthouse which flashed behind him and the scattered lights of Paimpol to keep him on his course. He brought Monsieur Yffiniac back with him in time to save the cow.

"Ah, Perrik!" cried Madame Guélou, "if you had not been here, we should have lost our cow." Perrik said nothing, but something new began to swell in his heart. Monsieur Yffiniac

9

stayed for morning coffee. He was an old man, too old for the
sea, and he was wise in the ways of both sea and land. In the
clear morning sunlight he looked about the little patch of farm.

"You have a good place for artichokes here," he said.

"Artichokes!" cried Perrik angrily. Was Monsieur Yffiniac
making fun of him, too?

"Yes," said the old man. "They are a great delicacy in Paris,
and they say that there is good money in them. I have seen
great fields of them near St. Pol-de-Léon and Roscoff. You have
the same kind of soil and climate here. Why don't you try
them?"

April and May slipped by, and the stern Breton coast began
to blossom into lines of gentleness. Perrik thought of Yann with
the dark sea rolling about the *goëlette*. The hold would be half
full of salted cod by now. The masts might still be white with
frost, and the decks would certainly be white with salt. The
little china Virgin would still hang smiling behind her lamp in
the smoke-stained cabin. It was a brave life, but the first sting
of Perrik's disappointment was past. He bent his back in sun
and wind over Madame Guélou's little patch of ground, and
around him in June billowed a sea of artichokes. They were like
big, green roses, and Perrik carried them in to market, when
Madame Guélou carried in her baskets of flowers.

At the end of July Perrik and Madame Guélou had made a
tidy profit on the artichokes. So artichokes were not a joke after

10

all! And then early in August the first of the Iceland ships came in. It was not *La Paimpolaise*. Perrik went in town to see it come to dock. He helped unload and weigh the slabs of yellow fish until his hands were stiff and cracked with salt. News of *La Paimpolaise?* No, she had not been sighted for months.

This was the uneasy time of year. Old men, women, and children climbed to the top of Tour de Kerroch or out to the high point where the Widow's Cross stood, and looked far out to sea, straining their eyes for the sight of a schooner. One by one the boats returned—all but *La Paimpolaise*.

It was almost the end of August, and Madame Guélou's little, wind-browned face grew drawn and lined with anxiety. She and Perrik said little, but Yann's return was always in their minds. When the last of the other boats had been in for several days, Madame Guélou made a pilgrimage to St. Loup le Petit to light a candle before the image of the saint. Perrik knew the old tradition of the country, which so many of the women believed, that if the candle flame burned brightly, the son or husband was still safe; if it flickered and went out, he had been lost at sea.

When Madame Guélou returned, her face was relaxed into lines of peace.

"The candle burned," she said. But Perrik's faith in the old superstitions was not as strong as Madame Guélou's. He found it hard to sleep at night, knowing that Yann was still at sea. Often he rose and went down to the beach, standing beside the little light that flashed its beacon to the returning ships before they entered the narrow channel that led to the harbor of Paimpol. A very old man, who had long returned from the Iceland fishing, kept the light, and sometimes Perrik wondered how long the old man could continue to keep it, and who would succeed him when he had grown too old.

Toward the end of August, stormy weather blew in from the sea. The pines around the Tour de Kerroch lashed and groaned in the wind. The waves burst in bombs of spray on the rocks outside the channel and harbor. Inside the harbor, the returned ships lay snug and still, but *La Paimpolaise* was still missing.

11

Perrik rose in the dark and lighted his lantern. He could not sleep with the sound of wind in the chimney and waves on the open sea, and, as he ran, he knew that something was wrong. It was the light. The little tower that held it was silent and dark. There were no warning flashes over the sea. He ran to the door of the tower and shook it, but it was locked and there was no reply to his pounding.

Suddenly, borne on the sea wind, Perrik heard the creaking of cordage, the faint shouts of men. A ship was coming in, and there was no light to tell her how near to the rocks she was. Going as far out on the rocks as he could, Perrik ran up and down, swinging his lantern back and forth and shouting. Now he could see the lights of the ship. Would they see *his* light before it was too late? His voice was hoarse with shouting, his arm ached with swinging the lantern. Still he shouted and ran, the foam breaking about his feet on the slippery rocks. Would they never see him? But at last there was a hail from the ship. She began to put about for deeper water. She was safe. Clear on the wind came the sound of her anchor chain dropping.

In the morning Perrik was the first to see her, lying at anchor in the clear summer dawn—and she was *La Paimpolaise.*

"Yes," said Yann proudly, with his arm about Perrik's shoulder. "It is best that some young men stay at home. We came through the perils of Iceland, but we should have been lost at the very doors of Paimpol, if Perrik had not stayed at home to save us."

"And another thing!" cried Madame Guélou. "It was a disgrace to the town that only old men should be left to tend the lights. Think of that poor old man in the tower, struck with paralysis and unable to move to tend his light! Assuredly we need some brave *young* men in Paimpol."

Perrik smiled. The sting of being left behind was all gone now. He, Perrik, was to be the new lighthouse keeper, the youngest keeper on the Breton coast, and he would have time for his artichokes, too. One could be brave and steadfast on land as well as sea, it seemed.

13

A story about Chi-wee, a little Indian
girl in America.

Grace Moon

THE DESIRABLE SHAWL

ILLUSTRATED BY *I. Heilbron*

What matters the shade of a little maid's skin
If her heart is the kind that is right, within?
If it sings with the song of the nighthawk's cry,
And leaps to the pink of the pale dawn sky?
There are hearts that are wild, and
    hearts that are tame.
But hearts that are true are ever the same!

IT WAS a beautiful shawl. Chi-wee, the
little Indian girl could see that across the Trader's store: dark
blue on one side and glowing red on the other, with a fringe
of the same two colors, and it looked warm and soft and *much*
to be desired.

Chi-wee saw the look in her mother's eyes as she passed her
hand over its surface, and in her heart a fierce little voice said:

"My mother shall *have* that shawl. The Good Spirit made
that shawl to be for *my mother.*"

It was trading day for Chi-wee and her mother. In the early
morning they had come in the wagon of Mah-pee-ti, the sheepherder, with the jars that Chi-wee's mother had made, to trade
them at the store for food and clothing.

It was a long ride in the bumpety old wagon from the high
mesa town to the canyon store, a ride over the wide desert of
many-changing colors and up and down sandy washes, but it
was a ride that Chi-wee loved and of which she never tired.

There were so many living things to see on the way: prairie
dogs and lizards and horned toads; sheep and, sometimes, away
in the distance, an antelope or a gray coyote. And then there
was always the excitement of wondering, when they bumped
down into a very deep wash, whether Mah-pee-ti's old wagon

14

would hold together until they got up the other side.

But it always did and it always had for as many years as Chi-wee could remember, for once a month they had taken this ride in the same old wagon ever since Chi-wee had been old enough to sit by herself instead of being carried in the shawl on her mother's back. The wagon looked now as it had looked then. Like the desert and the pueblo where she lived, it did not seem to change.

Chi-wee came close to the shawl and felt it with her fingers. It was as soft as it looked, and very warm.

"You will buy it, my mother?" she asked, eagerly, laying her cheek on the soft wool.

Her mother shook her head a little sadly.

"No, my little one," she said. "We must trade today for food and not for things we do not need."

"But you *need* a shawl, *this* shawl," said Chi-wee. "You *know*, my mother, that you need it!"

"We will not speak of it more," said her mother, turning away. "We have money for food only." And she spoke to the Trader of the flour and sugar and grain that she needed.

Chi-wee stood looking down at the shawl, and queer thoughts were in her mind, but above them all was the firm resolution: My mother *shall have* this soft, beautiful shawl!

She waited until her mother had carried some of the food out to the wagon and then she went to the Trader. He was a pleasant man and had always spoken kind words to Chi-wee, so she had no fear of him.

"What is the price of that shawl?" she asked him. "The soft blue one with the red underside?"

"Six dollars," answered the Trader, with a kindly smile for Chi-wee. "It's all wool and very warm." There was a thoughtful look in Chi-wee's eyes as her little hand went to her throat and opened the collar of her cotton waist.

"Look," she said, softly, to the Trader, "this is a very beautiful necklace that I have on. See, the shells are the color of the sky when the sun comes up—pink. I—I—think it is a very beautiful necklace." The Trader stooped and looked at it.

15

"Yes," he nodded, "I would give you two dollars for the necklace, if you care to sell it."

Her face fell, and her fingers touched the pink shells tenderly.

"Two dollars? I—I—thought—you see, it is the shawl I want—"

"I'm sorry," said the Trader, gently, "but the shawl is worth more, little girl. No, I could not exchange it for the necklace."

Chi-wee felt her heart grow very heavy, and all the way home in the bumpety wagon she had no eyes for the lizards and little hares and prairie dogs that scuttled out of their way, nor for the wonderful colors of the tumbleweeds and cactus, or the far-away blue buttes. Her mind was busy with plans to earn money for the wonderful shawl, but *how?*

There were very few ways to earn money in the high mesa town. She could weave a very little. An old man in the pueblo had taught her that. But that took a long time and money, too, to buy the colored wools, and pottery she could not yet make well enough to sell.

She could help pick peaches and apricots, but now it was not the time for them, and anyway they gave her but a few pennies for that. And she had nothing to sell, nothing but the necklace, her one treasure. The Trader had told her that was worth only two dollars, and the shawl cost six!

Oh, but it was a very difficult thing, this earning money. She could not understand how other people did it. But not for a moment did she give up the thought of getting the shawl for her mother. It was just *how* to get it that puzzled her.

When next they went to the Trader's, Chi-wee looked eagerly for the shawl, and she felt that her heart almost stopped beating when she did not see it where it had been before. Of course others would see how beautiful it was and buy it; others who had six dollars and even more, others who did not have to wait and plan. She felt the hot tears stinging her eyelids. *Never* had her heart been so set on anything as on that beautiful blue shawl with its red underside!

"Has it been sold?" she asked the Trader, in a voice she could not quite keep from shaking, "That—beautiful shawl—has it been sold?"

16

He looked at her for a moment with a little puzzled frown.

"The shawl?" he asked, and then a look of remembrance came into his eyes as he laughed a little. "No, it is still here, did you want to buy it?"

A sudden resolve came into Chi-wee's heart, it almost frightened her.

"Yes," she said, quickly, and looked to see that her mother was beyond hearing. "I want to buy it, but I have not the money, not *all* now. Here!" And with trembling fingers she unclasped the little shell necklace and thrust it into his hand. "I will bring more next time. Could you, oh, could you keep it a little while for me?"

There was such eagerness in the little voice, such a look in the eyes, and such a tremble all through the small figure that the Trader could not help but see it. From surprise the expression in his eyes softened, and he put his hand on Chi-wee's head.

"How old are you, little girl?" he asked, unexpectedly.

"Seven, I think," answered Chi-wee, in a surprised voice. "My mother tells me, yes, she tells me, seven."

"Ah," said the man, slowly, and the look in his eyes was far away but very tender, "my little girl would have been seven now. Yes," he added, suddenly changing his voice, "I will keep the shawl for you, little girl of the mesa, until you bring the rest of the money," and he turned to the others who had entered his store.

Chi-wee felt as if she walked on air as she went to the wagon. The shawl was hers, *hers*—almost! And "almost" was such a *little* word that she nearly forgot it altogether. Those warm, soft folds would rest on her mother's shoulders, and that lovely red would gleam as she walked. How proud she would feel that *she*, Chi-wee, had bought and paid for it herself. Yes, and her heart dropped a little at the thought, but *how* was she going to pay for it herself?

The next month was a very busy one for Chi-wee and a happy one, too, and had her mother not been very occupied with her own work she must have noticed something strange about Chi-wee's actions. She seemed to be hiding something,

17

and there were trips she made into the desert for which she gave no explanation.

When the next trading day came there was a bumpy place under the little girl's shawl that had not been there on other trips, and when she handed the Trader a great jar of wild honey her heart was beating fast with excitement and happiness.

She did not tell of the labor she had had in getting it, nor of the painful lump on her arm that told of the angry stinging of a bee, but there was deep pride in her voice as she said: "I have brought this to pay some more for the shawl. Next time I will bring something else."

There was a look she could not understand in the Trader's eyes as he took the honey, but he turned to a white stranger who was standing near. She could not catch the words, and when he turned back to her she still could not understand the look in his eyes.

"I have other shawls," she suddenly heard him saying to her. "You will not mind that this gentleman has bought the blue one with the red underside?"

To Chi-wee it seemed as if the world turned black. Her shawl! Her precious shawl! To go to this stranger! She could not speak. Words would not come. Everything began to swim through the sudden tears in her eyes. She saw the stranger man walk to the door with a bundle under his arm, and the Trader turned his back to her to attend to those who waited at his counter. It could not be true. People could *not* be so cruel!

Chi-wee stumbled out of the store and into the waiting wagon with a storm of anger and grief in her heart. But she did not cry. She sat in silence all the way home and tried to think why white people did things that no Indian could ever do.

At their home door her mother called to her to help with the parcels in the wagon.

"And take this great one," she said, "that the white stranger said you had bought from the Trader. With what could you buy, little daughter?"

Chi-wee opened her eyes wide and stood still. What could it mean? Her mother placed a great bundle in her arms,

18

wrapped in white paper. Soft it felt, soft like a baby!

She did not wait to think, but tore open the paper, there before her door. IT WAS THE SHAWL—HER SHAWL! And tied to one corner was a little card with words printed on it in ink. She could read them with difficulty. She wished now she had taken more lessons from the teacher lady at the Mission school.

"It is your love for your mother that has bought this shawl, little girl of the mesa. And it is my love for another little girl like you that gives you back your precious treasure. White hearts are just the same as Indian ones, inside!"

And there, beside the shawl, wrapped in a bit of paper, was her pink shell necklace!

Now Chi-wee *did* cry, but the tears were just for happiness as she hugged the shawl and her mother who did not yet understand, and the pink necklace that had come home again!

She did not know then or afterward whether it was the Trader himself or the white stranger who had given her the shawl, as the Trader would not say, but to Chi-wee it did not matter, for she had learned a great secret, one that you and I know already; that "white hearts are just the same as Indian ones, inside!"

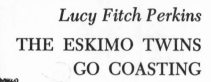

Lucy Fitch Perkins

THE ESKIMO TWINS
GO COASTING

ILLUSTRATED BY THE AUTHOR

THIS is the true story of Menie and Monnie and their two little dogs, Nip and Tup.

Menie and Monnie are twins, and they live far away in the North, near the very edge.

They are five years old.

Menie is the boy, and Monnie is the girl. But you cannot tell which is Menie and which is Monnie—not even if you look ever so hard at their pictures!

That is because they dress alike.

When they are a little way off, even their own mother can't always tell. And if *she* can't, who can?

Sometimes the Twins almost get mixed up about it themselves. And then it is very hard to know which is Nip and which is Tup, because the little dogs are twins, too.

Nobody was surprised that the little dogs were twins, because dogs often are.

But everybody in the whole village where Menie and Monnie live was simply astonished to see twin babies!

The name of the Twins' father was Kesshoo. If you say it fast it sounds just like a sneeze.

Their mother's name was Koolee. Kesshoo and Koolee, and Menie and Monnie, and Nip and Tup, all live together in the cold Arctic winter in a little stone hut, called an igloo.

One spring morning, very early, while the moon still shone and everyone else in the village was asleep, Menie and Monnie

20

crept out of the dark entrance of their stone house by the sea.

The entrance to their little stone house was long and low like a tunnel. The Twins were short and fat. But even if they were short they could not stand up straight in the tunnel.

So they crawled out on all fours. Nip and Tup came with them. Nip and Tup were on all fours, too, but they had run that way all their lives, so they could go much faster than the Twins. They got out first.

Then they ran round in circles in the snow and barked at the moon. When Menie and Monnie came out of the hole, Tup jumped up to lick Monnie's face. He bumped her so hard that she fell right into the snowbank by the entrance.

Monnie didn't mind a bit. She just put her two fat arms around Tup, and they rolled over together in the snow.

Monnie had on her fur suit, with fur hood and mittens, and it was hard to tell which was Monnie and which was Tup as they tumbled in the snow together.

Pretty soon Monnie picked herself up and shook off the snow. Then Tup shook himself, too. Menie was rolling over and over down the slope in front of the little stone house. His head was between his knees, and his hands held his ankles, so he rolled just like a ball.

Nip was running round and round him and barking with all his might. They made strange shadows on the snow in the moonlight.

Monnie called to Menie. Menie straightened himself out at the bottom of the slope, picked himself up and ran back to her.

"What shall we play?" said Monnie.

"Let's get Koko, and go to the Big Rock and slide downhill," said Menie.

"All right," said Monnie. "You run and get your sled."

Menie had a little sled, which his father had made for him out of driftwood. No other boy in the village had one. Menie's father had searched the beach for many miles to find driftwood to make this sled.

The Eskimos have no wood but driftwood, and it is so precious that it is hardly ever used for anything but big dog

21

sledges or spears, or other things which the men must have.

Most of the boys had sleds cut from blocks of ice. Menie's sled was behind the igloo. He ran to get it, and then the Twins and the pups—all four—started for Koko's house.

Koko's house was clear at the other end of the village. But that was not far away, for there were only five igloos in the whole town.

First there was the igloo where the Twins lived. Next was the home of Akla, the Angakok, and his two wives. Then there were two igloos where several families lived together. Last of all was the one where Koko and his father and mother and baby brother lived.

Koko was six. He was the Twins' best friend.

The air was very still. There was not a sound anywhere except the barking of the pups, the voices of Menie and Monnie, and the creaking sound of the snow under their feet as they ran.

22

The round moon was sailing through the deep blue sky and shining so bright it seemed almost as light as day.

There was one window in each igloo right over the tunnel-entrance, and these windows shone with a dull yellow light.

In front of the village lay the sea. It was covered with ice far out from shore. Beyond the ice was the dark water out of which the sun would rise by and by.

There was nothing else to be seen in all the Twins' world. There were no trees, no bushes even—nothing but the white earth, the shadows of the rocks and the snow-covered igloos, the bright windows, and the moon shining over all.

Menie and Monnie soon reached Koko's igloo. Menie and Nip got there first. Monnie came puffing along with Tup just a moment after.

Then the Twins dropped on their hands and knees in front of Koko's hut, and stuck their heads into the tunnel. Nip and Tup stuck their heads in, too.

They all four listened. There was not a sound to be heard except loud snores! The snores came rattling through the tunnel with such a frightful noise that the Twins were almost scared.

"They sleep out loud, don't they?" whispered Monnie.

"Let's wake them up," Menie whispered back.

Then the Twins began to bark. "Ki-yi, ki-yi, ki-yi, ki-yi," just like little dogs!

Nip and Tup began to yelp, too. The snores and the yelps met in the middle of the tunnel, and the two together made such a dreadful sound that Koko woke up at once.

When he heard four barks he knew right away that it must be the Twins and the little dogs.

So he stuck his head into the other end of the tunnel and called, "Keep still. You'll wake the baby! I'll be there in a minute."

Very soon Koko popped out of the black hole. He was dressed in a fur suit and mittens just like the Twins.

The three children went along together toward the Big Rock. Monnie rode on the sled, and Menie and Koko pulled it. The Big Rock was very straight up and down on one side, and long

23

and slanting on the other. The Twins were going to coast down the slanting side.

They climbed to the top, and Menie had the first ride. He coasted down on his stomach with his little reindeer-skin kamiks (shoes) waving in the air.

Next Koko had a turn. What do you think he did? He stood straight up on the sled with the leather cord in his hand, and slid down that way! But then, you see, he was six.

When Monnie's turn came she wanted to go down that way, too. But Menie said, "No. You'd fall off and bump your nose! You have hardly any nose as it is, and you'd better save it!"

"I have as much nose as you have, anyway," said Monnie.

"Mine is bigger! I'm a boy!" said Menie.

Koko measured their noses with his finger.

"They are just exactly alike," he said.

Monnie turned hers up at Menie and said, "What did I tell you?"

Menie never said another word about noses. He just changed the subject. He said, "Let's all slide down at once."

Koko and Menie sat down on the sled. Monnie sat on Menie. Then they gave a few hitches to the sled and off they went.

Whiz! How they flew!

The pups came running after them. In some places where it was very slippery the pups coasted, too! But they did not mean to. They did not like it. The sled was almost at the end of the slide when it struck a piece of ice. It flew around sideways and spilled all the children in the snow.

Just then Nip and Tup came sliding along behind them. They couldn't stop, so there they all were in a heap together, with the dogs on top!

Menie rolled over and sat up in the snow. He was holding on to the end of his nose. "Iyi, iyi!" he howled, "I bumped my nose on a piece of ice!"

Monnie sat up in the snow, too. She pointed her fur mitten at Menie's nose and laughed. "Don't you know you haven't much nose?" she said. "You ought to be more careful of it!"

Koko kicked his feet in the air and laughed at Menie, and

the little dogs barked. Menie thought he'd better laugh, too. He had just let go of his nose to begin when all of a sudden the little dogs stopped barking and stood very still!

Their hair stood up on their necks, and they began to growl!

"Hark, the dogs see something," said Menie.

Monnie and Koko stopped laughing and listened. They could not hear anything. They could not see anything. Still Nip and Tup growled. The Twins and Koko were children of brave hunters, so, although they were scared, they crept very quietly to the side of the Big Rock and peeped over.

Just that minute there was a dreadful growl! "Woof!" It was very loud, and very near, and down on the beach a shadow was moving! It was the shadow of a great white Bear!

He was looking for fish and was cross because everything was frozen, and he could not find any on the beach.

The moment they saw him, the Twins and Koko turned and ran for home as fast as ever their short legs could go! They did not even stop to get the precious sled. They just ran and ran.

Nip and Tup ran, too, with their ears back and their little tails stuck straight out behind them!

If they had looked back, they would have seen the bear stand up on his hind legs and look after them, then get down on all fours and start toward the Big Rock on a run.

But neither the children nor the little dogs looked back! They just ran with all their might until they reached the Twins' igloo. Then they all dived into the tunnel like frightened rabbits.

When they came up in the one little room of the igloo at the other end of the tunnel, Kesshoo and Koolee were just crawling out of the warm fur covers of their bed. Menie and Monnie and Koko and the little dogs all began to talk at once.

The moment the Twins' father and mother heard the word *bear* they jumped off the sleeping-bench and began to put on their clothes.

They both wore fur trousers and long kamiks, with coats of fur, so they looked almost as much alike in their clothes as the Twins did in theirs.

The mother always wore her hair in a topknot on top of her

25

head, tied with a leather thong. But now she wanted to make the bear think she was a man, too, so she pulled it down and let it hang about her face, just as her husband did.

In two minutes they were ready. Then the father reached for his lance, the mother took her knife, and they all crawled out of the tunnel.

The father went first, then the mother, then the three children and the pups. At the opening of the tunnel the father stopped, and looked all around to see if the bear were near.

The dogs in the village knew by this time that some strange animal was about, and the moment Kesshoo came out into the moonlight and started for the Big Rock, all the dogs ran, too, howling like a pack of wolves.

Kesshoo shouted back to his wife: "There really is a bear! I see him by the Big Rock; call the others."

So she sent Monnie into the igloo of the Angakok, and Menie and Koko into the next huts. She herself screamed, "A bear! A bear!" into the tunnel of Koko's hut.

The people in the houses had heard the dogs bark and were already awake. Soon they came pouring out of their tunnels armed with knives and lances. The women had all let down their hair, just as the Twins' mother did. Each one carried her knife.

They all ran toward the Big Rock, too. Far ahead they could see the bear, and the dogs bounding along, and Kesshoo running with his lance in his hand.

Then they saw the dogs spring upon the bear. The bear stood up on his hind legs and tried to catch the dogs and crush them in his arms. But the dogs were too nimble. The bear could not catch them.

When Kesshoo came near, the bear gave a great roar, and started for him. The brave Kesshoo stood still with his lance in his hand, until the bear got quite near. Then he ran at the bear and plunged the lance into his side. The lance pierced the bear's heart. He groaned, fell to the ground, rolled over, and was still.

Then how everybody ran! Koko's mother had her baby in her hood, where Eskimo mothers always carry their babies. She

26

could not run so fast as the others. The Angakok was fat, so
he could not keep up—but he waddled along as fast as he could.

"Hurry, hurry," he called to his wives. "Bespeak one of his
hind legs for me."

Menie and Monnie and Koko had such short legs they could
not go very fast either, so they ran along with the Angakok,
and Koko's mother, and Nip and Tup.

When they reached the bear they found all the other people
crowded around it. Each one stuck his fingers in the bear's
blood and then sucked his fingers. This was because they
wanted all bears to know how they longed to kill them. As each
one tasted the blood, he called out the part of the bear he would
like to have.

The wives of the Angakok cried: "Give a hind leg to the
Angakok."

"The kidneys for Koko," cried Koko's mother when she stuck
in her finger. "That will make him a great bear-hunter when
he is big."

"And the skin for the Twins' bed," said their mother.

Kesshoo promised each one the part he asked for. An Eskimo
never keeps the game he kills for himself alone. Everyone in
the village has a share.

27

The bear was very large. He was so large that though all the women pulled together they could not drag the body back to the village. The men laughed at them, but they did not help them.

So Koolee ran back for their sledge and harnesses for the dogs. Koko and Menie helped her catch the dogs and hitch them to the sledge.

It took some time to catch them, for the dogs did not want to work. They all ran away, and Tooky, the leader of the team, pretended to be sick! Tooky was the mother of Nip and Tup, and she was a very clever dog. While Koolee and Koko and Menie were getting the sledge and dog-team ready, the rest of the women set to work with their queer crooked knives to take off the bear's skin. The moon set, and the sky was red with the colors of the dawn before this was done.

At last the meat was cut in pieces, and Kesshoo and Koko's father held the dogs while the women heaped it on the sledge. The dogs wanted the meat. They jumped and howled and tried to get away.

When everything was ready, Koolee cracked the whip at the dogs. Tooky ran ahead to her place as leader, the other dogs began to pull, and the whole procession started back to the village, leaving a great red stain on the clean white snow where the bear had been killed.

Last of all came the Twins and Koko. They had loaded the bear's skin on Menie's sled.

"It's a woman's work to pull the meat home. We men just do the hunting and fishing," Menie said to Koko. They had heard the men say that.

"Yes, we *found* the bear," Koko answered. "Monnie can pull the skin home."

And though Monnie had found the bear just as much as they had, she didn't say a word. She just pulled away on the sled, and they all reached the igloo together just as the round red sun came up out of the sea and threw long blue shadows far across the fields of snow.

28

A Mexican mystery.

Melicent Humason Lee

THE SECRET STAIRCASE

ILLUSTRATED BY *Carol Stoaks*

SLOWLY Pancho left his little blue house on the hilltop in this village of Mexico. He carried three square tiles on his head—the last tiles his father had made before he was killed a week ago in a street accident. The tiles were bound together by a strong rope. He held up one hand to keep them steady. In his white homespun jacket and trousers, he swung down the narrow trail to the market far below.

His mother stood in the yellow-trimmed doorway and waved good-bye to him.

"*Vaya Usted con Dios!*" she called. "God be with you."

Down the trail Pancho trudged with his burden. The burden was heavy, but his heart was heavier still. When he had sold the last three tiles, what could he do for his widowed mother? It would take him a long time to learn to make good tiles like those of his father. The red clay was on the bank near the little blue house, the brick kiln for firing the tiles was in back of the

29

house, but some years and patience must come before he could make tiles good enough to sell. And in the meantime . . .

"What shall I do? What shall I do?" whispered the song of his bare brown feet on the earth. "What shall I do in the meantime?"

Down, down to the market he trudged—down between little twisty streets and houses of rainbow colors, and gardens behind mud-brick walls, and pigs and goats and dogs in the alleys. Down, down.

Many Indians passed him on the way to market, calling out a cheery *"Adiós!"* They were not so poor as he, and they felt sorry for him, and their greetings were as merry as they could make them. A buxom Indian woman with long braids swinging trotted past him with a basket of fresh eggs on her head, and an old woman with a turkey tucked under her arm brushed so close to him that the turkey feathers tickled his cheek. A strong man with a homemade ladder on his back, and an old man with a net of squashes hurried by, and so on.

Nobody but Pancho had just three last tiles.

Now Pancho came into the village park. Trees with sun-splashed leaves lined the walks, a bright, foaming fountain

shone in the center where Indian women were filling water jars, and children were sitting on the fountain's rim stringing queer seeds that had fallen from the trees. Everywhere were chucklings and laughter and merry calls. Everyone had a happy heart but Pancho.

"What shall I do? What shall I do? What shall I do in the meantime?" he thought.

He pattered along the tile walks of the park to a long, cobbled road that led downhill to the market. At the foot of the road near the market was a little blue church with a tower, and from the belfry of the tower jangled cheery bells. Streams of Indians were trotting down the street with their wares, and some of them were passing into the church to rest a while and pray.

Indians were coming from all the villages around Pancho's village, for it was the big Saturday market day. Indians came from the hot country with armadillos to cook for supper, bouquets of orchids, baskets of bananas, pineapples, papayas. Indians came from the mountains with warm wool blankets in natural color, or dyed scarlet and green, with designs such as only Indians can make. Indians came from the middle lands with sacks of corn.

Nobody but Pancho came with just three tiles.

Pancho reached the busy market at the foot of the street and pushed his way into the crowd. Soon he found a sunny seat on a mud-brick wall where he could watch the venders and buyers, or over his shoulder see the cattle and sheep and baby calves and pigs and oxen for sale in the outdoor pen.

A great feeling of loneliness swept over Pancho as he watched the crowd. What could he take to market the next day and the next day and the next day?

"What shall I do? What shall I do? What shall I do in the meantime?"

Then, while he was looking at two black goats butting each other in the pen, he heard someone calling to him in Spanish, "Boy! You have just what I want! Three tiles in the right size."

Like all village Indians, Pancho knew Spanish. He turned quickly, hopped down from the wall, and faced an old lady.

31

She wore a rusty black scarf around her head, and a long, black, crinkly dress with a white, patched collar and a small gold brooch, and her shabby shoes were square-toed.

"Good day, señora!" said the boy, politely, making a neat bow such as his mother had taught him. "Do you wish to buy the tiles?"

Soon a bargain was made, for Mexicans always bargain before buying, and the three tiles belonged to the old lady.

"I will give you three more *centavos* for carrying them home for me," she said. "Come!" And she led the way up the hill.

Pancho was very much surprised when she turned into an old street which had once been one of the finest streets. Walls of mellow, creamy white rose up on either side, with barred windows and carved doors tucked into them. Spanish nobles had lived there in the days when Mexico was a Spanish colony.

The old lady took a rusty key from the folds of her faded skirt and opened a small carved door. A knocker in the shape of a pig hung from the door. She led the way into a cobbled passage, which pierced the thick walls of the house. She rustled down a long tiled gallery which lined one of the four sides of a patio where bright hollyhocks and four o'clocks and Job's tears were blooming. She vanished into a doorway far beyond.

Pancho peeked into the rooms he passed as he followed her. They were almost bare. Only a few pieces of rude, homemade furniture were scattered among them. He followed the señora into the last room. It was a curious room. The ceiling was gone, letting in the blue sky, black buzzards perched on cracked walls, and a heap of tiles lay in one corner on the bare ground.

"Earthquake," explained the lady in black.

" Sí, señora. Yes, señora," said Pancho, who thought nothing of earthquakes. "Where shall I put the tiles, señora?"

"On the other tiles in the corner," said she.

Pancho carefully laid down his tiles. He felt sorry for the old lady. She would have much work to do to restore this room, and she seemed poor.

"May I help you lay down the tiles again?" he asked. He knew how to lay tiles even if he didn't know how to make them.

32

"You may help me today," said she, "but I can use you no longer."

Pancho guessed that she didn't have enough *centavos* to pay him for more than one day's work. He would give her a good start. He imagined that she was renting this cracked old house for a few *centavos* a week.

He began scraping the earth with a shovel which he found in one corner. The old lady left him and rustled down the gallery. Soon he could smell pink beans cooking. The smell of the good beans made him hungry.

He smoothed out the earth in one corner of the room. He laid one tile—his own. He laid another tile—his own. He laid a third tile—his own. Then he found that the earth was not quite smooth enough for a fourth tile. The earth was very hard at this spot. He seized a pick which he found in the corner where the shovel had been. He picked the ground with it, and suddenly the earth fell away into a cavity below, and at the same time he felt the cold air rushing into his face. He peered down into the hole he had made and found a tiny stone staircase, leading down into the darkness!

His heart jumped. His mother had told him about secret staircases in the old Spanish houses. She had been a serving maid in an old house once. He made the hole a little wider and crept through it. He began slipping and sliding down the worn steps of the staircase into the dark and dampness beyond.

At the foot of the staircase he found a small, wooden jewel box with a fancy iron lock. The lock was rusty and gave way at his touch. He pushed back the rounded lid of the box. A long string of something that looked like the Job's tears in the garden leaped to his sight. Soft, cloud-colored pearls!

He pulled them out of the box. They shone in his hands from the light that fell into the opening above. Pearls! A fortune, he knew, for his mother had told him stories about pearls.

Then a secret look stole over Pancho's face. He peered upward. No one was in sight. He heard no one. No one would know. The pearls belonged to him! He had found them. The old lady didn't own the house—he felt sure of that. She was

33

renting it for a few *centavos* a week. Perhaps the owner was a German rancher who lived on a coffee ranch in the mountains, or a Swiss rancher who lived on a pineapple ranch in the lowlands, or a Spaniard who lived in Spain. The owner would be rich. He would not need the pearls. And the old lady would never know. They didn't belong to her, anyway.

He tucked the string of pearls into the pocket of his jacket. He closed the lid of the old, worn, jewel box. He started creeping up the stairs.

Then suddenly, the words of his mother as she waved good-bye floated down the staircase to him.

"God be with you!"

He stopped. He became the same Pancho again, the same Indian boy who had taken his last three tiles to market. He ran down the stairs, tucked the pearls into the box, closed the lid, and ran up into the sunlight.

"*Señora! Señora!*" he cried, darting into the kitchen where the fragrance of the pink beans met his nose. "I have found something. Come, quick! Please!"

The señora followed him back into the little room, wiping her hands on her apron. "What is it? What is it, boy?" she cried, and then her face grew pale. "Is it . . ."

The boy pointed down the secret staircase. "Pearls in the little chest!" he said.

"*Madre de Dios!* Mother of God!" cried the old lady. "They are the pearls of my grandmother. She hid them in this house when the bandits came a long time ago, and then she died of a bad heart, and nobody knew where they were."

"But I thought. . ." began Pancho.

"Ah, my young friend," said the old lady, not scolding him for opening the box, "I know what you thought—that I was a

34

poor old woman renting this house for a few *centavos* a week.
The fortunes in my family have been lost for years, but I am
Señora Teresa Ramirez de Espinosa, and I am the only one of
my family that is left. The pearls belong to me. Now I can restore my house to its early beauty, and you will be the boy
who guards my house from bandits." (Little did she know
how nearly he had become a bandit himself!)

"A thousand thanks, *señora,*" said Pancho politely, "but my
mother is a widow, for my father was killed a week ago in an
accident, and she needs me at home. Besides, I am going to
follow my father's trade. He made tiles for a living, and I am
going to make tiles, too. My grandfather made tiles, and my
great-grandfather made tiles, and other grandfathers before
that."

"But," said the old lady, "what will you do in the meantime?"

(What shall I do? What shall I do? What shall I do in the
meantime?)

Then the Señora Teresa Ramirez de Espinosa smiled and
said, "Give me your hand, boy, and we shall go down the secret
staircase together. If the pearls are really there, I will give you
one to help you and your mother while you are learning your
trade. You deserve it for finding them. I will take it to Mexico
City and sell it for you, for the jeweler knows me well and will
ask no questions. Come! And let us hope the beans do not burn
while we are down there, for they are all we have for dinner!"

35

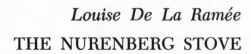

Louise De La Ramée

THE NURENBERG STOVE

RETOLD BY *Dixon Burket*

ILLUSTRATED BY *Fiore Mastri*

AUGUST lived in a little town called Hall. It was a charming place. It had wide meadows and great mountains all about it. It had paved streets and enchanting little shops that had latticed windowpanes and iron gratings. And it had a very grand old Gothic church that made August feel strong and peaceful when he looked at it.

August was a small boy, nine years old. He had curly hair and rosy cheeks and big hazel eyes. He had no mother. His father was poor, and there were many mouths at home to feed.

One night he was trotting home through the snow. He was very cold and he was very tired, but he kept up his courage by saying over and over to himself, "I shall soon be at home with dear old Hirschvogel." The snow outlined with white every gable and cornice of the beautiful old houses. The moonlight shone on the quaint gilded signs, the lambs, the grates, the eagles that hung before each doorway.

August hurried along and at last came to his own door. He knocked on it, and the solid oak door, four centuries old, flew open. The boy darted in and shouted as loud as he could, "Oh, dear Hirschvogel! I'm home with you at last!"

It was a large barren room into which he had rushed. The bricks on the floor were bare and uneven. In the room was a walnut cupboard, handsome and very old, a broad deal table, and several wooden stools. But, at one end, sending out warmth and color as a lamp shed its rays upon it, was a tower of porcelain, burnished with all the hues of a king's peacock and a queen's jewels, and surmounted with armed figures, and shields, and flowers of heraldry, and a great golden crown upon the highest summit of all.

It was a stove made in the year 1532, and on it were the letters H. R. H., for it was the handwork of the great potter of Nurenberg, Augustin Hirschvogel.

The stove, no doubt, had stood in palaces and been made for princes, had warmed the crimson stockings of cardinals, and the gold broidered shoes of archduchesses. No one knew what it had seen or done or been fashioned for. Yet perhaps it had never been more useful than it was in this poor desolate room, sending down heat and comfort to the children now tumbled together on the wolfskin rug at its feet.

"Oh, dear Hirschvogel, I'm so cold, so cold!" said August, patting the gilded lion's claws and smiling at his brothers and sisters. "Is Father in yet, Dorothea?"

Dorothea, who was seventeen, and the oldest daughter of the Strehla family, smiled back at him. "No, dear, he is late," she said. "But Father says not to wait for him; so we'll have supper at once."

Supper was a huge bowl of soup with big slices of brown bread swimming in it and some onions bobbing up and down. Ten bowls were soon emptied by ten wooden spoons, and then the three oldest boys slipped off to bed. They were very tired for they had been working in the snow all day. Dorothea soon drew her spinning wheel by the stove and set it whirring, and the little ones got August down upon the old worn wolfskin. "Tell us a story, August. Draw us a picture!" they cried.

August had a big wooden board that his father had given him and some sticks of charcoal. With these he would draw a hundred things he had seen in the day, sweeping each out with his elbow when the children had seen enough of it, and sketching dogs' heads and men in sledges and old women in their

37

furs, and pine trees and cocks and hens. And now and then—very reverently—he drew a Madonna and Child. His pictures were all very rough, for no one had taught him how to draw. But they were all very lifelike, and the children watched him breathlessly, shrieking with laughter when he made a funny animal. Even Dorothea, though she was troubled about where they would find money to buy bread the next day, laughed as she spun.

August was now warm again, and he looked up at the stove that was shedding its heat down on them all.

"Oh, dear Hirschvogel, you keep us so warm and happy," he said. "Just a little bit of wood to feed you and you make a summer for us all the winter through."

The grand old stove seemed to smile back at him. No doubt, though it had lived for over three hundred years, it had known very little gratitude. All the Strehla family knew about it was that their grandfather, a master mason, had dug it up out of some ruins where he was building. He had found it was without a flaw and so he had taken it home. Indeed, he had put it just where it now stood in the big empty room, where, for sixty years, it had been warming three generations of the Strehla family.

"Tell us a story, August," cried his brothers and sisters when they had seen enough of his charcoal pictures. And August looked up at the stove and the figures on it and made up many adventures about them.

The old stove was eight feet high. And how the children all loved it! In the summer they laid a mat of fresh moss all around it and decked it out with green boughs and beautiful wild flowers. In winter they were always glad to hurry home from school, knowing that they would soon be cracking nuts or roasting chestnuts beside Hirschvogel. But it was August who loved Hirschvogel the most of all. He used to say to himself, "When I grow up I will make such beautiful things, too. Then I will set Hirschvogel in a beautiful room of a house I will build in Innsbruck, just outside the gates where chestnuts are by the river. That is what I will do some day."

August opened the door. "You shall never touch it!" he cried.

He did not say this out loud for fear that the others would call him a silly dreamer. But he thought about what he would do when he was grown-up, every summer day when he drove the herds of cattle up through the blue gentians in the high mountains. Here there was stillness, and the sky was all around him. The mountain air was cool and clear. Here he was very happy and could dream his dreams.

On this winter's night, however, August was too busy thinking up new stories for the children to remember his grown-up dreams. Suddenly the door burst open, and in came their father.

The younger children ran joyously to meet him. Dorothea pulled the one wooden chair up to the stove for him, and August flew to fill his long clay pipe.

Their father, however, did not smile at their welcome, but slumped down heavily in his chair and let his pipe grow cold.

For a moment he did not speak. Then he said suddenly, "Take the children to bed," and Dorothea did so. August, who did not consider himself a child, stayed behind, curled before the stove.

There was a long silence. The cuckoo came out from the clock and struck the hour. August dropped asleep, and Dorothea's wheel hummed like a cat.

Suddenly Karl Strehla struck his hand on the arm of his chair, sending the pipe to the ground.

"I have sold Hirschvogel," he said, in a husky dogged voice. The spinning wheel stopped. August woke up and sprang to his feet.

"Sold Hirschvogel!" cried August and Dorothea.

"I have sold Hirschvogel!" repeated Karl Strehla. "I have sold it to a traveling trader for two hundred florins. I had to. I owe so much money. He saw the stove this morning when you were all out. He will pack it and take it to Munich tomorrow."

August stared at him in a daze. "It is not true! It is not true!" he muttered. "Surely you are joking, Father?"

Strehla laughed drearily.

"It is true. Would you like to know something else that is true too? The bread you eat and the meat that you put into

39

this pot and the roof you have over your heads have not been paid for for months and months. Your grandfather can lend us no more. There is no work to be had. And I have ten hungry children to feed. Boy, stop staring at me that way! The stove is no human being. It goes—tomorrow. Two hundred florins is something. It will keep us going until spring—"

August kept on staring, and he choked back a sob. "It is not true! It is not true!" he echoed stupidly. How could they take away Hirschvogel! His Hirschvogel!

"You will find it is true," said his father doggedly. "The dealer paid me half the money tonight and will pay me the rest tomorrow when he comes to take the stove away to Munich. No doubt it is worth more, but I will take what I can get. The little black stove in the kitchen will warm you all just as well. Who would be silly enough to keep a gilded painted thing in a poor house like this when it will bring two hundred florins?"

"Oh, Father, Father," cried August, convulsively. "You cannot mean what you say! This is not a piece of hardware. It is our dear Hirschvogel that we all admire and love. Listen, let me try and get work tomorrow. Perhaps I can cut ice or make paths through the snow. There must be something I could do, and the people we owe money to are our neighbors and they will be patient. But sell Hirschvogel! Oh, never, never, never! Do give those florins back, dear Father, give them back!"

August's father looked down at his boy. He was sorry that he had to cause pain, but he did feel that he must earn that money.

"The stove is sold," he said loudly. "I can do nothing about it. Children like you do not understand. The stove is sold and goes to Munich tomorrow. Be thankful I can get bread for you. Now stop this nonsense and go to bed."

As he spoke he took the oil lamp that stood at his elbow and stumbled off to his own bedroom.

"Come to bed, dear," sighed Dorothea. "Oh, August, do not look like that! Do come to bed."

"I shall stay here."

"Here! All night!"

41

"They might take it in the night; besides I can't leave it *now.*"

Beside the stove Dorothea left him, and he stayed close to it all night long.

Early in the morning, while it was still dark, his three elder brothers came down the stairs, each holding a lantern. Then they went outside to work, one to the stoneyard, another to the tinder-yard, and a third to the salt works. They did not notice August; they did not know what had happened.

A little later Dorothea came down holding a lamp. She laid her hand timidly on his shoulder. "Dear August, you must be frozen. August, do look up. It is morning now."

The boy rose slowly to his feet.

"I will go to grandfather," he said in a low voice. "He is always good. Perhaps he can save us."

Loud knocking at the front door drowned his words. A strange voice was calling. "Let us in! Quick! There is no time to lose. More snow like this and the roads will all be blocked. Let us in! We have come for the great stove."

August opened the door. "You shall never touch it!" he cried. "You shall never touch it!"

The big Bavarians who had come for the stove looked down at him and were amused. "Who shall prevent us?" one said.

"I!" said August. "You shall never have it!"

Just then his father came forward and pushed him out of the back door, roughly. The buyers of the stately and beautiful stove started to pack it carefully. Soon they carried it away.

August, blinded by his tears, leaned against the back wall of the house. A neighbor hobbled by and said, "Child, is it true your father is selling the big painted stove? How foolish! The stove was worth a mint of money!"

August swallowed hard. "I don't care what its value was," he muttered. "I loved it, I loved it!"

"Well, go after it when you are bigger," said the neighbor, goodnaturedly. "Don't feel so bad. The world is small, and you may see your stove again some day."

Then the old man hobbled away to draw his big pail of water at the well.

42

"Go after it! Why not?" thought August. He ran out into the courtyard by the little gate and across to the huge Gothic porch of the church. He hid himself in the doorway. Presently his heart gave a great leap. The straw-enwrapped stove was brought out and laid with great care on a low sleigh driven by bullocks. As the sleigh slowly crept over the snow, August hurried after it.

After the stove reached the station and was lifted on to the train, August crept into the freight car, found a hiding-place behind the stove, wedged in among cases of woodcarving, of clocks, of Turkish carpets, and of Vienna toys. He had only one idea now; where Hirschvogel went he would go, too.

By good luck August had found some money in his pocket and before he had got on the train he had purchased some bread and sausage at the station. Now, in the darkness, as he listened to the thundering, pounding noise of the train, he munched on part of his sandwich.

After he had eaten, he set to work like a little mouse to make a hole in the straw and hay in which the stove was packed. He nibbled, he pulled, and he pushed just where he thought the opening of the stove was. Nobody heard him and nobody came into the freight car. As the train went lumbering on and on, August saw nothing of the beautiful mountains and the shining waters and the great forests through which he was being carried. All he could see was straw.

Finally, through the straw and hay and twisted ropes he made his way to the door of the stove. Then he curled up inside it, and leaning out, he rearranged the ropes and the straw so that no one would know even a little mouse had been at them. The air came in through the brass fretwork of the stove, and he curled up again safe inside his dear Hirschvogel. Then he went fast asleep as though he were in his own bed at home.

The train rolled on in its heavy slow fashion, and the child slept soundly for a long while. When he did awake it was quite dark outside. Every time the train stopped he heard a banging, shouting, and jangling of chains. Then his heart seemed to jump up into his mouth.

When they came to lift the stove out, would they find him?
And if they did find him, what would they do with him? That
was what he kept thinking of all through the dark night that
never seemed to end.

In the morning the train seemed to go slower. There had been
a heavy snowfall. When it reached Possenhoffen it stopped,
and the Nurenberg stove was lifted out. August could see
through the fretwork of the brass door that the stove stood
facing a bleak and wintry lake with snow-covered banks and
mountains in the distance.

It was now nearly ten o'clock.

Before he had time to look long at the scene, the stove was
lifted up again and placed on a large boat that was waiting. It
was a very long boat on which lumber and freight were often
carried. The stove was heaved and hoisted up, and poor August
was growing rather giddy. Then the big boat crossed the lake
to Leoni, a small town about three miles away.

"If we should be too late!" cried the two dealers to each
other. "He said eleven o'clock."

"Who is he?" said August to himself. "The buyer, of course, of Hirschvogel!"

At last they touched the pier at Leoni.

"Now, men just a mile and a half further," said one of the dealers to the men who shouldered the Nurenberg stove. All of them grumbled over its weight. They didn't realize that they also carried inside it a small panting boy. August was beginning to tremble now. He was about to see the future owner of Hirschvogel!

"If he is a good kind man," he thought, "I will beg him to let me stay with it."

The porters started on their long journey, moving away from the village pier.

After a long, long time, August no longer felt the fresh icy wind blowing on his face through the brasswork of the stove. He felt, instead, that the porters were mounting a great many steps. They were going so softly he knew they must be moving on carpets. Warm air came in to him, too, so he knew he must be inside some building.

45

"I hope we are nearly there," he said to himself. "I am so hungry and so thirsty and oh, dear Hirschvogel, I feel so very, very strange!"

The porters walked on and on and on. At last the stove was set down again. It was set upright so that August's feet were hanging downward. He was thankful for that.

There was a lovely fragrance in the air—the fragrance of flowers. "Only how can it be flowers?" thought August. "It is November!"

From afar off he heard some lovely music. Presently someone stepped near him and a low voice cried, "So!" Someone was looking at Hirschvogel and admiring its beauty.

Then the same voice said, after a long pause, "I am glad you bought it. It is very beautiful and it is undoubtedly the work of Augustin Hirschvogel."

Then the hand of the speaker turned the round handle of the brass door, and August held his breath.

The handle turned. The door was slowly drawn open. Someone bent down and looked in, and the same voice that he had heard praising the stove cried out in surprise, "What is this in it? A child!"

August, very terrified, sprang out of the stove and fell at the feet of the speaker.

"Oh, let me stay! Please, sir, let me stay!" he cried. "I have come all the way with Hirschvogel!"

Two men seized him roughly and muttered in his ear, "Be quiet, boy! Hold your tongue! This is the King."

They were about to drag him out of the King's presence when the kind voice spoke again. "Poor child, let him go. Let him speak to me."

The astonished chamberlains let August slide out of their grasp, and he stood there in his rough sheepskin coat and his thick, mud-covered boots with his curly tangled hair standing up on end.

He was in the midst of the most beautiful room he had ever seen. A young man with dark friendly eyes was looking down on him and said, "My child, how did you come to be here hidden in this stove? Do not be afraid. Tell me the truth. I am the King."

August was too much in earnest to be nervous in the presence of such a famous person. He threw his great battered black hat with the tarnished gold tassels down on the floor and clasped his hands. Here was someone who could help him.

"Oh, dear King," he said shyly, "Hirschvogel was ours, and we have loved it all our lives. Father sold it, and when I saw that it was really going away from us I said to myself that I would go with it. So I have come all the long way inside of it. Last night in my dreams it spoke to me and said beautiful things. Please, please, let me live with it! I will go out every morning and cut wood for it. No one has ever fed it with fuel but me since I grew big enough to do so, and it loves me. Yes, it does. Last night in my dream it said so. It said, too, that it had been happier with us than in any palace."

His breath failed him and he lifted his sad, eager young face to the King.

The King looked down at him and smiled. "What is your name?" he asked.

"I am August Strehla. My father is Karl Strehla. We live in Hall in the Innthal. And Hirschvogel has been ours so long—so long!"

He swallowed hard.

47

"And you have really traveled inside this stove all the way from Tyrol?"

"Yes," said August. "No one thought to look inside until you did."

The King laughed. "Little fellow, you are very pale. When did you eat last?"

"I had some bread and sausage with me. Yesterday afternoon I finished it."

"You would like to eat now?"

"If I might have a little water I would be glad. My throat is very dry."

The King called for water and wine and cake also, but August, though he drank eagerly, could not swallow anything. He was too excited.

"May I stay with Hirschvogel? May I stay?"

"Wait a minute," said the King. "What do you wish to be when you are a man?"

"A painter, oh, a painter! I wish to be what Hirschvogel was— I mean the master that made my Hirschvogel."

"I understand," said the King.

He looked down on the child and as he did so he smiled once more.

"Will I let you stay with your Hirschvogel? Yes, my boy, I will. You shall stay in my court and you shall be taught to be a painter. I shall send word to your father that you are here. I shall see, too, that your father has work. As for you, you may paint in oils or on porcelain, just as you wish, and you must grow up worthily. Then, when you are twenty-one years old and have done well in our schools of art, I will give you your Nurenberg stove. If I am not living then, those who reign after me shall do so. Now go away with this gentleman and do not be afraid. You shall light a fire every morning in Hirschvogel, but you will not need to go out and cut the wood yourself."

The King smiled again and stretched out his hand. August was almost too happy to speak.

"Oh, thank you, dear King," he said.

Louise A. Stinetorf

THE FIRST LAMB

ILLUSTRATED BY *Clarence Biers*

HIS name was *Abd el Karuzeh,* and his
father and mother pronounced it deep down in their throats so
that each syllable sounded almost the same as all the others,
like the echo of pebbles dropped into a deep well. It was a big
name for a small boy, but his size was deceiving. He was older
than he looked. None of the men and women who make their
homes in the limestone caves in southern Algeria, in that low
range of hills which separates the coastal plane from the desert,
are big people.

Abd el Karuzeh was ten years old, and for two years now he
had helped herd the village flocks. Every morning he and the
other boys of his age went from cave to cave and called out
the sheep and goats of the family or families living within. Then
uphill they all trooped, following trails which only familiar eyes
could recognize and scaling slopes which only sheep, goats, and
boys bred to mountains could climb.

One by one, Abd el Karuzeh and the other boys rounded up
out of the flock a dozen or so ewes with their lambs and stopped
on some slope where the African sun had coaxed a faint tinge
of green out of the jutting rocks and sour soil. Sheep were stupid
creatures, Abd el Karuzeh's father said, and there had to be an
abundance of food under their very noses—else they would
starve to death! Farther on, where only weeds and thistles

From *Children of North Africa* by Louise A. Stinetorf, copyright, 1943, by Louise
A. Stinetorf, published by J. B. Lippincott Company.

struggled against the rocks, the older boys pastured the goats. While beyond even that, among the crags where human eyes could discover almost no green thing, the boys who were no longer children but not yet men, foraged along with the tribe's camels for a precarious existence. They did not return to the caves at night, but lived and slept with their grumbling, ungainly charges for months at a time. Therefore, each of them carried a spear, for no one knew when a lion would spring from a rock.

Abd el Karuzeh carried a dagger stuck through his belt, but lions seldom came close to the caves. He had only hyenas to fear—and then only after dark. Darkness comes quickly in the mountains once the sun has set. And well he knew that when shadows to the east of the rocks began to grow blue, he must gather his ewes and their lambs together and hurry down the hill. The patter of hooves on the rocks was a dainty and light sound, but a hyena made no sound at all until its powerful jaws snapped through a lamb's neck.

The old men of the tribe said a hyena could follow a man unnoticed until its hot breath scorched his heels. There were evil spirits, Abd el Karuzeh had heard from these men, which lived among the rocks and roamed the hills at night. Sometimes they took the form of a hyena and followed travelers. Whenever one rose up onto its hind legs and whispered into a man's ear, that man spoke only foolishness from then on and became a burden to his tribe, said the old men.

But Abd el Karuzeh was not thinking of hyenas or foolish men one particularly sunny afternoon. He was swinging his bare legs over the edge of a huge rock and pitying himself a lot. His father was poor, to begin with. Poor, even for the cave dwellers of southern Algeria. He owned only a half dozen sheep, and he had not, like other fathers, given his son a lamb with which to start a flock of his own.

"You must earn your first lamb," he had replied shortly to Abd el Karuzeh's pleading. But he turned his face away when he said it, for Abd el Karuzeh's father loved his son, and it was hard to deny him this thing.

Like all fathers he dreamed of the day when he would sit among the old men and listen to Abd el Karuzeh, then become a grown man, help direct the tribal council. But like all fathers he also knew that if Abd el Karuzeh did not own flocks of sheep and goats and camels, no one would listen to him. Poor men can be as good as rich men, but no one asks their advice. And how was any boy to start a flock without even one lamb to call his very own? So Abd el Karuzeh's father could not meet his son's eyes as he had replied, "You must earn your first lamb!"

So the boy sat perched on a big rock and dangled his legs down its warm sides as he wrestled with his problem. What could he do to earn a lamb? He asked himself the question a thousand times, but there was no answer. The only way Abd el Karuzeh had ever known a boy to get a lamb was for his father to give it to him. If his father was too poor—

Abd el Karuzeh did not like the thought. So he banged his bare calloused heels against the rock and squinted across the valley at the cliff ten miles away. He knew that above and below that cliff other boys were herding sheep and goats. Almost every one of those boys could look at his flock and point out a lamb, or perhaps a ewe and her lamb that belonged to him!

Abd el Karuzeh knew they loved their sheep. That when the anemones and cyclamen splashed color over the hills after the rainy season, they wove wreaths for their sheep's necks and tied bouquets to their legs and fat tails. That on frosty nights when the fires died down and the heat had gone out of the caves, they crept among the animals in the corner and snuggled up to their own sheep for warmth.

But what could a boy do to earn a lamb? Even a sickly lamb? Or a crippled lamb? If he could kill a lion or a leopard and bring the skin to the Headman, then the tribe would give him almost anything—a sheep, a goat, even a camel! But Abd el Karuzeh knew that not many grown men had killed a leopard, and even fewer had killed a lion. No, he would have to think of some other way.

What could he do? And when could he do it? He arose every morning before the sun had cleared all of the mist away from

51

the cave entrance, took the bit of bread and cheese his mother gave him, and set off for the hills with the other shepherds. There he kept one eye out for eagles which might carry off a lamb that had strayed too far from its mother, and watched with the other for any small animal he might kill with a rock and roast over a little fire of thorns for his midday meal.

A shout aroused Abd el Karuzeh, and he looked up to greet another shepherd. The sun was already red in the western sky, and the shepherds were rounding up their flocks to return to the caves. Abd el Karuzeh, being one of the youngest boys, did not go so far into the hills as the others, so he waited as they brought up their sheep. The sun sank lower and lower, and the crags to the west pierced its red disk.

"Fuad and Feragi are late," one shepherd murmured uneasily, looking at the blue shadows already stealing across the lowest rocks.

"Do you see them anywhere, Abd el Karuzeh?" asked another. "Your eyes are sharp."

Abd el Karuzeh scanned the slopes, but there was no sign of the two boys and their flock. The uneasiness among the boys grew. Fuad and Feragi were brothers and sons of the Headman, but the boys would have waited for their poorest comrade. No shepherd deserts a fellow shepherd in the hills at night. For the hyena, which is a skulking coward under the sun, is feared by grown men under the stars. Where were Fuad and Feragi? Even the sheep and goats bunched together as though afraid.

But what was that? It sounded like the patter of raindrops on dry leaves. A sigh of relief broke from the boys, and even the flock started milling about as though glad. Hurrying down the pathway came the Headman's sons and their sheep. But they were not happy boys.

"We have had to abandon a lamb," said Fuad, the elder.

Relief among the boys changed to dismay. Not only are his charges wealth to a shepherd; he loves them as a mother loves the baby that depends upon her helplessly. And just as no mother will desert her baby, neither will a good shepherd desert one of his flock.

52

"What happened?" someone asked in a low voice, and every boy strained forward listening.

Feragi pointed to a big white ewe that kept sniffing the lambs of the flock and bleating softly now and then. She was hunting for a lamb which was not there!

"She-of-the-Nimble-Toes strayed off a bit from the flock," he said, "and I went after her to bring her back. When I was but several steps from her, I saw an adder among the stones between us, and I threw a rock at it. I crushed the poisonous snake's head, but our ewe, She-of-the-Nimble-Toes, was frightened and leaped sideways, knocking her lamb over the cliff."

"Could you not reach it?" Abd el Karuzeh knew the answer before he asked.

"No," Fuad replied. "It fell on a small ledge and if we could have gotten down to it, we could not have climbed back up again. It is a pity, too, for She-of-the-Nimble-Toes comes of good stock, and her lambs make fine sheep."

"And it was unhurt," Feragi put in.

"It will not remain unhurt long," Fuad remarked shortly. "Even now a hyena or the jackals may have it. Oh, we tried to get it, of course, but the rock was brittle and snapped under our hands, and the bushes broke under our weight. We were each too big and heavy."

"I thought Fuad was going to fall once," Feragi interrupted.

"And you dangled your cloak over the cliff for me to hold on to—and risked being pulled over after me. Didn't you? You are a brave, good brother!"

"I'd rather have you than a lamb any day," Feragi grinned, although he was embarrassed by his brother's praise.

"Well, you have me. But it is late, and we must get the rest of the flock back to the caves before we lose any more," Fuad replied as he started his companions and the animals down the trail.

A lamb, a fine lamb, alive and unhurt on a ledge where a boy might reach it! It seemed wicked to Abd el Karuzeh to abandon it to wild animals.

"Yah hya ris!"

The shepherds were singing as they always did on the way home at night, one boy carrying the melody and the others joining in on the chorus in a sad minor key:

"Yah hya ris!" Yes, my Captain!

They did not notice that Abd el Karuzeh had fallen behind them. He stopped short. Back there in the gathering darkness was a lamb, a good lamb, alive, unhurt—on a ledge where he might rescue it. Back there, too, there might be jackals or hyenas ready to devour either lamb or boy!

"Yah hya ris!" came the chorus of the shepherds' song. That way lay food, fires, companionship, safety. As Abd el Karuzeh looked after the boys, he saw Fuad stride over to a tired lamb, pick it up, and swing its soft body around his neck like a collar. Fuad was a good shepherd. He would never have deserted a lamb if it had been at all possible for him to rescue it.

With sudden determination, Abd el Karuzeh turned and trotted off into the darkness. One by one the stars pierced the Algerian sky, and the moon swam in a faint azure glow.

"Yah hya ris!"

Abd el Karuzeh found himself singing under his breath as

54

he hurried along. When he thought of the words of the song he could not think of what might lurk in the shadows. And when he sang, even faintly, he could not hear what might creep up behind him.

A stone rolled down the hillside, and he began to run in terror. Was there really anything following him? He clasped his hands over his ears so he could hear no evil. He had no desire to go through life talking foolishness! On and on he sped, his heart in his throat and his pulse pounding in his ears.

His foot dashed another stone downhill, and his pulse struck a new note. Or was it his pulse? He jerked his hands from his ears and listened.

Baaaaaaah!

Only a lamb—a cold lamb—bleated like that!

Ba-a-a-a-a-a-h!

He followed the quavering sound. Here was the cliff. Here was a clean space where Fuad's and Feragi's bodies had brushed all the dirt and stones aside as they had tried to worm their way down the cliff. And there, looking up at him, from below, was She-of-the-Nimble-Toes' lamb!

Abd el Karuzeh took off his cloak, slid on his stomach over the cliff, and with his toes felt for a bit of jutting rock. Almost inch by inch the boy descended, his body plastered to the rock in front of him, his skin wet with sweat from exertion and the nervous strain. Time after time as he eased his weight from one foot to the other the rock crumbled and went crashing down the mountainside. Only his strong fingers saved him. Fuad had been right. The shrubs were too small and the rock too brittle and crumbly to have held a larger boy.

At last he stood on the ledge beside the lamb. He picked it up, and it nuzzled its head against his chest. As he stroked its warm wool, he could see in the pale moonlight that there were stains on its back, and he saw, too, that his fingers were bleeding.

Blood has a very strong odor to animals. Abd el Karuzeh cowered back against the cliff and peered to the right and left of him. There was no time to waste. The smell of blood would surely bring animals, and quickly. He slung the lamb about his neck as he had seen Fuad do, took off his belt, and tied its feet together.

Climbing down the cliff had been slow, hard work. Climbing up was even slower and more difficult. He was tired. His fingers hurt. The lamb about his neck made him feel awkward and off balance. Its feet scraped the rock. He could not plaster his face as close to the cliff as he wanted to—as he knew was safe! If the lamb grew nervous and kicked, even a little bit, it might plunge them both into the abyss below. There might be a hyena jumping for his feet—or one waiting for him above. His pulse pounded in his ears so loudly he could hear nothing.

It seemed an eternity before his hands had struck a broad expanse of level rock and he had wormed his thin little belly back over the top of the cliff. To safety?

Abd el Karuzeh was not quite sure how far he was from his father's cave. He looked down the long pathway he must cover, and his breath caught in his throat. A gleam of light! Was it a hyena's eyes? Now many gleams! A pack of jackals?

Then he laughed aloud—animals' eyes are in pairs, and they

are steady in the darkness. These lights bobbed up and down singly. Too, animals tread softly, and Abd el Karuzeh's keen ears caught the sound of footsteps almost as soon as he had seen the torches.

"*Saiida,*" he shouted, pulling the second syllable out into a long high-pitched note: e-e-e-e-e-e-e!

"*Saii (e-e-e-e-e-e-) da!*" "Hallo-o-o-o-o-o-o!" came back his father's voice before his own echoes had died away. The rocks rattled beneath his feet as he sped down the path; but there was no need to slip along quietly now. No animal, however hungry or fierce, attacks a party of men with fire in their hands.

Fuad and Feragi were in the group, and their father. Abd el Karuzeh untied the lamb and placed it in Fuad's hands.

"Why do you do that, Abd el Karuzeh?" the Headman asked.

"Did not your sons tell you?" Abd el Karuzeh asked in surprise. "It belongs to you. It is the lamb of your ewe, the one we shepherds call She-of-the-Nimble-Toes."

"It is a lamb my sons abandoned to die," the Headman replied slowly, "therefore, it no longer belongs to anyone in my family. We could not wear its wool with satisfaction. We could not claim its lambs with honor.

"Fuad," the Headman turned to his son, "return the lamb to its rightful owner!"

Tears slid from Abd el Karuzeh's eyes and sank into the lamb's soft wool. It was not manly to cry, he knew; but now not only his fingers throbbed—but his heart was very full.

"Abd el Karuzeh!" His father spoke sharply as poor men the world over are apt to do when they are very proud of their children. The boy sank on one knee before the Headman and laid his forehead upon the palm of the Headman's hand in sign of thanks and tribal submission.

Then, with Fuad on one side and Feragi on the other, and his lamb—*his very own lamb*—cradled in his arms, Abd el Karuzeh followed the men back to the safety, warmth, and companionship of the caves.

A day with a Chinese boat-
girl in Foochow.

Elizabeth Foreman Lewis

HOK-HWA
OF THE WATERFRONT

ILLUSTRATED BY *Janet Laura Scott*

HOK-HWA yawned, drew her bedding tightly about her for another nap, breathed deeply of the sharp, salty air, and then she remembered. Drowsiness cleared from her brain, and her eyelids lifted. Truly this morning was not one for sleeping, indeed no! Had she forgotten so swiftly the plans made by her parents only last night? At the time, excited as she was, sleep had seemed the farthest of all things from her mind, for Father, coming home with an unusual catch of fish, had announced that on the following day—and that was now—he would remain on the houseboat and repair damages made in the hull by a recent storm. Immediately Mother had offered to carry the fish into Foochow City for sale and had added that the return trip would furnish good opportunity for gathering straw. Better, Hok-hwa should accompany her—two bundles would be twice the use of one—and Father, settled on the boat, could look after the two smaller children, the pig, and the fowls.

Suddenly Hok-hwa sat up in the cramped quarters of the cabin and peered out at the heavy blanket of mist enfolding her world. As yet she could distinguish none of the craft crowding about her own home in this great colony of Foochow's boat-people, but the darkness was paling gradually, and in a little time dawn would again come up from the sea. The others in her family were sleeping soundly, much to her dissatisfaction. If they were not stirring by daybreak, perhaps a slight cough might arouse them.

58

She huddled, debating the wisdom of such a course—for it had its risks—while a little breeze sighed itself into being, grew stronger and then, heady with its own capacity for mischief, pushed mightily at the curtain of fog and tore it into ragged, uneven fragments. In the clear spaces between these Hok-hwa saw silver points of light dance on the background. Fascinated, she counted and lost them, star by star. One only, larger than the rest, remained to hang like a lantern over Pagoda Anchorage, several miles down the river. Perhaps, it had to wait for the sun's arrival, Hok-hwa told herself, so the great steamers and junks might come through the treacherous shoals of the China Sea safely into port. Then, too, though this thought made her shiver, so long as light remained, the pirates who infested the rocky islands and coastline were less likely to swoop down on the ships that brought such rich cargoes of the world's goods into Fukien Province, and carried out with them equally valuable loads of China's finest tea.

Without warning, the horizon was aflame and the star gone. Cocks crowed and, on the next boat, Neighbor Sing's wife crawled up from her bed under the deck planks and fumbled with the cooking-pot. "Good!" thought Hok-hwa, for the noise

had wakened Father, and she would not have to cough the little cough. She waited for her parents to finish yawning and stretching, then jumped up.

"What affair is this?" asked Mother. "Have you been awake all night?"

Hok-hwa smiled happily in reply, straightened her cotton jacket and trousers which at this season of the year were both day and night garments, smoothed her hair backward with a coarse willow comb, and crept on deck to start the fire under the iron food-pan.

Each moment the activity and clamor increased about her. Bare feet flapped on the decks; women hurried about the preparation of morning rice; men called from one boat to another, arranging fishing expeditions; children demanded attention; ducks quacked, dogs barked, and pigs squealed. From each floating home, spirals of smoke ascended; brown sails bellied in the wind; and a thousand hulls, rising and falling with the lap, lap of the Min River, tugged at their moorings and reached longingly toward the sea.

Hok-hwa looked after her younger sister and brother while her mother caught up a soiled garment and leaned over the gunwale to wash it. Neighbor Sing's wife reached into the river and rinsed a small sieve of grain; then with a gourd dipper ladled up water and put on the rice to steam. Ducks swam in the narrow spaces between boats and gobbled greedily at scraps of refuse on the surface. A chicken, envious of such fare, strained at the twisted bamboo cord that connected one of its legs with a stout peg on the deck and slipped over the edge. There it flopped, squawking half in water and half in air, until its owner pulled it back to safety. Chopsticks now clicked against rice bowls; nets were gathered up; sampans darted out between houseboats and junks; and Foochow's boat colony settled down again to the daily routine of living.

In a half hour of time Mother and Hok-hwa were on their way. The washed garment hung stretched on a pole to dry. The children were fastened, like the fowls, securely to the deck with ankle cords, and all wore on their shoulders cylinders of

60

bamboo which, in emergency, would keep them afloat. The fish had been lifted from the river, where they had spent the night suspended in a covered basket, and transferred to a bucket of water in which they would travel to Foochow Market. Mother led the way over the uneven floor of decks until they finally reached the land. What an adventure to feel earth under one's feet, Hok-hwa thought as she ran ahead. In all of her life she had been on dry soil four or five times only. The narrow path they now trod lay between inundated paddy-fields, in which men bent double over the task of transplanting young rice. One more skillful than the others stood erect, stuck the plants between his toes, and pressed them firmly down into the mud.

In terraces above grew tea-plants, and close by, fields of jasmine whose yellow flowers would later be dried and packed with some of the choicer tea leaves.

Hok-hwa halted abruptly as a water buffalo blocked her progress. She was not very familiar with these beasts, and the ugly lowered head was frightening. From a higher level of farmland, a small boy's laughter jeered at her fears. The animal took a step forward, and with relief Hok-hwa saw Mother's arm reach out, grasp one of the great curving horns and turn it gently until a safe passageway had been achieved. The water buffalo made no further move, and the two went on, but not too fast for Hok-hwa to retort impolitely to her tormentor.

After a time they found themselves on the hard-packed road which led into the city. Here in the outskirts were great houses, and over their garden walls eucalyptus and palm and tall poinsettias cast shadows. Birds flew about; one, singing as it soared, moved toward the clear spring sky. Hok-hwa followed its flight with shining eyes. On the boats one did not hear music like this—only the mewing of gulls. A small green lizard darted across the ground, and a ricksha coolie swung out of step to avoid touching it. Mother sucked in her breath; she, too, disliked lizards—they were snakes that were not snakes!

Shops began to appear, most of them devoted to the work of craftsmen in silver and lacquer. Hok-hwa glanced into each doorway as she passed. One worker held in his fingers a minute junk, no larger than the first joint of his thumb. On it he was tying threads of silver to the full spread sail of the same gleaming metal.

"Look, Mother!" Hok-hwa cried out.

The artisan glanced up and smiled at the child's eager face. "Big Sister, do you like the boat?" he asked.

Embarrassed, Hok-hwa bowed and shrank back against her mother. As they went on, she voiced her thought. "Some day, perhaps for my wedding, I wish for a little silver boat like that one."

"In three or four years when you go to live on Sia Fisherman's houseboat as wife for his son, you will forget all about small silver toys. You will want, as does every bride, silver bracelets for your wrists and silver knives for your hair."

"But if the government will no longer let boatwomen wear knives in the hair, Mother, why must I want them? When you brought me to Foochow City a year ago, I saw women whose hair ornaments were silver flowers and moths. Very beautiful they were. If I might have one of them—I would be happy."

"When boatwomen have money to buy silver hair-ornaments they spend it on knives," her mother remarked. "It is the custom. Centuries ago there was much trouble between the people living on the boats and those on the mainland. It was then that each boat-wife had knives made with which to protect herself while her husband and sons were fishing. What more sensible place to carry them than in the knot of hair on her head!"

But Hok-hwa was not listening to this explanation she had heard many times before. Her interest had wandered to a lacquer shop. From its open front the pungent odor of burning paints and oils swept into the street. The articles on display were rich in color—Mandarin red and deep maroon and soft olive green. An occasional vase or tray of brighter green was flecked with gold dust. On the boat was a red lacquer box in which Mother kept her few treasures, but even though Hok-hwa admired the flowers and butterflies on its lid, she knew it did not compare with these objects before her.

The streets grew narrower, and traffic increased. Yells from vendors and load-coolies deafened the ears. Just before Wan-sui-chiao (Bridge of Ten Thousand Years) in the heart of the city was reached, Mother turned into a doorway where fish of all kinds were offered for sale. After lengthy bargaining with the proprietor, she emerged with an empty bucket and some small money. The bucket was less convenient to carry than a basket, but it had kept the fish alive, and won her a decent price for them. They halted for the second time to purchase water-melon seeds and condiment for cooking purposes. Hok-hwa received a handful of the seeds and wedging them between her teeth, cracked and threw away the outer coverings and chewed the kernels.

They made faster headway on the return trip until the country fields were once more in view. To the right lay meadowland and a hillside, dotted with the horseshoe-shaped graves peculiar to the section. There they began to gather grass for use of the pig and fowls on the boat. In no time each had a rolled bundle which could be carried on the shoulders with little difficulty. Mother adjusted hers and started off.

Hok-hwa stood still in the afternoon sunlight and looked about her. She wriggled her toes in the grass and wondered if it would be pleasanter to live all of one's days on land. Trees and flowers and birds; interesting shops and crowded streets! In the distance could be seen the feathery bamboo groves of Kuliang Mountain and the temple on Kushan's sacred peak. A whiff of salty air touched her nostrils, and she turned in response to the odor. Beyond gleamed a broad expanse of water, the Min River, and still farther away lay the shimmering China Sea. For a day's visit the land was good! But there on that ever-changing surface of the water was her home, and she was suddenly glad that this was so.

Her mother's voice interrupted these thoughts. "Come, we must hurry a little!"

Hok-hwa answered, "I come,." and swinging the straw to her shoulders hurried down the hillside.

THE Larsson family—seven children and mother and father—found living in their apartment a bit crowded. So when a rich uncle willed them two horses, they made a trailer with a living room, kitchen, and bedroom, and decided to tour Sweden selling the Peep—a singing saucepan invented by Papa. Their first day on the road brought exciting adventures. They stopped for lunch in a grassy nook near a bright lake.

Edith Unnerstad

THE SINGING SAUCEPAN

ILLUSTRATED BY *Frances Eckart*

MIRRE and I helped unharness the horses. Rosalind looked through all her things, hunting for her bathing suit, and as soon as she found it, she was off to the lake.

We tied Laban and Lotta with long ropes to a couple of birch trees and got water for them from the lake. They started eating the grass at once. Mama was already well under way with the food, and Papa went around and gave the wagons a good close inspection to see how they had stood the first stage of the trip. He wasn't exactly pleased with the wagon coupling, so he fussed with it a bit.

Then the rest of us went in swimming. The water was cold, but after all it was early in June, so you could hardly expect it to be hot. Rosalind was already a long way out in the lake. She was a regular Olympic swimming champion. She'd rather live in water during the summer than on land.

Mama called out after us, "See if you can find some plants for your collection; I mean something you haven't already."

Oh, dear! The press! We had promised Mama and Papa to take the flower press with us and collect specimens during the entire trip. And now we had left it at home. Personally, I thought it was a bad thing well forgotten. But I knew what would happen when Papa and Mama found out. Here we were, probably gone for the whole summer, and we couldn't press a single flower for our collection.

I decided not to say anything yet. They'd find out soon enough. And our energetic Mama would be sure to find some way so that we could get those blooming plants pressed!

I found a stone and skipped it off into the lake. Mirre snorted into the water like a hippopotamus. Dessi sat on a stone, looking at the lake and the birch trees and everything, until I yelled at her. Then she slowly got up and walked into the water.

I swam out and played with Rosalind. She was as slippery as a piece of soap and much quicker than I. On land, though, it's different.

Knutte just dipped himself quickly. Then he came out and played with his airplane. It flew beautifully until it got caught in a tree, and he had to climb up and get it. Its nose was dented a little, so he didn't dare fly it any more. There isn't anybody so careful of his things as Knutte.

Mama wouldn't let Pysen go swimming. It was too early in the summer. He went crawling around on all fours, and raced Laban and Lotta to see who could eat the most grass.

Then Mama called to us, "Come on and get out now or you'll all of you be frozen blue!"

Rosalind pretended not to hear until Papa came and called her.

"I never want to go home again," she said, as we lay and sunned ourselves. "I just want to live like this always. I'm going to swim in every lake I see."

"Then you'd better get moving," Papa said, "because Sörmland is full of lakes, and we don't have time to wait for you."

Rosalind and I raced each other to get warm, and then

Knutte wanted to run, too, so we made him lean over and played leapfrog. Dessi and Mirre went back to the wagons to help Mama set the table. Dessi wanted us to sit out in the grass among the cowslips for lunch, but we booed at that idea because we wanted to try our new dining-room table.

Suddenly there was quite a commotion up on the highway. A crowd of people had collected, and they were standing looking at us and watching what we were doing. We couldn't help noticing that they laughed and pointed at the signs.

"We have an audience," Mama said, as they started coming toward us. "I wish we could have eaten in peace first. The food's about ready. I'm glad we set the table inside!"

There were two boys, who had parked their bicycles beside the road, and an old woman with a couple of milk bottles, and a middle-aged man in shorts, with a rucksack. He looked as if he had never been out on a walking tour before but that he would show the world he was quite a man. And once those four had decided to pay a visit, more people followed. Cars, bicycles, and wagons stopped on the highway, so that it began to look like a traffic tie-up.

"Peep-Larssons! What's that supposed to be?" one of the boys asked and grinned.

Just then the food finished cooking, and Peep gave its signal. It began with a peep and got louder and louder until it was a scream. Mama was in the parlor, so it was about a minute before she got to the kitchen to take the saucepan off the fire. I had always thought it was a little noisy, but now, out-of-doors, it sounded hair-raising. The old woman with the milk bottles dropped one of them and couldn't collect wits enough to pick it up until half the milk had poured out onto the grass. The man with the rucksack jumped and got gooseflesh on his skinny, white legs.

"Police!" he yelled. "They're whistling for the police! They're trying to murder someone in the wagon!"

"Police!" someone else shouted. "Someone get the police!"

"Hey, Gosta," one of the boys said, "get going. Run to the store down the road and call the police!"

"Run yourself!" the other one answered and went closer to the wagon. "I want to see what happens."

People were now running toward us from all directions. But Mama got a good grip on the handle and turned happily and proudly to her audience with the screaming saucepan held high in the air. The noise began to fade, became a peep, and then died with a sigh.

Everybody stared with amazement at Peep. Little O, who lay sprawled out half-naked on her blanket among the cowslips, imitated the racket.

"Ee-eee-eee-ee!" she shrilled. "Eee-eee-eee!"

The only creatures who seemed completely undisturbed were Laban and Lotta. They had flapped their ears at the noise and then continued calmly to eat. And that was good, because they were going to hear that sound rather often. If it had made them nervous, they might sometime run away with the whole caravan.

"What on earth is that?" asked the milkwoman.

Mama had just cleared her throat and opened her mouth to

68

begin her first lecture demonstration on Peep's remarkable qualities, when someone said, "The police!"

A motorcycle with a sidecar had stopped up on the highway, and two policemen came striding down at us with giant steps. If Rosalind hadn't grabbed Little O out of the way, she might have been trampled.

"What's the meaning of this?" one of them asked and looked around. "Let me see your driver's license—well, I mean—no—that is—ahem! Who was doing all that whistling?"

"Ha, ha!" laughed one of the boys. "Driver's license! The police thought this was a car!"

Everyone started snickering.

"This is all a mistake, officer," Papa began.

Mama interrupted him.

"You see, Captain, it was this," she said, and held up the saucepan.

"That thing!" the policeman said gruffly. "You trying to put something over on me?"

"I assure you it was this," Mama said and beamed at him.

We pushed up to the wagon and gathered in a little clump at Mama's feet.

"That's right," we said. "It was our pan that whistled."

The audience burst out laughing. The other policeman took hold of the gruff one's arm and pointed at the wagon and the signs. And they began to laugh a little, too, although they looked as if it were against regulations.

"Yes," Mama said, "this is Peep. And we're the Larssons. How do you do? We were only getting a little lunch ready. And Peep always lets us know when the food is cooked, Captain."

"It certainly lets you know in a loud voice," one of them said.

"Doesn't it though?" Mama sounded happy.

Several of the audience looked disappointed.

"Was that all it was?" they said. "We thought they'd murdered someone."

Mirre heard this and decided to give our fallen reputation some help.

"But we've got an uncle who's dead," she said.

69

"What did she say?" someone asked from the back of the crowd.

"She said they've got the body of an old man there," someone answered.

"Where? In the wagon?"

"Guess so."

"Well, well," said one of the policemen as he pulled out his notebook. He sounded gruff again. "What did he die of?"

"He was run over," I said.

"They've run over someone with those wagons." It was the same voice that had said we had the body of an old man. It sounded pleased.

"Horrible! Just horrible!" said the man with the rucksack. "And so, of course, they hid the body in the wagon. Isn't that so, officer?"

Everybody rushed up to the parlor wagon to look in the windows. They looked disappointed when they saw only a table set for lunch.

"He's probably in the other," said a boy. "It looks more mysterious."

Papa tore after the people who wanted to climb up on the coupling to look in the sleeper window.

"Let me explain the whole thing," he yelled.

The policemen said, "Everyone stand back so we can clear this matter up. All right. Now then. Your name is Larsson, you said. First names?"

Mama set Peep down and picked up the frying pan and spoon and pounded so that the birch trees rattled. She announced loudly that she had something to say. And the policemen were so stunned that anyone should dare interrupt a cross-examination, they didn't even protest.

Mama then delivered the greatest speech of her life, as Papa said afterwards. She stood there in front of the silver curtain and told the audience exactly what the whole story was and how we happened to be on the road. She showed them Peep and told them what a remarkable invention it was. She took off the lid and let them see the three pans where our lunch lay

70

steaming: potatoes and pork sausages and Little O's cereal. She asked if there were a law against getting your own lunch in your own wagon.

"And Peep is made in three sizes," she added, "and this one is the largest, because as you can see, we're a large family." And then she told them the price of each size and that a "Directions for Using" came with each one.

She finished by saying that she thought they were an enchanting audience, and that she was convinced that both the friendly captains and the audience now understood that everything was all right. And if anyone wanted to see how we lived, they were welcome to come up one at a time and go through the wagons. And while they were doing that they could see for themselves that we didn't have the body of an old man anywhere. Uncle Enok was run over right near Katrina Hissen in Stockholm on April 19, she added.

Well let me tell you, everybody laughed. Some of the audience paraded into the wagons and said they thought we had the perfect solution to the perfect way to live—if only they could come along! And some others asked Mama to explain the wonderful Peep all over again, and she was only too glad to do so.

You could see that the policemen were trying very hard to maintain a serious expression, but it didn't work out too well. So they said that they had to go make sure there wasn't a traffic jam up on the highway, and they added loudly that anyone who had a car or bicycle, would they please be so kind as to move them? They went back up the hill to the road, and I could see how their shoulders shook, once they had turned their backs to us and thought we weren't watching.

The old lady with the milk bottles said that Peep was just the kind of saucepan she needed. She only had to go home to get the money, because she didn't have any with her.

After she'd gone, Mama asked Papa if they could cut the price a little for the old lady, since maybe she didn't have so much.

But one of the boys, who happened to hear, said:

71

"She's the owner of all those big farms over there."

A couple of men who had driven their car down the little road, and had been very anxious to peer into the wagons, said that they were from a newspaper and were out on a reporting trip. They asked if they couldn't photograph the whole Peep-Larsson family and Laban and Lotta and the wagons. Mama said that it would be silly to refuse because it was such good publicity for Peep. So we hitched up the horses again—although not too well because it wouldn't show—and then we all stood up, and they took pictures and asked a million questions.

Mama said that Dessi painted, and Dessi looked horrified and said: "Oh, Mama!!"

But Mama felt they might as well know that our family had artistic talents, since it wouldn't hurt the Peep business a bit. Quite the contrary.

Then one of the men asked me what my name was and what my talents were.

"Lars Larsson Peep," I answered, "and I haven't any talents at all, so I'll probably be a newspaper reporter and drive around and take pictures."

"Lars!" Mama said, a little shocked, but the men laughed.

Then one of the men told me that if I were going to be a reporter, I'd have to begin young.

"You can begin by writing about your adventures on this trip."

I didn't think that was such a bad idea. Later I even thought a lot about it. So I guess you could say that it was that newspaperman who gave me the idea for this book.

We unhitched the horses again, and one of the men bought the smallest Peep to take to his wife. And the milkwoman came back and bought another small Peep.

We were all about to die of hunger, so Papa finally told everybody who stood around that they'd have to excuse us. The food had naturally grown stone-cold, because so many had looked to see if the potatoes were really done and whether the cereal had been scorched. But it all tasted good anyway.

Mama boiled coffee in an enamel pitcher and served rusks

with it. Then one of the policemen came back and wondered how large the middle-size Peep was, and if there would be room for it in the sidecar. He was thinking of giving it to his fiancée as a little kitchen present. The little one wasn't large enough, because he liked potatoes so well that a lot had to be boiled at one time. He bought the saucepan and looked quite pleased with it, except he seemed also to be a little embarrassed.

"Good luck with the Peep business!" he said when he left.

"Oh!" Mirre said, "I'm going to be a policewoman. I thought he was awfully sweet!"

"Oh, you and your crushes!" I said. "Here all of us were about to go to jail just because of what you said. You would have loved that, of course."

Papa started to laugh at the whole incident, and the first thing we knew we were having one of the Larsson-double-special family laughs. We don't just giggle when we once get started. Mirre laughs louder than the rest of us, but we're almost as good.

Papa said that now it was all over, we did have to admit it had been wonderful fun, every bit of it, and that Mama had done magnificently.

"Yes," Mama said and wiped away laugh-tears from her eyes, "this was a real nice première, and thus far everything has gone the way I'd—we'd planned. We've already sold three saucepans, and that's only the beginning. Speaking for myself, I think I'm going to like this life very much. Time was when I went on the road in Shakespeare. And I really don't think the saucepan journey is a bit harder."

"You're smart, Mama," I said.

"Noble, you mean," she said and laughed. And she gave us all second cups of coffee—for once.

"What do you have principles for, if you can't abandon them sometimes?" she said.

"The man with the rucksack is still standing outside," Dessi piped up. "He looks very unhappy about us somehow. Look at the way he's staring!"

74

"Shall we offer him a cup of coffee?" asked Mama while she poured herself a third cup. "It might cheer him up; might make him as cheerful as we are!"

I went out and asked. He looked me up and down. Then he raised his eyebrows and said very pointedly: "*Nej tack*. No, thank you, Mr. Peep-Larsson!"

"My name's Larsson Peep," I said because I thought it sounded better.

"I don't drink poison," he said.

"We weren't planning on offering you any," I said.

"Coffee is a poison," he said. "Coffee in small doses induces an anxiety neurosis and heart flutterings. Coffee in large doses induces grave disorders in the heart and ultimately death."

"We don't drink coffee in doses," I said. "We drink coffee in plastic mugs from the five-and-ten."

He left, looking puzzled as he walked off.

After each of us had washed his own plate and mug in the lake, we began to break camp.

Laban and Lotta each got several lumps of sugar before we drove off. They seemed very willing to get back into the traces, just as if it were a great honor for them.

Little O went to bed again, and Pysen went to sleep because it was time for his nap. He fell asleep the minute his head hit the pillow. Since he usually slept a couple of hours, Mama decided she might as well sit with us in the parlor for a while and knit. Mirre and Rosalind quarreled about whose turn it was to sit on the driver's box, so Papa said that, for the sake of keeping a little order, we'd have to take it by age. So Mirre won.

There were a number of people standing around and looking at us, but we were already so used to it that we hardly noticed. We got back to the highway without any particular difficulty.

Dessi looked back and said that we must remember that place for some other time.

Kate Seredy

EASTER EGGS

ILLUSTRATED BY THE AUTHOR

WHEN Jancsi hears that his cousin Kate from Budapest is coming to stay with his family because she has been ill, he expects her to be a delicate city-bred girl. But on the way home from the station Kate pushes Jancsi out of the wagon and drives off with the team of frightened horses! She and Jancsi soon become good friends, and this is the story of how they spend Easter in Hungary.

BUT for her long black braids anybody would have taken Kate for a lanky little boy. She was perfectly satisfied with Jancsi's old clothes. "I'd rather be a boy anyway," she said. She was always trailing after Jancsi now. Followed him from house to barn, from barn to pasture, asking a million questions. Pretty soon she began to help him. She wouldn't have anything to do with the pigs. "I like them only after they're made into sausages," she declared. But she liked to drive the geese and ducks to the brook or feed the chickens. The milking was still a mystery to her. Why anybody should go to all that trouble just to get *milk* she couldn't understand. She loved horses. Whenever Kate was missing, she could be found in the stables. Jancsi taught her to saddle, feed, and currycomb the horses. He was very proud of the way she rode. After the first painful lesson she listened to his sound advice and was rewarded one day by Father.

76

He looked on one day while Jancsi and Kate put the horses through all their paces. "Pretty good," he said. "Kate, the first week after Easter I'll take you with me when Jancsi and I ride out to inspect the baby lambs—providing you keep out of mischief."

She was off her horse and in Father's arms before he knew what had happened. She was hugging and kissing him until he gasped for breath.

"Uncle Márton! Oh, I'm so happy! I'll never eat your sausages again, an' I'll *try* not to scream, an' I'm so glad you'll take me because—I'd have sneaked after you anyway."

"And gotten a boy's size licking for it!" laughed Father.

"Let's see, it's a whole week until Easter. Wish it wasn't so long. I don't like Easter anyway; you have to be all dressed up and nothing to do," said Kate.

"Oh, but Easter is wonderful!" cried Jancsi. "We make Easter eggs, and everybody goes visiting, there are millions of good things to eat and . . . !" Jancsi gasped for words to describe the wonders of Easter.

Kate interrupted: "Make Easter eggs? How can you make an egg?"

"Mother just dyes them, silly, and we write all kinds of flowers and patterns on them."

This was something new for Kate. She contemplated it in silence for a while. "What else do you do?" she asked.

"Go to church and sprinkle the girls an' everything. Wait and see—it's fun!"

"Sprinkle—what—sprinkle the girls!!?"

" 'Course. All the boys and young men go to all their friends who have girls to sprinkle them with water. The girls and mothers give them meat and cakes to eat and Easter eggs to take home."

"Oh! but that's silly. Slosh water on girls for no reason at all and get cakes! What do the girls get for getting wet?"

"Wait a minute, Kate," laughed Father. "It does sound silly if you put it that way, but there is a beautiful reason for it. Do you want me to tell you?"

77

"A story?" asked Jancsi eagerly.

"No, Jancsi, the truth," said Father. "Come on, let's sit under the apple tree and I'll tell you." He spoke seriously, almost as though he were thinking aloud.

"Easter is a holiday of joy and love and giving. We welcome our friends and offer them the best we have. For us, who live on the land, Easter means the real beginning of spring—and spring for us is new hope, new life, after the long bleak winter. Spring brings warm sunshine, life-giving soft rain. Every living thing depends on sunshine and water. So we celebrate Easter by giving each other the sunshine of hospitality, and we sprinkle each other with fresh, pure water. How does your Easter greeting go, Jancsi? Say it for Kate!"

Jancsi recited:

"My song is the song of hope,
The voice of spring is my voice,
All my dear friends, let us rejoice;
God gave us sunshine, God gave us rain,
Our prayers have not been in vain.
Gone is the cold, cheerless winter,
Here is glorious Easter again!"

Kate nodded. "I like it, Uncle Márton—only—I—well—I can't understand why only the girls get sprinkled."

"You can sprinkle us on Tuesday after Easter. That's when girls have a good time," laughed Jancsi, jumping up. "Come on, the horses are waiting for a rub."

The last days before Easter were busy and exciting ones. Father and Jancsi whitewashed the house inside and out. They painted the window boxes and shutters a bright blue. Jancsi and Kate selected the largest, most perfect eggs, and they were laid aside for decorating. Mother made piles and piles of nut-cakes and poppyseed cakes, baking them in different shapes. Some of them looked like birds or lambs, some were crescent-shaped, some looked like stars and crosses. The cousins were always sniffing around the kitchen, waiting for "tastes."

Evenings Mother got out her dyepots and the fascinating

work of making dozens and dozens of fancy Easter eggs kept the family busy. There were two ways to decorate them. The plainer ones were dyed first. When they dried, Father and Jancsi scratched patterns on them with penknives. The fancy ones were lots of work. Mother had a tiny funnel, with melted beeswax in it. With this she drew intricate patterns on the white eggs. After the wax hardened, she dipped them in the dye. Then she scratched off the wax, and there was the beautiful design left in white on the colored egg. In this way she could make the most beautifully shaped designs by covering up parts of the pattern again with wax before each dipping. The finished ones were placed in baskets and put on a shelf until Easter morning.

"I'll make some extra fancy ones for Kate. She can give them to the boys she likes best," Mother said, smiling.

"Could I try to make one or two myself?" begged Kate. "*All* by myself. I don't want anybody to see them."

"Look out, Kate, you'll get all messed up, and this dye doesn't wash off. You have to scrub it off with sand," warned Jancsi.

Kate went to a corner with her dyepots and labored for a long time in silence. When she finally put her eggs away and came back to the table, she was a sight!

"Oh, Kate, you clumsy," cried Jancsi. "Now you look like an Easter egg. Oh, you look funny." She was red paint from head to toe. Her fingers were dripping, her nose looked like a red cherry.

Jancsi's hands were wet with the dye, too, but he carefully kept his face and clothes clean.

Kate looked at him seriously.

"Jancsi, dear, there's just a little smudge of black on your nose," she said, pointing a red finger at an imaginary spot.

"Don't touch me! I'll wipe if off," cried Jancsi and, forgetting his wet hands, rubbed his nose vigorously.

"M-m-m. That's off, but your forehead is smudged, too. The smoke from the candle, I imagine," said a very sweet and solicitous Kate.

Jancsi rubbed his forehead.

"Your chin, too. My, my, these old-fashioned candles."

Jancsi rubbed his chin. Father and Mother were laughing hard, but he didn't know why.

"It's perfect now, Jancsi," smiled Kate. "Now you look like an Easter egg yourself."

"Oh, my boy," laughed Father, "won't you ever learn the ways of our sweet pussy? You are decorated for Easter all right."

Jancsi ran to the mirror. He couldn't help laughing.

"I should have known better," he admitted. "She had her angel face on. I'll tell the boys to scrub your face for you, sprinkling isn't enough."

Saturday, Mother packed all the meats, bread, and cakes in big baskets lined with snow-white napkins. They would take them to the church Sunday to be blessed by the priest. She put the finishing touches on the family's Sunday clothes. Kate didn't pay any attention to her own dress Mother had promised for Easter; she was satisfied with her boy's clothes.

On Sunday they started to dress after a very early breakfast. Kate's clothes were laid out on her bed. Suddenly a wail came from her room. "Oh, Auntie, which skirt shall I wear?"

"Which skirt? All of them, of course, it's a holiday!"

"But there are eighteen on my bed!"

"That's because you're only a little girl. I'm wearing thirty-six, but I'm a married woman," said Mother, appearing in the doorway. She completely filled it. Her pleated and starched skirts were all the colors of the rainbow, standing away from her body like a huge umbrella. She wore a white shirtwaist with puffed sleeves, a tight black vest, laced in front over red buttons. Her head was covered with a fringed, embroidered shawl, tied under her chin. She wore tight black boots with high heels. Kate gazed at her with awe.

"I'm really very young," she said meekly. "Couldn't I wear just one or two skirts?"

"All nice girls wear at least ten," was Mother's firm answer.

When Kate finally emerged from her room, she looked like a small replica of Mother. Her dress was even more colorful, with

a scarlet red vest. Her sparkling, shimmering bonnet had long red and green ribbons on it, cascading almost to her knees. But Kate's face was sad. "My old boots," she said, "they look awful with this pretty dress."

"Oh, you poor lamb!" cried Mother. "We clean forgot your boots! Father! Jancsi! We forgot Kate's boots."

Father came in, solemnly shaking his head. "Hm-hm. Think of it! Our pussy hasn't any boots. What can we do? She will have to wear mine!"

He went to the cupboard. When he turned around, he held

81

the prettiest, trimmest pair of little red boots in his hand.

"Oh," said everybody. Kate flew to him, crying: "Uncle Márton! You are the sweetest, best, dearest uncle!" She was trying
to hug him and put her boots on at the same time.

Father left them to get the wagon while Kate was still dancing around happily. She was kissing Mother and she even at-
tempted to kiss Jancsi. But he balked at that. "Only girls kiss,"
he declared and stalked out after Father.

They drove to church in great state. The wagon had been
freshly painted, the horses were brushed until their coats shone
like black satin. They overtook and passed more and more
wagons as they approached the village. "Our wagon is best of
all!" said Kate proudly.

The streets around the village church were lined with ve-
hicles. The church square was packed with people. They were
dressed in brilliant colors, the women in immense skirts, swaying, their hair-ribbons floating in the breeze. The men all had
bunches of flowers in their hats and wore snow-white pleated
shirts and pants, and black, blue, or green sleeveless jackets.
It made the prettiest picture Kate ever had seen. "Like a big
flower garden," she whispered.

Slowly the church filled, and the service began. After the last
prayer and hymn, the priest blessed the food in the church
square. Groups of friends stood around for a while, talking.
Kate was introduced to many people. Everybody had heard
about the runaway horses. She was the subject of open admiration from the village boys and girls. Here was a city girl who
not only had had the measles, but wasn't afraid of anything!

"We'll come to your house tomorrow!" promised the boys.

When Kate woke up Monday morning, Father and Jancsi
had already left for the village. Mother and Kate spread the
best white tablecloth on the big kitchen table and placed huge
platters of meat, bread, and cakes on it. "What a beautiful
tablecloth," exclaimed Kate. "I never saw anything like it in the
stores."

"I made it myself, Kate, when I was your age," said Mother.
"I planted the flax, reaped it, prepared it, spun the thread, and

wove it into this cloth. It's more than twenty-five years old now, but it's as good as new." Kate wanted to know more about spinning and weaving, but Mother was too busy. She promised Kate to teach her all about it in the winter.

They were still arranging the baskets of eggs when the first wagon drove in. The men and boys walked in, and one of them spoke a piece:

> "Glory be to the Holy Father
> Who gave us food and pure water.
> As we water the rose to make it bloom,
> We sprinkle the rosebud in this room.
> May you live long,
> Old and young,
> Peace be with you on this holy day of Easter."

They all repeated the last line. Kate saw the flasks of water in their hands. "It won't be so bad, the bottles are very small," she thought. Just the same she squealed and ran when the boys stepped forward and began to throw water on her. There was great shouting and laughing in the kitchen. "We want eggs! Give us some eggs, Kate, we'll stop sprinkling if you do," cried the boys. She ran to the basket and gave them handfuls of eggs. Mother invited them to eat anything they liked. Another wagon drove in. Young men came on horseback. It was great fun for Kate! She was pretty wet by now, but didn't mind it.

Visitors came and left; the kitchen was always full of people and laughter. She liked the verses they spoke, she liked the boundless hospitality, she liked ever so much to be there and enjoy it all!

The food supply was almost exhausted when the last wagon drove off. There weren't any more eggs. She slumped in a chair, tired but happy.

Jancsi and Father came home in the afternoon, loaded with eggs. "Well, Kate," asked Father, "did you give everything away? Not one egg left for us?"

"I saved one for you and one for Jancsi," said Kate, walking to the small basket where she had hidden the eggs she had made all by herself.

"You said I had to give the best ones to people I like best." She smiled, holding out her hands to Father and Jancsi.

"Mine has a nice flower on it and—oooh—little ducks! Aren't they, Kate?"

"Yes, I drew them for you because we had such a good time with the duckies."

Father took the egg offered to him. It wasn't a very good Easter egg, being a tiny bit smeary, but to Father it was the most beautiful gift in the world. This is what Kate had written on it: "I like you best of all, Uncle Márton!"

THE six Mitchell children, Peter, Patsy, Joan, Angela, Timmy, and Catherine move from Washington to Montreal when their father takes a job there. And in Canada they have many happy adventures. One day, when they are caught in a thundershower, they seek shelter at the nearest house and meet Pierre Jolicoeur, a French-Canadian boy, who soon becomes their good friend.

Hilda van Stockum

A VISIT WITH PIERRE

ILLUSTRATED BY THE AUTHOR

WHEN Daddy came home Friday evening he seemed discouraged. "I am looking for a house for the winter," he told Mother, "and I cannot find any. Everybody wants to sell his house; no one wants to rent it. If it goes on like this we shall have to live in a snow hut, like the Eskimos."

"Oh, could we, Daddy?" asked Peter, much taken with the idea.

But Mother seemed to think that there were grave disadvantages to living like an Eskimo.

"Why don't we buy a house, then?" asked Joan.

Daddy shrugged his shoulders. "Not enough money," he stated briefly. "The move here took almost all our savings."

"And our war bonds?" asked Peter. "You can have mine."

"No, no, I won't touch those," said Daddy. "They are for your education when you are older. No, we must find another way out. I keep looking at the papers and following up advertisements."

85

"There are still two months," Grannie consoled him. "We don't have to leave here until September."

The children worried very little about the house. Winter seemed so far off. Besides, Daddy made them work. Daddy was very industrious himself. He made railings on the porch for Mother, he chopped up several dead trees for fuel, he made a raft for the older children from which they could dive into the lake and a sandbox for Catherine in front of the hut where Mother could keep an eye on her. All the while he was whistling soldiers' songs. He said this sort of work made him feel rested. The children didn't feel rested. They had to fetch and carry nails and hammers, lug wood, haul pailfuls of sand, and stand holding pieces of wood while Daddy sawed them. When Daddy finally went back to town the children felt relieved. At last they could sit down.

Mother, however, was pleased with this activity. She said everything was much easier with plenty of wood stacked near the kitchen and several safe places for Baby.

"Today we may go and play with Pierre, Mother, mayn't we?" begged Peter. "We've worked so hard for Daddy."

"Yes," said Mother. "You go. It's a lovely day. Grannie and I'll manage."

It was lucky, thought Peter afterward, that they happened to go to the Jolicoeurs that Monday. As they came walking down the road they could see from afar that Mr. Jolicoeur had taken out his *calèche,* or carriage. He and Pierre seemed just on the point of leaving. Joan, Patsy, and Peter began to run. They always wanted to know everything that went on.

"Hi, Pierre" cried Peter. "*Qu'est-ce que c'est que ca?*" It was a mouthful but a very useful one. With that sentence you were on the way to learning the whole French language. Peter had learned some of it already.

"We make a veeseet," said Pierre, "to *Grandmère et Grandpère.*" He looked elegant in a blue suit with breeches. Peter noticed the difference from his own knickers, which usually slobbered halfway down his ankles. Pierre's breeches were held tight under the knees with laces.

"Perhaps you would like to come for the ride?" asked Monsieur Jolicoeur, who already had climbed on the driver's seat. "We have only Pierre and me."

"Don't the other children want to come?" asked Joan, astonished.

"*Maman* wants the older, to help," explained Pierre. "And young ones make *beaucoup* trouble for *pauvre Grandmère*."

Joan nodded. That made sense to her. Peter and Patsy didn't have Joan's scruples. They were already sitting in the *calèche*, pink with joy. Joan climbed in beside them.

"Good," said Mr. Jolicoeur. "My mother, she will be pleased to meet young *Américains*. She will be talking about it all winter when the snow is deep and the fire burns. She is a great story-teller, my mother, and very wise. She knows a little English. She had education, my mother, she went to a convent when she was young." An affectionate smile lit up Mr. Jolicoeur's good-natured face. You could see he was very proud of his mother. "*Allons*," he said, and chirped at Ste.-Marie. Ste.-Marie trotted off.

Blissful, the three Mitchells sat in the back seat and feasted their eyes. You could see better from a horse-drawn carriage than from a car. The sun shone on their heads, they smelled the good horse smell and heard the musical clopping of the hoofs. All around, nature seemed to reach out her arms to them. Sometimes trees arched over their heads, and then again the road would open up to a glorious mountain landscape with hill upon hill receding in all shades of blue.

At last Mr. Jolicoeur stopped Ste.-Marie in front of a lonely farmhouse. A woman with a large hat on her head straightened up from weeding a cabbage bed.

"*Voilà Jean et Pierre!*" she cried joyously.

The wrinkles in her face showed she was old, but she made quicker movements than Grannie. Monsieur Jolicoeur jumped from the *calèche* and kissed her. Then Pierre followed, hugging her so tight her hat fell off and he had to pick it up and hand it back to her.

"That my granmother," explained Pierre unnecessarily. "*Grandmère, ceux-ci sont mes amis américains.*"

The grandmother exclaimed over the young visitors who had come from so far.

"*Oh, là, là,*" she said. "That America, grand country, eh? You must tell me many things. Come inside."

Grandpère met them as they entered the house. He wore high boots and a cap. Around his middle he wore a colorful sash, and he was smoking a long pipe. The kitchen was large and roomy. On one side there was a very high bed made like a press, with lots of drawers under it. Grandmère saw the children looking at it and smiled.

"I have my clothes now in the drawers," she said. "But one time they were beds for my little ones. I had ten children, and six are still alive." She looked proudly at Pierre's father.

The young Mitchells wandered from one unusual piece of furniture to another. The chairs and table were quite different from those they knew at home. Grandpère had made them all himself, with a bit of carving on them to finish them off. Grandpère could not speak English. He listened to his wife's words of praise with a smile on his face, puffing at his pipe.

"Grandpère great worker in wood," Grandmère told the children. "Look how he made," and she showed them a crucifix which hung on the wall, carved with skill and tenderness out of a block of rough wood. Other things hung on the wall, too. Patsy noticed them first.

"Pictures made on cloth," she said. They were rugs worked, not into patterns, but like paintings, with scenes of Canada in winter: sleds pulling wood out of snowy forests, or a village street with brightly painted houses, gay under their white blanket.

"Grandmère made those," Pierre told them proudly. "They are 'ooked rugs."

"What is this?" asked Peter curiously, turning the wheel on a wooden machine.

"That's a *rouet*," said Grandmère. "*Qu'est-ce qu'un rouet?* a . . . how you say? spinning wheel. . . ."

"A spinning wheel. . ." Patsy and Peter eyed it reverently. So this was the thing that had sent Sleeping Beauty into her hundred years' rest!

"Where can you prick yourself?" asked Patsy curiously, but Grandmère didn't understand her question. There was no time for long explanations, anyway, for Grandmère suddenly let out a fierce yell.

"*Là, là, c'est affreux, il est échappé encore, ce Tonnerre de Dieu!*"

She rushed out of the house, accompanied by the other Jolicoeurs. The Mitchells followed more slowly, wondering what it was all about. They saw soon enough. A great big goat was scampering all over Grandmère's flower beds and cabbage patch. She was too quick for Grandmère to catch. She threw a yellow beam out of slanting, wicked eyes, kicked up her sharp, vicious heels, and bounded over the fence and up the mountain.

"*Ah, c'est une misère,*" moaned Grandmère. "I cannot follow, I am not a goat." The children had to laugh at that.

"We'll follow," they said.

"Yes, we'll follow," Pierre promised. "Come."

The three Mitchells ran after Pierre, and Pierre ran after the goat. But the creature was too quick for them. They stumbled and fell where she scarcely needed to touch a foot. Soon the children were panting, dirty, disheveled, and hot. They had to sit down and rest while the goat disappeared behind a rock.

"*Oh, là, là,*" said Pierre, wiping his face. "That is why she is called *Tonnerre de Dieu,* 'God's Thunder.' "

"But why do you call her 'God's Thunder,' then," asked Patsy curiously. "Why not just 'Thunder'?"

"Because God made 'er," said Pierre. "Ee makes t'ings sometimes we don't like. They good for us all the same. Tonnerre de Dieu very good. Gives much milk."

"But what do we do now? She is out of sight," said Peter. "Someone else will get her good milk."

"I know where she gone," Pierre answered calmly. "She 'as boy friend. She will make Madame Joubert ver' angry, it is to be feared. But, *que faire?* I cannot 'elp it."

"Who is Madame Joubert?"

"You will know soon," Pierre told them lugubriously. He got up and walked in the direction they had seen Tonnerre de Dieu go.

"*Voilà la maison de Madame Joubert,*" said Pierre, stretching out his hand. "*Et voilà Tonnerre de Dieu,*" he added dramatically.

The three Mitchells burst out laughing. The hill on which they stood sloped down into a valley. Farther on there was another hill and on that hill stood an old frame house with two porches, an outside staircase going to the top porch. Down that staircase ran a small woman shouting many French words so quickly they seemed to run into each other. She was shaking her fist at Tonnerre de Dieu, who was frolicking about on the hillside with another goat. Unfortunately the goat had run into Madame Joubert's clothesline, and now she was trailing Madame Joubert's wash all over the rocks and grass.

"*Hi, ho, heu,*" cried Madame Joubert frantically.

She had reached the ground and was now running to catch the loose end of the clothesline. Behind her came a small girl, with a small boy after her, behind that two more little boys.

Six little girls were still descending the staircase, and the house was not yet empty. All those children were shrieking at the top of their voices just like their mother.

Now the door of the downstairs half of the house opened and a lady came out. She had her arms at her sides and talked French angrily. She pointed at Madame Joubert's children and shook her fist. Several more children now came through the downstairs door and gathered around the second lady.

"That is Madame Desanges," giggled Pierre. "She even more angry than Madame Joubert. *Oh, là, là,* but they are fond of fighting."

The Desanges children now began to shout at the Joubert children, and into this medley the goats charged, blind with the clothes they had managed to collect around their horns. Tonnerre de Dieu wore a beautiful pair of red flannel underwear, and the other goat had a baby's nightgown draped across her eyes.

The children fled in all directions, for there was enough point left to the horns to hurt.

Pierre and the Mitchells now abandoned their role of spectators. Since Tonnerre de Dieu couldn't see because of the red flannel, they hoped to catch her. They fell over several small Desanges babies before, at last, they caught hold of the clothesline and pulled. Startled, Tonnerre de Dieu was brought to a standstill. Meanwhile Madame Joubert had captured the other goat.

She was breathless, but not wordless. She addressed Pierre with great vehemence. Though they couldn't catch one single sentence, the Mitchells understood that Madame Joubert was not pleased. She did not love Tonnerre de Dieu. She had much work to do, and now she had to do the wash over. Her twelve children would go hungry, as she had no time to cook dinner. Hereupon the twelve children all started to weep, and Pierre was greatly affected. Now, however, Madame Desanges came to the rescue.

"It does not matter," she said in very clear French. "I have a soup just made; you shall all eat of my beautiful soup."

Whereupon there was great peace. All the little Desanges
children looked pleased and proud, and all the little Joubert
children stopped weeping. Madame Joubert went to her wash-
tub, and Madame Desanges went to her stove.

Only the goats and the children were left standing in the sunshine. The oldest Joubert child proposed a game, which the
Mitchells were eager to join. So Pierre tied Tonnerre de Dieu
to the porch railing, and all the children old enough to play
joined hands. The smallest Desangeses and Jouberts sat and
watched, sucking their thumbs. They sang,

> *"Petit' hirondelle qui n'a qu'une aile*
> *Tu t'en vas voler, vole, vole, vole,*
> *Tu t'en vas voler, vole, vole, vole,*
> *Tu t'en vas voler,"*

which is, in English:

> Little swallow with one wing,
> You go flying, fly, fly, fly,
> You go flying, fly, fly, fly,
> You go flying.

One little Joubert girl stood in the ring and tried to get out,
but the others wouldn't let her. So she sang the rest:

> *"Non, vous ne m'aimez pas,*
> *Gentils petits enfants,*
> *Non, vous ne m'aimez pas,*
> *Pour m'enfermer comme ça."*

> No, you do not love me,
> Sweet little children,
> No, you do not love me,
> Because you hold me fast.

Then she broke loose, and the ring was suddenly scattered as
the "swallow" tried to catch her captors. At last she caught hold
of Peter, who was too interested in everything else to take care
of himself. Now he had to go into the ring and be a swallow,
which he did bashfully.

There was not much time for the second game, as Madame Desanges called the children to her beautiful soup. The Mitchells had a brief glimpse of the Desanges kitchen, sixteen children gathered around the table, silenced by steaming soup, which they ate standing as there was not enough furniture for them to sit. In a corner Madame Joubert was rocking her baby to sleep. The Mitchells would have liked to linger a little, looking at the cozy scene, but Pierre said his grandmother would be waiting, and he unfastened Tonnerre de Dieu.

"I wish *we* had sixteen children," sighed Patsy, tearing herself away.

Grandmère was indeed waiting, and very relieved to see them all, including the goat, which she put away safely. "You are in time, the bread is done," she said.

With fascination the Mitchells watched her as she went to the outdoor oven with its pointed roof and, opening the door, pulled out loaf after loaf of delicious fragrant bread.

"I bet you hungry." Grandmère smiled.

She had laid the table in the kitchen with flowery china, and soon the Jolicoeurs and Mitchells were feasting on the excellent hot bread, spread thickly with homemade butter and honey, and washed down with goat's milk.

"I had some *confiture,* too," Grandmère murmured, bustling about. "Where is my *confiture?* Where have I her laid? I don't find her." She was pulling out all the drawers under the bed, but no jam anywhere.

"She is rationed, I hide her for feast, and behold, she has flown," Grandmère cried dramatically, throwing up her hands. Pierre looked at her with a smile which grew broader and broader. He shook his head.

"Grandmère always lose t'ings," he said. "I 'ave a *petit cadeau* for Grandmère I made myself, *voilà.*" Slowly he pulled an object out of his pocket. It was wrapped in tissue paper. Grandmère took it and unwrapped it.

"*Tiens, c'est beau, ça,*" she commented reverently, clucking her lips.

It was a little statue of St. Anthony carved out of wood. He

94

had an almost round halo on his head and a string of beads around his middle. If you looked close you could see mistakes, but from a distance it was perfect.

"I made him myself, with knife," said Pierre. "Saint-Antoine good for Grandmère, good at finding t'ings." He looked roguishly at his grandmother, and she pulled a face at him. Then she handed the statue to Grandpère, who nodded approvingly.

"*C'est bien, ça.*"

The Mitchells now had to feel and touch the little statue. They were astonished at Pierre's skill.

"Was that what you were doing when we first met you?" asked Joan.

Pierre shrugged his shoulders. "I don' know too many t'ings. I will show you at 'ome."

"Too much carving you do," said his father, rumpling his hair affectionately. "It is better to look after the cows."

"O-oh, don't you want Pierre to be an artist?" asked Patsy. Her eyes were solemn. "Sometimes people become rich and sometimes they become famous. I don't know what I would choose," she continued slowly. "I should like to be rich *and* famous, but that never seems to happen. If you want to be famous, you have to be poor," she sighed.

"*Tiens*, a philosopher," Grandpère said, smiling.

It was now time to go home. Grandmère had to rest in the afternoon. So Monsieur Jolicoeur gathered up his passengers, and after a hearty farewell they were clip-clopping down the road again, watched after by the old couple.

It was well toward the end of the day when the three Mitchells returned to their hut. They opened the door, and there sat Mother, putting her finger to her lips. She was in the rocker with Catherine on her lap. Trusty was curled at her feet, and behind her sat Timmy and Angela, munching homemade cookies while they pored over a picture book. Joan, Patsy, and Peter looked at one another.

Home is not a bad place either, their eyes said. And then they tiptoed inside.

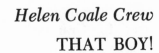

Helen Coale Crew

THAT BOY!

ILLUSTRATED BY *Salcia Bahnc*

"WHERE is that boy?" growled old Tommaso Marchi, laying down the hand lens through which he had been examining the mosaic work he was doing. His little shop on the Via Sistina was a small one, wedged in behind a large building and approached by a narrow alley. The window where he worked looked out upon a court in which a tiny fountain played and a thick lilac bush bloomed in one corner. All around the court ran an arcade, and usually when Old Tommaso could not find "that boy" at his elbow, he would see him chasing along the arcade with his dog Bimbo, or sitting on the edge of the fountain teasing the goldfish, or otherwise wasting his time when he ought to be at work.

"Where is that boy!" growled the old man again. And then he bent his head over his work and forgot the boy completely. For fifty years his capable hands had been making mosaics; sometimes even making, in his small laboratory opening from his shop, his own glass, coloring it to suit his need or fancy, and fitting the tiny cubes into charming pictures and borders. Old Tommaso thought very little of the cheap mosaics turned out by the hundreds in the big factories to sell to travelers and tourists. He made his only to order, and many handsome automobiles drove up to that alley entrance, whose owners wished to order a fine bit of mosaic work for a wedding or birthday gift, or for the adornment of house or table.

This morning Tommaso had just finished the making of a shallow tray. In the bottom of the tray was a bed of cement,

96

and in this while it was still soft he had carefully placed, using pincers for the purpose, the little cubes of colored glass that were to make the picture. Before him stood the picture he had copied, a picture of Apollo in his chariot, driving the horses of the sun, with the graceful Hours grouped about him, and Aurora scattering flowers in his path. The cubes of glass were all in place, their surfaces level, their edges so close that no least crack had been left anywhere. And now the cement had become hard, holding the cubes firmly in place, and he had smoothed and polished the picture. His last polishing he was now doing with his finger tips, and such sensitive finger tips were they that he would have been aware at once of the slightest unevenness. The background he had made of gold cubes, and in all other respects he had imitated the coloring of the picture before him as closely as possible. The picture itself was a copy of a painting hanging in a palace not far away, and he had gone more than once to look at the real picture during the making of his mosaic.

Such a piece of work may seem difficult to the reader of this story, but Tommaso had done something still more difficult. He had made up bundles of long rods of colored glass in such a way that the ends made pictures, heated them hot, which melted them together, and pulled the hot mass out into a long slender rod. Then, by cutting a slice off the rod he had a mosaic so small as almost to require a reading glass to see it clearly These little mosaics he set into rings or brooches. He had made one just recently of a little Cupid with bow and arrows, swinging in a rope of roses. Of course from that long bundle of glass threads he could cut many sections, and so have many tiny pictures of his little Cupid.

And now once more, having assured himself with his finger tips that the picture in the tray had a smooth and flawless surface, he looked up, and for the third time growled, "Where is that boy!"

This time a voice at his elbow said gaily, "Here, Master!" and there stood Toni, breathing hard as though he had been running fast, and Bimbo with his red tongue hanging out.

"Where have you been?" asked Tommaso.

"Nowhere, Master," said Toni, smiling sweetly.

"What have you been doing, rascal?"

"Nothing whatever, dear Master!"

"Would that you did your work as cheerfully as you do nothing," said Tommaso. And then he gave the boy a note, with very careful instructions as to where he was to leave it, and told him to return at once to the shop, without any loitering on the way, else he would forfeit his dinner.

Tommaso knew that Toni would do anything rather than forfeit the good, hot dinner he had every noon at the shop, brought in from a near-by restaurant. For Toni's mother was very poor and his father no longer living. Their home was in a tall tenement house near the river, and there, during his first ten years, Toni had had to play nurse to his four younger brothers and sisters while his mother went out to work. She was a washerwoman and every day went to one of the public washing troughs scattered here and there throughout the city. The people of Rome have always had plenty of water, and it is said that even if you are out of sight of a fountain, you are never out of hearing of the cool splashing of one. At the washing trough eight or ten women can wash at once, beating the clothes with wooden paddles, old and young alike chattering and singing as they work. Sometimes Toni carried the heavy basket of clothes to the trough for his mother, and he thought to himself that he would much rather beat and scrub and rinse, laughing and chattering with the rest, than stay at home and keep the four little ones from stumbling down the steep and dirty tenement stairs or getting lost in the narrow, winding streets. Even the baby, the *bambino*, was quick at running off on his short but sturdy legs. Toni was glad enough when their neighbor the barber got him his job with Tommaso. Yet oddly enough, bright and quick though he was, he had never become interested in Tommaso's mosaic work. He liked to leap about and jump and climb and use his strong, splendid muscles. But to potter with little bits of glass and marble—*ahi!* there was nothing to that!

98

Now it so happened that at about the same time that old Tommaso, bent over his work in his shop at the Via Sistina, was wondering impatiently why Toni had not returned from his errand, a well-dressed woman in a fine auto, sitting behind a solemn chauffeur, became very restless indeed, and finally said fretfully to the chauffeur, "Giuseppe, where is that boy? What can have become of him? He has been gone fully a half hour, and he promised to be only ten minutes. You'd best run down the stairs and find him."

She had started out that morning, it seems, to show the sights of the city to her nephew, Stefano, come to Rome for the first time on a visit. Stefano had not wanted to go riding at all. His home was in Venice, that city on the sea, where all the streets are canals, and where instead of walking on sidewalks one rides in a gondola—a slow business at best. Stefano wanted to use his feet this lovely spring morning, here where there were miles and miles of sidewalks. And so he had persuaded Aunt Cecilia to let him get out of the automobile and run down a great stairway that curved about a big church on both sides, joined together in front of it, and ran like a cascade down to a piazza below. At the foot of the stairway there was a foam of lovely flowers, where flower sellers had spread out their wares, and beyond that a fountain in its marble brim. And so the chauffeur had stopped the car, and Stefano had jumped out and gone down the stairway in a flash.

Everyone who goes to visit Rome goes to see the Spanish Stairs, as the great flight, reaching from a higher to a lower street, is called. As to the church, "halfway up the stairs it stands," like the clock in Longfellow's poem that says *"Never! . . . Forever!"* At the lowest level is the flower market, with its baskets of flowers of all kinds and colors, and graceful little growing shrubs and trees in tubs or pots. The market women wear shawls quite as colorful as the flowers, and the men have silver earrings in their ears and red or blue handkerchiefs about their necks. Among them little boys with picture post cards run about, trying to make sales; and there are always some saucy little chaps, who, having nothing to sell, joyfully stand on their

heads before tourists, thinking this sight to be quite worth a penny. And, because of the twinkling smiles and the wiggling bare toes, perhaps it is!

Stefano did not pause to look at the church. He knew that Aunt Cecilia was going to show him plenty of churches before the day was over. He simply ran down the Spanish Stairs so fast that at length he could not stop if he wanted to, and he would probably have tumbled headlong into the fountain in the piazza had he not run full tilt into another boy, which knocked them both over. The other boy was Toni.

"I say!" cried Toni, jumping up smilingly. "What are you doing, anyway?"

Stefano got up and brushed off his clothes. They had both been thrown against the brim of the fountain. "Well, you saved me from a bath," he said, "and I owe you thanks for that." Taking a penny from his pocket he tossed it at Toni, and Toni caught it deftly. Then they smiled at each other.

The flower sellers and the post-card sellers and the boys who stood on their heads for a penny all gathered about, expecting a fight. They would have enjoyed seeing a good fight, as business was dull at the moment. And the fight would have been a fair one, as the two boys were just of a size.

"They are as alike as two chestnuts," said old Granny Brigida, who had sold flowers at the Spanish Stairs for a round half-century, and whose face was as brown as a chestnut itself.

"As like as twins," said her little granddaughter Vanna, setting down an armful of lilac branches to look at the two boys.

"As like as twins," echoed Nello, the seller of little lemon and orange trees, and he gave an ear of each boy a tweak.

"As like as twins!" echoed everybody. And then, as it seemed there was to be no fight, they all gradually went back to their own business.

But Stefano and Toni stared at each other. Stefano felt as though he were looking into a mirror when he looked at Toni. Toni had never looked into a mirror, but he had seen a dim reflection of himself in the glass of a shop window occasionally, and Stefano's face did not look unfamiliar to him. As they stood staring, a great idea came to Stefano. He drew Toni around to the other side of the fountain to tell him about it. And the great idea was this, that since they looked so much alike, it would be the best fun in the world to change clothes and be each other for a whole day. Stefano had read a book in which two boys had done that, and they had had some great adventures.

"*Ahi,* no!" said Toni. "I might not like the things you do."

"Yes, you would," said Stefano. "I'm riding around Rome in an automobile all day today. Riding, you understand. Leaning back on soft cushions, seeing shops and fine buildings, and maybe a squad of soldiers go by, or buglers playing, and having a fine lunch somewhere—"

Toni began to get interested. "Will you have *gelati?*" he asked. *Gelati* is what the Italian people call ice cream.

"*Gelati,* of course," said Stefano; "white or pink or maybe both."

"It's a go!" said Toni quickly. He had never been in an auto at all, and had seen only a very little of the city he lived in. As to *gelati,* well, he had seen other children eating it. Without another word they hid behind a row of little lemon trees in green tubs and exchanged their suits, caps, shoes and stockings. When they stood up again, they were more alike than ever. Then Toni told Stefano how to find Tommaso Marchi's shop, straight down the Via Sistina, and gave him a note to be given to the old mosaic-maker. And Stefano told Toni how he would find Aunt Cecilia in a plum-colored auto just back of the church.

"But," said Stefano, looking sharply at Toni, "you'll have to wash behind your ears before Aunt Cecilia sees you. She's very particular about that. She washed behind my ears this morning." And as Toni prepared to make a thorough job of it by plunging his whole head into the fountain, Giuseppe the chauffeur laid a firm hand on Toni's arm and said, "You're to come to your aunt at once, sir, and no more nonsense."

The two boys winked at each other behind the chauffeur and each went—no, not his own way, but the other's!

Let us first follow Toni. When he and Giuseppe reached the waiting auto, Aunt Cecilia was looking out from it with a very angry face. But Toni, swinging off his cap, saluted her in cheerful and care-free fashion.

"It has been hours and hours—" began Aunt Cecilia sharply, but Toni interrupted her with a laugh.

"Well then, Aunt, we must hurry along," he said. "There are so many things in Rome I want to see."

Aunt Cecilia could hardly believe her ears. "But you said this morning—"

Toni interrupted her again. "But that was this morning," he said, and stretching himself back luxuriously on the softly cushioned seat, he smiled sweetly at Aunt Cecilia.

Aunt Cecilia was pleased to think that her nephew had changed his mind about driving around Rome. She told Giuseppe to go first down the Corso, a broad avenue running south to the Forum. And presently Toni ceased to lean back comfortably in the seat, but sat bolt upright, looking at the fine shops and famous palaces along that famous avenue. Toni had to cross the Corso every day going from his home to the shop, and again going from the shop back to his home. On those two daily occasions he crossed it on foot, and usually barefoot at that. And now he sat in lordly fashion in a fine auto, with Stefano's neatly polished shoes on his feet! He had to be careful not to point out places he knew, for of course if he was Stefano he had never seen them.

Aunt Cecilia began to tell him about the wonderful Carnival that swept up and down the Corso once a year—people in fancy costumes laughing and jostling in the street, and people in the balconies of the houses throwing down *confetti*, tiny scraps of bright-colored paper, poured out like a rainbow that has been splintered into a million pieces, and flowers, and candy. And she told him that centuries ago on Carnival day riderless horses were made to race down the Corso. And she told it so well that Toni seemed to hear the heavy clattering hooves beating on the stone pavements, and the screams of people hurrying to get away before the horses were upon them in that mad race.

Also Aunt Cecilia told him wonderful tales of the men who had built those great palaces that lined the Corso, and every

103

time she stopped for breath Toni would say, "Tell me more, Aunt Cecilia!" And Aunt Cecilia thought, "What has come over the boy? This morning he wasn't interested in anything."

At the foot of the Corso they saw the great monument put up in memory of the king's grandfather, he who first joined all the parts of Italy into one united kingdom. At the foot of the monument, which is really a great building with corridors behind white pillars, Toni saw the tomb of Italy's "unknown soldier." Now he was in a part of Rome that he had never seen. Soon they stopped to look at the Forum, an empty space containing here and there a group of ancient marble pillars still held together by a fragment of marble cornice, here and there a cracked and battered pavement of marble or stone. Aunt Cecilia told him the story of the Forum: how at first it was a mere market place for the long-ago people; how later, lined with splendid temples it became a place where impassioned speeches were made by the men whose very names are the history of Rome; how in the Middle Ages it went to ruin, the marble temples being pulled down and carried off to make those very palaces they had just seen on the Corso, until the once stately Forum became nothing more than a cow pasture; and how now it was being carefully preserved as the very heart of Rome.

Then they went on to the Colosseum, that great ruin that was once a mighty circus for the people. Toni looked, shivering with excitement, at the huge enclosed space where gladiators fought together, or men with wild beasts, while in rising rows upon

104

rows of seats sat the people of Rome—Emperor, statesmen, generals, soldiers, women and children, slaves—all being amused by these cruel sports. By this time Toni's eyes were round and big and his heart beating. Never before had he dreamed that his city had had a long and wonderful history, or that it was a place to be proud of, or that it was called the Eternal City because of its long glory. Had he gone to school every day he would have learned these things, but he had gone to school very few days indeed of his life. At first his help at home, and then the money he earned at Tommaso's shop, had been so badly needed by his mother, that she saw to it that when the truant officer came around looking for children that should be in school, Toni was nowhere in sight.

At last noon came, and they went to a white-and-gold restaurant that Toni thought must surely be a part of the king's palace. Here, while they sat eating a most delicious dinner, topped off with *gelati*, Toni, comfortably full of good things to eat, fell into a state of dreaming. Perhaps he could be a great man! And make speeches in the Forum like that Cicero that Aunt Cecilia told about! Or fight and win battles like that Julius Caesar! Or make a united kingdom, like that grandfather of the king! Or even—Tony grew very grave—be an unknown soldier with flowers and tears dropped daily upon his tomb! Toni's heart swelled with these many new thoughts. They were like growing pains in his heart and brain. And presently he asked Aunt Cecilia a question.

"How do men get to be great?"

"By doing their duty, first of all," said Aunt Cecilia.

"But if you had some little piece of work to do every day, like making mosaics in a dark shop, and nothing else, could you get to be like that Cicero man?" asked Toni.

"That would depend upon how well you made the mosaics, first of all," she answered.

And then Aunt Cecilia looked sharply at Toni, and the more she looked the more suspicious she became. She saw that his hands were not slender and white, but broad and muscular, and not any too clean, and his fingernails broken. She saw that his

105

curly hair had evidently not been cut by a barber, but had evidently been rather roughly snipped off by an inexperienced hand. And when he finished his *gelati*—oh, horrors!—he did not wipe his mouth with his napkin, but upon his sleeve! And at that she jumped up and shook him by the shoulders.

"You are not Stefano at all!" she cried. "You are dirty behind the ears! I don't know who you are, but I'm going to take you straight home with me and put you in the bathtub!" Which was just like Aunt Cecilia, who always did the first duty that came along and did it as promptly as possible. Toni rode meekly beside her in the car back to that bathtub, wondering if she could have made a Cicero if she had been a man in the days when great speeches were made in the Forum.

Meanwhile Stefano, in Toni's shabby clothes and shabbier shoes and cap, went east along the Via Sistina with Bimbo sniffing at his heels. Bimbo could not understand what had happened. Those were certainly the clothes that his little black nose sniffed at and his four short legs followed every day of his life. But something was different. He felt uneasy. Always before Toni had gone whistling along the street, with his cap on the back of his head. This time there was no whistling, and the cap was pulled down over its wearer's eyes. Bimbo had to show him the entrance to the alley they must take to reach the shop.

When they entered the shop, Tommaso was in the laboratory. He was going to make a bracelet for a young bride, and he was looking over his stock of glass, neatly arranged by colors in the drawers of a tall case. When Stefano entered, Tommaso looked at him over his spectacles.

"You almost missed your dinner," he said.

Stefano said nothing. He fumbled about in the pockets of Toni's coat, found the note, and handed it to Tommaso.

"Well?" asked Tommaso, still peering over his spectacles.

"Sir?" said Stefano, wondering what he ought to say.

"Why don't you make your usual excuses for your delay?" asked the old man.

Stefano, not knowing what to reply, looked around the room.

He had never seen a room like it before. He pointed to a queer black stove and asked what it was.

"You've seen me melt glass in there a thousand times," said Tommaso impatiently.

"And what are those little clay pots?" went on Stefano, his interest making him forget that he was supposed to be Toni.

"Are you losing your senses?" cried Tommaso. "You broke one of those only last week."

"Let's see you melt some glass," said Stefano. "And what's the pair of bellows for? Oh, and all those little glass blocks— what do you do with 'em?" And then he caught sight of the mosaic tray lying on a table and he hung over it entranced.

The old man was as puzzled as Bimbo for a few minutes. He knew that a boy could have a change of heart, but he did not think that it could occur in the flash of an eye. Stefano ran his fingers softly over the picture of Apollo and Aurora, and Tommaso saw that they were not blunt and muscular fingers, but long and shapely and sensitive. The boy could feel through his fingers as Toni never could have done. Tommaso wiped his spectacles, and took a good look at the boy through them. A change of heart cannot change one's fingers, not in a lifetime!

"Boy," he began, and was about to ask Stefano who he was, but Stefano did not give him a chance.

"Did you make this?" asked the boy. "I never saw a better one in Venice. How do you color your little pieces of glass?" And all this in one breath. And Tommaso, only too delighted to have an interested visitor, nodded to himself knowingly, and then showed Stefano everything in the laboratory and in the shop. He explained how he made the beautiful colored glass. Usually he bought good clear glass, melted it in his furnace, and added the coloring matter to suit his own taste. Sometimes, however, he sent to Venice for his colored glass, for the Venetians are famous glass-makers. And now it was Stefano's turn to tell Tommaso about the glassworks on the Island of Murano, near Venice, for he had been there and Tommaso had not. He had always been too busy to leave his shop. They talked about the fine mosaics on the wall of the cathedral at Venice, with the wonderful gold background, and the figures clothed in brilliant reds and blues, as bright now as when they had been put there centuries before.

At noon Stefano went to a little near-by restaurant and brought back their simple dinner, macaroni and cheese, beans with olive oil, and two hot, crusty rolls. As they sat there eating, and still talking of glass and the part it has played in the world, from ancient days to the present time, both as something useful and as something beautiful—the vases and dishes, the necklaces, the clear glass windows of homes, the stained-glass windows of churches, the mosaics on walls and floors, the lenses of telescopes and microscopes, the crystals of watches—suddenly Bimbo became very much excited, and rushed barking to the door. The door was pushed open from without and there was Toni, bringing in Aunt Cecilia.

108

"Enter, Aunt Cecilia!" said Toni, with a fine flourish and a beaming smile. And as Aunt Cecilia sailed into the little dark room, Toni said to Stefano, "She found me out when she looked behind my ears. How did *you* get found out?"

"I haven't been found out yet," said Stefano. But old Tommaso winked a knowing eye at Aunt Cecilia over his spectacles.

Then the boys told the whole story, while Aunt Cecilia and old Tommaso listened without saying a word. But when the boys had finished their story both their elders were ready to say something, but, as you guess, Aunt Cecilia got in ahead.

"That boy of yours, Mr. Marchi, must go to school every morning," she said, "and I am going to see that he does it. As to that boy of mine, if he were half as polite and attentive to his aunt as Toni has been, he would be doing well."

"That boy of yours, Madam," said Tommaso, "is a very intelligent boy, indeed. I recommend an art course for him, and designing in particular. Travel, too, he should have, to see the world's works of art. As to that boy of mine, if he were one tenth part as interested in the marvels of glasswork as your boy is, he would soon make his fortune."

Then Aunt Cecilia and Tommaso shook hands, and the ship with all sails set started off, Stefano following, with Bimbo jumping from one boy to the other as uncertainly as the famous donkey that couldn't choose between two bundles of hay. At the door Aunt Cecilia turned for a last word.

"Toni," she said, "I shall see your mother tomorrow."

Toni burst into merry laughter, seeing a vision of Aunt Cecilia taking his four little sisters and brothers home with her and putting them all at once into that big shining tub of hers. His own mother had a mind of her own, and when she stood with her arms akimbo, it wasn't easy to get around her. But if anybody could do it, it would be Aunt Cecilia.

"There is nothing to laugh about—" began Aunt Cecilia, but Toni interrupted her by giving her a loud kiss. Then he opened the door with a flourish. But as Stefano went out behind his aunt, Toni held him long enough to say, "*Ahi!* That Aunt Cecilia! What a Julius Caesar she would have made!"

109

A young Navajo Indian boy comes to
the rescue.

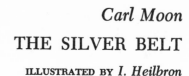

Carl Moon

THE SILVER BELT

ILLUSTRATED BY *I. Heilbron*

DAH-CHEE was a little Navajo Indian boy,
who lived far out in the west. The big desert was his home,
and not far from where he lived was a wonderful canyon. He
was never allowed to enter this canyon alone, for there were
snakes to be found on the warm sandy bed in summer, and in
winter the rains made big patches of quicksand that were not
safe to walk upon.

But Dah-chee liked this big canyon best of all play places.
He loved the big dark walls, and the eagles' nests high up in
the cliffs, and the places to climb and hunt for little animal
trails. Sometimes his father would take him into this wonderful
place, and he loved these little journeys, as his father always
pointed out so many interesting things.

Most of the Navajo men wore beautiful belts, made of bright
silver disks strung on a leather thong, and none were more
beautiful than the one worn by Dah-chee's father. Always he
had wanted one, too. He thought if he had one for his very
own—well, he would be the happiest Indian boy in the world.

When he became eight years old, his grandfather brought
him a new bow and a lot of bright red arrows. My, but Dah-
chee was happy! He had never owned a real bow before, and
he danced up and down for joy. Out he ran into the desert and
began to look for something to shoot at. A big cottonwood tree

110

stood close by, and on the side of it, his grandfather tacked a piece of sheepskin. It shone white against the dark wood and made a good target. Then he set a large stone on the ground, about twenty feet from the tree, to mark the place where Dah-chee was to stand when shooting.

"Tomorrow," said his grandfather, "I go back to my home in the desert. In seven days I will come again to see you. If, when I come, you can shoot well enough to hit the sheepskin mark once out of five shots, I will give you a silver belt. If you do not hit the mark, the belt will not be given to you. Only Indian boys who shoot well should wear the belt that warriors wear."

Then the old man went away, and each day little Dah-chee tried very hard to hit the mark. At first he couldn't even hit the tree. The arrows simply wouldn't go where, he was sure, he was aiming them. Then one day he found that he could hit the tree every time, and at last, on the day before his grandfather was to come again, he was able to hit the piece of sheepskin twice out of five shots.

That day was a long one for Dah-chee, and he felt that the morrow would never come. He not only wanted the long-wished-for belt, but he was going to show his grandfather how well he had learned to shoot. He was very sure he would have no trouble hitting the mark, at least once with five arrows. Again and again he thought of how wonderful the new belt would look about his waist. Wouldn't he be proud of it?

When the long-expected day came, he was up before the sun, testing the string of his bow, to make sure that it was just right. As soon as it was light enough to see he began shooting at the mark, and he kept on shooting until his arms ached and his little legs were weary with running after the arrows.

It was late in the morning when his grandfather rode up to the hogan, which is just the Indian name for home. With him was a white man, a lady, and their little daughter. The little girl looked to be about Dah-chee's own age. Parties of white people often came to visit the wonderful canyon in summer-time, and as they were almost always guided by his grandfather, Dah-chee was used to seeing them stop at his home.

111

On this particular morning it seemed an age before his grandfather had finished attending to the white man's horses, and had the many camping things packed, for the party was to start up the canyon later in the day, after the lady and little girl had rested. But at last the old man came to Dah-chee, and seeing he held five arrows and the bow in his hand, he said,—

"Well, Dah-chee, we will now see how well you can shoot."

They went over to the big cottonwood tree, and taking his stand by the stone, Dah-chee quickly shot the first of the five arrows. It missed not only the sheepskin mark, but the tree as well. It may be that he was a little too excited, or too anxious; anyway he had four arrows left, and only one was needed to hit the mark. His grandfather said nothing, but waited for him to shoot again. The second arrow hit the tree, but struck the bark some distance from the sheepskin. At last, when four of the five arrows had been used, the old man spoke kindly to his little grandson.

"I believe you have saved the last arrow just to show me how easily you can hit the mark. Though you now have but one arrow, it is as good as ten, if it hits the sheepskin."

At his grandfather's words, Dah-chee grew more calm, and his arms were more steady as he raised the bow for the final shot—the shot that *must* hit the mark, if he was to get the belt. Just as he was taking careful aim, he heard the little girl and her father coming. Anxious to shoot before they came up, he let the arrow fly a little too quickly, and it struck the tree far below the bit of sheepskin.

His grandfather walked away without saying a word, for he was a wise old man and knew that his promise to his little grandson must be kept. The little boy hung his head and turned away without stopping to pick up his arrows. Then, fearing that the little white girl might follow him, he ran as fast as he could to some great rocks that stood far out in the desert. Dropping behind one of the rocks, he lay with his face to the sand and cried as though his heart would break. It didn't seem real, or true, that he *could* have missed the mark each time out of the five shots.

He had lain there a long time when he suddenly heard the sound of footsteps near at hand, and a moment later his father stood beside him. He did not seem to notice the tears that still stood in Dah-chee's eyes, as he said,—

"Your grandfather is ready to take the white people into the canyon, and he says that, if you wish to, you can go with them."

Dah-chee was on his feet in an instant, and soon had forgotten the great disappointment of the morning as he rode along in the wagon, pointing out the many interesting things to the little white girl. Later in the afternoon, when they had ridden a long way, his grandfather told them all to get out of the wagon and to walk a while to stretch their legs. All were glad to obey and jumped out on the smooth white sand.

The high canyon walls cast big cool shadows, which were welcome, as the day was very warm. Dah-chee's grandfather drove the wagon slowly, and behind it, in single file, came the white lady, then her husband, and the little girl, with Dah-chee the last in the line. This just suited him, as he had his bow in hand, with an arrow on the string, ready to shoot at any bird or animal that might be careless enough to show itself.

Soon both he and the little girl were some distance behind the others of the party, each gazing delightedly about them at the many things to be seen.

"Oh, look at the lovely red rocks over there by the canyon wall!" cried the little girl. Then she called to her father, "Look, Father! What a fine place for a playhouse! Let's all go over and see it." And she pointed toward the place as she ran.

Without waiting for her father, who had turned back when he heard her call, she ran on to the pile of rocks, followed by Dah-chee who was some little distance behind her. She reached the spot, and stopped short as she heard a queer, dry rattling noise that was not like any sound she had ever heard before.

As she turned to see what could be making the sound, she saw, so near to her that she could have touched it, a great rattlesnake coiling itself on the flat top of a rock. For some reason she found she was unable to move. Her father, who had heard the noise of the snake, ran forward as fast as he could

and cried out with fear as he realized that he was too far away to reach his little daughter before the snake might strike her.

Then above the dry rattle of the snake was heard a far different sound; it was the twang of Dah-chee's bowstring, and a second later the big snake was twisting harmlessly on the rock with a red arrow through its body.

Then the white man acted very foolishly; at least Dah-chee thought he did, for as soon as he had caught up his little girl and realized she had been saved, he picked up Dah-chee also and hugged him close, while tears of joy ran down his face. Surely, thought Dah-chee, no Indian man would ever do a foolish thing like that.

When the little boy's grandfather and the little girl's mother had heard the white man's cry of alarm, they came running up to learn the cause. The white man and the little girl told them all about the big snake, and of how Dah-chee had made the wonderful shot, just in time to save the little girl from being bitten. Dah-chee did not care for the praise of white people— what could *they* know about good shooting?—but his grandfather, well, if *he* was pleased, that was a different matter, for he knew all about such things.

The old man, who had said nothing, reached into a large leather bag, that was suspended from his shoulder by a thong, and drew out a package. From this he produced a beautiful new belt whose bright silver disks shone in the sun like polished mirrors. And still without a word, he knelt beside Dah-chee and fastened it about his waist. Then he rose and said,—

"Dah-chee, you have given proof that you are worthy to have the silver belt, and I believe you will some day be a good guide and a good warrior."

But Dah-chee scarcely heard his grandfather's words, though they were words of greatest praise, for his little hands were wandering over the smooth silver disks of the beautiful belt, and it was really *his*, his very own.

Helen Coale Crew

THE BAEDEKER BOY

ILLUSTRATED BY *Matilda Breuer*

YOUNG John Stow did not know that he had been given the name of a man much more famous than himself. He had heard of Shakespeare, but he had never heard of that old John Stow who had studied every nook and corner of the City of London in the days when Shakespeare was a young man and had written down all he had found out in a fascinating book. Whether young John got his name from old John, who can say? But like that old John he was fond of prowling about in odd, out-of-the-way corners when he had a spare half-day. When this story begins young John had never come across old John's book, but you shall hear how he came across another book about London that became a great delight to him —a book that is as conspicuous in the hands of tourists seeing London as is the red cross on an emergency kit.

Young John Stow was a bellboy in the Bailey Hotel in the West End of London. When he had gone to answer the advertisement saying that a bellboy was wanted there, he had found a dozen other boys ahead of him in the small room off the office where they were told to wait, and where a good bit of lively scuffling was going on. John, being a quiet boy, with a pair of grave eyes, was afraid he had no chance at all, with these lively chaps ahead of him. But to his great surprise and happiness, the job was given to him. On the day when first he put on the neat suit with its shining buttons which the Bailey

116

bellboys wore, his heart thumped joyfully beneath it, and his solemn face almost smiled.

It is not the easiest thing in the world to be a bellboy in a big hotel. Bells are forever ringing that he must answer, and he must carry up to those "Beautiful Ones," as John called them, who rang their bells so frequently, everything from a newspaper to a mustard plaster. Often a Beautiful One sent him out to buy flowers for her, or took him with her, by special arrangement with Mr. Simpson, the clerk at the desk, to carry her purchases home. Always there were suitcases and hat boxes to carry up and down for those arriving or leaving. And when the Beautiful Ones, dressed like queens, went in the evening with their husbands to the opera, John Stow opened the front door with a solemn flourish for them to pass out. These Beautiful Ones used to wonder among themselves why John Stow never smiled. But they had never seen John when he was sent to buy a rose or a bunch of violets in the morning for them to wear at the breakfast table. For then John always ran quickly to the station, two blocks away, of the underground railway, and bought the flowers from his own sister Joanna, who was flower girl there. John always smiled when he saw Joanna standing there with her basket of flowers.

Joanna got up very early every morning and went to the Covent Garden Market. Under one of its great sheds is the flower market. Here the gardeners from the country round about unloaded from their wagons great boxes and baskets of all the kinds of flowers you ever heard of, and quite a good many that you never heard of at all. Joanna bought little bunches of white and purple heather, branches of broom with its yellow flowers, violets and maidenhair fern, daffodils, cowslips, primroses—whatever was in season. Then she hurried by the underground, and got off at the station near Bailey's Hotel. There the men going to their business or the ladies going shopping often stopped to buy her flowers. The people of London are fond of flowers, and all over the city the flower girls serve them. There was one old white-haired Scotchman whose work was at the British Museum. One morning he asked Joanna if she

117

never had a thistle to sell. The thistle is the flower of Scotland as the goldenrod is the flower of America. Joanna had never seen any thistles at the market; they did not seem like flowers at all to her. She supposed that they were prickly weeds that the donkeys were contrary enough to eat. But she asked Mr. Crum at the market if he wouldn't bring some. And every morning after that she sold the old Scotchman a great prickly, purple thistle. And when he paid her he always said, "Thank you, my dear," and put it into his buttonhole.

One day somebody left in one of the rooms at the Bailey Hotel a rather battered-looking book, with a cover, and with many pencil marks inside. John was hastening along a corridor when he saw a chambermaid putting it into a wastebasket. He ran and snatched the book from the basket and held it up before her.

"Ho!" cried John. "That's a book!"

"So I have eyes to see," said the chambermaid, who was very busy and a little cross.

"Would you throw away a book!" said John reproachfully. To him a book was a very precious thing.

"Ain't you smart!" said the chambermaid. "Why, this book is no good. There are enough of them left behind here in a year's time to make a bonfire for Guy Fawkes's Day."

"May I have it?" asked John.

"Help yourself; nobody else wants it," said the chambermaid, and walked off with a great pile of sheets and pillowcases in her arms.

John pounced upon the book and buttoned it up inside his jacket while he went along the corridor to answer the bell of Room 56. At his first chance he put it away in the locker where he kept his home clothes. All day, which was an unusually busy one, he had no opportunity to look at the book. But he was off duty early that day, and at five o'clock, when he had put on his own clothes and folded the uniform neatly away in the locker, he took the book and hurried home. Joanna was not at the underground station at this time of day. She sold her flowers between seven and eight in the morning and then went to a small restaurant where she waited on table the rest of the day. When John got into the underground train to ride home—it was too far to walk—he did not look at the book. He leaned his head wearily back, closed his eyes, and contented himself with wondering what it would be about. But when at last he reached the rather forlorn place that he called home, he opened the door, shut it behind him with a bang, and cried, "Ho! Dad! Mother! Kit and Kitten! Look what I've got!"

Did I say forlorn? Oh, but that was only on the outside, I do assure you! The great building was indeed rather dingy and dilapidated, but the five rooms on the third floor, which were home to the Stows, were bright and cheerful and spotlessly clean. John went through the tiny hall directly to the kitchen, where he knew everybody would be. Mother was there cooking supper; and Father, who had to sit all day in a wheel chair, was reading the paper. The twins, Christopher and Crystal, known as Kit and Kitten, were setting the table and getting very much in the way in spite of their help. John went at once to his father and laid the book on his lap.

"There!" he said, knowing how well his father would be pleased with something new to read, for he had read the shelf of books in the parlor, from the Shakespeare at one end to the fat old dictionary at the other, more than once over.

"Why," said Mr. Stow in pleased surprise, "it's a Baedeker's 'London'!"

Such a furor as that castaway book did make! When supper was over and the dishes all cleared and Mr. Stow's chair wheeled up close to the table, he laid the book on the table, spread out the maps one after the other, explaining meanwhile what a Baedeker was. The Baedeker people, he said, were publishers in Germany, who for many years had prepared these guidebooks telling everything about the various countries and cities of the world that travelers and tourists would like to know. There were maps and plans and directions; there were the names of hotels and how much it cost to stay at them; there were lists of the famous pictures in the art galleries; there were bits of history; there were the names of men who had made certain houses famous just by living in them—everything! Joanna came in late and joined the family around the table. Father read them paragraphs here and there from the book, and they had no idea that their own city was so full of interesting things.

At last Kit and Kitten were sent to bed; then Joanna and Mother went also. But John and his father sat over the maps until the clock struck twelve and the cats were yowling and prowling on the back fence. And after that the Bailey Hotel's youngest bellboy lay wide awake, his head so full of Old London Bridge and Guild Hall and the Tower and Sir Christopher Wren and Shakespeare and Sir Walter Raleigh and quaint old taverns and ancient signboards and dark and crooked alleys that it is a wonder he ever fell asleep at all.

And that is how young John Stow of the twentieth century took to hunting up all the interesting places and all the out-of-the-way corners of London, as Old John Stow of the sixteenth century had done before him, only that young John had had very little education, and certainly did not dream of writing a book about what he saw. He took to walking home instead of riding on the two afternoons when he got off at five o'clock, and was always late to supper by an hour or two. Indeed, when summer made the days long and twilight was still not night at nine o'clock, he was often later than Joanna. But nobody minded it, because when he did get home, he always had something to tell, and opening the map of the Baedeker, would show where he had been. Often he and his father planned beforehand where he would go.

If only the Beautiful Ones who thought that Bellboy John never smiled could have seen him bursting into that little kitchen, his grave face one beaming smile from ear to ear, they would have changed their minds. Or if they could have heard his voice—"Ho, Dad! I saw the Cheshire Cheese Inn today and the very seat where Dr. Samuel Johnson sat for his tea, at the time he was writing that old dictionary of ours! And the cook in his apron and cap was fetching in a big pie, Mother, and I up and asked a cook's boy what's in that pie, and he says, 'Larks.' And I says, 'What, songs and all?' And then I went to the house where Dr. Johnson lived, up an alley from there; and

I went in, Dad, because it is free to the public, it says so in the Baedeker, and I'm the public—well, you needn't laugh, I'm part of it, anyway!" And all of this he said in one breath, so that really it should have no commas or periods in it. And then he laughed at himself.

By the end of the summer John had had as much education as if he had gone to school—and perhaps more. For he not only had learned the ins and outs of his native city, from Westminster Abbey to London Tower, but he had learned, helped out by his father, much of its history and the names of many of the people who had helped to make that history. And when now and then he found that the London County Council, the group of men who determined what old buildings should be torn down to make way for new ones, had given orders for the destruction of some ancient house that he had just been looking up and reading about in his Baedeker, he was quite distressed.

Meanwhile he was doing his work at the Bailey Hotel as well as he knew how. He kept his uniform neat, his buttons polished, his shoes blacked, his fingernails clean, and his temper sweet; and if that isn't pretty nearly the whole duty of man, at least it is an important part of it. And still the Beautiful Ones wondered why this obliging and swift-footed bellboy was always so grave. They had no idea how happy the heart was that looked out of those solemn eyes and beat behind those well-polished buttons. John wouldn't have changed places with the Prince of Wales himself! "Poor child!" said the Beautiful Ones to each other. "He must have troubles of his own."

And then one day at the end of the summer trouble came, sure enough. Kit and Kitten, seven years old, had gone on an errand to the nearest greengrocer for their mother, and did not come home. They had gone off hand in hand, Kit with the basket and Kitten with the money held tight in her hand, at ten o'clock. At eleven o'clock Mrs. Stow began to be anxious and went herself to the greengrocer's. Mr. Bumper was wrapping up a cabbage for a customer. Mrs. Stow, without waiting for him to finish, asked anxiously if her two children had come in at about ten o'clock.

"Yes, ma'am, they did so," said Mr. Bumper, "and bought some stuff and put it into their basket and went off with it. Ain't it so, Mrs. Bumper?"

Mrs. Bumper, who had been stooping down behind the counter, rose up like a jack-in-the-box. "Yes, ma'am," she said, "they were here, bless their pretty faces, and they left as soon as they got their packages, ma'am."

Mrs. Stow wrung her hands in distress. What should she do? Why, of course, get John and Joanna at once. So she 'phoned to the hotel and to the restaurant and told John and Joanna that the children had been lost for more than an hour and that they must come home at once, and then she hurried home herself.

When the office clerk at the Bailey Hotel called John to the 'phone and he had heard the message, his face grew quite pale. Without getting permission to leave, without stopping to change his uniform, he went home as fast as he could. He knew he was breaking two rules and he knew he would lose his job, but he had no time to think of that. He could only think of his anxious father in the wheel chair, his mother frantic with distress and not knowing what to do, and two helpless little children lost in London! Now that John knew his city so well, he knew that it was not all made up of fine buildings and handsome parks. He knew there were dark streets and darker alleys where harm could come to the two little ones.

Straight home he went first of all, and after hearing his mother's story he went to Mr. Bumper's store, and with that as a center, went about that neighborhood in widening circles. And now, to his surprise, he found that in his walks about London he had made friends here and there without knowing it, people who had become interested in the boy with the book and thought of him as "the Baedeker boy." The cook's boy at the Cheshire Cheese came to help him hunt. The Fleet Street policemen added several hunters from their force. Newsboys took up the cry of "Two children lost!" By one o'clock a crowd of boys and men were hunting, up Fetter Lane and around St. Paul's and up Milk Street and around the Bank and back by Threadneedle Street, and even down to the fish market, the slipperiest, messiest place in the world. Joanna went to Covent Garden Market, remembering she had once taken them there. Four o'clock came. Mrs. Stow ran distractedly from one place to another and Mr. Stow sat at home, looking at the Baedeker map and groaning over the great maze of streets, in any one of which his lost children might be.

But bless you, they found them! And it seems that a poor hungry woman, seeing their basket of food had snatched it from them and run down an alley, the twins chasing after her to get their basket back. According to their own tale, they had run about a hundred miles in every direction after the woman, and then walked about a thousand miles more, trying to get home. And the thousand miles had gotten them to the British Museum. As they sat forlorn and weary and frightfully hungry on the steps of that great building, an old white-haired man came out and walked down the steps. Kit, looking at him, jumped up and said, "Sir!"

The old man stopped and looked at Kit.

"That's a thistle you have in your buttonhole, sir," said Kit.

"It is, but not a Scotch one, as it should be," said the man.

"Did you buy it from my sister Joanna?" asked Kit. "She sells one to a Scotchman every day." And at his own mention of Joanna, Kit burst into tears, which is easy to do when one is only seven and home a thousand miles away. Kitten, being also seven, did likewise. Then Mr. MacGregor, for that was his name, wiped their tears on his own big handkerchief, heard their story, and calling a cab, took them home.

John was too weary that night to do anything but fall into bed, leaving Mr. MacGregor and his father and mother talking together. Next morning, with a face so grave that the Beautiful Ones would have been horrified, he reached the Bailey Hotel early, and went at once to the office. There he stood quietly at the clerk's desk until the clerk looked up. There was a lump in his throat, and the world looked gloomy. He hoped none of the other bellboys would come in.

"That you, Stow?" asked Mr. Simpson.

"Yessir," said John, gulping at the lump.

124

Mr. Simpson drew a number of shillings from the drawer and tossed them out on the desk.

"You're fired, Stow," said Mr. Simpson. He did not mean to be unkind by his unfeeling brevity, but he had "fired" so many bellboys that he was quite hardened to it.

"Yessir, thank you, sir," said John. He looked at Mr. Simpson with big, mournful eyes, picked up the shillings, and went to the locker room and took off his uniform. He folded it carefully, running his hand over the buttons he had been so proud to wear. It was even more of a blow than he had thought it would be, to part with that uniform. He sighed, put on his own suit, and went slowly out. Turning around as he crossed the street, he looked up at the Bailey Hotel. One of the Beautiful Ones, at her window, nodded and smiled at him. But John had no heart for smiling. He walked the few blocks to the underground station, and there was Joanna selling a thistle to Mr. MacGregor.

"You look very blue this morning," said Mr. MacGregor to John. "Have you lost the twins again?"

"I have lost my job," said John, and blinked manfully to keep the tears back.

Mr. MacGregor fixed the thistle carefully into his buttonhole. "Thank you, my dear," he said to Joanna. And then to John, "I need a page in my department at the British Museum. Would you like to apply for the job this morning?"

Would he! All of John's soul rose up in a glorified smile to those grave eyes of his.

"Come with me, then," said Mr. MacGregor. "You will have to carry many books for me if you become my page."

He handed John a book, just a small book with a sober blue cover, but John stared in surprise and fascination at the gilt title on the back—*The Survey of London, by John Stow.* Then Mr. MacGregor tipped his hat to Joanna, and followed by John, dipped down into the earth to take the train. Young John Stow, holding old sixteenth-century John Stow's book under his arm and stumbling down the stone steps after Mr. MacGregor, must have felt as Alice did, falling down the rabbit-hole into Wonderland.

126

How a boy of Greece made his wish
come true.

Alice Geer Kelsey

THE SKELETON WINDMILL

ILLUSTRATED BY *Clarence Biers*

ARE there any errands I can do for you,
Mother?" asked Manoli. His eyes were as twinkling as the sunlight on the seas that surrounded his own island of Crete.

Kyria Zacharakou looked up in surprise from the coarse gray
sock she was knitting. "Can this be my Manoli asking to help?
You usually think of nothing but play, play, play. Why do you
suddenly want to do something for me?" She smiled in playful
reproach at her son, with his shining black eyes and his dim
dimples in cheeks that were not so plump as his mother wished.

"Oh, I see!" The mother noticed that Manoli held in his
hands a toy he had finished making the day before. It was a
scooter on which he had been busy ever since he had found a
pair of small wheels in the shop at Erakleion where second-
hand iron was sold. The toy was a crude affair made of old
boards, bent nails, and the two proud wheels. "So you want
to go on an errand? Let's see. Suppose you carry some oranges
to the old widow Elene who lives over the hill."

Manoli's smile disappeared as he looked at the narrow
cobblestoned trail built many years ago by the Turkish in-
vaders. It led over the hill to the one-room stone hut of the
widow Elene.

"But that wasn't where I wanted to go, Mother!" Manoli
protested. "I could not use my new scooter on that old paved
trail."

"Oh, so it was using the new scooter, not going on an errand
for me, that you were thinking of?" Kyria Zacharakou laughed.
She, of course, knew that all the time.

127

Manoli's smile came back. He had known his mother would not fail him.

"How about going to the city and telling your Aunt Katerina that we shall be coming to visit her after church on Sunday morning?" she asked.

"Oh, father!" Manoli called to the tired-looking man who was just coming into the yard of their tiny stone house, carrying a rush basket of fresh oranges on his head. Such golden balls of sweetness Manoli was sure grew nowhere as sweet as on his own island of Crete. "Father, I am going all the way to Erakleion. I am taking a message to Aunt Katerina. Is there any errand I can do for you?"

"Yes, indeed!" Manoli's father gave a tired, patient smile. "Bring me home a few *pics* of strong canvas cloth to make new sails for our poor dead windmill. I'm tired of carrying water."

Manoli knew that his father was joking. Cloth for windmills was one of those things that simply could not be found in the markets of Erakleion. Crete had become an island of silent windmills. The canvas sails had gradually during the war years been whipped to shreds, with no chance of being replaced. A few people had found cloth of one sort or another to bring their

128

skeleton windmills to life. Manoli himself had seen in the "valley of the thousand windmills" that some of them had come to life with new sails of assorted colors. They had begun to draw water again to irrigate the fields and orchards. But Manoli's family had not yet been lucky about the canvas. There was no reason to hope that a ten-year-old boy on a homemade scooter would come home with a few *pics* of it under his arm.

"I wish I could get some cloth for you, old windmill!" Manoli looked up at the ten silent arms of the skeleton windmill which stood unmoved by the fresh breeze blowing in from the Aegean. "You are a disabled war veteran just like any soldier who lost his legs on the Albanian front. You stand there looking as brave as though you would never give up hope of getting five new sails again. I'm sorry, old windmill, but I'm afraid I can't do anything for you."

"Run along with you now," said his mother. "You may stay all day with Aunt Katerina, if she asks you. Just be home before the sun goes down."

Tucking his new scooter under his arm, Manoli started toward the macadam road by his own favorite short cut. The grownups of his family insisted that it was a long cut instead of a short cut. They had forgotten what fun it was to play King Minos while threading one's way through the labyrinth of the five-thousand-year-old palace of Cnossus. Manoli had spent so much time watching the men who worked at the excavations and listening to what the guides told visitors that he could name most of the rooms as he went through them. He always liked to enter the grounds through the bath chamber at the southern edge of the palace. This was the palace where caravans of Egyptians had stopped to bathe themselves after their long journey north across the Mediterranean and across the island of Crete. They must wash off the soil of travel before they came within the outer courts of the great palace. There were other bathing pools and even the tiny bathtub of the queen elsewhere in the palace ruins, but this outer pool was the only one where there still was water.

Manoli loved to climb the stone staircase that led to what he

129

believed were the balconies where the king and queen had sat to look at the sunset or to gaze over the hills at their grazing flocks or at the ships whose sails dipped and bowed on the sea. Manoli usually went down the stairs that led to the king's council chambers—one where the king acted as ruler and one where he acted as priest. If he found the guarding gate unlocked, he sat down for a quiet, impressive moment on the great gypsum chair where the king used to sit when he was conducting sacrificial rites to the sacred bull.

Today Manoli's short cut could not be quite so long as usual. He had the road to Erakleion to follow on his new scooter. Today he took the shortest route through the old ruined palace. He did not stop to wonder about the big storage jars in the king's storeroom which had once held olives, wheat, raisins, and wine. He did not pause to study the meanings of the brightly colored paintings which had recently been made on the walls in imitation of the pictures that were known to have once covered them. Manoli would be glad when the museum, closed because of the war and the unsettled times that followed war, would be open again so that he could see the treasures—pictures, vases, statues, jewels—that had been found when Sir Arthur Evans and others excavated here at Cnossus. Manoli did not take time to peer into the deep pits that were near the eastern entrance by which he left the grounds. He usually

stopped to imagine King Minos's servants coming out to throw their broken pottery into one of these pits, or to imagine palace guests offering sacrifices to the sacred bull in the other deep pit. Just before he left the enclosure of the ruins, he always gave a little good-bye salute to the bronze statue of Sir Arthur Evans, the patient Englishman who had dug and studied for many years to unravel the old secrets of Cnossus. It was a very tiny salute today, because, interesting as five thousand-year-old palaces were, it was not every day that Manoli had a new scooter to try out on the macadam road that wound down the hillside toward Erakleion on the water front.

This road was safe for a boy just getting the hang of riding a rather wobbly scooter. Manoli met only one automobile in the entire four miles, a weary old car puffing lazily up the hill. He met two shepherds driving a herd of black goats and white sheep which scattered up and down the banks when they saw him rattling toward them on his noisy scooter. He passed several men and women driving donkeys laden with baskets of oranges, cauliflower, or cabbages. But nobody and nothing passed Manoli as he speeded down the hill toward Erakleion.

How surprised Aunt Katerina will be, he thought, as he pushed across the bridge spanning the ancient Venetian moat that once guarded the city but now was filled with gardens and vineyards. In the city at last, he chose one narrow street after another, twisting nearer to the house where his aunt lived.

He started the brass knocker clanging and tried to lift the latch. Locked! He knocked again. He rattled the doorknob.

"Aunt Katerina!" he shouted. "Aunt Katerina! It's Manoli!"

"There, there! Don't break down the door!" A scarfed head poked from the upstairs window of the house next door.

"I've come with a message for my Aunt Katerina." Manoli was trying to sound more cheerful than he really felt. "Do you know where she is?"

"Down at the quay," said the woman. "There's a wheat ship unloading. She's in charge of the women and girls who go into the hold of the ship to scoop the spilled wheat into bags and sew them up before they are lifted out by the ship's cranes.

131

Manoli was soon in the wider streets which were smooth enough for him to have a bumpy ride on his scooter. As all the roads leading to the water front went gently downhill, he found himself going at a speed which made it necessary to dodge smartly now and then. At last he reached the breakwater that curved out into the sea, making a wide quay where boats could tie up and discharge their cargo.

He had to stop a minute at the entrance to the breakwater to admire the carved white lions on the front and on the back of the old fortress which had guarded the sea approach to the city in the days when the Venetians had ruled Crete, before the coming of the conquering Turks. In the tiny enclosed harbor which was once the pride of the Venetians, there were now small fishing boats and cargo caïques drawn up to the quay.

Manoli looked at the brightly colored patched sails and thought of his skeleton windmill. But he knew the fishermen's canvas was far too precious to be spared even to bring his windmill to life. The inner harbor where the small boats lay was all right for medieval ships or for the small boats owned by modern Cretans, but it was beyond the Venetian fortress on the new breakwater that the ocean-going vessels were moored. It would be there that Manoli would find his Aunt Katerina in command of the women repairing the leaking wheat bags.

"Oh, look at the surf!" said Manoli to himself. He was both glad and sorry to see that the water raging in from the Aegean was rough today. It meant that he would have an exciting game of dodging when a big wave dashed over the breakwater, wetting everything that got in its way. He decided that it would be wiser to go on foot with the scooter tucked under his arm. The mole of the breakwater would be slippery where the waves had washed over it. And there were trucks coming and going, taking up the lion's share of the passage. He was not good enough yet at dodging on his scooter.

"That must be the wheat ship." Manoli looked at a big gray freighter, freshly painted, drawn up to the quay. "It's a Greek boat flying our good blue and white flag. No, that's not wheat

being unloaded. They are loading something onto the boat. It must be something grown on our island. My father says we Cretans will be poor until we start selling something we have raised again."

Manoli was now within reading distance, but the labels on the boxes being loaded onto the ship were in English, to be read in the land to which they were going. He knew, however, from the size and shape of the boxes that they must be filled with the good Sultana raisins for which Crete used to be famous in the days before the war, when Greek ships could carry Greek produce to far places.

"Raisins, olive oil, and oranges," chanted Manoli to himself. "My father says no place in the world can beat Crete in raising them. I wonder if that is why King Minos chose Crete as the site for his great palace."

But Manoli did not think long about King Minos' possible reasons for settling at Crete. Tied to the quay just beyond the Greek ship was a big battered-looking freighter, flying the flag of red, white, and blue which every Greek boy had learned to respect.

133

Manoli, with his homemade scooter under his arm, was soon at the side of the American Liberty ship. He drew close to the wall of the mole to keep away from all the busy doings of the Cretan water front. It was all very confusing to the boy used to his quiet farm, where even the windmill was silent now that it needed new sails before it could do its work of drawing water to irrigate the fields. The four great cranes of the ship were whirring and screeching as each carried a dozen bags of wheat at a time from the hold of the ship. Two of the cranes were filling a barge and a caïque drawn up to the opposite side of the ship. Two cranes were piling bags on the quay.

"Aunt Katerina is in the hold of that ship," Manoli said to himself. "How can I get in to see her? There's a ladder going up the side of the ship, but there's an American sailor at the top of it. He would ask me why I wanted to go on board. He would ask it in his own queer language, but I would know what he meant."

Just when Manoli was about ready to give up hope of getting aboard, a Greek workman called down over the ship's rail to the Greek stevedores, "We need more empty bags in the hold. Send some up."

One of the stevedores picked up a heavy armful of bags and looked about him. "Who will carry these onto the ship?" he shouted to anyone who might be listening.

Before his words were finished, the stevedore saw a small boy flash out of the shelter of the wall and dash across the mole to him.

"Let me carry them," said Manoli in a small hopeful voice.

There proved to be enough bags for two trips. The first armful Manoli dumped from the deck into the deep hold without stopping to look for his Aunt Katerina. He could see that women were busy far down in the hold, sewing the bags with neatly eared handles.

As Manoli came up the ladder with his second armful of empty bags, he said to the sailor, "Please, I'd like to carry these down into the hold instead of dumping them."

. . . just getting the hang of a rather wobbly scooter.

Of course the good-natured American sailor could not understand Manoli's Greek a bit better than the boy could understand the American's English, "Okay by me, Bud, whatever it is you want to do. You don't look like the sort to be blowing up the ship or hiding as a stowaway."

Though Manoli could not understand the words, he understood the smile that went with them. He knew he was on a friendly ship.

It was hard tucking the bags under his arm so he could hang onto the steep ladder with both hands as he climbed straight down into the deep hold. By good luck, he happened to go down just where Aunt Katerina was working. He might just as easily have gone into one of the other four holds. This was his lucky day.

Aunt Katerina was waving both arms wildly and talking to a woman who sat slumped and frowning in a corner. "You can't stop now! Of course you are tired. We are all tired. But we have promised to work another three hours. If we want American ships to bring us wheat, we have to do our share. And you know very well we would go hungry without this wheat."

"But my poor back! How it aches!" groaned the woman. "Can't you find someone else to work in my place? I can't stoop over that broom another minute, let alone three hours."

"We haven't time to hunt up someone for your place," argued Aunt Katerina. "I would let you go if there were even a child here to sweep while the rest of us sewed the bags. But there's no one."

"Yes, there is, Aunt Katerina," came a chuckling young voice which made Aunt Katerina jump and turn quickly. "I can sweep wheat and scoop it into bags."

"All right, Manoli." Aunt Katerina was businesslike. "There's the broom, and there's the spilled wheat. You just sweep it into a pile, and the women will fill the empty bags and sew them up."

Manoli looked, wondering, at his Aunt Katerina. She was talking to him just as though he was one of the gang working under her, instead of her favorite nephew. Her straight back

135

was turned toward him so he could not see the laughter in her eyes as she set her play-loving nephew to work at the hardest job he had ever faced.

At first it was fun attacking the wheat-strewn floor with the short-handled broom. But soon it became monotonous. The dust from the wheat filled his nostrils and made him sneeze. He tried to remember how necessary it was to get the wheat onto his hungry island, but he found himself thinking instead of the new scooter lying idle on the mole while he worked in the hold of this ship.

Once he felt someone looking at him. He straightened his tired back enough to look up through the opening where the faraway sunlight was streaming in. His American sailor friend was grinning at him. When the sailor caught the boy's eye,

he called down something that sounded to Manoli like, "Atta-boy," which probably made sense in the strange language of Americans. Manoli worked better after that.

At last a bell rang, and Aunt Katerina said, "Time to eat. We can climb up onto the deck and eat in the sunshine while you tell me why you came to find me. There will be a new set of workers after lunch. Your job is finished."

Manoli and his aunt sat in a sunny spot on the deck, sharing her lunch of dark bread and white cheese. They talked about the big freighter, the Sunday visit, the new scooter, and the skeleton windmill which was so terribly in need of five strips of canvas to cover its ten bare arms.

Soon the big American appeared, accompanied by a dark-skinned sailor who had lived in Greece when he was a boy. He could speak Greek as well as English.

"My friend here has been watching you work," he said. "He thinks you ought to be paid for it now. You may not be around later when the others are paid."

Manoli stared at the men, openmouthed and silent. It had not occurred to him that he would be receiving pay. He had been working to help Aunt Katerina and the tired woman, because he was finding it fun not to play all the time, and because he knew the people of Crete needed every grain of wheat the ship had brought.

"My friend wants me to ask what sort of pay you would like," said the sailor. "Shall he pay you in drachmas, or is there something else you would rather have?"

Aunt Katerina, looking at the big American, realized what Manoli did not, that he had taken a fancy to the boy and was planning to make a present to him. She knew that Manoli's name was not on the payroll and would not be. But Manoli was proud to have the sailor think he was worthy of being paid.

His eyes wandered over the deck as he thought what he should answer. Should he say he would like drachmas? Should he ask for something else? Such a thing had never happened to him before. But then, he had never met a big American sailor before. This must be the way they did things. Manoli's

137

eyes, wandering over the deck, suddenly came to a stop. They grew bigger, rounder. The smile played all over his face.

Manoli did not move his eyes from a heap of worn canvas as he asked, "There wouldn't be, anywhere on the ship, some old canvas to bring a dead windmill to life? There wouldn't, would there?"

Then Manoli's eyes left the pile of limp canvas and turned to the sailor's face with a look that made the American stop smiling even before the other had translated the boy's question for him. Never in all his life had the American dreamed that a small boy could want some old thing so much as this one seemed to want old canvas.

"Tell me about the dead windmill," the American asked through their interpreter.

Manoli's answer was translated into English for the big sailor. "Did you ever see a windmill that was only a skeleton? It stands limp and still, no matter how the wind blows. It has bare sticks where it should have sails to catch the wind. When there is a war in a country, things wear out and there is nothing new. Dead windmills are sadder than other wornout things, because they should be so very much alive. When windmills are dead they cannot draw water to irrigate the fields. Then the crops are not so good. Dead windmills cannot draw water for families to use, so water has to be brought from faraway springs. Windmills ought to sing, but dead windmills do not make a sound except sometimes a little groaning when the wind blows, to remind them that they should be dancing."

"And would some old canvas bring your windmill to life?" the American asked quietly through the other sailor who knew Greek.

"Yes. Enough canvas to fit a sail to each of the five pairs of empty arms," answered Manoli.

"Wait a minute!" The American disappeared while the other sailor explained to Manoli and Aunt Katerina that he had gone off to speak to someone.

Manoli's eyes were still measuring the canvas, lying in its limp heap, when the sailor came back, smiling.

"It's all yours, Bud!" He scooped the pile of canvas into Manoli's arms. "It's your good luck that you came here on the day when lifeboat number three had a new cover and when the mate had no plans for using the old canvas. It's all yours, Bud. And may your windmill dance and sing as never before."

It was dark that evening when the last bit of canvas had joined the windmill arms together. Manoli and his parents had worked without stopping except for their bowls of pea soup for supper.

"May I carry my bed near the windmill tonight?" asked the boy. He always spread his thin mattress and blankets outdoors on nights that were not too cold, but usually close to the house.

Manoli was so tired that he fell asleep almost the minute he had spread his bed—almost, but not quite. He lay awake for five perfectly happy minutes listening to the wind playing its old familiar tune, *Creak—whir—creak,* in the windmill which was alive again.

In China, lonely Bei-ling searches for
a runaway monkey and finds a new
friend.

Martha Lee Poston

THE MONKEY SPIRIT

ILLUSTRATED BY *Clarence Biers*

BEI-LING was the daughter of a wealthy
man. Her clothes were of richest silks and satins. The house in
which she lived had a hundred beautiful rooms. Everything
that heart could desire was hers. Yet she was not happy.

For so rich a man was her father that Bei-ling did not go to
school as other children do. A teacher gave her lessons at home,
and only the children of the very rich, her father's friends, could
be her playmates. Always she must stay inside the walls of the
great House of Wu.

Often she was so lonely that she slipped off to the gatekeeper's house where she stood watching the poor children who
played outside. Her heart was filled with envy for the dirty,
barefoot boys and girls who raced and fought, worked, and
played, all up and down the city streets.

"See how that boy rolls his hoop!" she cried one day as she
watched. "He goes through a puddle, and the hoop never falls!"

"That he does, Little Miss," said Old Man, the gatekeeper,
who sat near on his bamboo stool.

"*I* could roll a hoop so, with a long street to roll it in," said
Bei-ling wistfully. "But our courtyards are too closed. Nor have
I any toy that I love as, that boy loves his rusty iron hoop."

"Shame on you, Little Mistress!" grumbled Old Man. "Does
not your father give you playthings that any common child

140

would marvel to see? How can you envy that poor lad who never had so much as a full meal in his life? Go back to your courtyard and play as you should."

"Oh, let me stay here!" begged Bei-ling. "Surely there is no harm in my watching a little longer."

Before Old Man could reply, there was the crash of a gong, far away, coming quickly nearer—a gay, lively sound.

"A candy man!" cried Bei-ling, "or perhaps it is an idol procession. Now surely you will let me stay!"

"It is no candy man, nor yet a parade," he laughed, turning back to his stool and his water pipe. "It is only a rough, common fellow with his goat, dog, and monkey show."

"Call him in, Old Man!" begged Bei-ling. "My father will pay him. Let us see the show!"

So in a moment a merry-faced showman stepped over the high wooden doorsill into the great outer court.

"A monkey show! A monkey show!" The news was whispered along corridors and in courtyards until servants and maids came running.

"Oh, dog with shaggy hair, go out for the people to see!" sang the showman, beating loud on his gong. Out ran the dog, bells sounding from the collar at his neck. Proudly he trotted around the courtyard once; then sat down beside his master.

"Oh, goat with an old man's beard, trot quickly for the people to see!" chanted the showman. With neck arched in pride, the little goat trotted daintily around the ring.

"A very fine show this will be," muttered Old Man, drawing at his brass pipe until the water in it purred with its most comfortable sound and smoke came out in great puffs. Bei-ling, standing beside him, smiled with joy. Such a show as this made her forget her loneliness for a while.

"Oh, monkey with the sad, wise face, can you not do better than these beasts? Go out before the people!" At the sound of the gong, the monkey climbed nimbly from the showman's back.

"Old Man," whispered Bei-ling, "is not that monkey the most precious small animal you have ever seen? I wish he were my own—like a little live doll!"

"A clever little beast," smiled Old Man. "But none except showmen own monkeys, Little Miss!"

Bei-ling said no more. She only thought, "That monkey would be a thing I could truly love!"

As the show went on, she felt that her heart would surely burst with longing to have this monkey for her own. She hardly saw the tricks of the dog. It was only the monkey in his dingy crimson jacket that she watched with all her eyes.

"Swing, Little One! Climb! Twist! Turn!" chanted the showman as he fixed a stake between two paving stones. And the monkey swung by hands, feet, tail: twisting, turning, dropping, until Bei-ling was breathless lest he fall.

"Now! Ride to rest thyself!" sang the showman. There was a sigh of joy from the watchers, for this was the best-loved part of the show.

"See him ride the goat—like a little man!" whispered Cook.

"Now! He dresses in fine clothes," murmured the gardener. Coolies, amahs, and maids cried out for more. Only two who watched were silent—Bei-ling and a little kitchen maid about her own age. They stared at the tired monkey from places far apart among the onlookers, the same expression of deep longing in their eyes.

"This is only half a show! Give us more!" cried everyone but these two.

"There can be no more," said the showman.

"You have not showed us the masks that your monkey wears," said Old Man. "He has not dressed up to be a pig, nor yet a donkey or a mouse. What manner of show is this?" He turned away in disgust.

"This is the best show of all shows!" shouted the showman. "For this reason it cannot go on without more pay."

"Oh! Ah! Ah-yah!" murmured many voices. Some were a little angry. Some laughed. All began feeling for their money belts to find a copper or two.

But as the big pennies dropped into the showman's bowl, there came a sudden scuffle underfoot, a shrill bark sounded.

143

Foh-foh, Bei-ling's poodle, rushed for the center of the ring and the tired monkey sitting there. Quickly the monkey darted away between feet and legs, Foh-foh close after him. Up to the carved wooden archway above the corridor he scrambled. There he clung, trembling, to the latticework, while many hands reached for the dog to pull him back.

"Ah-yah! I am ruined!" cried the showman. "Catch that monkey quickly, or I shall starve!" Seeing his master come after him, the monkey slipped away along the rafters.

"Go after him! Catch him!" commanded Old Man sharply. Away raced the servants this way and that, and Bei-ling, with wildly beating heart, watched them go. Suppose he were not caught? What then!

This same question the showman wailed aloud. "The great Master shall hear of this!" he cried again and again. "What way have I now to earn my rice?"

His noise was so great that a crowd began to gather at the gates to see what went on at the House of Wu.

"My father will pay you that you may buy a new monkey," said Bei-ling suddenly. "Wait for me here!" She ran off to find her father, who heard her story, laughing, and finally agreed to pay the showman.

So it was that the showman received more than the price of a new monkey and went off, secretly pleased, but grumbling still. The household settled into quiet. The monkey was forgotten.

Bei-ling alone set out through the dim, winding corridors of her home, to search patiently. She had only to find him now, and the monkey would be her own. Had not her father bought him? Never had so wonderful a thing happened to her. Not once did she doubt that in a few short hours she would hold the precious small beast in her arms, give him food and water and coax him to be her friend.

But, alas, she found no trace of him that day, nor in the many days that followed. Every afternoon, when lessons were done, she hurried along the great halls, her eyes on the rafters above, looking for any sign of the bright little eyes or small, darting

figure that would end her long seeking. How hungry the monkey must be! Perhaps he had crept into some dark corner and died. Then she would never find him. And it seemed to her that this was a thing she could not endure.

One day toward evening, Bei-ling came upon a dim, wide hall, far from the courts where the family lived. Here among the rafters were stored sedan chairs, their curtains neatly folded, their shafts laid dusty beside them. "Perhaps the little monkey hides here," mused Bei-ling, staring at the old sedan chairs used now only for a great wedding or funeral.

A sudden noise startled her—a sound of soft footsteps hurrying near. Bei-ling went toward the sound, her heart pounding. Who could it be? None came to this old part of the house any more. Then she caught a fleeting glimpse of a girl's figure, ragged and small, in the shadows ahead of her.

"Who is there?" she called out. The girl stopped, crouched against the wall.

"It is only I, Little Mistress." The voice was small and low.

"And who are you?" asked Bei-ling, astonished.

"I am Mei-whan, your kitchen maid," said the girl. Her eyes looked this way and that in fear. Her hands, hid in a coarse blue apron, trembled.

"Well, are you truly?" said Bei-ling. "What brings you to this place?"

"Cook—Cook—he sent me here to carry him back some herbs quickly. I must go before he is angry with me."

The girl darted away, leaving Bei-ling to wonder at herbs being stored in so strange a place.

By evening she had almost lost hope of finding the monkey. Yet how could the little beast so disappear that none who went about the house saw any trace of him? This, Bei-ling could not understand. She sat by a pool in her own rock garden, discouraged, until two amahs began to whisper close by. Then suddenly, Bei-ling found herself listening with all her ears.

"That was no monkey lost here the day of the show!" she heard one say.

"No monkey! What was it then?" gasped the other amah.

" 'Tis said it was a Monkey Spirit!"

From their talk, Bei-ling learned that something was stealing meal, candies, fruits from the kitchen each night. It could not be the monkey, for it unlocked boxes and cupboards, untied sacks, and fastened each one of them again with care.

"Cook is frightened. He says the Monkey Spirit will bring misfortune to all," said the amah. "Moreover, this Spirit has great power. He keeps himself invisible, that none of us may see him as we go about our work!"

"Hm! Ah-yah! Indeed! This must be an evil spirit, true enough!" whispered the other amah. "Now you have frightened me until I shall not eat or sleep again!"

Bei-ling laughed aloud, suddenly happy. "Now they are afraid of so foolish an idea! Now I know the monkey is still here, alive and well! Soon I shall find him."

But tales of the Monkey Spirit spread and grew until fear was in the hearts of all the servants. They hurried through the halls, not daring to look anywhere, lest the Spirit suddenly appear to seize them and carry them away whence they might never return. The great House of Wu grew so quiet, so full of terror, that it was no longer a pleasant place in which to live. Even Old Man, usually too wise for servants' talk, locked his little gatehouse each night with special care.

Bei-ling only laughed again at the servants' fears, until one day Old Man said to her, "This business of the Monkey Spirit is now settled. Cook has had new bars put on the kitchen windows, new locks on all cupboards and boxes. No food can be reached by any but himself. Thus he will starve the monkey's body until his spirit must leave this place and we shall be safe again."

"Oh, he must not do this!" cried Bei-ling. "The monkey is no evil spirit. He is only a clever beast whose master taught him more tricks than we knew. Tell the servants I will give money to the one who finds him. Help me, Old Man!"

But Old Man only shook his head. "Perhaps this affair is more serious than a little one can understand," he said. And Bei-ling went, full of sorrow, back to search alone.

147

That night she lay long awake. "Tomorrow I will ask my father to let me leave my lessons that I may search all day. Unless the monkey is found quickly, he will surely starve." So thinking, she was ready at last to fall asleep, when a sudden sound made her sit up in bed. It was no sound a monkey could make, surely. It was the noise of someone crying—sobbing as if her heart would break.

"Can it be that the monkey is truly an evil spirit?" thought Bei-ling. This sound in the still, dark house filled her with terror. Then she rose quickly and slipped into her shoes. "Only servants believe such things," she told herself. "We of the House of Wu are more wise." She set out to find the soft, pitiful sound.

Along the dim corridor outside her sleeping room she made her way quietly. As she turned the sharp corner where this hall met another, she drew back. For there on a doorsill crouched a small figure, bowed down crying. It was no monkey, but a girl about her own size. It was Mei-whan, the kitchen maid.

"Mei-whan, why do you cry?" Bei-ling asked gently, going nearer.

The girl raised her head. From the circle of her arms jumped the monkey. He chattered, darting along the paving stones; then ran back to Mei-whan to cling lovingly to her shoulder.

"Do not have me beaten for my wickedness, Little Mistress!" pleaded the girl. "Only take the monkey you have sought."

"What wickedness?" asked Bei-ling. "Where did you find the monkey?"

"I found him long ago," said the little maid, her voice shaking. "At the monkey show I thought no monkey was ever so pretty or so clever as this one. When Foh-foh chased him away, I followed and caught him. He was very tired, Mistress. He was so frightened he could hardly run. He was poor and thin; I caught him easily and have kept him ever since. Forgive me!"

"Oh! And so it was that I could never find him!" said Bei-ling slowly. "And so it was that I found you creeping in the old hall of sedan chairs!"

"It was so," said Mei-whan humbly. "It was I who stole the

148

food to carry it to the monkey hidden in the old hall. I locked boxes and cupboards, thinking then it would not be noticed. Now Cook has barred the kitchen and the monkey will starve."

"Yes," said Bei-ling. "But why are you crying here?"

"I was bringing the monkey to put him in your room tonight. Then you might care for him, and none would ever hear of my wickedness." Tenderly, she set the monkey in Bei-ling's arms and turned to run away.

"Wait! Come back!" called Bei-ling softly.

As she spoke, the monkey leapt with a strong bound from her arms and clambered to Mei-whan's shoulder.

"See, it is only you that he loves," said Bei-ling. "You must keep him. I have many playthings. You have none. No harm shall come to you for keeping this little live one you have cared for so long."

So Mei-whan went about her work with a joyful face. The monkey came with her and grew to be the pet of all. Day by day Mei-whan whispered among the servants of Bei-ling's kindness, until at last the tale came to the ears of the Master.

"Little Daughter, you have done a thing both just and brave," he said to Bei-ling proudly.

So pleased was he that he allowed Mei-whan to become the special maid of Bei-ling, to live in her court as her friend and companion.

Thus was Bei-ling's loneliness ended. Here was a playmate she could love indeed. Moreover, the monkey soon became as much her pet as Mei-whan's, as the happy three played together in the courtyards of the House of Wu.

Only Old Man was displeased. "The Little Mistress never comes to my gate to watch any more," he grumbled.

A young boy of India finds his greatest treasure.

R. Lal Singh
and Eloise Lownsbery

BIM'S GIFT
FROM THE FOREST

ILLUSTRATED BY *Ann Vaughn*

AT SUNUP, the moment that Bim heard the gate open, he ran out to greet the servant who came every morning from the village to milk the cow.

"A happy day to you, Bim sahib," said the tall, thin brown man.

"The same to you, Bukaru," said Bim. "It *will* be a happy day for me because my grandfather is coming. And in just one more day I shall be another year old. Then I am certain that my grandfather will tell my father to let me go along to the jungle."

Bukaru rolled his eyes upward. "Rama forbid!"

They both looked off beyond the high mud walls to the green treetops towering into the blue sky. To Bim the jungle was the most mysterious and beautiful place on earth, and the most longed for, but forbidden. To Bukaru it was a fearsome place never to be entered unless one had to.

Now, as they walked along to the cowshed, the man turned sideways to look down at the boy. "I'd not let my little Kamala go to the forest."

"But Kamala's only a girl," said Bim.

"Nor my Narada either. Old Suk says the forest is the home of Yama, king of Death." Bukaru held up one brown hand, bending down each finger at a time as he counted, "Death from serpents, tigers, lions, elephants, baboons—"

150

"Aie!" said Bim. "Who's afraid of the free people? They won't hurt you if you are harmless to them and keep wise witted. Grandfather says so."

"Won't they then? What of poor Ramdas's son, snatched by a tiger as he minded the cows? What of Suk's prophecy of cobras that lie in waiting for woodcutters?"

"But my grandfather is wiser than Suk. He knows the truth about everything." Bim ended the argument by calling his pets. "Here, Bindi. Come, Danu."

"Meow," said Bindi, who sat in the tall grass patch, washing his face in preparation for a bowl of milk. Now he lifted a plumy gray tail, swishing it from side to side, in a gay greeting. For though he slept with his master every night, he liked to steal away very early in the morning, before the morning star paled.

That swishing tail was invitation-to-mischief for Danu. Scrambling down from his perch in the jack-fruit tree, he dropped lightly to the ground, made a running leap and grabbed the tail with both small black hands.

"Ya-aow!" yelled Bindi, humping up his gray back and whirling about.

With two running steps and a jump, Danu now swung himself up to safety. Hanging by his tail, he gleefully held out two hands full of cat fur, jibbering in triumph.

"Tongues chatter best when they have something good to say," Bim reminded him. "A fur thief had better hide for shame. Never mind, Bindi," he consoled his cat. "Danu hasn't yet had his sugar cane so he feels like stirring up trouble."

Bindi glared up at the big monkey, but thought better of chasing him just then. So he licked and smoothed his injured tail and crept closer to Bukaru who squatted beside that white smell-of-milk streaming into his earthen pot.

By the time Grandfather arrived, the two friendly enemies had had their usual romp and chase with Bim, and had called a truce. Danu loudly announced the visitor, and Bim and Bindi ran to greet him.

"Aie, Grandfather!" cried Bim, looking up into the calm

peaceful face. The deep-set eyes were brown pools of kindness. The cheeks were sunken. The smiling mouth was nearly lost in a white beard.

The Bapu bent down over the boy whose arms were thrown about him. He stroked Bim's head; he pinched his cheeks. "My son of India—are you happy today?"

"Of course I'm happy to see you, Grandfather, especially today."

With his hand on the boy's head, the Bapu stooped to pick up Bindi who rubbed against his legs, in and out, in and out, for joy of seeing him again. Danu, who had swung down to Bim's shoulder from the big wooden gate, squeaked happily as Grandfather shook his tiny hand. Quickly the two wee black palms were lifted together to his protruding forehead in the accepted sign of reverence.

The Bapu's shoulders shook in silent laughter.

"Good Danu," said Bim. "For remembering, you shall have a sweet." It was his newest trick, and the monkey was so delighted at Bim's praise that he turned a somersault and danced wriggle and stamp, wriggle and stamp.

Now came Mother Lakshmi from her spinning, pulling her rose-colored *sari* over her black hair. She too greeted the old man with the sign of reverence, and brought him his favorite drink of sweet mango juice. They all sat down on the veranda bench, Bim as close as he could squeeze.

"Guess what day is tomorrow?" asked Bim.

His grandfather guessed: Krishna-day, Rama-day, Brahma-day, Vishnu-day, his eyes crinkling into smiles at the corners.

"No, it's my birthday," Bim told him. "And do you know what I want more than anything in all the world?"

The Bapu couldn't guess that either.

"I want to go alone to the jungle. And I am glad you came because you can tell my father so when he comes home tonight."

Bim's mother and grandfather exchanged a look. "Why not invite some of the village boys to go along with you then, Bhimason?"

152

"Oh, no, sir," said Bim quickly. "They are all afraid to go, even Narada. Suk tells them fearful stories of how Yama stalks about the forest, looking for them in every tongue and claw of the wild free people there. Suk is so old and wise that they all believe her."

The Bapu shook his head. "Suk may be old in years, but in wisdom she is not as old as Danu here."

Bim's mother nodded. "She keeps the whole village cowering in fear by her superstitions. If only they would listen to you, Bapuji." She sighed. "It seems strange that other, distant villages sit at your feet, while our own—"

Grandfather laid his long slender hand over her small one. "Can they hear words of truth in their hearts, when their minds are already darkened by Suk's sorcery?"

"Yes," agreed Bim, "our village boys are afraid of everything; of serpents, of ghosts, of the dark. It's no fun going to the forest with them."

Grandfather lifted his bushy gray eyebrows. "Can it be said of you that you separate yourself from your kind? That you are fonder of animal brothers than of human?"

"It is true," said Bim's mother, "that our boy is too fond of his pets, perhaps; but, as he says, he does not enjoy the boys, so I do not insist on his visits to the village. And when they come here, I am afraid Bim prefers his secret hiding-place under the banyan tree."

"Taking his manners there with him, no doubt, and his sense of 'I-am-better-than-thou?'" The Bapu's eyes twinkled. "Well, then, what of the cousins?"

"Oh, those cousins!" scoffed Bim. "They are such children!"

Grandfather smiled. "Last time I visited their village I thought Rewa a manly little fellow, nearly nine, I dare say. And Jal must be all of seven."

"As a matter of fact," Mother Lakshmi added, smiling, "I shouldn't wonder if Bim were not to see his cousins tomorrow. They might be coming to visit us for a day or so."

"Oh, Mother!" Bim's voice was full of reproach. "Why have you sent for them? I have set my heart on going to the forest

153

tomorrow. I don't want to stay at home to play with those cousins." Bim's face looked like a thundercloud.

"Well, then," his grandfather suggested, "why not make up a party for the jungle trip? Mother and Bukaru might take the cart and gather wood, while Bim enjoys the wonder of the jungle with his cousins. I'm very certain that Rewa has no fear."

Bim looked up quickly, a ray of hope in his face. "Do you agree, Mother? Would you leave us alone, quite by ourselves, and go off to cut wood?"

"I dare say I might manage to be quite out of sight, Bim, since you want that so very much. But just what would you do if you were to meet an elephant, or a wild pig?"

"I would make a noise to frighten it, like this." And Bim gave such a fearful yell that his mother jumped.

The Bapu nodded, smiling. "You have remembered our jungle games, I see. But suppose your bear or your buffalo or wild pig were very cross just at that moment, not with you, but because it had found no dinner, so that in its quick anger, it charged you boys instead of running away from your noise?"

154

"Then I would command the cousins to climb a tree quickly. I would tell them and the wild beast, 'Grandfather says we are never to fear.' Because when you fear, you make a bad odor which the beast wants to tear apart. And fear keeps you from thinking and acting with quick wits."

"And where are your eyes?" asked the Bapu.

"On the eyes of the elephant or the tiger. I must never take my eyes from his. And if he decides to be friendly, I shall talk to him softly."

"And just suppose that a jungle beast, mad to kill, should actually claw you?"

"Then I must go limp—pretend I'm no more alive—like this, until I can think how to outwit him." And Bim threw himself down, keeping still and more still, even to his breath.

His grandfather nodded to his mother. His brown eyes crinkled into a smile. "There, my daughter, there, wife of my son, can you doubt now that your son is ready for a jungle birthday party?"

She nodded, her beautiful face glowing. "Since he has never harmed so much as a mouse, I ought not to fear for him. And he will enjoy the forest all the more because he is responsible for his cousins, too."

Bim was less certain of this last than she. Still, at sunset, he met his father at the gate with the important announcement, "Tomorrow, my father, on my birthday, the cousins are coming, and Grandfather says we are to go to the jungle."

His father pinched his cheek. "I see how happy that has made you, my son. Then if your grandfather says it, it must be so."

And next morning, Bim met his cousins at the gate with the same news. "Today is my birthday, and we are all going into the big jungle."

"Aie!" said Rewa. "I hope we shall take a gun." His black eyes snapped.

Bim stared at him. "No one about here has a gun, not even my father."

"That's because he's only a Jemadar and not a soldier like my

155

father. My father says that all the men at Khyber Pass have muskets, even the boys. When I am nine he has promised to bring one home to me."

"Me, too," said Jal.

"No, only to me. You're too small."

"Not even my grandfather takes a gun to the forest. He takes only his flute," said Bim. "I suppose I shall take mine."

Rewa shouted with laughter. "A flute! You couldn't kill a tiger with a little reed pipe!"

"Who wants to kill a tiger?" asked Bim with scorn. "I'd rather tame a wild beast than have only its skin."

"Let's see everything again, at your house, Bim," begged Jal, tired of being left out of the argument.

So the three boys went exploring. For Bim's house and yard were larger than theirs. His yard, like their own, was enclosed on all four sides by a thick wall made of sun-dried mud bricks. This they called a compound; it shut them away from the brown road that trailed one way to the great forest and another way to the village. Within this safe world-of-its-own lived humans and animals and trees in one intimate family. Bim seldom left it.

"Let's play hide-and-seek," cried Jal, darting into the heart of a spreading banyan tree. "I'm It."

Long ago the mother tree had sent down long air roots to the earth, each of which took root and became itself a tree. So the mass of big green leaves had become so broad and so thick that the whole village might find shelter there from the burning sun. It was Bim's favorite hiding-place.

"Let's go down to the shed," said Rewa, when they had finished their game. They could not visit Rani, the cow, because every morning, after milking, the village chief herdboy, Bukaru's tall son Narada, came to drive her out to pasture. And each evening, at cowdust-time, he drove her home again.

Beside her shed grew a thicket of bananas; next a canebrake, and then a clump of jack-fruit trees, with green and yellowing fruits sticking out from the trunks like large melons. Here the boys found Danu and Bindi.

"Come, Danu, come, Bindi," called the cousins.

But both cat and monkey, usually so friendly, had fled upon their arrival. Bindi remembered how well Jal liked to squeeze him. And Danu thought of the many times when Rewa had pulled his tail.

"*Ao bhai,* come brother," called Bim softly. "Rewa and Jal are staying for a visit," he explained. "They are older now. They want to play with you and see your tricks."

For answer, Danu only bared his yellow teeth and made funny faces, scolded in a high squeak, and spat; while Bindi turned his back and curled round and round for a nap.

"Don't mind them," said Bim. "They forget their manners. Bukaru will cut some sugar cane for you to feed Danu. And Bindi will soon come running, if we pretend not to notice him. He really does love to be petted. But he can't get his breath if you squeeze him, Jal."

"No, I won't," promised Jal, opening and closing his small hands.

"Cluck, cluck," cried the brown hens, running out from their patch of thick, high jungle grass.

"*Ahjao!*" Bim answered. "They think we have come with corn. Tomorrow morning early, we'll come to search for eggs. They like to lay them in the tall grass."

On the right side of the yard, which was of hard-packed mud, stood a clump of lime trees. One, larger than the rest, formed an umbrella patch of shade over a big flat rock. Here sat Bim's grandfather, cross-legged, his eyes closed, swaying with the music as he played the Krishna-hymn on his flute.

"Let's ask him for a story," said Jal.

But Bim held a finger to his lips. "Yes, later. Now he's making the sacrifice. We can't speak to him now. Later, he'll tell us how the tiger got its stripes."

So the boys strolled on to the kitchen. This was a small hut, standing by itself under its sloping thatched roof. The mistress of the little house welcomed them with wide-opened arms.

"Aie, how tall and big you have grown, Rewa! And Jal will have so much to do that he won't miss his mother this time."

157

"No, my aunt, I'm not a baby any more," said Jal proudly.

Both pairs of shining black eyes were darting about the kitchen hut, noting the clay stove, like their own; the round pats of cow dung to burn; the hanging brass pots, pale yellow from much scouring; the tall earthen water jars; the bundles of dried herbs hanging from the rafters with strings of onion and garlic. And on the shelves, beside the baskets of spices, both boys stared hard at a big block of molasses and honey, covered with banana leaves.

Their aunt smiled. "Yes, you shall have some sweets when we return home from the forest tonight."

"Oh, Mother, can't we start now?" begged Bim.

"Just as soon as I prepare the food for your grandfather and your father, who are staying at home today. You boys may play until I call you."

"Well, first, let's see your house again, Bim," said Jal. He remembered that in Bim's room were often treasures of sweets and little pets.

The house or *bungla* was made of the same mud-dried bricks as the wall, roofed with thatch and plastered with cow dung. Across the front stretched a veranda with benches and a cot

bed, criss-crossed with palm-hemp rope. Here Grandfather slept on his frequent visits.

Inside were three rooms. In the one where Bim's parents slept, the cousins could see that the little light was burning on the shrine, the altar niche to Lord Krishna. Jal stood on tiptoe to see the small statue of him, playing his flute to the birds. He laid on the altar a jasmine blossom he had picked from the vine over the veranda.

The treasure room Bim shared with sacks of rice and of barley, a heap of melons and jack fruit, vegetables and ripening bananas.

"Shut your eyes," Bim commanded. "Tight shut."

Sure enough, when they opened them, each found in his hand, from Bim's private treasure store, a small ball of rice rolled in coconut, rather grubby with dust, but nonetheless sweet.

The treasure room boasted a window-frame, barred with wood, which looked out toward the village down the road, its one-room huts like a clump of anthills.

In the front room the Jemadar looked up from his desk, smiling. He wore a pink turban and a linen *dhoti*. Bim was proud of his father, straight and tall, with well-trimmed brown beard. He collected rents for the land and houses of the villagers, since all belonged alike to the Maharajah who lived in his big palace beyond the village.

"Well, my little men, it is a long time since you have paid us a visit. And now that you have both grown so tall and strong, you will have good times playing here together."

"Yes, my uncle," said Rewa, making a quick sign of reverence with his palms.

"Yes, my uncle," said Jal, echoing him. "And will you take us to see the Maharajah's wild animals?"

"Oh, no," said Bim quickly. "You wouldn't like them. The Rajah keeps them shut up in small houses. They glare out and they pace up and down, up and down. I don't like to see them!"

Bim's father laughed heartily. "Well, run along now, brothers, I dare say Bukaru is ready for that great journey to the jungle."

159

Indeed, they were just in time to see the man leading in Meta, the work-buffalo. Now they could help with the important process of harnessing him to the high, two-wheeled cart made of heavy teakwood, hand-hewn.

Bim darted back into the house for his reed pipe that Grandfather had made him. His mother came, bringing two well-sharpened heavy knives. She called the boys for a bowl of curds and gave to each a large crisply baked *roti*. Then she climbed into the cart beside Bukaru. Bim and Rewa and Jal sat on the cart floor, munching their bread as they rumbled out of the gate, with Father and Grandfather waving good-byes.

"Mind you keep your eyes sharp and your wits keen," said Father.

"Mind you have plenty of courage," called Grandfather. "If you will neither fear nor hate but bless all things, the jungle will greet you as brothers."

"All the same, I wish I had a gun," said Rewa as they jolted on past the neem tree outside the gate, past Meta's mud wallow, past the rice fields. They choked as a cloud of dust rose from Meta's shuffling hooves. With all his eyes, Bim stared up at the approaching green wall of treetops that raised their heads to the sky.

To him the forest was an enchanted world, perhaps all the more longed-for because forbidden. Forbidden because of the many times he had run away there as a child. Yet at this season of the year, this dry season, when the free people were driven from the depths of the jungle out to the fringes, where the villages huddled, was a most dangerous time to enter. That was why no child in Haripur village was allowed to go in alone. Old Suk made them all fearful.

In other years, there had been attacks by old, man-eating tigers. Each year, fruit trees were stripped by wild deer; vines and gardens by jackals. Wolves howled too close for comfort as they snatched away a yellow dog, or a sheep. Wild hogs grubbed up sugar-cane brakes. Little red foxes came slinking out to gobble up a stray chicken. Bim knew all this, but he wasn't afraid of them, not only because he had so often played

160

jungle games with his grandfather, but because more than anything else in his life, except his family, he loved the jungle.

So now he hugged to himself the truth that at last, in spite
of old Suk's fears, just because his grandfather was fearless,
and he was another year old, he was actually entering again
this enchanted world.

Now the bright glare of sunshine was left behind. They came
into a sudden twilight, a blue and lavender and green twilight,
broken by flecks of yellow sunlight as it came sifting through
the thick green roof.

The boys stilled their happy chattering, hushed by the deep
silence broken only by the crunching of a stick beneath their
groaning cart wheels, or by the whir of wings as jungle fowl
fluttered out of their path.

Meta bent back his ears along his curving horns. His nostrils
quivered. He was longing to stop, to turn around; but Bukaru
urged him forward, with bamboo smacks along his broad
humped back, on to a small clearing, large enough to turn the
cart about. Here they stopped. Bukaru jumped down, helped
out his mistress. The three boys tumbled down to the soft dry
moss, blinking their eyes in the dim light. Jal kept close to his
aunt. Rewa caught up a stout stick.

"Aie, who's afraid of the jungle?" he demanded. "I'm not
afraid of wild beats like Jal. Nothing can hurt us now. I've
got a gun."

Bim looked about him with big eyes. He was shivering from
excitement. It was a wonderful world. Above his head giant
butterflies sailed slowly. Rewa began running about, trying to
catch them. Bim looked at them in wordless delight. Although
he lived so close to the forest, he had to come inside to see such
butterflies: bright green ones, blue, yellow, and lavender. He
let one alight on his arm, breathlessly watching as its wings
slowly rose and fell. When he followed its flight then, he could
see gay birds darting about: parrots and parakeets; cuckoos,
and quadrils; with brilliant scarlet or green or blue or yellow
on wings or boots.

"They are all talking to us at once!" Bim told his mother.

161

She nodded and pointed higher still, up to the tallest tree-tops. "Listen!"

Bim could hear a reedy chattering. "*Bander!*" he cried to the cousins. "The *bander-log!*" Sure enough, a troop of monkeys came running along their sky road.

"They imagine that we are warrior demons come to invade their palace," said Rewa, brandishing his stick.

"I'd like to catch one," said Jal, "to take home."

Now the monkey clan came swinging down the long creepers which hung in festoons from the treetops to the ground.

"You are all as curious as Danu," said Bim, laughing. "We are friends, not enemies. Can't you see? Rewa's stick is only for pretend."

At that announcement, the little people jabbered faster than ever. "Come down to visit us," shouted Bim, craning his neck; "we are your friends."

Out of the dense forest shadows came the reply, "Friends." Then, more softly still, "Friends."

Bim stared at his mother. He had never before in his life heard an echo. "Did you hear, my mother? They answered me."

Mother Lakshmi laughed. "Yes, now you have heard the voice of Aranyani, son. She is the forest-nymph, the mother of beasts. She will always answer when you call."

"Will she answer me, too?" asked Rewa. And he shouted, "Tell me—"

"Tell me," came back a faint reply.

"Mother," shouted Jal.

"Mother," answered the voice.

"You see," Jal said, "she knows my mother too."

His aunt smiled. Now that Bukaru had tied Meta's head thriftily beside a patch of jungle grass, she took from the cart their sharp cutting knives. "When you are tired of playing, sit together on this fallen tree trunk," she said, "while we go to gather wood."

"You'll leave us all alone?" asked Jal.

"Are you ever all alone, little one?" She smiled at him. "If a large animal should come near, climb up into the cart and call me. Remember Grandfather's warning to have plenty of courage."

So she left them in a new world, to Bim, a world at once beautiful and thrilling.

But Jal looked at the two tall backs and then into Bim's face. He said in a small voice, "I think I should like to cut wood too."

Bim put an arm across Jal's shoulders. "Why not stay to watch the monkeys with us? Look, there's a mother carrying her baby."

They shouted with laughter at the comical sight of the wee black wrinkled head peeking out from under its mother's body, to see what it could see. Nearer and nearer drew the monkey band, curious to see what manner of beings these boy visitors might be. But as soon as the boys tried to approach them, the whole *bander-log* scrambled back up their creeper ladders again, loudly jibbering their protests.

Suddenly something flew directly over their heads, screeching fearfully. "Waw, waw, waw, waw, waw, waw, waw," seven times, each screech louder than the last. The noise was so unexpected, so terrifying, that even Bim found himself cowering beside his cousins beneath the cart. Presently, very much ashamed, he crawled out.

"It was only a peacock!" he said. "Look at him there in the tree. I suppose he doesn't want us in his own compound. So he's telling all the jungle: 'There are humans about.' He's warning the little people."

"I'll show him," cried Rewa, shaking his stick at the bird poised on a near-by branch. "If this were a real gun, I'd shoot him. Bang!"

For answer, the cock screeched again and began preening and shaking out his blue-green feathers. Slowly he lifted his gorgeous plumaged tail.

"Perhaps he would like to hear us sing," said Bim.

The three sat down on a big fallen log. Bim ran his fingers lightly up the holes of his flute to make trills that sounded like birdcalls. A white peahen flew up to join her mate and to cluck her approval of his tail show. Again the gray monkeys swung

163

down the vines until they sat in a wide circle at the edge of the clearing.

"They have come to our concert," said Bim in delight. "If we sing to them, then the peacocks and forest people will know we are not afraid of them."

So Rewa and Jal sang, the Krishna bird-song that Bim played on his reed pipe, the first song his grandfather had taught him, the song every Hindu child knew by heart: *Cheeria login—* little bird people, I will make you a song: I have roamed your kingdom, all the day long."

From out the purple shadows something moved. A leaf stirred. A dry branch snapped. Bim thought he saw spots and eyes. Perhaps a musk deer? The monkeys took flight again, screeching and scolding. Bim tilted his flute as he followed them with his eyes, but he played on. Now he was attracted by a slight movement at the end of the log. There, coiling itself on the bark he saw a long ebony snake, a cobra in the very act of out-puffing its hood. Its head upreared until it was on a level with Bim's.

For an instant, the Krishna song faltered as an instinctive fear gripped the boy. Then he remembered his grandfather's warning. "He who fears—"

Bim's big brown eyes met and held the small bright black eyes of the serpent, while he played on, just as he had seen the snake-charmers in the village bazaar. The cousins beside him still sang on, unmindful of the flat head peering through its hood, swaying from side to side, keeping time to the music, with a gentle, even motion.

Bim repeated the names of his hero-gods, but his notes quavered, and he felt queer in his stomach and breathless. His forehead was moist with perspiration. At the same time, he began to push backward along the log toward the cousins.

And just then, Rewa and Jal both saw the cobra too. Their song ceased abruptly as the forest rang with their screams. They tumbled off the log, clutching each other.

Then Rewa looked at the stick in his hand; this made him feel brave. "Take that, Mr. Cobra," he shouted, flinging the

164

stick at the serpent with all his might.

Surprised, the cobra reared high and hissed, preparing to strike.

Bim edged slowly backward, still playing on.

Meanwhile Mother Lakshmi and Bukaru came running. The cousins shrieked out the news.

"He's going to eat Bim," cried Jal.

"I threw my stick, but I didn't kill him. I wish I had a gun," said Rewa.

"Hush, children. Quiet them," Bim's mother told the serving-man. "Do not move, my son. Play on and on, softly."

She came close behind Bim, fearlessly facing the angry serpent that upreared several inches, transferring its unwinking black gaze to her eyes.

With her hands touching her forehead she bowed.

"*Namaskar*, O Nag. O Wise One."

She spoke to the cobra in a singsong voice like a chant, until finally it lowered its head. Gradually, its hood receded; slowly the cobra uncoiled. Turning, it slithered away, down off the log, a noiseless ebony streak, down and away through the jungle grass into the purple shadows.

Bim's mother sat down on the log and gathered the three boys into her arms. Jal sobbed. She dried his tears with a corner of her rose *sari*.

"See," she said, smiling, "there is no place for fear or for tears in the forest. That was great Nag, the wise one, come to bid you welcome to his world." Over the cousins' heads, she smiled at her son.

"Did you see the beautiful big hood?" cried Bim, with a sudden feeling of exultation. For the first time in his life he had looked into the eyes of a cobra. He felt somehow older, larger than before. He had been afraid, and then not afraid, well, almost not afraid. But his mother, she was the brave one. He stroked her smooth black hair, where her *sari* had fallen off as she ran.

"I almost killed that cobra with my club," Rewa gloated. "If I had had my father's gun, now—"

"Hush, child," his aunt reproved him. "If you strike he will strike you in return."

Bukaru came to stand before her. His face was long and very pale.

"*Namaskar*," he said. "But surely, Sahiba, surely there is great danger here. Old Suk would say that evil spirits are about. With one strike of its fangs, it could have killed Bim, then the boys, and then us too. You know the saying: 'When the time comes, Death bites like a serpent and is gone, and none can stay him.' "

Bim looked quickly into his mother's face. It was calm. Her brown eyes were pools of quiet.

"And the Bapu would say, 'The Shining Ones protect the fearless.' So, my brother, our time has not yet come. Now let us return for our wood."

Bim recognized clearly her quiet tone of authority. Bukaru could only bow and follow her, however unwillingly.

The three boys scrambled again onto the log. They straddled it, pretending it to be a hippopotamus.

"We'll ride through the jungle to the king of all the nagas," cried Bim.

"And we'll visit all the wild elephants," said Rewa.

"And cheetahs and tigers and panthers," added Bim.

"And big lions," said Jal.

"If I had a gun," said Rewa, "I'd shoot them all."

"Then you'd lose caste, and be no better than a foreign white man," said Bim. "Listen."

Out of the forest, which had seemed so still at first, they heard now a curious humming sound, as of millions and trillions of insects. They all tried to imitate the zooming sound, and ended by giggling at the faces Jal made.

"Let's go on a treasure hunt," said Bim.

"What kind of treasure?" asked Rewa. "Jewels?"

"Yes, jewels, or—well, just anything we can find. You two search while I count to ten times ten. Then you come back and count and I'll search."

So the hunt began. "Back to the stump," Bim shouted. "What have you discovered?"

167

Jal has filled the folds of his turban with jungle nuts, red and black. "I shall string them into a necklace for my mother," he announced.

Rewa had captured two praying mantises. "I mean to train them to fight each other," he said, "as our village barber does."

When it was Bim's turn, he hid his treasure behind his back and made them guess. "No, not an animal; yes, a kind of jewel." In the end he showed them a peacock's feather, green and blue, with a black and gold eye. "It's for my birthday," Bim said, well pleased. "I'll take it home to Sri Krishna, for his shrine."

All too soon the two grownups returned, nearly hidden under their bundles of wood. Bukaru looked up at the sky. "What time is it, Sahiba? Night falls quickly here. We must soon leave. It is never safe in the jungle after four."

"Yes, we will soon leave, Bukaru. Only one more load each to bring. While we are here, we should take advantage of so much good wood, thanks to the Maharajah."

But she had been gone into the thicket only a few moments when she called, "Bim, Rewa, Jal! Come here, little ones."

They ran to her. She pointed down beneath a tangle of vines and ferns at the foot of a large stump.

Jal thought it must be another serpent and hid his face in her skirts. Rewa reached for a stick.

"What is it, Mother?" Bim asked, blinking in the forest gloom at something round, brown and gold.

His mother stooped and lifted it out carefully. She held it in her two slender brown hands—a soft fluffy round ball.

"What is it?" all three asked at once.

"A royal jungle tiger kitten," she said quietly. "So new a baby cub that it doesn't even know it is being looked at by three human brothers."

Bim touched it. "Oh, it's alive. It's warm and soft." He laid both his brown hands over it, his heart tingling with a strange joy.

Rewa poked it with one finger. "What big ears it's got!"

Jal touched it. He made a gurgling sound of delight. "And what big paws it's got!"

168

"So," said Bim's mother, "here's another pet for you, son. How kind the great forest is to you on your birthday."

"Let me hold it," begged Bim, feeling a sudden sense of possession.

"No, me," said Rewa.

"Yes, each in turn. And soon it will be old enough to play with you. Would you like that?"

"Oh, Mother, I must take it home, I *must*." Bim was determined.

"Could we play with it too?" Rewa and Jal wanted to know.

"Of course you may. Carry it carefully, Bim, while I bring the wood. For we must return home at once. Bukaru!"

"Coming, Sahiba, coming." Bukaru stumbled along toward them as they ran out to the cart. He was bent double under his load of wood. In his hands he carried a big coil of creeper ropes.

Rewa burst out laughing. "You look as if the forest were walking out on two legs."

"Have a look at what my mother found for me," said Bim, showing his furry treasure. "It's a birthday gift."

Bukaru gave one look and jumped back as if he had been struck. He looked behind them, around them, then up to the sky, his eyes rolling fearfully. Dumping his wood into the cart, he called to Meta sharply to wake up and be off. He turned the cart around in a great hurry, with ungentle hands. He hustled the boys up on top of the load.

Bim heard his mother's quiet voice. "Are you so fearful then, Bukaru, of the jungle's gift to our boy?"

169

"Were your ears stopped, Sahiba, that they have heard no tales of the fierce anger of a tigress who defends her young? Of the wrath of a father tiger deprived of his son?"

"It is nonsense to fear any such thing. You know well that the tiger would only eat the kitten if he found it. And this mother must have abandoned her cub, left it to die, perhaps, because it was only one. Perhaps she was startled away, or she may be a young mother not yet wise in motherhood. Without milk tonight, the little thing would only die."

"Yes, Bukaru," added Bim, "we must save it, because I want it for a pet. I mean to tame it; to make it my jungle brother."

Again the man rolled his eyes to the darkening sky. "Then again, the mother may only have gone off for a drink or for food. What is to prevent her returning this night and taking her revenge on our village, on my own little Kamala, first of all?"

"May the Lord of all creatures protect you," replied Mother quickly. "I have no such fear for your daughter, Bukaru. The children were blessed this day by the forest. Was not Nag wise as a yogi, harmless as a wood dove? This gift of a royal Bengal tiger kitten must mean that Bim and his cousins were accepted by the jungle. His grandfather will be well pleased. It is a good sign."

"Yes, my mother, it is a good sign," said Bim, with blissful contentment. "And I shall call it *Heya*, the abandoned one, the little left-to-die one."

Bukaru glanced backward over his shoulder at the tawny ball of fur asleep in Bim's arms, and clicked sharply to Meta to hurry. With his long pole he thwacked the blue-black humped back. "*Jao! Chello!* Get along!"

The buffalo sniffed the air heavily and laid its ears flat on the horizontal head. So, fearful of heart, he rolled them along, as fast as he could walk out of the deepening shadows of the mysterious jungle.

A story of South America.

Alida Malkus

THE SILVER LLAMA

ILLUSTRATED BY *Matilda Breuer*

YAMA had nearly reached his second summer when Cusi found him on the mountainside, near the corral where he had slept as a baby, high up among the Andes. The snowy peak that looked down on him was reflected in the blue waters of Lake Titicaca.

"This is my Yama," Cusi cried. "How tall and handsome he has grown!" He threw his arms around the young llama's neck, stroking and petting him.

Yama's coat was matted and torn from his lonely wanderings since he had been driven from his mother's side, but it was still a beautiful soft silvery white.

"I will take him home and comb his hair," cried Cusi.

He put a colored rope around Yama's neck and led him very gently down the path. His father was loading dung for the fires upon the backs of a flock of big shaggy llamas. They pressed close to Yama; they did not kick or bite him. They hummed a little note of welcome. Yama crowded into the middle of the herd.

"Let him follow his father," laughed Cusi's father. For the leader of the animals was Yama's father, and he wore a bell around his neck. He was large and haughty and spotted white and brown.

Now Yama led a fine life. He slept with Cusi. Bright gay new woolen tassels were put in his ears. He was petted and combed. Cusi rarely combed his own hair, but Yama was different. "One must look after one's herd," said Cusi.

171

"He is a true silver llama. Good luck goes with him," said Cusi's father.

"We shall take him to the Fair at Puno," said the mother, "when we go to buy the plow. I have seen a thing called a plow that makes the earth very nice for the potatoes."

"I would like a cart with a wheel in front, a cart called a wheelbarrow, that a man pushes," said the father. "Then I could carry a load in the new way, instead of on my back."

On the morning of the Fair, Cusi's father threw a hair rope around the necks of his twelve llamas and drew them into a ring with their heads together. Then they all stood still while he put their packs on.

There was a good deal of wood and potatoes to take into the Fair at Puno. Cusi's father filled the sacks. Then he thought, "I will give each one a little more to carry this time, a stick or two."

Cusi's mother thought she would give each llama a few extra potatoes to carry, just a few. She hid them under the sacks when no one was looking. But Yama's father knew his rights. He would not carry one stick over his regular load. So he lay down.

"But it is only a handful," cried the mother, and took off the potatoes.

"I beg forgiveness," apologized the father. He threw off a few sticks.

Yama's father rose up again. "Without the sticks he can still carry the potatoes," said Cusi's mother to herself. She tucked away another little sack of the frozen potatoes under the faggots. But she could not deceive Yama's father. He lay down again. And all the llamas lay down with him.

"Come, my good friend, I beg of you, rise," begged Cusi's father. "What offends you, revered person?"

Cusi's father scratched the llama's head. But the leader of the llamas only twitched his nose and remained on a sit-down strike. Yama did as his father did.

So Cusi's mother had to take away the hidden sack of potatoes, and then the leader of the flock stood up and the other

172

llamas all stood up. Now they were ready to go to the Fair. The father dug up his gold. There were three pieces; he counted them and put them in a little pocket in his purse. The mother carried the extra potatoes herself, along with the baby.

Yama himself carried only a beautiful blanket on his back. For he *was* the only pure white llama in the herd and still young. When he was two years old, he would carry a load too.

So they went merrily up over the mountain and down along the winding trail to the pampas. The mother spun as she walked; when she had no more fleece to spin she would pluck a handful of hair from the backs of the pack animals. Whenever they came to good pasturage they stopped for breakfast, lunch, or supper. Then the mother would sit down to knit on a new cap for Cusi. The father would do a little weaving on a

173

handsome belly-strap for Yama. All he needed to make ready was to hook the top of the loom over a stick. Cusi played on his cane pipes.

In this way nobody got tired. When the sun was going down they came to an "untying place," and there they stopped for the night. When their packs were taken off, the llamas all lay down and began to hum, they were so pleased. It sounded like wind humming through the grasses.

"In olden days," said Cusi's father, "before the white men came, there were hundreds of thousands of llamas in these ancient corrals. They belonged to the King of the land, the Lord Inca. Among the royal flocks was a certain silver one, like Yama, pure white. He was taken to the temple for a sacrifice. But my great-great-great-grandsire did a service to a prince of royal blood, and he was rewarded with that same white llama.

"A silver llama; and he was the grandsire of Yama, of this we may be sure. For has there not always been a silver llama in the flocks of this family for as long as a grandfather can remember? And all the silver llamas were sacred. Silver images both big and little were made of them and buried in the tombs, so that silver llamas might go with the spirits of the departed into the next world. To find one of those little silver llamas today is very good luck."

"When the gods of the mountain were angry," said Cusi's mother, "the volcano above us spouted fire. The earth shook. The great stones which two hundred men would not move fell down. The floors of the temple were tilted up on edge. You will see them as we pass on the way to the lake."

"There is treasure there," said the father, "gold and silver, buried with the great ones. Gold and silver llamas, too. If one dared dig among the stones . . . but it is forbidden."

"I would rather have my Yama," said Cusi. "He is alive, and he is silver too, and good luck."

The father fanned the fire and they gathered round it. "The grandsire of Yama carried precious cargo to the palace of the Inca," he said. He was pulling a piece of meat for each one out of the pot which the mother had set over the fire. The llamas

174

had lain down; they were all yawning. Cusi was yawning too, his cheek bulging with potato.

"What did he carry?" he murmured.

"He carried jewels and gold from the mountains to the sacred city of Cuzco. He brought back orange fruit and cocoa from the hot valleys to the beautiful Princess Coiar. He lived to be more than twenty winters old, and as he was pure white, he never grew gray. He was always very proud. That is why his children are so proud. They remember."

"Can we not get a cargo of jewels for Yama to carry?" Cusi asked sleepily. They all lay down together; nothing is so warm as llama fur. There was no answer as the father and mother were already asleep, and Cusi did not notice for at once he was asleep, too.

In the morning Yama was the first one up. He shook his blankets out; quite simple when they grow upon your back. He walked over and stood waiting by the bags of fuel.

"How quickly he learns!" cried Cusi's father, much pleased.

The father was very careful to load each animal, not a stick over his load. They left the "untying place" and struck out across the pampas towards Puno.

In the center of the pampas that morning they came up to a man with a drove of asses and little burros laden high with sacks and shovels and picks. He was shouting and laying about him with a stick. He was a stranger.

"I have been here since yesterday," he cried, "with these wretched beasts. I am worn out whipping them."

"Put your strength into helping with the burden," said Cusi's father. "The creatures carry too heavy a load."

"They can carry it," shouted the man, "already they have carried it for the five days past, so it is not too heavy. Here, you have some animals without packs. Sell me one. I will buy that white one."

"No, we cannot sell any of our creatures." Cusi and his father and mother went on over the pampas shouting, *"Héya, héya,"* to bring their animals together.

At sundown they came to the Fair in the town by the great

175

blue lake. The mother put on three skirts over her old blue skirt—a red, a turquoise, a violet one. She took out three pairs of sandals and they each hung them at their belts so the village folk would know they had shoes for their feet if they wished. They all put on their holiday ponchos.

The father felt in his little man-woman bag. "One, two, three," he counted the pieces of gold; no more, no less.

The Puno Fair was full of people and pelts and potatoes and peppers. The mother spread her potatoes on a blanket in front of her and went on with her knitting. The father unloaded the llamas and led them back just outside the town. He put the hair rope around them so they would know they were in a corral.

Cusi ran about looking at the things to eat: white potatoes and rose-colored potatoes and yellow ones, cocoa beans from which you made rich chocolate, and cocoa leaves to chew when you were hungry and cold and tired. There were custard apples and oranges from the valleys at the foot of the great Andes Mountains. Cusi traded some dried meat for oranges.

"I'll trade you two little pigs for your silver white llama," a valley man offered. "I'll give you a sack of oranges and a gold piece," said another. But Yama was not for sale.

"We have meat, we have wool to spin and weave, we have milk for cheese, we have everything when we have our llamas," said the family.

But out on the pampas Yama's adventures were just beginning. Father had been in such a hurry to return to the Fair that he had not put the rope around Yama's neck, too. So Yama moved away from the flock, nibbling here and there. Farther and farther he strayed until at last he was way off on the pampas. Here and there other llamas grazed, so he was not lonely.

"*Héya, héya,*" cried a voice. It was the mining man. He came forward and stroked Yama's neck, and Yama looked proudly down his nose, permitting the man to admire him. Suddenly a rope was drawn around his neck, and the man was leading him along towards a distant hill. Just before dark they came to a gate in a high wall. Inside, among the stones of a ruined temple, were the man's pack animals.

176

"Now, my fine friend," said the miner, "you can carry these extra tools." He put a dirty pad on Yama's beautiful silver coat and began strapping on his back a bundle of tools—a pick, a shovel, a hoe, an adze.

The load seemed very heavy to Yama; that was just because he had never carried anything before. Yama held up his head proudly and did not move.

"Ah," said the man, "this is a beast of intelligence." He lifted a heavy thing with a small wheel at one end and set it on Yama's back. "We will get away from here now, tonight," said he.

But the added weight hurt Yama's back. This was too much. With great dignity he lay down. He would not rise; he knew his rights. The man flew into a rage. He cursed and prodded and shouted. Night was coming on. Finally, he took a hoe out of Yama's pack and threw it down. Yama got up, but it was hard to do, and his back seemed to be bending in the middle.

Now the man gave him a sharp cut with the whip and Yama

whirled around upon him. The man began to back away; he was frightened. But Yama came at him, and when he could see the whites of the man's eyes in the moonlight, he spat, as all good llamas do when pushed too far.

Then in the darkness he turned and ran, the tools on his back clanging and clattering. He didn't know where he was going and presently came up sharply against a wall. It smelled and looked like the wall of the corral on the mountain side, where Yama had been so happy as a baby. Perhaps this was a good place to stop. Yama lay down and began to chew his cud.

What a terrible night that was for Cusi and his father and mother. They ran here and there hunting for Yama. A big white man had given the father a lovely tin bathtub in exchange for his poncho, but even that did not console them when Yama was nowhere to be found.

They searched for Yama around Puno. They searched for him on the near-by pampas. Finally, Cusi's search for Yama led him to the place of the ruined temples. He nearly turned back then, fearing to disturb the spirits of the departed and bring bad luck on them all. But stronger than his fear was his anxiety for Yama. Cautiously, Cusi followed down a long wall till he came to an opening. A long time later he saw his silver llama lying patiently by the fallen stones, chewing his cud and smiling sweetly.

Yama bleated for Cusi and raised up on his front feet. In the earth before him a little silver llama glinted in the moonlight. Cusi snatched it up and threw himself on Yama's neck. Beneath them in the earth was a treasure of gold and silver for whoever would dig, but Cusi never thought of that. He had found enough good luck for one day.

He tore the heavy load off Yama's back and Yama rose up with dignity. Then Cusi tied on only the pick and the spade and the adze. He himself took the wheelbarrow bottom, for that is what the strange-shaped object turned out to be, and crying *"Héya héya,"* he led the way back over the stones. His feet were good and horny, almost as hard as Yama's except that he had more and better toes.

178

And so they returned to Puno. When the mother saw the pick and the spade and the adze, she knew they would not need to spend a gold piece for a plow. What a lucky creature Yama was! The father put the little tin bathtub on top of the wheelbarrow bottom, and there was his wheelbarrow.

"I will carry it home myself," he said. "We are rich, with all these tools and these fine pack animals. Let the good creatures eat and rest on their way home." He lifted the wheelbarrow on his back, the mother put her marketing into her shawl beneath the baby, Cusi carried the adze, the pick, and the spade.

So they set out across the pampas, and the rising sun shone on Yama's coat so that it looked like silver, and all the llamas followed him slowly and elegantly over the pampas. Their eyes were bright and gentle, their heads held proudly, as though they remembered that once their grandsires had carried gold and jewels for emperors, and fresh fruits from the valleys for the lovely Princess Coiar.

A Hopi Indian finds a treasure.

*Alice Crew Gall
and Fleming H. Crew*

TUNGWA

ILLUSTRATED BY *Keith Ward*

ON ONE of the great deserts of Arizona, in a village built on a flat-topped hill, lived Tungwa, a Hopi Indian boy.

These flat-topped hills are called "mesas," and there are many of them scattered about over the Arizona deserts.

The village that Tungwa lived in was a queer little place. All the houses were made of sun-dried mud and stones and were built, one on top of the other, like stair steps, so that the roof of one house served as the front porch of the house just above it. And each flat roof was reached by a ladder, which was the only way the Hopis had of getting in and out of their houses.

On one of these flat roofs Tungwa sat one morning, watching his mother as she wove a willow basket.

He liked to watch his mother make baskets—her fingers moved so swiftly. And he liked to see the little white bone awl that she used flash in and out as she wove the soft grasses and strips of willow into place.

Tungwa, like all Hopi people, had brown skin and straight black hair. For clothes he wore only a pair of old trousers, cut off to make them the right length for his short legs.

They were active little legs, and they carried Tungwa into all sorts of places, so that his mother found it a task to keep his trousers mended. But she did not mind. When her little son came to her with a fresh hole to be patched, she would only

180

shake her head and smile, and tell him to hold very still so that she would not stick him with her needle.

This morning as the two of them sat on the roof together, Tungwa's mother was thinking of other mornings, not so long ago, when Tungwa had lain here in the small cradle she had made for him with her own hands, out of leaves and willow. How proud she had been of him then! How proud she was of him now!

From time to time she raised her eyes and looked out across the desert, and when she did this, Tungwa would turn to follow her gaze. There was something mysterious to the little Indian boy about this great empty stretch of sand with its hummocks of coarse grass and sagebrush, and the blue Arizona sky coming down to touch the world, away out there.

Not far from the foot of the mesa he could see patches of green where springs of water came up out of the ground, moistening the sand. It was there the Hopis had their fields of corn and beans and melons. And Tungwa knew that somewhere out in those fields his father, with the other Indian men, was at work.

"Soon I shall go out there, Tewa, my mother," he said, "and help my father with the corn."

"You are not big enough for that yet, Tungwa, my little son," she told him. "Work in the cornfields is hard, and the sun is very hot."

"I like the sun, and I am strong," said Tungwa, beating his little brown breast with his small fists. "I am strong enough to work."

"You can go with the children to scare the birds away, after the corn begins to ripen," his mother told him and, bending over her work, she began to sing, a song about falling rain and Indian maidens and yellow butterflies.

Tungwa listened for a while, but presently he got up and went to the low wall that ran around the edge of the roof. Standing with his arms resting on the top, he looked down.

On the roof just below, Watika, the weaver of blankets, was at work. He sat on a grass mat before his loom which hung

181

from wooden pegs in the wall of his house. On this loom was a blanket, not yet finished, and the old Indian was patiently weaving bright-colored yarn in and out, in and out.

"I am going down to talk to Watika," Tungwa called to his mother. And at once he climbed down the ladder.

Watika, the blanket-weaver, was very old. His hair was gray, and his face was wrinkled. But his hands were as steady as they ever were, and his ears were very keen. He heard the boy coming and, without looking up from his work, he said, "It is Tungwa, the little son of Tewa the basket-maker. It is late morning for you to be on the housetops, Tungwa. The other children are already at play. Their voices come up to me from down by the water hole."

"I shall go down to the water hole after awhile," Tungwa told him, "but just now I would rather stay here with you and learn to make a beautiful blanket like that one."

"Umph!" grunted the old blanket-weaver, and for a time neither of them spoke again. Tungwa could hear the laughter of the children at play down by the water hole. He could hear the singing of the women as they went about their household tasks. Now and then a dog would bark. These were the usual morning sounds that he had heard all his life.

But the little Indian boy was very young, and he soon grew tired of sitting still. "Watika," he said, pointing out across the desert, "have you ever made a journey out there? Have you ever been away yonder, beyond the purple mountain?"

"No," Watika answered, "I have never been beyond the purple mountain. But when I was young I traveled a long way out across the sand to another mesa of our people. Many corn plantings have come and gone since then. I shall never again make such a far journey."

"I shall make a journey some day," Tungwa said. "When I grow big I shall make a far journey. I shall go away yonder, farther than the cornfields. Even beyond the purple mountain, Watika! And I shall see many wonderful things."

The old blanket-weaver slowly shook his head. "You are a Hopi Indian, Tungwa," he said. "You will always love your

182

mesa best, and your village and your desert. We are not wan-
derers, we Hopis. We had our time of wandering long ago,
before we came to live here at the mesa."

"What do you mean?" Tungwa asked. "Have not the Hopi
people always lived here?"

The blanket-weaver made no answer for a time. His long
brown fingers moved swiftly and surely as he drew the green
yarn through his loom.

"It happened a long time ago," he said at last, "so long ago
that no one can remember when. But our wise men have kept
the story, handing it down to one another. It is a story that will
never die. It is the story of our people, Tungwa. Today, Watika,
the weaver of blankets, tells it to Tungwa, the young son of
Tewa. And when Tungwa grows old, perhaps he, too, will tell
the same tale to some small child, here in this very place."

Watika stopped his weaving now and, sitting very straight,
he folded his arms across his breast. "Far to the south," he
began, "there once lived a mighty people—Indians like us,

183

Tungwa. The land they lived in was fair and green and full of growing things. Great trees gave a pleasant shade. And through soft fields, clear fresh streams of water ran."

"Have you seen that land, Watika?"

"No," the old Indian replied, "I have not seen it, and just where it is I do not know. I only know it lies yonder, somewhere to the south. Even old Mugwa, the Medicine Man, can say no more than this."

"It must have been a pleasant place to live in," the little Indian boy said.

"Such was the home of our people in those days," the old blanket-weaver went on. "But evil times came down. Our gods were angry with us. They sent fierce warriors, unfriendly Indian tribes, who seized our flocks and destroyed our fields and homes. There were wars then, and many of our people were killed. Many were carried off to serve our foes as slaves."

"How could that be?" Tungwa asked angrily. "Are not the Hopis braver than all others?"

"Our gods forgot us," old Watika said slowly. "Our people fought bravely, but still our foes came on like a plague of locusts, sweeping everything before them. Then our people fled. They left their flocks and fields and all the things they loved, and fled, hoping to find new homes in some far place. But they found no peace. Farther and farther they were driven, until these desert lands were reached. And here, upon the flat-topped hills, at last they found shelter."

The old blanket-weaver pointed a long thin finger toward the end of the mesa. "They built their village out there," he said, "in a great hollow under the cliff. There, where you see the big red sandstone boulder, a path leads down to it. Not much of their village is left now, but you can still see the crumbled walls of some of the old houses. They were once the homes of our people, Tungwa."

"What became of the people who lived there?" Tungwa asked.

"They are gone," Watika told him. "Those cliff-dwellers are gone. Their houses have been deserted for no one knows how

184

long. Now only bats live in those silent rooms." The blanket-weaver lowered his voice almost to a whisper. "They call the place the Cavern of the Dead."

The little Indian boy shivered. It frightened him to think of those old houses, so long deserted, there under the cliff. Suddenly he gave a cry of surprise. "Look, Watika," he said. "Look, there by the red boulder."

The blanket-weaver turned his head. "It is only Mugwa, the Medicine Man," he said. "He often goes down to the old village. And sometimes he hears strange sounds there, far back under the cliffs. He says they are the voices of the dead."

"Have you ever seen that place, Watika?" the little Indian boy asked curiously. "Have you ever gone down to the old village where the voices are?"

"Yes," Watika answered, "I have been there."

"And did you hear the voices?"

"Our people spoke to me there one day," Watika told him.

"What did they say?" Tungwa asked excitedly. "What did the voices of our people say to you, Watika?"

"They did not speak in words," Watika answered and then, pointing to some small figures in the edge of the blanket he was weaving, he said, "These little figures are the voices that came to me that day, Tungwa."

The little Indian boy was puzzled. He looked at the figures and then at the old blanket-weaver. "I do not understand," he said.

"Come closer," Watika told him, "and I will show you what I mean. These little figures that I have worked into my blanket are meant to represent the sacred Snake Dance that our people dance, each year, so that the Rain God will not forget to make the rainclouds spill their water upon the thirsty ground. Look," he went on, "here is a raincloud. Here is a thunderbolt. Here are the Indian boys who attend the priests. And here are the women carrying trays of sacred meal."

Tungwa grew more confused. He knew about the Snake Dance, for he had seen his people dance it every year. Though he did not understand all that this sacred dance meant, he knew

185

the Rain God understood, and that was all that mattered. But what had the Snake Dance to do with the Cavern of the Dead?

Old Watika saw the question in the boy's eyes, and after a moment he went on. "I was the first of our Hopi weavers, here at this village, to weave these figures into blankets," he said proudly. "The design is not my own. I found these figures on a piece of broken pottery in that village in the hollow of the cliff. They are the work of some old Hopi potter, now long gone. And that is why I say my people spoke to me that day, there in the Cavern of the Dead. I copied the design as nearly as I could, just as I found it on that broken pot, weaving it into a blanket. But part of the design is missing, for there was one piece of that broken pot that I never found, though I searched for it in the piles of dust and stones in the deserted village."

"Maybe you will find it yet, Watika," Tungwa said.

"No," replied the old weaver of blankets, "I shall not visit the Cavern of the Dead again for the pathway down the cliff is steep, and I am very old."

These words made Tungwa sad. "Oh, you are sound and strong," he said quickly. "You will live a long time, Watika."

The weaver of blankets put his hand on the head of the little Indian boy and looked deep into his eyes. "Some day, Tungwa," he said, "you will be great among the Hopi people. You have brave eyes."

Many times that day the little Indian boy thought of the old blanket-weaver's words. And that night, asleep on the floor of his mother's house, wrapped in his warm woolen blanket, he dreamed strange dreams of Watika and the broken pot and of Mugwa, the Medicine Man, who listened to the voices in the Cavern of the Dead. And he was glad when morning came again with its familiar sounds.

Tungwa did not stay on the rooftops that day, but went early to the water hole.

This water hole was a large natural basin in the hard sandstone of the mesa and, long ago, the Hopis had made it still larger by digging and scraping it out with their rude homemade tools. When it rained, the water would pour down from the mesa, filling the basin so full that it looked like a little lake. But it did not often rain in the desert, and there were times when this basin was almost empty.

Just now there was plenty of water in it, and Tungwa sat down on the ground, close to its edge, and took a deep breath of the clear desert air.

Not far away, eight or ten little burros stood drowsing in the sun. But there was no sound to break the early morning stillness, and for a long time Tungwa sat there without moving.

Great thoughts come to a little boy, alone by a quiet pool of water.

"The blanket-weaver says I have brave eyes," Tungwa whispered at last and, rising to his feet, he folded his arms across his breast, as he had seen old Watika do, and stood facing the sun. "I am a Hopi Indian," he said proudly, "and some day I shall be great among my people!"

That morning little Tungwa went alone to visit the Cavern of the Dead.

He could not have told why he went there. The thought of that crumbling old village, where no one had lived for so long, frightened him. But, somehow, the place drew him, and he had to go.

By the big red boulder at the end of the mesa he paused, but only for a moment. Then, slowly making his way down the narrow passage between the jagged sandstone walls, he came to the end of his journey.

It was a strange place—a great pocket in the cliff, a huge cavernlike opening in the side of the mesa. Its high roof of solid sandstone arched above and came down to form a wall at the back and sides. The front of the cave was open and from it the cliff dropped almost straight down, to the sandy desert far below.

For some time Tungwa stood looking about him in wonder. The place was silent and deserted, but he knew that here in this great cavern there had once been a village of his people, where young Indian boys, like himself, had lived.

Under the arching roof stood the ruins of a number of little

187

houses. Many of the walls had long ago crumbled away but, here and there, he could make out an opening that had once been a door or a window.

He peeped in at one of these doors. It was dark in there and very quiet. Cautiously he slipped inside and, instantly, a queer feeling came to him, a feeling that he was not alone, and that those who long ago had lived here were looking at him from the dark corners and through the cracks in the broken walls.

A bat passed silently above his head, and he felt the rustle of cool air.

And then he heard a noise!

It was not a very loud noise. It sounded like a loosened stone rolling across the floor of the cave, and almost at the same instant Tungwa saw something moving in the darkness.

It was like a living shadow and it startled the little Indian boy so that he jumped quickly back. As he did this, one of his bare feet came down on something hard and sharp.

Tungwa did not know that he was hurt. He was too frightened and excited to feel any pain. What was this thing that was moving, here in the cave with him? He crouched close to the wall and waited. Nor had he long to wait, for suddenly, moving out of the dark, the shadow took form and stood sharply outlined against the blue sky at the opening of the cave.

Tungwa was relieved. It was not a ghost after all, for ghosts were like thin smoke, and you could see through them. This was solid and real, and he could see it plainly.

It was only one of the village dogs!

But now that his mind was relieved, Tungwa began to notice the pain in his foot. "What was it that hurt me?" he wondered and, stooping, he felt around on the floor until his hand touched something hard and smooth.

He picked it up, but in the darkness of the little room he could not see what it was. "It is only a stone," he decided and was about to toss it from him when a strange thought flashed through his mind. Holding tightly in his hand the thing he had found, he hurried out of the cave.

The sleepy little burros were still drowsing by the water hole, and the Hopi children were playing in the sun, when Tungwa reached the edge of the village. But he did not stop. He kept straight on until he came to the sun-dried walls of the little Hopi houses.

Up one ladder he climbed, then up another, and as he jumped down onto the flat roof, he saw old Watika, the blanket-weaver, sitting before his loom drawing in and out the bright-colored yarn.

"Do you know where I have been, Watika?" asked the little Indian boy.

Watika did not look up from his work. "No," he said, "I do not know unless you have been with the other children at play, down by the water hole."

"I did not stop to play at the water hole," Tungwa told him. "I have been on a long journey, Watika. I have been to the Cavern of the Dead."

The old blanket-weaver looked at him in wonder. "The Cavern of the Dead!" he exclaimed.

"Yes," the little Indian boy answered. "I have been to the great hollow under the cliff. I have seen the village where our people lived so long ago. And look, Watika," he added, holding out his hand, "I found this in one of the little rooms. It is a

189

piece of broken earthenware, and there are some figures on it. I thought you might like to copy them into your blankets."

The blanket-weaver took the piece and examined it eagerly. "Tungwa," he exclaimed, his voice trembling, "Tungwa, son of Tewa, you have done a great thing today! This is part of the broken pot. It is the missing piece that I could not find! You have made old Watika very happy!"

Little Tungwa was very happy, too. Never had life seemed quite so pleasant as it did just then. Never had the Arizona sky seemed quite so blue.

A song came floating down from the roof above. It was his mother's song—the one he liked so well—the song about raindrops and Indian maidens and yellow butterflies.

Turning, he climbed up the ladder as quickly as he could. At the top he looked over the low roof wall. His mother was standing in the doorway of their home. How beautiful she was, he thought.

"Tungwa, my little son," she said gravely, though her eyes smiled at him, "where have you been so long?"

Tungwa climbed one round higher on the ladder and jumped down upon the roof, forgetting all about his sore foot. "I have made a far journey, Tewa, my mother," he answered proudly, "and I am hungry. I have great things to tell you of, this day!"

WALK ON THE RAINBOW TRAIL
Indian Song

Walk on a Rainbow Trail;
Walk on a Trail of Song,
And all about you will be beauty.
There is a way
Out of every dark mist—
Over a Rainbow Trail!

190

"MOTHER, are there then goblins—*real goblins*—in this Iowa where we go?"

His mother had laughed. "No, Johann! Thy great-uncle speaks of a different kind of goblin. . . . He means only the strange customs we will meet, the unfamiliar people, the new language."

Well, Johann's heart was young and strong, but now it hid a deep, growing worry. Oh, he didn't fear the new language . . . but strangers . . . other boys his age . . .

Nan Gilbert

HOUSE OF
THE SINGING WINDOWS

ILLUSTRATED BY *Clarence Biers*

JOHANN RIEHL lay flat on his stomach behind the low stone wall and peeked out cautiously at the children going by.

There were two of them . . . a boy who might match Johann's own nine years, and a girl a little younger. Every morning they passed Johann's home on their way to the white frame house down the road, and every morning Johann lay breathlessly behind the stone wall and watched them.

"Goblins!" he whispered when they were safely gone. "Hobgoblins!"

They weren't of course, and Johann knew it. But the word had a special meaning for Johann.

Way back in Bavaria, across the sea, Johann's great-uncle Fritz had used it when Johann's father and mother had urged him to come with them to America.

"*Nein, nein!*" he'd shaken his head positively. "Once I have been there, and that is enough. I am too old to go fighting hobgoblins now!"

191

Johann's eyes had nearly bulged from his head. He had followed his mother to the kitchen, words sputtering out of him like corn popping.

"Mother, are there then goblins—*real goblins*—in this Iowa where we go?"

His mother had laughed. "No, Johann! Thy great-uncle speaks of a different kind of goblin, one that needs no tickling spear to scare the old and timid. He means only the strange customs we will meet, the unfamiliar people, the new language. To him, those are as fearsome as goblins, and he has no longer the young stout heart to beat them off."

Well, Johann's heart was young and strong, but now it hid a deep, growing worry. Oh, he didn't fear the new language—hadn't he spent a whole year learning it painstakingly from the Englishwoman across town? But strangers . . . other boys his age. . . .

He'd asked his great-uncle about it, very casually to show that it didn't really matter.

"The American *junge*, Uncle Fritz, the boys and girls over there—they were not so different from me, *hein?* "

Under his great bushy eyebrows, his great-uncle's eyes had twinkled secretly. "Ach, such creatures! They do nothing but play baseball and eat apple pie and ice cream and dream of being cowboys! And their talk, it is outlandish! 'Holy jumping catfish' they say. And 'Nuts!' "

Johann was quite subdued during the rest of the preparations for their journey. Baseball. Ice cream. Cowboys. Holy jumping catfish. Anxiously, he said the strange words over and over, struggling with their meaning.

It was March when they embarked—Johann, his mother, his father, and the twenty-two canaries Mother could not leave behind. The voyage was wintry and dismal, across a sea as gray with fog as Johann's own heart. But spring reached America almost as soon as the Riehls did, and Johann thought the bewildering number of miles they crossed to Iowa were like layers to a towering cake, each layer more richly plummed with beauty than the last.

Oh, this was a good land, a fine, generous, strong land. Johann loved it already. If only—if only its people loved *him!*

For the first week, he didn't have to find out about that, though. Mother kept him too busy. They scrubbed and polished every inch of the snug farmhouse that was to be their home. It was an old, old house, built of stout, warm-hued stone, and in it Johann could almost believe himself back in Bavaria. Mother had set up her many little pots of vines against the living room and kitchen walls by the staircase; she had spread the familiar braided and crocheted rugs over the floors. Father had taken time off from planting to screen the front windows inside and out (the sills were more than a foot deep), and now the windows made fine big cages for the twenty-two canaries.

"Next week," Mother decided briskly, "thou must start to school, Johann, with the other *kinder!*"

Johann's heart dropped straight to his hiking boots. School. Strange American children like the two who passed his hiding-place each morning. Now surely Johann was up against the biggest goblin of them all?

Soon after eight o'clock, the following Monday morning, Johann's mother pronounced him ready for school. His hair was slicked flat under the little pancake of a beret; his short tight jacket and brief pants were freshly pressed. His bare knees, like his hands and face, shone pink with scrubbing.

"Now shall thy father go with thee, Johann?" his mother asked kindly. "Or I?"

193

"*Nein,* neither!" Johann said hastily. "Let me go alone, Mother!"

"Alone?" she looked at him doubtfully. "You have the school report, *hein?* And the letter from the schoolmaster? . . . Ah, well, go then, little one."

Once outside, Johann circled quickly to the barn.

His heart beat furiously fast; if he hadn't been nine-going-on ten, he'd have almost thought he was scared. Soon now he must face the American children—do battle with his biggest goblin— but oh, joy, he had found the right uniform for his fight!

He had discovered it yesterday, quite by accident, hanging dusty and forgotten on a hook in the barn . . . a tattered, enormous pair of overalls!

Just such a garment, though smaller, had the boy worn who'd passed Johann's house each day . . . so different a looking garment from Johann's own clothes that Johann had been sick at heart.

But now—

Diligently, Johann smacked and smoothed the precious overalls, pinning them to his size with many, many safety pins. Perhaps Mother could have cut them down to fit, but Johann hadn't told her of his prize. She'd worry because there was no money this spring to replace his foreign clothes.

The overalls bulked a little oddly when he was finished, but even so, Johann decided anxiously, they looked better, more American than his own suit. Carefully he hung his jacket and cap on the hook, and ventured at last out into the road.

Ahead of him walked the girl and boy.

The boy was first to hear the scuffle of Johann's boots in the gravel. He looked back and stopped, staring at Johann unblinkingly the whole minute it took Johann to overtake them.

Then, finally, he spoke. "Hi!"

The careful "how-do-you-do" Johann had learned from the Englishwoman choked in his throat. He swallowed hard, and faintly echoed, "Hi."

"You going to school?"

Johann nodded. They fell into step.

"My name's Peter Janus, and this here's Paula. What's your name?"

"Jo—" Inspiration struck Johann, and boldly he chopped off the balance. "Joe Riehl."

Johann gestured back toward the stone farmhouse. The little girl squealed suddenly, "Oh Peter, he lives in the house with the singing windows! I *told* you somebody nice must live there!"

Peter looked more sharply at Johann. "They said some Germans bought that. You German?"

Johann took a deep breath and mustered the words well in his mind before trying them. "Holy jumping catfish, no! I'm American!"

They reached the schoolhouse. Peter led Johann up to the teacher's desk. "We gotta new boy, Miss Iverson. His name's Joe. Joe—what did you say?"

"Riehl."

Miss Iverson held out her hand. "Hello, Joe. We're glad to have you." She had a smiling face and corn-yellow hair, and Johann knew instantly that he wanted to please her above all else.

There was no time then to find out what class Johann would belong to. He took a seat in the back of the room and listened and looked with all his might. Here all about him were American children, real Americans. Already they accepted Johann as one of them. But if they found out he *wasn't*—

When the recess bell rang, Peter came straight to Johann. "Whatcha want to play?"

Johann plunged bravely. "Baseball."

"Baseball, huh?" Peter's face brightened. "What's *your* act—pitch or catch?"

Johann gulped. His eyes roved wildly in search of help. Miss Iverson chose just that moment to come up to them and say, "You run out and play, Peter. Joe's had recess all morning, and now I must find out what class to put him in."

"Now, Joe," she went on briskly, drawing paper and pencil toward her, "have you a report card from your last school?"

Automatically, Johann reached into his pants pocket beneath the tremendous overalls. Then his hand stopped; his face became a picture of woe.

"You forgot it?" Miss Iverson smiled. "Well, never mind. Tomorrow will do. Now what subjects were you studying this year?"

Johann brought his hand out of his pocket guiltily, leaving the report card where it was. His mind was a whirl of giddy fireworks, and all he knew clearly was that he *couldn't* show that record from a foreign school. He just couldn't.

"Reading, I suppose?" Miss Iverson prompted him. "Geography?"

"Oh, *ja!*" Johann said hastily. "And Script and French and Political Science—" He stopped short, silenced by the puzzled look in Miss Iverson's eyes. Now what had he said wrong?

Slowly, Miss Iverson pushed the paper away from her. "I believe we'll wait for the report card after all," she said with a friendly nod of dismissal. "I'll put you with Peter today."

Johann drew a mighty breath of relief. For today, then, he was safe. Tomorrow was a goblin he'd not battle till it came.

The rest of the morning went smoothly. Johann recited with Peter's Reading Class, and found the words he'd learned from the Englishwoman quite adequate. His sums were correctly

196

done, too, and he went out to lunch very satisfied with himself.

Peter sprawled beside him in a shady corner of the school-ground. When Johann opened his basket and got out the fat roll with the good *leberwurst* inside, Peter's eyes popped greedily. "Oh, boy! You got hot dogs, huh?"

Johann looked curiously at his sandwich and then nodded violently. "Sure. Hot dogs. You want one?"

He gave Peter a roll, and Peter said generously, "Here, you can have my pie!"

Johann took it gingerly. It had thin flaky crust top and bottom, and it tasted not unlike his mother's *apfel-torte*. Johann gobbled it down to the last bite and sighed contentedly. These American ways, they weren't so hard to take!

The afternoon got off to a bad start. Miss Iverson opened it by talking about a party. Apparently it was to be quite a party, the last event of the school year, and the children must have discussed it often from the way everybody chattered at once. Peter leaned over to whisper noisily, "It's gonna to be fun! An all-American party. Our folks are comin' and everything!"

Johann's heart curled into a tight little ball. All-American. Then it would be just for those who were completely American. Johann felt suddenly cold and left out; he could never pass for an all-American, never!

Afternoon classes didn't go as well as the morning ones. Johann stumbled badly in Spelling, and in History he could only stand dumb. Then, shockingly it was recess again and Peter was pushing a great long sort of club into his hand and shouting, "First bat! Joe's first bat!"

He was shoved and jostled into an awkward position facing a boy with a ball. Johann's eyes were huge and black with fright; he didn't know what was coming next. But it turned out to be the ball that was coming—coming right at him and fast!

Johann gave a startled yelp and put up the strange club to ward it off. The ball cracked briskly against it and shot back over the big boy's head. Everybody was yelling and screeching in a deafening way. Urgent hands pushed Johann wildly. "Run Joe! RUN!"

197

What had he done? What must he run from? His pounding heart took his breath away; he tried to force more speed into his trembling legs. Something tangled with his feet and almost threw him. An open pin pricked sharply at his heaving side; he felt his overall slipping, slipping from his shoulders, and the tangle was growing more desperate around his feet.

But still he ran, and still urgent hands thrust at him, turning him in a big circle until suddenly he tripped and fell flat, right where he'd started.

"Yay! Home-run!"

Johann thought his poor ears would split. Peter pounded him on the back. He tried earnestly to get up, and now the cause of his tangle was hopelessly apparent. The pins in his overall legs had come loose. Terrible lengths of blue denim, like rolls of elephant flesh, cascaded around his ankles. Even the sides of the suit gaped open limply.

The roar around him was sharpened by laughter. "Hey!" the big boy who'd thrown the ball howled. "You shrinkin' or some-thin', kid?"

But suddenly Peter was squared away before the big boy like a bristling terrier. "Maybe he likes his clothes that way, see? Maybe he likes room to grow! You wanna make something of it?"

The recess bell cut across the argument. Peter hurried back to Johann and helped him with the pins. "Don't you give a hoot about that ol' smarty!" Peter said strongly. "You are swell!"

The spreading warmth around Johann's heart was damped out coldly at four o'clock when Miss Iverson closed the school-house door and joined Johann and Peter and Paula.

"I believe I will just walk home with you," she told Johann companionably. "It'll be a good time to pick up your report card!"

Johann couldn't say a word. All his words were strangled inside him. A last desperate hope loosened his tongue. "I'll go ahead!" he stammered. "I—I'll tell Mother you're coming!"

He tore away from them faster even than he'd made the home run. Panting, he crossed the fields, flung open the front

Proudly he ushered them into his home.

door. "Mother! Mother! They are coming!"

His mother hurried anxiously out of the kitchen, wiping her hands on her big apron. "What is it, boy? Who comes?"

"The teacher, Mother! Oh, you must hurry, hurry—make yourself fine in the good dress—talk only the American—oh, Mother, you do understand, don't you? They are coming!"

"Ja, ja!" She ran up the steps, too rushed and bewildered to notice Johann's strange costume. He trotted swiftly back to meet the others and slow their pace. Now if Mother put on the American dress Uncle Fritz had bought her when he was here— oh, it was just a kitchen work dress, but it was *American!*— maybe, even yet, his secret would still be safe.

Slowly, slowly, Johann guided the trio through his front gate.

"See, Miss Iverson!" Paula cried. "See the windows!"

"Oh, beautiful!" Miss Iverson exclaimed, and then she repeated softly, "Beautiful. . . ."

But her voice was different, and she wasn't looking at the windows now. Johann followed her glance to the front door.

His Mother stood there. Her face was flushed pink from hurry, but its gentle dignity was undisturbed. She had done what her son asked: she had put on her finest . . . the full, embroidered skirt and tiny jacket, the fine-tucked floating-sleeved blouse of her Sunday best back in Bavaria. Proudly, now, she held out her hands to them while her eyes went shyly to Johann for approval, and she said in her careful English,—

"Welcome!"

Johann's throat choked with a great love for her. Oh, it didn't matter that she'd torn his poor secret wide open! She'd tried hard to please him . . . they'd just better like her! They'd just better!

Fiercely he strode to her side and faced them. "Miss Iverson, this is my mother, Frau Riehl!" And just so there'd be no mistake, he added defiantly, "And my name's not Joe, either. It's Johann!"

But oddly, nobody seemed much concerned. Paula and Peter had run over to look at the canaries, and Miss Iverson said casually, "I daresay it will be Joe soon enough. The boys will see to that." She started to follow his mother into the house.

Johann said bewilderedly, "But we're not Americans like you. We come from across the sea—"

Miss Iverson smiled. "Don't we all, Joe? Isn't that what America is, a gathering place for everybody with the courage

200

to cross the sea and find it? Why, that's why our country is big and strong, Joe, because it takes big, strong people to leave all that's dear and familiar behind them and to strike out to find a new world! People like you and your parents . . . like Peter's grandfather who came from Greece, like my own mother and father who left their home in Norway. Oh, you'll see us all, dressed in our own particular Old World clothes at the all-American party! Your mother must be sure to come and wear that lovely costume."

Johann's head was swimming with happiness. "But the all-American . . . I thought it meant . . ."

"Just that we, who were Norse and Greek and German, are all Americans now, Joe—that's what it means." Miss Iverson went on into the house, and Johann swung around open-armed to Peter and Paula.

"Come on in!" he invited warmly. "The windows look much prettier from inside!"

Proudly he ushered them into his home, and sunshine poured into his heart through a thousand singing windows.

From AMERICA THE BEAUTIFUL
Katharine Lee Bates

O beautiful for spacious skies,
For amber waves of grain,
For purple mountain majesties
Above the fruited plain!
America! America!
God shed His grace on thee,
And crown thy good with brotherhood
From sea to shining sea!

201

A Scottish adventure.

Helen Coale Crew
THE MACDONALD PLAID

ILLUSTRATED BY *Helen Prickett*

"TAG!" cried Donal, giving Kirstie a thump on the back and springing away on nimble feet.

"I'll taggit you!" screamed Kirstie, and away she went in pursuit of Donal over the great moor. They were like young foxes, the two children, with their reddish hair, bright sharp eyes, quick feet, and noses keen for scents. Over the brown earth they ran, through the purple heather and the golden gorse, trampling down clumps of waving ferns and crawling through the slender stems of the broom plant. And now Donal is panting. Kirstie has her tongue hanging out. Their hearts are thumping. Their ears are singing. And then Donal runs down to the side of the moor to where a little stream slips along between moor and hill, takes a flying leap across it, and turns to jeer victoriously at Kirstie. Kirstie's legs are far too short to make that jump.

No, they are not always playing, these two Scottish bairns. They have lessons to do in wintertime, just like the rest of you. Even when the freezing winter weather has settled down over the country and they cannot walk the long miles to the school in the Town, Grandfather sets them sums to do upon their slates, and Father has them read Aesop's Fables to him—in

Latin, if you please! And too, there's the woodcutting work, at which they help, and the carrying of kindling wood to the Town to sell. Oh, they're busy enough! Want to hear their story?

We are so used to reading in Grimm's Fairy Tales stories of woodcutters in the Black Forest, that perhaps we think that all woodcutters, Hop-o'-my-Thumb's father and the rest, cut their wood there. But there are still many forests left in the world, in spite of all the cutting that has been done, and axes still ring in them, with flying chips where they bite into the stalwart tree trunks, and piles of fragrant logs to show what they have done. Woodcutters ring the world around with their sweet-smelling work. And in this story we have to do with a woodcutter in Scotland.

Away up north in Scotland, not so very far from where King Macbeth lived in olden days, a great lord, or laird as they call it there, had an estate that covered more than one rugged mountain, and at least one wide moor. This moor, rolling up to the sky at one end, was covered with bracken and gorse in the summertime, out of which birds would start up suddenly and go whirring into the air until they were mere dots. In the springtime wild flowers made a pleasant carpet there, but in November the first snow spread its chilly coverlid out of which a few dry stalks of weeds stood up and rattled in the wind, while from the hills surrounding the moor drifted down the song of the pines.

On the edge of the moor, where it began to dip down into the valley of Pebbly Brook, stood a woodcutter's house, a very humble house indeed, but at the same time a very happy home. It had stood there for many years, built strongly of stone and plastered over, with a thatched roof on which sometimes a bracken seed would lodge in windy spring to become a waving green feather in midsummer. The thatch was thick and warm, and came down well over the windows like eyebrows forever frowning. There were but two rooms, and in each the floor was of stone. Here John Macdonald had been born when his father before him was woodcutter to the laird, and here he had brought his wife Janet when they were married. His father,

Old Jock, was still living, and sat most of his days, for he was very old, beside the wide fireplace, lonely when the family was off in the woods at work, and happy when they sat about the fire with him, listening to his tales of the days of yore.

Sometimes on winter evenings, when the windows were covered with frost and the moon rose over the windy stretches of the moor, the old man went to a little cupboard over the chimneypiece and took out his most precious possession, a book of the "Poems of Ossian," old and worn, which he handled with reverent care. These strange and lovely old tales of the early chieftains and warriors of Scotland were handed down from generation to generation by word of mouth for centuries, before they were gathered together and printed in a book. Many of them had to do with the old heroic chieftains, Fingal and Ossian. Old Jock could have told the tales quite as well without the book, but he loved the feel of it in his hands, he said.

When Old Jock spread the book open on his knee, Janet settled herself in her corner with her knitting, John sat near by smoking his pipe, and the two children, sturdy Donal and bright-eyed Kirstie, sat one at each knee of Old Jock, listening with eyes and ears and hearts. Old Jock pushed his long white hair back from his face, and his eyes looked as though he could see those ancient heroes before him. And with a solemn voice he began, "A tale of the times of old! The deeds of days of other years!"

When he had finished a tale, he allowed the children to recite the parts they liked best, for they had learned their favorite parts by heart, having heard the tales so often. Donal liked best of all the address of Ossian to the sun:

> O Thou that rollest above,
> Round as the shield of my fathers!
> Whence are thy beams, O Sun?
> Whence thy everlasting light?
> Thou comest forth in thy awful beauty;
> The stars hide themselves in the sky;
> The moon, cold and pale, sinks in the western wave;
> But thou thyself movest alone.

Who can be a companion of thy course?
The oaks of the mountains fall;
The mountains themselves decay with years;
The ocean shrinks and grows again;
The moon herself is lost in heaven;
But thou art forever the same,
Rejoicing in the brightness of thy course.
When the world is dark with tempests,
When thunder rolls and lightning flies,
Thou lookest in thy beauty from the clouds
And laughest at the storm!

Donal's eyes always flashed when he recited these words, but when Kirstie recited her favorite part she very often ended up with a tear in each eye:

I have seen the walls of Balclutha,
But they were desolate!
The fire had resounded in the halls,
And the voice of the people is heard no more.
The stream of Clutha
Was turned from its place by the fall of the walls.
The thistle shook there its lonely head:
The moss whistled to the wind.
The fox looked out from the windows:
The rank grass of the wall waved round his head.
Desolate is the dwelling of Moina:
Silence is in the house of her fathers.

Old Jock, getting out his handkerchief and wiping away Kirstie's tears, would ask the little lassie tenderly what it was that touched her so, and sometimes Kirstie would say, "Why, that lonely thistle, Grandfather," and at other times she would say, "Well, there was nothing for the little fox to eat." Kirstie half wished she might have been the lovely Moina, but Donal was sure he would have gladly been the great Ossian.

In the mornings, from the moment the sun gilded those little rattling weeds lifted above the snow, there was no time to think of brave heroes and lovely heroines. Then the children must get up at once, for there was much to be done. Donal made the fire, Kirstie stirred the porridge, while Mother milked the cow and Father fed the donkey. Eppie the donkey must also work, and especially at the woodcutting seasons. John Macdonald cut wood for the laird who lived in the great stone house perched on a crag high up the mountainside. It was from up there that Pebbly Brook came tumbling down into the valley and reached at last the Town, six miles away, where it turned the mill wheels. John had as his pay for the woodcutting his little farm rent free, and all the branches of the trees he cut down that were below a certain size.

When they had eaten their porridge and milk, and Old Jock had drunk the cup of hot tea he needed to keep him warm, they got ready for a day in the forest. John fastened two large, deep baskets on Eppie's sleek gray sides, Janet filled a little basket with newly baked scones, Donal put a ball of twine and a pair of shears in one of Eppie's baskets, and Kirstie carried a bag of eggs very, very carefully. They started out in good spirits, singing some stern old Scotch hymns as they went. At first they walked downstream for a mile or so, and then turned up a

206

rough cart road on the right. As they mounted slowly upward the forest grew deeper, the underbrush thicker. Sometimes a startled rabbit ran across the road; sometimes a deer went crashing through the bushes by the roadside. There were many wild gooseberry and blackberry bushes in the underbrush, and the fruit of these the children had gathered in the summer for their mother's jam making. At last they came to a broad level shelf on the hillside. Here, in a clearing, stood a wooden hut. Back of the hut a young man, Sandy McGill, John's helper, was already swinging his axe. Here and there stood neat piles of logs cut to the proper length for the laird's huge open fireplace in his great hall. From the clearing they could look across the valley and see the laird's great stone house, its windows all afire with the light of the sun, now high enough to peer over the shoulder of the opposite hill.

John Macdonald took a key from his pocket and opened the door of the wooden hut. There was a stove inside, a table, a few chairs, and a great wooden chest, padlocked, which contained tools. John unlocked this and took out the tools they would need for the day. Then Donal built a fire in the stove, and Janet sat there knitting as contentedly as though she were at home. Janet did not always come up to the clearing with them, but now and then she enjoyed a day in the forest.

John and Sandy worked steadily all morning, sometimes with axes, sometimes with a long two-handled saw. Meanwhile the children were far from idle. They gathered up all the smaller branches, broke or cut them into even lengths, and tied them up with the twine into bundles to be used for kindling wood. When their hands got cold in the sharp November air they ran into the hut and warmed them at the stove.

At noon they all stopped to eat. Janet unpacked the scones, boiled some eggs, and made some hot tea. And then, while John and Sandy smoked their pipes and told stories and jokes, the children raced up and down like wild young creatures until they were warm through and through and their cheeks like winter apples.

"Ye are good Macdonalds to the marrow," said John, proud

207

of his children's vigorous bodies contented with plain food, and their wholesome young minds joyous over simple pleasures.

"And that makes me think," said Janet, nodding and smiling at her bonny bairns, "if 'tis as cold as this tomorrow when you start for the Town, you may take the Macdonald Plaid to keep you warm."

This was great news to the children. Always they had wanted to be trusted with the Macdonald Plaid, a great, long woolen shawl of the colors of the Macdonald Clan that even Old Jock could remember as being a family treasure away back in his boyhood days.

"We will take turns wearing it," said Kirstie.

"Yes, Kirstie first and then me," said Donal.

But their father laughed and said, "When I was courting your mother, we found it big enough to keep us both warm at once, did we not, Janet?"

"Indeed, yes!" said Janet. "And I remember we walked home in it the frosty day we were married, all the way from the Kirk in the Town to the wee bit hoose on the moor's edge. The moon came up before we reached home, and the broad back of the moor was as silver as a lake."

All the afternoon again they worked. When Kirstie's bundles of kindling wood were uneven, or too loosely tied, or not big enough, her father made her do them over again. He said that there would be no flaw in the tuppenny bit she would be paid for each bundle in the Town on the morrow, and so there must be no flaw in the bundle. Donal, two years older than Kirstie, who was only eleven, always had neat and even bundles, firmly held by two twists of twine tied into knots that would not come undone.

At last the day was over. The fire in the stove was carefully put out; the tools were wiped dry and put away in the chest; the house door locked. While John and Sandy did these things Janet and the children filled the baskets on the donkey with the bundles of kindling wood, and tied some long bundles of twigs, which Old Jock could make into brooms for Janet, across the patient creature's back. Eppie was handsome, as donkeys go,

208

with smooth gray hide, patient eyes, and ears that could sometimes be alert, sometimes wag reproachfully.

Sandy said good-bye and went whistling away up over the brow of the hill, for he lived in the valley beyond, with his axe over his shoulder. They had so much wood cut now that in a week's time John and Sandy would drive up to the clearing with a big wagon, load on the logs, and take them up to the laird's woodhouse on the hill opposite. There had been one particularly big and beautiful log that they thought would surely be chosen for the Yule log at Christmastime, now almost here.

That night, in the little house by the moor, when a story of Ossian had been read by Grandfather, and a chapter or two from the Book of Job by Father, who insisted that Job was a greater hero than Ossian, the children were so full of spirits that they begged not to be sent to bed at once. Could they not just dance the Highland Fling before they went? John growled a bit first and then consented. Donal ran joyfully and got the bagpipes from a nail behind the door, and then, upon the hearth in the glow of the fire, the two children danced that joyous dance to the skirling of the pipes.

Next morning, which was a Saturday, it was a proud moment to the children when Janet got out the Macdonald Plaid from the chest, unwrapping it from the clean white cotton cover in which it was kept. Its colors were a little faded, but as Old Jock said, "Any man with a drop of the Macdonald blood in him would thrill at sight of it." The donkey was loaded with the two baskets of kindling wood, Donal put on a warm worsted vest under his coat, and Janet wrapped Kirstie up in the Plaid. Then away the two children and the donkey went, down the valley along Pebbly Brook, towards the Town.

Six miles is a long way for a heavy heart, but for such light hearts as Donal's and Kirstie's it was no length at all. Whether or no Eppie's heart was light we cannot say, but at least her neat little gray legs moved briskly. In summer the children always took this journey barefoot, to save their shoes, but it was too cold for that now.

"How many bundles have we today, brother?" asked Kirstie.

"Fifteen in each basket," said Donal. "That makes thirty. And at tuppence each that will bring us five shillings."

"Mother said," said Kirstie, "that if we sold every bundle we might buy a few raisins for a mealy pudding."

"Losh!" said Donal. "It makes my mouth water. If you'll give me the raisins out of your part of the pudding I'll give you all the mealy part of mine."

"Not me!" said Kirstie. "I shall eat every raisin I find in my piece and then wheedle at Mother for more."

After a while they came in sight of the Town. It lay in a silver loop of the stream, which by now had widened to quite a river. On one side of the river stood the woolen mills, and on the other, at the edge of the Town in a grove of trees, they could see the gray stone towers of the big school where lads for miles around went to prepare for one of the big universities.

When they reached the Town they went at once to the square and tied Eppie to a ring in an iron post in front of Mr. Craigie's shop. In Mr. Craigie's shop you could buy garden tools and seeds, soap, a few dry groceries, smoked hams, cough drops, camphor, tobacco, and toys. Mr. Craigie welcomed the children and told them he would take ten of their bundles of kindling wood. Donal brought the bundles in and put the money deep down into his safest pocket.

"Have ye got a cold, now, either of ye?" asked Mr. Craigie, looking at their rosy cheeks. They both shook their heads.

"Or a cough?" went on Mr. Craigie. Both children coughed the best they could, considering that they had never had a cough in their lives.

"Aha!" said Mr. Craigie, with a wink. "Ye surely are bad this morning!" He took down a jar from a shelf and gave them each a little black licorice drop.

"They are ugly little black things," said Mr. Craigie, "but would ye believe it, now, the licorice plant has beautiful blue flowers! Think of that and chew them slowly, and maybe ye won't cough any more today. Blue, mind ye. As blue as the flax flowers." And with a laugh he went off to attend to a customer, and the children went out.

And then—can you believe it?—Eppie was gone! Bag and baggage, she had disappeared. Not a trace of her left. Kirstie choked on her cough drop and burst into tears, but Donal said gravely, "Macdonalds do not cry until they are really hurt," and dragging Kirstie by the hand, started off to look for the missing donkey. Up and down and around they walked, but nowhere could they find any trace of Eppie. Footsore and weary, they returned to Mr. Craigie's shop and told him their tale of woe. Mr. Craigie was full of sympathy; he gave them each a hoarhound lozenge.

"There!" he said. "Try those. You might not know it, but the hoarhound belongs to the mint family. Very respectable plants. 'Tis a fact." Then he went to the door and looked out and all around. "Aha!" he cried. "This is Saturday, and the school lads are free. Best go over and look about on the school green. There's twelve chances out of nine the little beast is there."

"Eppie is not a beast, she is a lady," said Kirstie, so emphatically that the hoarhound lozenge leaped out of her mouth and across the narrow sidewalk into the street.

"Have ye looked for the lady on the school green?" asked Mr. Craigie gravely.

"No, sir," said the children.

"Better try it," said Mr. Craigie. "Strange things happen over there."

So Donal and Kirstie went over to the school campus, a lovely stretch of rolling lawns under tall elms and oaks. They went in through the great stone gates rather timidly, but no one was in sight anywhere. In and out among the ivy-covered buildings they went, but nowhere was Eppie in sight. And yet—

"Hark!" said Donal.

He seized Kirstie by the arm. Surely that was Eppie's plaintive bray. It seemed to come from the air. Both looked up. There on the edge of a gray roof, with her little gray legs braced firmly and her ears full of reproach, stood Eppie.

"Come down! Come down!" screamed Kirstie, dancing up and down in her excitement and distress. Donal clapped his hand over her mouth.

"Silly blatherskite!" he said. "Don't you know she is as likely as not to come right down the side of the house if you call her?"

Kirstie stopped screaming but went on dancing, and the ends of the Plaid waved like banners. At this moment a group of students came around the corner of the building. At sight of the little dancing figure and the distressed face of Kirstie, they stopped short. Then one of them exclaimed, "The Macdonald Plaid, as I live!" And putting his hands to his mouth in megaphone fashion he shouted, "Macdonalds to the rescue! Macdonalds to the rescue!"

In answer to this call there presently came running up five more lads, and the six crowded about Donal and Kirstie, while the others went on about their own affairs. Donal and Kirstie soon told their trouble, pointing to poor Eppie.

"That's one of the Freshmen's childish tricks," said the first Macdonald, who had himself done the same thing with a stray cow the year before. "We'll have her ladyship down in a jiffy." And in less time than it takes to tell it, the six had rushed into the building, appeared shortly upon the roof, and with the combined effort of twelve strong arms and six determined wills brought poor Eppie safely to the ground.

"But where are her baskets?" cried Donal, while Kirstie's tears began to flow afresh. And he explained to the big lads that two baskets and twenty bundles of kindling wood were missing.

"See here, you young Macdonalds," said the first Macdonald, "we'll buy the lost baskets and bundles. Anything to comfort kinsmen in distress!" And whipping off his cap, he passed it around among his five fellow students. There was a pleasant clink of shillings in the cap. The lad handed the cap to Kirstie with a flourish.

Donal and Kirstie bent over the cap and counted the money and calculated gravely on their fingers, and at last Donal said, "There's enough to buy two baskets and pay for the wood and two shillings over." He put two shillings back into the cap and handed it to its owner.

"But," said Kirstie, "this isn't fair. You do not get anything for your money."

"Yes, we do, too!" said the first Macdonald, with a laugh. "We get the Freshmen!"

And at that, with a shout, the six of them cried, "We get the Freshmen! We get the Freshmen!"

"Hold on," said one of them. "Why can't our young kinsmen give us some amusement for our money? What can you do, youngsters? Can you dance the Highland Fling?"

Could they! If there were but bagpipes—That was easily fixed. One lad hastened with flying heels into the building and came back with pipes, skirling as he came. Then in the clear, crisp November air Donal and Kirstie, their eyes like stars, their cheeks like June roses, danced with all the joyous abandon and

213

grace of happy children. When at last they stopped for lack of breath, there was warm applause and a cry for more. At that Donal stepped forward and recited Ossian's address to the sun, followed by Kirstie with the lament for the desolation of Balclutha. After that there was a respectful silence, and then such a ringing cheer that it brought an inquiring student face to every window of the big building and caused Eppie to tremble in the legs.

Next, things happened so quickly that the children are not clear to this day as to just what did happen. But as the great bell on the courthouse struck twelve o'clock, followed by the mill whistles, they found themselves on the homeward road, Eppie stepping jauntily along beside them with two new baskets hanging at her sides. In the bottom of one basket lay a package of raisins. In the bottom of Donal's safest pocket lay five shillings. And tucked beneath the tongue of each child, where it would last the longest, was a hoarhound lozenge, a parting gift from Mr. Craigie. They walked in blissful silence. After a while Donal shifted his lozenge to one cheek and said, "Losh! What doings!" But Kirstie said nothing. She remembered the lozenge she had so indiscreetly lost.

That night around the peat fire at home, you may be sure Donal's and Kirstie's story was listened to with the deepest interest. When the last question had been asked and the last answer had been given, Janet rose and put away the Macdonald Plaid, laying it tenderly in the chest.

"Well," said Old Jock, "the Macdonald blood is good stuff, wherever found."

"Aye," said John, " 'tis so. Thick and red."

Whether Eppie had dizzy dreams that night of high roofs and slippery footholds, we cannot say, nor can she.

Helen Train Hilles

GOING UP!

ILLUSTRATED BY *Marguerite Davis*

T HE four Sherwood children, Jock, Ricky, Twig, and Bumps, were hanging in midair!

They were in a cable railway that ran up the side of a mountain. None of them had ever been in one before, and to see the little box you were sitting in, tied from the top to a cable that pulled you up the mountain, was really quite thrilling. As they hung above it, they got their first view of Switzerland from way high up. They could hardly believe they were on their way to Mademoiselle's house.

"We're *still* going up!" said Jock.

"We must go higher steel," answered Mademoiselle with pride.

"I do hope that sort of rope thing won't break," said little Bumps, as the other children called Eleanor, the youngest.

"Silly!" said Jock, who knew everything. "That's a steel cable!"

Below them stretched green valleys. Above, the towering peaks of glistening white mountains. Twig sniffed in the thin, cold air. There wasn't a trace of dust or fleas. There was a cheery tinkle from the big low bells on the necks of the cattle grazing on the soft green slopes.

Ricky glowered as he watched. The tinkling annoyed him. He refused to admit, even to himself, that there could be anything beautiful or even mildly interesting about Switzerland.

"Oh, look!" Bumps shrieked. She seemed to have adopted Switzerland. "Look at all those teensy villages! Sort of little clumps!"

215

"Those are Alpine villages," said Jock, as though he owned them.

"*We* can see," said Ricky loftily.

"Just because you're in a bad humor you don't need to act like that," said Twig, in her most grown-up tones. She brushed a speck off her dark blue traveling skirt.

Ricky could hardly control himself. It was bad enough to have to go and spend a whole month marooned in Switzerland under the thorough chaperonage of Mademoiselle, their retired French governess, without the others acting as if they didn't mind!

He opened his mouth—then shut it again in a thin, straight line. He could hardly say everything he thought with Mademoiselle right there!

How he had hated this whole miserable summer, until they reached Montenegro, which they had just left. Europe with its sappy languages and queer people (particularly the French) was certainly a flop compared to America! That was why he was so particularly incensed at being dragged away from Montenegro, which was the first place that he had felt things were picking up.

He had tried every way he could think of to get out of coming to Switzerland. But Father and Phil had said the month was all arranged for, that Mademoiselle needed the money she would get for their board, and it would do the children no harm to be settled somewhere for a change. Ricky raised a row. But he came—fuming.

It took a long time to get to Switzerland. He got glummer and glummer the farther they went. And when the Family really left them, and Mademoiselle really materialized, he felt that life could hold no worse.

To Ricky's never ending shame Mademoiselle kissed him. She spoke of him playfully as *"ce cher Reeckee"* till he smarted with humiliation and thought lovingly of the Montenegran dagger that he had unfortunately promised to keep in its sheath, and high up on the wall.

She told all the children she *"se rejouie"* to see them, and had the same funny clothes and smell, and the same bustle and worry about time and railroads, so that the three others rather enjoyed the prospect of the pleasant, familiar hate she inspired in them.

"We change again, here!" said Jock.

Ricky's thought reeled back to the present. The children got out of their cable railway, and got on an electric one. This one ran along a mountain terrace with panoramas of beauty below

217

that Mademoiselle pointed out each inch of the way, while Ricky winced. At Murren they got out again.

"What do we do next?" asked Bumps.

It was then that Mademoiselle, the unathletic Mademoiselle whom the children remembered as screaming at a mere mouse, seemed to change her spots.

"From here we walk!" she announced briskly. "Haf you all goot shoes? Bien! We leave the baggage here. Hans weel fetch it by de mule."

The children watched in wonder as Mademoiselle fished in her black bag and produced two stout mountain boots, with nails studding their soles. Right there in the station she peeled off the thin black-laced shoes, through which the shape of her joints showed, and put on the boots. They came way up under her black silk dress, and she looked so funny that the children could hardly help laughing when she stood up.

"*Allons! En Avant!*" she said, and started out ahead with the slow swinging stride of the Alpine guide.

The children were too surprised to do anything but follow. Could Mademoiselle's house be reached only by walking? They all felt cheered by the unexpected.

In a few minutes there was no town left, and they were walking along a well-marked mule-track. A green valley lay down to the left of them as they skirted the pine woods that poured from the pastures above them to the floor of the valley. As their trail wound in and out of the woods they saw the mighty snow-peaks and smooth silvery sheets of slick glaciers. Herds of moving cows and goats were tiny figures above and once, out of the clear air, they heard someone yodeling. Suddenly Mademoiselle stopped.

"There is our home!" she said. Her voice was soft.

The sun was setting, turning the sky to a blaze of fiery red. The valley to their left was splashed with blots of color. Knee-deep in the flowery meadow stood a high, brown chalet, all alone. Great snowy peaks crouched behind it, their edges rimmed with light. Farther down the valley was a clump of smaller chalets. Goats and cows wandered freely about.

"Oh, how wonderful! I love it!" cried Bumps, completely going over to the enemy. How big it was, thought Twig. Ricky wished it were ugly.

"Golly!" breathed Jock. "To think of Mademoiselle having a house like that!"

A solid figure came out of the chalet and stood facing them, hand shading its eyes. Mademoiselle started walking again.

"Hurry!" she said. "Maman has been expecting us, and we are late."

They crossed the valley on a little path, the grass and flowers on either side of them almost up to Bumps's waist. She almost got behind, because she kept saying, "Oh, look at that one! Twig—wait—I've got to have this one—"

Maman was out to meet them.

"She doesn't look a thing like Mademoiselle," whispered Jock in some surprise to the others.

Her gray hair was piled into a tight knot. She had bright red cheeks. The black eyes under their white brows looked piercingly at the children. Her ample, bulky figure was all but covered by the thick apron she wore. The children were surprised she had a German accent.

"How-do-you-do?" said the children, as each in turn shook her firm, rough hand. Bumps added solemnly, "You have the beautifullest house!"

"You tink you like it—hein?" said Madame. "Come, wash, and we will haf de supper, then Hans will be here wit de bags."

But the children, who had never seen a Swiss chalet—except the toy music box Bumps had been given for Christmas once— had to walk all around it first.

"It has almost as many stories as a skyscraper!" said Ricky.

"It looks like a gingerbread house!" said Bumps.

Four stories of lovely, rich chocolatey brown! A carved balcony ran all around it, one story up, and there was a flight of wooden steps you walked up. Funny little balconies ran for a few feet or so at various places outside the upper stories. The whole thing looked as though it might topple over any minute, like a house in a stage set.

220

"I want to sleep up there!" Bumps pointed to a tiny balcony perched up high.

"*A ça, mais non, donc,*" said Mademoiselle firmly. "The night air, *tu sais bien,* is onhealthy." Madame, sitting calmly on the front steps, almost hiding them, fixed Mademoiselle with her eyes.

"Phutt!" she said disdainfully. "You wit your old-fashion ideas! The night air is goot." She winked with a wide grin at the children. "Many a time I climb out that very window when a child—skinned, you call it—down to the ground, and sleep in the meadow wit de goats! And I live yet," she laughed a firm, hearty inward chuckle that bubbled up inside her.

"You did?" whispered Bumps.

What was Mademoiselle going to do, wondered Ricky, who at this moment decided that he liked Madame. To his great joy Mademoiselle murmured, "Oui, Maman," in a very meek voice indeed.

The children could hardly wait to get to their rooms to talk this over.

"She backed down quick as a flash the minute the old lady even looked at her," he cried exultingly. An expression of wicked glee was on his face. "Say, I'll bet Mademoiselle's not her daughter at all! They don't look alike. She's not even French! I'll bet—"

"Well, she *said* she was," said Jock slowly.

A cowbell sounded in the little hall below, and the children scrambled to get washed. It was almost fun, washing out of the heavy white pitchers and bowls of cold water that they found. Twig looked at the funny, top-heavy-looking wardrobe in her room. She hoped Mademoiselle would take care of her wrecked clothes as soon as Hans brought them. She certainly was sick of living in a suitcase. Twig pulled at the little window, which stuck, then creaked open. The clear, thin air rushed in. The fat featherbed seemed to flutter in the breeze.

"Come, Twig, for heaven's sakes!" sounded from below. Twig ran downstairs.

Madame was dishing out supper at the long table. She sat before the biggest tureen the children had ever seen. How good it all looked—the thick soup, full of unrecognizable things; the thick country bread in long loaves, the great slices of golden cheese piled high on a platter, and two pitchers of milk.

"Oh boy!" breathed Jock. Ricky's face brightened as he saw the great bowl of soup that Madame poured for him, so full that a little slopped over. Mademoiselle looked disgusted.

"Not so much, voyons, Maman!" she said. "These children haf not the appetites like peasants!"

Maman laughed. Her genial double chin shook. Bumps hoped that when she grew old she'd have lots of double chins. They made you look so good-natured, sort of like Santa Claus.

"You teach them mitt books—and leave the eatings to me!" boomed Madame. "In eatings there is no much difference mitt peasants and titles!" She gave a sly look at Mademoiselle. But Mademoiselle was nibbling meekly at a piece of cheese. Ricky, Jock, and Bumps lost no more time, and all but dove into the food. Twig, however, decided that Madame's coarseness revolted her, so despite her hunger she ate sparingly.

Madame ate hugely. The children, full by now, gazed at her as she ate slice after slice of cheese, washed down with enormous draughts of goat's milk from a great fancy stein.

"She ate nine pieces of cheese! I counted!" whispered Ricky, lost in admiration. Madame had offered goat's milk to the children, but in spite of Madame's disappointment they had stuck to cow's milk. Bumps, who hated having anyone's feelings hurt, almost took a tiny swallow. But she couldn't quite bring herself to do it, even for Madame.

Madame, meal finished, took the checked napkin out from under her chin and turned to Twig. The piercing eye made her wish that she could shrink under the table.

"She eat notting—that one!" she accused. "Like a mouse!" She forced a luscious piece of cheese on Twig, who ate it slowly, making a face, but enjoying it to the last inch.

"It ees time for de bed," said Mademoiselle, looking at the round gun-metal watch on her scrawny wrist. "You others go to your rooms—I will help Eleanor."

"She always *did* remember things like bed," muttered Jock.

The children trooped upstairs. Mademoiselle had Bumps firmly by one hand, but Ricky and Jock went in to talk things over with Twig.

"I think Madame's grand," admitted Ricky. "It's a scream the way Mademoiselle's meek as Moses with her!" Twig arched her neck.

"Well, *I* don't," she said. "I think she's a coarse old woman, and of the two Mademoiselle wins out—though I don't think she's so hot, either." Ricky opened his mouth, and Twig went on hastily. "*You* needn't talk, anyhow. You've been yipping all summer about how you hated foreigners!"

Ricky's face fell as he remembered. It didn't help to have Jock grin. "Well, that was about the French—mostly," Ricky said slowly. "And of course it's an awful bore being 'way up here with nothing to do—"

He felt that that sounded lame and was relieved when Jock burst out, "I've got all the low-down! About why she and Mademoiselle are so different, and everything!" He obviously felt pretty important.

"Well, why?" asked the others grudgingly. Jock settled down in a high, carved wooden chair.

"Mademoiselle *is* French—at least, half," he said. "But Madame isn't French *at all*—she's Swiss!" The others stared.

"That's silly," said Twig, "people are always the same nationality as their parents—everyone knows that!"

"That certainly shows *you* up!" went on Jock. "It's clear to the *dullest* mind! Madame was a German Swiss, a peasant, and her family kept a hotel in this very chalet when she was a girl. It was a great center of mountain climbing. A young Frenchman came here to climb mountains, fell in love with Madame, took her back to France, and they had Mademoiselle!"

"That explains it," said Ricky, feeling vindicated.

"Imagine anyone falling in love with Madame," Twig sniffed.

"Well, anyhow, they all lived in France," went on Jock. "Then—remember when Mademoiselle left us to go back to France to her mother? Well, her mother said everybody was dead, except Mademoiselle, and she wanted to go back to Switzerland to end her days. She was sick, and Mademoiselle was scared. So they took their savings and bought back this old house, and they're broke, but Madame says she's perfectly happy. She never did like France anyhow, and she's put on twenty-eight pounds and isn't going to die at all!" He paused, out of breath.

"I knew she had some sense," said Ricky. "Oh, gosh, then Mademoiselle may not have been fibbing about all the finest families in France being her relations! You remember, about her dear departed cousin, the Count, and all. Heck!"

But another idea had slowly crept into his mind, dwarfing Madame and Mademoiselle. Mountain climbing! Here was at least something they could do in this far-off spot. Something that you did in America and that he had no doubt about being able to do. Hadn't he climbed the ladder path on Newport Mountain, and wasn't he generally good at much harder and more violent sports than that?

"Come and see me! Come and see me!" Bumps's voice muffled, came from the next room. When they opened the door, they couldn't help laughing. Bumps, red from giggling, was almost lost, sunk in her big featherbed. All you could see was her small head, the rest of her buried down deep in the puffy mattress. Mademoiselle was just putting over her a great feather quilt, which billowed up like a balloon.

"It's too comfy for anything! Mademoiselle, don't pull that 'way up, I'm smothering!" gurgled Bumps.

The others, quite looking forward to going into their own featherbeds, leaned over to try and kiss her goodnight. There was so much soft spongy quilt in the way they could hardly reach her happy face.

"I think this is the nicest place in the world!" she said sleepily.

"Not bad a bit," admitted Jock. Twig and Ricky said nothing. They didn't want to spoil her pleasure with their own ideas.

Mademoiselle, saying briskly, *"Bon nuit, dormez bien,"* was going down the stairs. Ricky leaned over and called down.

"Mam'selle!" he said. "Can we go mountain climbing tomorrow?" Mademoiselle turned around.

"We have all arranged—even to engaging guides, for when Blaise and Emile come!" she said impressively.

Guides? What for? Blaise and Emile? Who the heck were they? There was an ominously French sound to their names. Ricky took a step after Mademoiselle.

But with her parting shot, Mademoiselle had gone on down the stairs, refusing to tell them any more that night.

"Well, I *must say*," growled Ricky, "it's bad enough being cooped up here, but to have Mademoiselle go and wish a lot of frogs on us is just about the limit! It beats the Dutch!"

"The French, you mean," giggled Jock. Ricky was too far gone even to throw him a withering look.

The children had retired to a small balcony after breakfast, for a conference. They had learned at breakfast that Blaise and Emile were two French lycée students who were to come and stay at the chalet for a month's vacation. They were the sons of Mademoiselle's mythical Monsieur le Comte.

"New people are always fun—" began Bumps, then stopped, looking at Ricky's face. Twig put her hand to her hair, smoothing it. She wasn't quite sure how far you could trust Mademoiselle to have attractive cousins. She yearned to ask how old they were, but was afraid of being laughed at.

"As though any sap relations of Mademoiselle's could possibly be any fun!" Ricky was scornful. He was going to *have* to hate them, he now saw, whether he wanted to or not.

"We'll wait and see," Twig said peacefully. She didn't want to commit herself in any way, until after a first glance, at least.

In the days before the boys were to arrive, the children had a good time. Even Ricky was unwillingly filled with a sense of well-being, though when he remembered the cousins and the fight with the Family, this mood vanished. But being grouchy was rather wasted, at this time, marooned up there in what was practically their own valley.

Blaise and Emile were arriving at eleven. Mademoiselle had gone to meet them at Murren, taking Jock and Bumps. Twig had decided to stay home, and Ricky had refused indignantly to go.

He stayed by himself all morning. At lunchtime, however, just as he was beginning to feel that *anything* would be a welcome break in the day, he heard the echo of voices. He looked across the meadow to the mule-track at the edge of the woods. He couldn't help looking with interest.

First came Mademoiselle, stalking with the swinging stride that seemed to fit in so oddly with her prim self—as though she were one person from the knees up, and another from the knees down. Jock, following, was turning his head so often it made him stumble, to get his remarks across to the trio behind him. Bumps was walking along the middle of the path, hopping between two tall youths, a hand in the hand of each. She seemed to have adopted them, Ricky thought fiercely. He hated their precise voices as he heard them approach.

Ricky ducked inside, and picked up a book. He heard footsteps outside.

"Ricky!" called Jock's voice. "Ricky, where are you?"

There were voices at the chalet door, and the party came in.

"I don't know where everybody is—oh, there you are, Ricky!" Jock said anxiously, as he saw his brother's blank, dour face.

"This is my brother, Ricky," he gulped. "These are Mademoiselle's cousins, Blaise and Emile." Blaise, the taller of the two by a head, stepped forward, an expectant smile on the face that was white in contrast to the shock of soft, dark hair.

"I am so pleased—" he began, holding out his hand. Ricky barely shook it, leaving his hand limp. He didn't rise.

"How-do-you-do?" he said coldly.

The smile vanished from the face of Emile, the younger, thicker boy. He bowed gravely to Ricky, not holding out his hand at all.

Twig appeared at this moment of silence. She looked very neat, and there was a slightly knowing look on her face as she looked up at Blaise.

"My sister, Therese, but we always call her Twig," said Jock in tones of relief. Both boys greeted her with ceremony.

MARGUERITE DAVIS

"Mademoiselle," said Blaise, and Twig looked, thought Ricky disgustedly, as though about to purr. This was getting worse and worse.

In the afternoon Ricky stayed by himself and didn't even ask where the others had been. But in the evening he couldn't get out of sitting around the tiled stove in the stuffy little parlor, which had, he noticed, been opened up in honor of the cousins. Ricky felt completely shut out in the cold. After the way he had behaved in the afternoon he had expected people to be mad at him—but not simply ignore him! Twig was being so bright and gay that the children had almost forgotten she could be like that. Bumps was sitting sleepily in a corner listening—while Jock was slowly shooting questions at these boys who seemed to be a perfect mine of knowledge about things Ricky knew nothing about! Even Madame looked at him a couple of times as though he weren't there—which was worse than not being looked at at all. He couldn't stand it any longer. He had to say something. He opened his mouth in a silence.

"I don't suppose," he began, his voice coming out more disagreeable and patronizing than he had intended, "that either of you play baseball or football, or anything like that?"

Emile didn't answer, but Blaise did, at once.

"I have never played, but I have watched football and find it very interesting. We have different games in France."

"Like—like throwing the discus, or something," said Ricky. "Ha-Ha-Ha." His laugh was mostly embarrassment, but it *did* sound rude. Emile flushed. Silence reigned.

"Guess I'll go to bed," said Ricky, and slipped out.

He got into bed and pretended to be asleep when Jock came up and Twig joined him for a talk.

"Aren't they grand?" said Jock. "They're fun, and they know more than any of the kids at school. Mademoiselle certainly does manage to hook herself a swell bunch of relations!"

"I find them charming, too," said Twig softly, "particularly Blaise. Emile is, of course, just a nice kid. But they both have perfect manners."

"Well, I think they're fierce, with their manners like two sappy girls and their white faces and their silly English with that ridiculous accent!" Ricky rose up like a thin wraith in bed. Jock turned on him hotly, while Twig made a gesture of despair.

"They know more English than I do, and they speak awfully well, and I don't know what's eating you, and *you* needn't expect *us* to stick up for you. Will we, Twig?" Jock burst out.

"See if I care," said Ricky, deeply hurt.

But in the morning he felt a little better and managed to nod to everyone at breakfast.

"Can we start mountain climbing now, Mademoiselle?" he asked.

"May we have Albrecht again, *ma cousine?*" asked Emile eagerly. Mademoiselle nodded.

"But he weel not be free for two days," she said.

"I am not surprised at that!" Blaise exclaimed. "He is one of the most expert guides here. How does it come to pass that he is not engaged throughout the season?"

Madame laughed. "The good guides do not wish to work all the time," she said. "Albrecht has been with a party of Englishers for six weeks. He will be glad of a rest before his next party."

"Ah," said Blaise, as if he understood. Ricky was puzzled. If Albrecht wanted a rest, why was he going to be their guide? An uneasy feeling started creeping over him. Blaise and Emile sounded as though they knew what they were talking about.

"We're in luck to have you boys to start off with," put in Jock.

"But no," insisted Blaise, "we are only beginners."

"I am glad we are not to start too soon," said Emile. "We should go to Murren and get some boots—and I need a new ice-ax. Jock, have you and—and your brother got the proper clothing?"

"We've only got suits like what we've got on and gobs of sneakers," answered Jock.

"We don't need anything else to climb these dinky little peaks 'round here," said Ricky. "And we don't need Al—what's his name, either." So these two, with their thin weedy figures, thought they were mountain climbers, did they? And Albrecht thought he'd take them on in his spare time!

"Oh, but it is better so," protested Blaise.

"I'll tell you, we'll go to Murren with you, and you tell us what to get. We'll go this morning," decided Jock, without asking Ricky's advice. But he went, having a desire, after all, to own an ice-ax.

In the small outfitting shop, Ricky watched with interest. Blaise and Emile picked over everything, talking in fluent German to the man who owned the shop, choosing some things, discarding others. Emile got an ice-ax, Blaise a new pair of husky mountain shoes, nail-studded. Then they got together the costumes they advised for the Sherwood boys. Jock buttoned himself eagerly into his new clothes and even Ricky had to admit they looked pretty professional. The suits were heavy, of thick stuff called loden. They were waterproof. The short coat was so full of pockets that Ricky wondered what you'd put in all of them, buttoned up high around the neck. They got heavy shorts, and an extra pair of wool socks to wear inside the mountain boots that Blaise advised getting large. They were to carry flat gourds for water.

"I do not believe we will need goggles for the snow," said

Emile regretfully. "If we do, Blaise has several pairs. But we must all have axes," he added, brightening. "They are most useful to stick in the ground to prevent slipping—or, if there *is* snow. Do you remember, Blaise, the excursion on which we sat and slid down the side of a hill on the ice, using the ax as a brake?"

For a fleeting instant Ricky wished that he were on better terms with the cousins. He wanted to know more about that excursion of theirs.

On their way back, knapsacks with their new clothes swinging importantly on their backs, ice-axes dangling at their sides, Ricky almost forgot to be miserable.

He didn't talk, but he couldn't help noticing that the cousins seemed enchanted when Jock talked. They were constantly asking what certain slang expressions meant. They would repeat them, their exact elocution making the slang sound very strange. Emile even had a tiny notebook, scribbled over inside with minute handwriting. He would solemnly jot things down. Once, glancing at him out of the corner of his eye, after he had made a remark, Ricky thought he jotted down one of *his* expressions, though there was no way to make sure. After that, somehow, Ricky found himself becoming slangier than ever.

As they walked, they could see a mule trail, branching off to the right amongst the trees. Blaise pointed to it.

"It is perhaps there we will start," he said. Jock looked at it curiously. It did look awfully easy. Ricky was frankly surprised.

"Why, that's just a mule trail—that's not mountain climbing!" he exclaimed.

"Of course," put in Emile a little impatiently, "but you *always* start on an easy one!"

"If you take only a few hours, a small walk, then you do not get so—so, how you say, dog-tired," said Blaise. The others laughed.

When they got back to the chalet, Madame had supper all ready for them.

"Why it isn't even sunset yet!" said Jock wonderingly.

"But we must have the eating early tonight," Madame ex-

230

plained. "Albrecht was here. He will call for you boys at five tomorrow."

"At five!" said Ricky. "Why so early?" Emile looked at him.

"You always start early. So's to get your climbing over before the heat of the day. All climbers know that!" he said.

It was hard to wake up. But the air was so cool and stimulating that Ricky found himself humming as he got into his stiff suit and the new boots that clumped heavily as he walked. He decided against the ice-ax. It had grown heavy as he walked back from Murren yesterday.

Blaise and Emile were finishing their coffee as the boys reached the dining room. With them was a tall, thickset young man who nodded silently. Twig, who never got up early in the morning, was sitting calmly by Blaise, remarking that she thought early morning the loveliest time of day.

Blaise and Emile looked less wasp-waisted in their thick suits. All waited for the Sherwood boys to eat, then Albrecht turned to them and said in halting English, "You are beginner?"

"Yes," said Jock.

"Well, we used to climb mountains in Maine," began Ricky, then stopped. Somehow, before Albrecht, his experience dwindled in his mind. Albrecht nodded shortly. He pointed to Ricky.

"Your ax?" he said.

"I didn't think we'd need it," explained Ricky. But Blaise said one must always carry it, to get used to it, so he went upstairs and got it.

They started out—the four boys and Albrecht. No one said a word. The morning was cool, the grade level. Ricky felt a little conversation would save it from being a dull walk. Jock made a few remarks, but noticing the others' silence, stopped.

Blaise walked ahead, Albrecht at the end of the line, walking slower than any of them. Though heaven only knows, thought Ricky, everybody's simply *crawling*.

The mule-trail sloped very gently upwards. After a few minutes, despite the snail's pace at which they were going, Ricky began to perspire. He wasn't tired—far from it—but the boots and his ax and the walk made him feel that he was ex-

231

ercising. He felt in a pleasant glow, all over, almost good-natured. This was about like Maine, he thought.

Then, rather unexpectedly, the trail grew steeper.

"Weather?" Blaise asked of Albrecht.

"Goot!" he said. They walked on, silent as the grave.

The trail grew rockier. Little bits of rocks found themselves unexpectedly under the feet of the Sherwood boys. It was hard to avoid them, with the heavy shoes that seemed to make them stumble and the heavy ice-axes that swung with each move they made. It was really quite steep, thought Ricky as he started panting, lips closed so the sound of his heavy breathing wouldn't carry. A steep place. For a few feet they must go slantwise up a large rock.

As they found their footing carefully, Albrecht came up to Ricky. Ricky's ice-ax was dangling from his left arm, to the side where there was a void. Without a word Albrecht took the ax from him and placed it in the boy's right hand, the mountain side. Ricky flushed. Jock hastily transferred his own ice-ax.

"The ax is so you can use it to prevent slipping," explained Blaise. Emile gave a sideways glance at Ricky and said, "That is one of the first things to learn."

Ricky said nothing, but tried with all his might, as he climbed, to keep his breathing quiet, and his ice-ax firm, not dangling aimlessly. Jock was panting, too, now, so that Ricky thought he could hear him—or was it his own breathing that came in hard, suppressed breaths? A glance at Albrecht's face showed him to look just the same. Blaise and Emile seemed quite undisturbed. Suddenly they came out of the woods, and Ricky noticed gratefully that the others had paused. His heart was hammering his forehead now, and he hastily swabbed his face with the sleeve of his khaki coat, leaving a dark smudge.

"Whew!" breathed Jock. "Guess I'll take off my coat!"

Below they could see the woods through which they had come, and far down in the paler green, the tiny speck that was their own chalet. For a fleeting instant Ricky thought of his soft featherbed.

"Is it—is it much farther?" asked Jock apologetically.

"We are about halfway," said Blaise. "Would you—do you wish to turn back?"

"No!" said the Sherwood boys in chorus. They started off again. Now they were in the open. Every so often, for a few blissful moments they would cross soft patches of grass, but mostly they climbed up rough uneven rocks. Then through the woods again, where treacherous roots caught at their feet.

"Is this never going to stop?" thought Ricky. "We must be almost there—it's been hours since we started!"

233

Soon he could think of nothing but that he must go on. His right arm ached so that it was pure pain. Veins stood out in his forehead and he felt that his lungs, miles too big for his chest, would burst at any minute. He felt he very possibly might die before he reached the top.

Sweat was running down into his eyes, so that it was hard to see the ground. He couldn't count the blisters that he felt coming on.

"We are there!" announced Blaise. Ricky, stopped in his tracks, looked at him, grateful for those words, even from Blaise.

Below them was a view so lovely that Blaise and Emile paused for a moment to look at it, but Jock and Ricky stood, unseeing. Albrecht wasn't even panting. Blaise and Emile were breathing hard, but quite able to talk.

The others stood, but Ricky, trying to look nonchalant, sank to the ground. How blissful it was! He hoped they'd stay there and look at the view for a long time. Going down would be easier.

"Are you tired?" asked Emile. Ricky looked at him suspiciously.

"No," he just managed to say. Jock let out a quivering laugh. "And how!" he said.

Albrecht had turned and started to go down. Ricky hoped he would be able to manage to get up. He finally did, and wished he had never sat. He was stiffer and sorer than the first time he had ridden a horse. It was harder going down than up. He wished he could fly across the space to the chalet—the space looked so small from up here!

It was his heels that bothered him now. They seemed to grind themselves into him every time he took a step. If this was mountain climbing—or descending, he wasn't so sure he liked it!

They reached the fork where they rejoined their mule trail and Ricky turned for a moment and looked back. That fork, which he had described as a dinky little walk!

"I don't know how you do it," said Jock, looking with admiration at the slim, wiry French boys, who seemed to take walking like this so easily in their stride.

MARGUERITE DAVIS

Ricky had room in his tired mind but for one thought. He *had* to keep on, to show them!

As they crossed the meadow to the chalet, Ricky, stumbling every so often in the long grass, began to limp. It was then that the most humiliating thing happened. Albrecht smiled as he watched him walk. But Ricky was too tired to care.

That evening, sitting in the chalet after supper, the boys were too tired to talk much. Twig and Bumps and the French boys were the only ones who seemed at all lively. Ricky's lids dropped over his eyes in that hot room, and his body felt heavy. He said only one thing, and that a little timidly.

"We got up quite high." Emile laughed.

"That was a little walk," he said.

Ricky was almost asleep when he heard Blaise's quiet tones.

"Albrecht comes for us at four tomorrow," he said. The words pricked through Jock's and Ricky's numb bodies like a pin.

"Are you coming?" asked Emile, of Ricky. Ricky summoned all his strength and answered, "Of course." For a moment he thought he saw something like a gleam of admiration in Blaise's eyes. But, of course, that wasn't possible.

The next morning Ricky groaned when someone knocked at the door. He just couldn't get out of bed! But Jock was up, and he had to go. It was barely light when they got downstairs. Albrecht said good morning. Ricky thought he looked a little surprised when he and Jock came in.

With coffee hot inside them Ricky and Jock felt that, sore as they were, they were at least alive, and that was something. This time they started off in a different direction from the chalet. As they walked down the valley, Ricky could feel his limbs loosening, like a squeaky engine that had been greased. It wasn't so bad today!

Several days went by, each climb a little bit harder. The first day Jock, after climbing a particularly steep slope, had suddenly sat down on the ground.

"I—can't—stand it any longer! D'you mind waiting a minute?"

Somewhat to Ricky's surprise, no one had minded. Albrecht had laughed, and Blaise said, "But that is not surprising, as you are not accustomed to climbing."

But Ricky wasn't going to let the Frogs get a whimper out of him. He couldn't admit that he was tired—so he got no sympathy.

As they kept on climbing, day after day, Ricky no longer felt the complete exhaustion he had felt at first. And that despite the fact that they were taking harder and harder climbs. It became fun to get up in the early mornings, and see what there was to tackle today. The evenings, when they all sat around the fire, became comfortable ones, with a pleasant, tired feeling. He began to sense, too, the thrill of getting to the top and the burning desire, each day, to have the top a little farther away.

It was impossible to go off with the French boys day after day and not realize that they were good mountain climbers and good sports (though he still wasn't on very good terms with them). And in a way he had gotten fond of sure-footed Albrecht. Almost without their realizing it, the desire to climb and climb was becoming a thrilling sport.

Albrecht's next party was almost due. He had promised the boys to take them on one climb, before he left, that was not strictly for beginners.

"Tomorrow," Blaise interpreted from Albrecht, "we climb to a hut, especially for such purposes. From there, the day after, we can get a really good start."

"You mean we spend the night in the hut?" asked Jock.

"But yes," said Emile.

"Golly, that really is something like," murmured Ricky, eyes gleaming.

The numerous pockets of their coats, that the boys had wondered so much about, were filled with bars of chocolate, tins of cocoa, condensed food of all kinds.

"We shall find utensils to cook with in the hut," Blaise explained.

Ricky had a sudden desire for some chewing gum to take along. He ransacked his luggage and found two packages of slightly stale and brittle gum. He stuck it in his pocket. He had noticed that Albrecht always chewed something on their walks.

Everyone was out to say good-bye to them, and they felt, as they left the chalet, that they were going on a real adventure.

"Don't get lost," Bumps begged anxiously.

"Good-bye! *Do* all take care of yourselves!" called Twig.

"Get along!" said Madame. "Ach, I wish I could go too!" She smiled a wide cheerful grin that included all of them, and her knowing glance rested for a moment on Ricky. He suddenly felt warm. Madame seemed to like him again.

237

The climb to the hut, which seemed easy to the boys, was pure joy. The air was crisp and sparkling, and it was so sunny that Ricky was glad Blaise had some extra goggles with him. The higher they got, the more alone they seemed and the wider and more beautiful the view became. Ricky found himself thinking, as he looked up speechlessly at the white jagged mountains that rose all around them, "I wish I could climb that one—and that—and that!" Only this time he said it with awe and respect for their height.

They reached the hut at sunset. The air was thin and cold. A wide expanse of sleek snow, stretched above them in a slanting field, bathed in brilliant red from the setting sun.

The hut was rough, and not very big, but that made it all the more fun.

"It's sort of like the Bar Harbor playhouse," said Jock.

"More like camping in Arizona!" said Ricky. He had already spotted well-worn kitchen utensils and logs with which to build a fire. As he busied himself efficiently working about the hut, he felt a pleasant glow of self-satisfaction. Funny that anything in Switzerland could give him an Arizona sort of feeling.

Albrecht watched as Jock and Ricky built the fire, and worked like beavers over the food. Even Blaise and Emile seemed to appreciate the cooking that the boys themselves modestly felt to be expert.

It was fun, too, to roll your tired body in a blanket on the floor of the hut. Ricky lay there with the fire flickering comfortingly on the rude walls of the hut, and making little patterns on the ceiling. The others were rolled in companionable dark bundles near by, and he could hear them breathe. He felt happy and comfortable.

"Well—good night, everybody!" he sighed.

"Good night!" they all answered.

After they had been asleep but for a minute, Albrecht waked them up. It was cold and dark, and they shivered as they drank their coffee. After they had cleaned up the hut and were ready to start, Ricky felt in his pocket for the gum. He unwrapped it.

"Here—want some?" he asked, offering it to everybody. Jock

took some as a matter of course. Albrecht shook his head.

"Thank you," murmured Blaise, and Emile stretched out his hand with interest. They were to cross the snow, it seemed. Ricky and Jock watched with interest as Albrecht unwound the long rope that he had carried coiled on his back. A sudden shriek from Jock made them all stand still.

"Hey! Don't swallow it!" Emile made a terrible face at his yell and managed to catch the gum before it slipped down. Ricky laughed so hard that he almost swallowed his own gum.

"Weather?" inquired Blaise. Albrecht peered at the sky in all directions.

"Goot," he answered.

They started. How high they were! They were walking slower than ever today. The thin air seemed to sap their strength. Ahead, sloping gently upwards, was the sheet of snow stretched across the valley to the dim black rocks beyond. The snow wasn't steep, but the expanse was long. Ricky was excited. Their first snow-walk!

"Bet none of the kids at school have ever done this," said Jock exultingly.

How blinding the glare was! How alone the figures of the others, black against the snow, as they started to cross, thought Ricky. They used the rope, though it didn't seem very necessary. It hung in loose loops between them, loops that could be let out if need be. Ricky let his drag for a moment, but Albrecht told him he must never drag the rope.

With small, careful steps the party made its way, winding like a many-jointed transparent snake across the field. They had discarded their tasteless gum now, and Ricky kept feeling for his canteen. How long it took to cross that field! Ricky, glancing quickly back, saw their footprints, stretched like a dark, winding chain to where they were. He felt for his canteen again. It was empty.

How parched his throat and lips were—parched by the blinding glare around them and the thin atmosphere. He looked at the cold clean white snow surrounding him like a sea. Why hadn't he thought of it? He paused a moment, rope in hand, and scooped up a big handful. He was just about to put it to his lips when Blaise's voice bit across the silence.

"You must not eat snow!"

It was almost a command. In a flash Ricky's resentment against Blaise flared up. He didn't have a right to tell him what to do, even if he *was* a better mountain climber! He turned and looked wordlessly at Blaise, then calmly ate the whole delicious handful. Albrecht, who had watched this performance, shook his head. He murmured something in German.

"He says it cracks the lips and gives indigestion," interpreted Emile in a flat voice. Ricky felt a touch uneasy. Was it possible that Blaise had been right after all?

"Oh, I feel fine," he said, a little embarrassed. The snow had felt slick and delicious and spicily cold as it went down, aching, into his chest. They *must* be wrong. It was silly to say snow was bad for you. Why, he'd eaten snow all his life! Loads of it! They even used to make snow ice cream at school, he remembered well, when there had been a good fall of snow.

They started walking again, and as no one made any more remarks, Ricky soon forgot all about the snow.

Suddenly Ricky saw Albrecht turn his head quickly and spit to the right. It left a dark brown stain on the snow. Ricky had seen Albrecht spit before, and didn't think anything of it until he noticed him spit again—the same swift jerk to the right. Ricky watched, fascinated, as he saw that Albrecht was spitting systematically at intervals. He turned back. All along their trail were the dark spots, in almost a straight line.

"D'you suppose he does that accidentally or on purpose?" Ricky whispered to Jock. Jock leaned forward and whispered the question to Emile. He felt that maybe Albrecht would not like it if they talked out loud about his spitting. Emile murmured something. Jock whispered back to Ricky.

"He says that all the guides in this district chew something that makes a black stain, like prunes, or tobacco, or licorice, and when they go on a new trail they always spit to the right, so the other guides, if they come along, will know they've been there and that it's safe.

They had nearly reached the other side of the field, and ahead they could see a flat ledge of rock and above it a small rocky cliff. Ricky felt that his lips were dry and cracked. He licked them. Then he smiled, to see what would happen. He felt his lip crack, and a small warm trickle ran down his chin. On the snow a tiny red mark showed. Ordinarily Ricky didn't mind anything like that, but somehow he didn't feel terribly well in his stomach. He didn't have *exactly* a stomach-ache but—well, no doubt it would pass.

241

They reached the edge of the snowfield. Albrecht paused and coiled his rope.

Ricky saw that they had stepped onto a level rock ridge right under a quite steep little cliff. The snowfield must have been a sort of upland plateau, for under their ledge there was nothing but sheer cliff way, way down. But it was quite a wide platform that they were standing on.

"I'm not just simply nuts about looking down," admitted Jock in a low voice.

Ricky almost forgot his stomach-ache as he watched Albrecht, rope on his back, start climbing the small cliff above them.

"What are we supposed to do?" he asked Blaise.

"Wait until he gets up. Then he will make the rope fast, and we will use the other end to help us ascend."

Carefully finding clefts in the cliff for footholds, Albrecht started climbing. Up he went, sure, quick as a monkey, till it made Ricky a little dizzy to watch him. He had reached the top now, and fastened one end of the rope to a firm jut in the cliff, high up. He sat perched up there, and let the other end of the rope down slowly over the cliff to the others. It slid down scraping the rocks, to just where Ricky stood. He looked inquiringly at the others.

"You go next," said Blaise, who stood next to him. He fastened the rope firmly about Ricky's waist. Ricky knew he was supposed to climb the cliff.

He looked carefully for his first foothold, and holding the rope taut with one hand, stepped up, the other hand against the side of the cliff. This wasn't so hard, for if you were only careful there were plenty of places to step.

He felt again the squirming stomach-ache he had thought was gone. He leaned for a second against the cliff. He was over the others' heads now. He groped against the rock, and stepped up again. His feet felt a little shaky, not quite as sure as he was used to having them feel. His hob-nailed boot slipped a little as he slid it into a cleft in the cliff. As he straightened himself he looked down. Down, past the rocky platform where the others stood. From where he was that seemed like nothing at all. You could see valleys and trees and sheer cliffs way, way below. A moment of sheer panic darted through him. He couldn't look. He couldn't. He felt weak and perspiring and everything seemed suddenly to turn over and over, making him dizzier and dizzier—He had to hold on. He felt himself falling.

The rope stretched taut as Ricky, fainting, fell.

Crash! Ricky's dark figure tumbled down the rock, striking against Blaise, who stood below, almost knocking him off the cliff. He lay, unconscious, on the platform. The little party stood transfixed. Then:

"Ricky!" sobbed Jock, running the few steps to where he lay. Emile's face was white, as he held on to Blaise's arm.

"Dieu!" he breathed, looking at Blaise, who was white, too. "He might have knocked you off!" Blaise swallowed.

"But he didn't," he then said quietly.

Jock was on his knees by Ricky, and Albrecht, who had climbed down the cliff as rapidly as he had gone up, was on his knees beside him, too. Ricky's face was dead white, except for the dark blot of his cracked lip. Albrecht had found a flask. Gently he lifted Ricky's head and forced a few drops down his throat. All watched, the silent horror of what might have happened still hanging over them, as Ricky gurgled a little and struggled to sit up.

Ricky didn't remember what had happened after that awful moment when the fainting feeling had come over him, except that as he fell he had struck something hard. He looked up weakly.

"I—I'm sorry I made such a fool of myself," he said, and tried to get up. Then, as he gained consciousness more fully, he sank back with a groan as a pain like fire shot through his knee. "I—I must have hurt my leg."

Silently, horribly ashamed of himself, he let Blaise and Albrecht help him to his feet, but when he tried to put any weight on his foot, the knee hurt so that he thought he was going to faint, and his leg crumpled under him. Moisture was on his forehead, though he didn't utter a sound. Albrecht sat him

243

down again and felt his leg. At his touch Ricky couldn't help
letting out a yell. Jock turned as white as Ricky and felt slightly
ill himself. Albrecht motioned to Blaise.

"We will haf to carry him," he said.

Ricky's leg hurt so that it took all his strength to keep from
groaning, and he didn't have time to think of what else he felt
at all. Blaise and Albrecht made a knotted-together sort of ham-
mock out of the long rope. Ricky was laid on it. They stretched
it between them. It was far too short for him. His head and
shoulders were up against Blaise's shoulder and his good leg on
one side of Albrecht's weatherbeaten neck, the bad one dangling to the side.

Back on the snowfield, the party was more silent than ever.
A different kind of silence, as Blaise and Albrecht panted with
the heavy weight of the limp boy. Jock and Emile thanked their
stars that their brothers were alive, and Ricky, hands clenched,
tried to keep from making a sound.

But as his knee began to throb in regular, darting pains, he was able to think in between. His thoughts were beginning to bother him almost as much as the pain. After being such a washout all summer, here he was being an awful nuisance again. And Blaise, his enemy, was carrying him home!

Ricky didn't dare think what they all must think of him, and the horrible humiliation of having fainted and fallen so dangerously near to where they all stood haunted him. He shot a glance at Emile. Emile was probably delighted that he'd made a fool of himself.

And then, after all, to everyone's surprise and relief, it was not so far back to Murren. Albrecht, who knew all these mountains so well, had taken them to the hut and across the snow-fields for fun—but there was a far shorter and easier way back.

How glad they were to see the town—Ricky, who winced every time his rescuers took a careful step; Blaise and Albrecht with their heavy load; and the other boys, who still felt a little shaky.

At Murren Ricky was taken at once to a hotel, where he lay on the bed until the doctor, that Albrecht had called, arrived. Ricky, his leg bare, and eyes closed tightly, let the doctor make his examination with grit. As he watched the others' admiring faces, Jock felt as though a load had been lifted from his shoulders.

"*Now* they'll know he's a good egg, even if he's seemed nasty," he thought as he watched Ricky's tense face, and saw him make not one sign of complaint.

The doctor said the leg was not broken, but badly sprained, and he was a little afraid of water on the knee. He did Ricky up in stiff bandages which eased the pain a good deal, and said that if his leg was tied to the saddle he might go the short distance to the chalet on muleback. He himself would come out during the week. Ricky must be kept quiet and keep his leg up until then—and then they'd see.

Albrecht had a burro at the door when they came out. Ricky was lifted cautiously into the saddle and his knee fixed as comfortably as possible. Then Albrecht led the burro as the party walked slowly back to the chalet. As Ricky could see the chalet approaching he shrank back farther into the saddle.

Madame and Twig and Bumps and Mademoiselle were *all* at the door as he was lifted off.

Bumps sobbed over him and said it was dreadful, but Twig, as soon as she found the injury wasn't serious, thought it might be quite exciting to have an invalid around.

But it was Mademoiselle, who was always so surprising on these occasions, who got him to bed and made him comfortable. Even Mademoiselle was being a good egg—and he had been so awful.

When all the others came in to say good night Ricky felt he couldn't stand it. He was afraid he might cry or do something further to disgrace himself.

"Oh c-cut it out—you'd think no one ever hurt his leg before!" he said gruffly. "G—get out!" Then he put his hand over his eyes, so as not to see their troubled faces.

All night long Ricky lay awake and thought, his mind keeping time with the throbbing in his leg. He'd had a good jolt and he couldn't go on kidding himself. If the French boys didn't like him, he couldn't blame them. He, *Ricky*, had been a bum sport —a thing he'd always had a horror of. The rest of his stay here he'd have to try and be friends, to make up for it.

But that wasn't so easy. The doctor came and said he must stay in bed, or on a couch, but that he hoped he'd be able to get up in a week or two. A week or two! That was nearly all the time they had left.

After the first couple of days, no one paid much attention to him any more. It was a maddening situation to be in. He had all the disadvantages of being sick, and none of the advantages because no one, not even the doctor, was worried about him at all.

Albrecht had gone to his party, and Mademoiselle suggested one evening that she should take the others off on a sort of field trip. Ricky lay on his couch, saying nothing, but thinking how much he would like to go.

"Will we be gone several days?" asked Emile.

"Could we go to one of the factories where they make Swiss watches?" asked Jock. Mademoiselle thought they could.

"And you could go through a chocolate factory," put in Ricky generously. Twig's eyes were bright. What a perfect way to end the summer! It would be just like a house party, going off with Jock and Emile—and Blaise. She gave a fleeting thought to Ricky.

"It's too bad you can't come, too," she said.

"I'll stay and take care of him," offered Bumps. She had weakened for a moment at the mention of the chocolate factory, but she wasn't going to be torn away from the chalet until it was time to go home. She climbed up on Madame's lap, and looked around her in satisfaction.

"Oh, nobody needs bother about me," said Ricky. There was a twinkle in his eye, but no one saw it. He had a plan forming in his mind.

They had gone. The morning they left, Ricky lay for a long time in the sunshine. It was peaceful, except for Bumps, who was fidgeting, anxious to be off in the meadow where the wild flowers were.

"Oh, for goodness sakes, go on!" Ricky said. "I don't want anybody around." So Bumps was off in a flash, with a last worried glance behind her.

Ricky mused. He would *try* being nice, anyhow. And if they were nice in turn, why—why he'd do something to startle them. What could he do? Suddenly he laughed. Why—naturally the thing he could do was to learn to speak the language he had hated. He'd learn to speak French!

The idea grew. Surely he could do it. He remembered the time in Paris when he had tried to imitate the waiter and had succeeded so well his stepmother had told him he had a really good accent. And, for all he pretended not to understand a word Mademoiselle said, he could, he well knew, if he tried.

In the midst of his plan Bumps came running up, hands full of wild flowers.

"Oh, Ricky," she said, "I didn't know I'd be so long. I've come to stay with you now. Here—I've got forget-me-nots—and I don't know what this is. There's a book that tells, but I can't spell them very well."

"Here, get me the book and let's have a look," said Ricky. He was so pleased with his good intentions that he was willing to help anybody. He searched, finding pictures of the flowers she held squashed in her hands.

"And will you write out the names? Then I'll press the flowers—"

The book she was pressing them in, leaving squashy yellow stains, was the heaviest she had been able to find. As she put a gentian between its pages, Ricky caught a glimpse of the title. It was a French-English dictionary!

"Hey, give me that!" he shouted so loud Bumps looked thunderstruck. Then he laughed. "I mean, you can use another book to press them in, can't you?"

In the four days that followed Ricky had so much to do that he hardly thought of his leg at all. He had found, amongst the books in Jock's suitcase—he had always laughed at him for

248

carrying them around—Father's English-French phrase book.

During the sunny hours of the day that he lay outside, he drew. It was too hard to manage to paint with his leg up and when he was half lying down, but he drew things with black crayon. Why hadn't he drawn for so long? He was often interrupted by Bumps, who had pestered him ever since he had been of use to her with her collection, but he meekly went on helping her. Madame came out every so often and handed him a piece of cheese or something she had been cooking, and stayed to praise his drawings. It *was* pleasant to relax and to be appreciated.

The rest of the time he studied French, with a gleam in the eye that would have surprised his school. He pored over the dictionary, which was discouraging, because a lot of words didn't do you much good if you couldn't put them together. He read the phrase book through and almost learned it by heart. "Do you see the cat? Yes, I see the cat. May I have your passport? No, my passport is in my trunk. I should like a double room with a bath." Not so good, but at least it was better than the dictionary!

Then he tried to think of all the things he had heard anyone say, and repeated them to himself as he lay there. Sometimes Bumps or Madame would see him lying there, lips moving, and wonder what was wrong.

When he had gone to his room at night, and before Madame carried him out in her strong arms in the morning, Bumps would hear strange murmurs from the room next door. And sometimes a giggle, muffled, as though by a pillow. Ricky was really having a good time, and would bow very solemnly to himself as he said, "*Bonjour, Monsieur,*" to himself with much ceremony, all alone in his bedroom.

Bumps didn't care much *what* he was doing as long as he was so nice and like himself all of a sudden.

But the day the others were due home Ricky had a moment of nervousness. Suppose they didn't like him any better when he was being nice?

"There they are!" called Bumps, who had been hovering

249

around, peering across the meadow that Ricky had gotten to know so well. She flew to them, and he waved eagerly as they approached.

"I hope your leg is well," Jock remembered to say, breathlessly. "Gee, we had the best time! We saw the watch factory— and that was swell—and we went all through the chocolate factory, and here, we've brought you gobs of chocolate!"

"Thanks, oh, thanks a lot," said Ricky, as Jock dropped bar after bar on his lap. Twig came up next, and Blaise and Emile, and asked him how he was and dumped more chocolate on him till he laughed and said, "Good grief, *I* can't eat all that!"

"We'll help you," said Twig generously.

"I—couldn't we begin helping you now?" asked Bumps.

"And what do you think's happened?" said Twig, a shadow falling on her happy face as she looked at Blaise. "Mademoiselle had a wire from Father and Phil at Murren. They'll be here tomorrow!"

"That's fine," said Ricky.

That evening, as they all sat around the couch in Ricky's room, they told him all about their trip. No one seemed surprised that he seemed interested and agreeable. Suddenly Twig thought to ask him what he'd been doing.

"You must have been awfully bored," she said.

"No, I wasn't," said Ricky surprisingly. "Say, Bumps and I have the swellest collection of wild flowers you ever saw."

The others stared at him. What *had* come over Ricky that he was raving about wild flowers? If he hadn't looked so well they would have thought he was going to die, or something. And when Ricky, a little gaspingly, brought out a few botanical facts that he had learned in their absence, he paused in the midst of a dead silence, scared that they were going to laugh at him or think he was crazy.

"I know nothing of botany," said Blaise, listening with interest. "I have always great regret I did not take it at the *lycée*."

"And he drew—lots of things," put in Bumps quickly. So Ricky brought out his drawings, and people looked surprised all over again.

250

As Jock slept that night, Ricky practiced his French softly to himself, singing "Au Clair de la Lune", one of Mademoiselle's favorites, under his breath.

Everyone was impatient, the next morning, for Father and Phil to come. Except Ricky. People were hanging around his couch and talking. It *was* fun having a gang—and being part of it again! That morning the doctor came. He said Ricky was discharged and could get up again. Ricky still lay there, French phrases dashing through his mind.

"Well, for heaven's sakes—why don't you get up, Ricky! I should think you'd be crazy to," said Twig, perplexed.

Ricky slowly threw off his cover and rose to his feet. He felt a little wobbly, but he kept one hand on the couch to support himself. At least he could stand. All the others were there—had been there to hear the doctor's verdict.

Suddenly Ricky burst into a flood of French. Mademoiselle's head cocked itself to one side. Madame sat there, silently laughing until the tears ran down her cheeks. Twig looked startled and Bumps shrieked with delight. Jock was thinking: Here is Ricky, on his feet again, and getting ahead of the rest of us. But life would be more fun from now on.

As he poured out everything he could think of, from "Clair de la Lune" all the way through great lumps of the dictionary, the phrase book, and Mademoiselle's pet phrases all jumbled in together, with his face all red, it was Blaise and Emile's faces that he watched. Blaise watched, a slow smile of wonder on his grave face. But Emile, who had stared open-mouthed at Ricky for quite a while, recognized some of Mademoiselle's pet phrases and mannerisms and suddenly doubled up with mirth.

"But the accent is really excellent," said Blaise when anyone was able to talk.

The excitement hadn't died down yet when Bumps, who had turned away for a second, shouted, "Here come Father and Phil!"

The others rushed off. Ricky tried to take a few steps but found he was too weak and leaned on Blaise's shoulder.

Father and Phil were delighted to find Ricky's leg all mended

251

and to find him up. Everyone talked at once, and the children had so much to tell and so many new friends to show off to the Family that they looked completely bewildered. But Twig saw them look at each other in a pleased way.

"We must hear all about the accident," said Father in his comfortable deep voice. So everyone told him at once.

"It was a shame, that accident," said Emile, who was still going off at intervals into silent giggles over Ricky's mimicry of Mademoiselle. "He had begun to be a good climber, and Albrecht said he had the—the makings of a mountaineer."

"No, did he really?" asked Ricky delightedly. "But I wasn't really," he added after a pause. "I was tired to *death* most of the time!"

"But so is everyone, when he starts," said Blaise.

"Now do the French again," said Bumps. So Ricky let out his astounding flow for Father and Phil, who looked flabbergasted.

Ricky happened to glance at Mademoiselle. She was smiling a self-satisfied smirk, just as though she had been responsible.

He never did anything except in a whole-souled way. He grew red in the face and looked very queer and suddenly he burst out:

"Look here! I've been horrid, and I didn't want to come here anyway, and hated everybody, and was awfully disagreeable. I thought I hated the French, but I really didn't know anything about them except from Ma—" he gulped, saving himself from a break. "Well, anyhow I'm *glad* I came here instead of Albania, and I think the French are swell, and I hope Blaise and Emile'll come and stay with us in New York and—and I don't know why I behaved like such a bum!"

A dead silence greeted his explosion, but it was a sympathetic one. At last Emile said curiously,—

"What is that—a bum?"

"*I* think," Blaise said gravely, "that you are a—what you say? —a good egg!"

William C. White

WHO IS WHO?

ILLUSTRATED BY *Kay Lovelace*

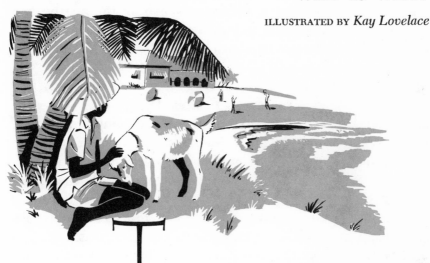

T HE news that General and Mrs. Kittleton were coming from London to Tobago to stay for three days had been known on the island for some time. Because the residence of Warden Leedon, the chief government official on the island, was being repaired, the General and his wife would stay at the Drake Hotel.

Mouseknees had heard the news, but he had not thought about it. He knew that many preparations were being made, but they did not concern him. Then, one afternoon, as he was drying dishes on the rear veranda, he saw an automobile drive up. Roderick St. Giles Buzby, one of the constables of the island, stepped out. On Tobago, "constable" means "policeman." Roderick was coal-black, more than six feet tall, and he wore as usual a spotless white coat, black trousers, a belt, and a cap. Mouseknees looked at that uniform in admiration.

"Hyah, Roderick," he said. He always called him by his first name.

"Constable Buzby, please," Roderick said, his face set as if he had eaten a sour mango. "I say there, my lad, is Mrs. Hudson about?" Roderick always spoke with a decided British accent that surprised anyone meeting him for the first time.

"Yep," Mouseknees said, and he saw Roderick frown. As he went to call Mrs. Hudson he wondered why Roderick was being so formal. This was a different man from the one he had known, for Roderick was usually a cheerful sort. At a distance he listened to him talk to Mrs. Hudson. Mr. Leedon, the warden, had sent Roderick along to inquire if everything was in readiness for the coming of the General and his wife.

When the work was done and Mouseknees was free for the afternoon, he was still wondering why the coming of a general should make such a change in the constable. He went down to town at once, sure that he could find Roderick near the wharf. There he was, talking to a few longshoremen and boatmen and looking very solemn. Mouseknees was interested at once. He pushed his way through the men and got close to the constable.

"Everybody will have to look sharp," Roderick was saying. "I dare venture to say that the General and his wife are the most important people ever to come to Tobago. I heard Mr. Leedon say so."

Mouseknees was not sure what the word "important" meant. "What's important?" he asked.

"Man," Roderick said, frowning, "General Kittleton is important because he's famous. He is an important government official. He gets his picture in the newspapers. Everywhere he goes people say, 'Here comes General Kittleton.' "

"Why?" Mouseknees asked, honestly wanting to know.

"Being important means they is somebody," Roderick said with his best British accent.

"Mr. Crumpf is somebody. Is he important?"

Some of the men laughed, and Roderick said pompously, "I wouldn't exactly say he is important."

"He could be if he wanted," Mouseknees insisted.

"Man, people rarely and seldom become important by just wantin'."

"Are you important, Roderick?"

254

"Constable Buzby, please. In some circles I should say I was important." Then he added modestly, "Of course, mind you, not as important as General Kittleton. Everybody in the whole world knows him."

"I don't," Mouseknees said simply.

Roderick frowned at him. "Man, you better hold your tongue." Then to the men around he said, "I am to be General Kittleton's chauffeur during his visitation." Having told that piece of news he said, "Now I must be going about my various and official duties which is several!"

Mouseknees watched him go. Just why Roderick should be so different because important people were coming, he did not know. He went to the edge of the wharf and sat down against a piling. Mouseknees was sure he had never seen an important man, and he wondered what the General would look like. Probably six feet tall, broad and strong, powerful, in bright uniform with medals and gold buttons.

It would be nice to be important and famous and to have someone shout, "Here comes Mouseknees!" and to wear uniforms and have his picture in the paper. The only trouble, Mouseknees told himself, was that he was not quite sure how a man became famous and important.

The General arrived and Mouseknees watched him alight from the automobile. He wore a gray suit, like any of the other tourists. He was not six or seven feet tall, but little more than five feet, with a thin pinkish face. He rode with Mr. Leedon, the Warden, a tall, grayed man who was very nice and a friend of Mouseknees. The General did not wear one medal, one gold button. He carried a cane, an umbrella, a camera, binoculars, and a briefcase, but Mouseknees had long ago ceased to wonder at the things these newcomers brought. The General's wife was in no way unusual, and to Mouseknees they seemed like any ordinary pair of tourists except for the fuss and for Roderick who was standing stiffly at attention, his white coat never whiter and starchier.

Yet there must be something different about this man, Mouseknees thought, or he would not be important. The only

difference that Mouseknees could see was when the General took off his hat. His hair was a funny half-gray, half-red color. There must be something else, and Mouseknees raced downstairs to help with the baggage. By getting near to the General he might be able to see differences.

He was about to take two bags when he heard Roderick snap, "Leave those bags." Surprised at the tone of Roderick's voice, Mouseknees put the bags down. A moment later, as Roderick picked them up, he was saying, "Yes, Mr. Leedon, yes, General," as soft and polite as ever.

"There's some difference," Mouseknees said to himself.

He wanted badly to serve at the General's tables, but Mrs. Hudson, who was excited and nervous, assigned some of the older boys. Mouseknees could watch the General, and that was something. He had time to notice that everybody around the hotel was sharp and snapping in speaking to each other but when they spoke to the General, they spoke softly and said,

"Certainly, General. By all means, General. Please, General!"

Mouseknees shook his head. The General sat down like other men. He ate like other men. He sneezed like other men.

After breakfast the General went to his room, and Mouseknees watched every step he took. He walked just like other men.

Mrs. Hudson and Mr. Leedon were in the dining room, and Mouseknees overheard a bit of conversation.

"Oh, dear," Mrs. Hudson said, as if she was worried, "he complained because there was no private balcony off his room."

Mr. Leedon said, "We'll do the best we can."

A few minutes later there was a roar from the General's room. Mrs. Hudson went running and after her Mr. Leedon and three or four of the boys. Then Mrs. Hudson called, "Bring the long-handled brush!"

Mouseknees was nearest, and he grabbed the brush. This would give him further chance to see the General.

Inside the room the General was pointing up to the ceiling and hopping about. Between hops he said, "A tarantula! A tarantula!"

Mouseknees knew what to do. He took the brush, reached for the ceiling, and a small object fell to the floor.

"A tarantula!" the General said, his face rosy red.

"No, sir," Mouseknees said, "a house spider. It's good luck!"

Mrs. Hudson look horrified at hearing Mouseknees contradict the General.

The General shook his finger at Mouseknees. "Young man, I've been in the tropics before!"

"Yes, sir," Mouseknees said. He went back to the kitchen with the brush. No one ever raised such a fuss about spiders before.

Mrs. Hudson came along a moment later. "Young man," she said, and Mouseknees had never heard her speak like this before, "don't you ever talk back to the General again. No matter what he says, you be quiet!"

The General certainly made a difference around the Drake Hotel.

There was the same excitement in the dining room at lunch. Everybody was hopping around. One boy dropped a bowl of soup in the corridor, another dropped a tray of dishes that made an awful clatter, and the General frowned. Mouseknees stood in a corner of the dining room from where he could watch the General without interruption. The General drank water like other men, he talked like other men, and he smiled like other men. Staring continually at him, Mouseknees could see no difference. Twice the General looked up and saw Mouseknees in the corner, staring at him. Then twice more. The fifth time the General spoke to Mr. Leedon and Mr. Leedon called Mrs. Hudson.

Mrs. Hudson motioned to Mouseknees to come outside. "What do you mean by staring at General Kittleton?"

"Nothing," Mouseknees said, wishing he could ask, "What's important?"

"I have enough trouble," Mrs. Hudson said. "You go in the kitchen and ask Elixir Cupid to put you to work."

Elixir, whom the boys called Ellie, was the cook.

Sadly, Mouseknees went to the kitchen. At work in the kitchen he would not be able to see the General.

"Humpf!" Elixir said to him. "Why you gotta humbug Mis' Hudson?" "Humbug" is a Tobago word for "annoy." "She got enough troubles."

Mouseknees said nothing. He had not meant to annoy Mrs. Hudson but he could not explain it.

"Clean these pots and pans," Elixir said sharply. "Is enough trouble aroun' here with important guests."

"What's important?" Mouseknees asked. "General look like other guests except maybe for his hair."

"You can't see important," Elixir said. "It don't stick out like goat's ears." She went about her work mumbling to herself. "Everybody excited, upset! Be awful glad when they go!"

"Yeah," Mouseknees said, polishing a frying pan.

"Be worse tomorrow up at the Warden's house," Elixir continued. "Goin' to be a fancy dinner. Gettin' fifty cooks, killin' nine hundred chickens, catchin' four hundred fish. Never been

258

such a dinner on Tobago. Didn't ask me to help cook. Be a awful poor dinner if I can't cook."

"Is too bad," Mouseknees said. The coming of the General had upset everybody, and he could not find out why.

From cleaning pots and pans, Mouseknees turned to cleaning the stove. He finished that and said, "What else, Ellie?" There must be some end to the number of jobs she could think of.

"Wash down the floor," she said.

He did that and when it was done he had a bucket of dirty water. Still wondering why the coming of the General made all the difference around the hotel, he went to the veranda railing and absently poured the water over the edge.

The resulting roar made him drop the bucket. There, below, peacefully dozing until the guests should want him, was Roderick St. Giles Buzby, his white coat now a beautiful streaked gray. Roderick looked up and saw Mouseknees and was about to yell when he realized that if he made any noise he might attract Mr. Leedon and that would mean explaining why he had been asleep. "You—you—!" he said, uncertain what to say next.

Mouseknees kept saying, "I'm sorry!"

"You come down here, I catch you and put you in jail!"

"I didn't know you were there!"

There was a step on the veranda, and Mouseknees turned. It was Mr. Leedon. "Where is Constable Buzby? I want him to go up to my house."

Mouseknees wanted to run for he knew what Mr. Leedon would discover in a moment. Then Mr. Leedon leaned over the railing.

"Constable Buzby! What's the matter, man? Who did that to you?"

Roderick was weak and confused. "That boy, Mouseknees. He pour water over me."

"I'll attend to him," Mr. Leedon said. "You change your coat and go on an errand."

Roderick went away mumbling, "When I catch that boy—!"

As if that were not trouble enough, Mrs. Hudson came to

Mouseknees a few minutes later. "I have just heard what you did. One more thing, young man, and you're through in this hotel for good. Understand? I have enough responsibility just now without any extra worries."

In the afternoon Roderick drove the General and his party around the island, and Mouseknees felt relieved. He was safe from Roderick for the time being. He lay in the meadow behind the house where Pahdetoo, his goat, was tied—a new place since Pigeon had discovered the old one—and he thought about the General. He wished he could get near enough to him to hear him talk. Possibly he said things that other men did not say and those things made him different.

Quiet vanished and excitement came again at five o'clock when the General and his party returned to the hotel. Mouseknees promptly went to the veranda, to be away from Roderick. The front veranda was soon filled with people, and Mouseknees helped the other boys set up tables and chairs. He wanted to get near to the General, but there were always so many people around. But he could hear bits of conversation.

"A beautiful day, a beautiful drive, a beautiful island, a beautiful ocean," the General was saying.

Other people said exactly the same things.

Then the General said, "My pipe! Where did I leave my pipe? In the automobile, I suppose."

"I'll get it," Mouseknees said impulsively, and he ran from the veranda and was halfway down the stairs before he remembered that he would have to chance running into Roderick and that would mean trouble. But if he got the pipe, perhaps the General would talk to him.

He looked carefully around the corner. Roderick was not in sight. Three quick steps and he was at the automobile. He saw the pipe on the seat, reached for it, and was about to pick it up when he heard a voice.

"Ah—ah! There you are!" That was Roderick.

Mouseknees grabbed the pipe and started to run, but Roderick had him by the shoulder. Mouseknees tried to wriggle free, and there was a little noise as the pipe fell from his hand

261

and clattered on the cement and its stem broke in two pieces.

Roderick let him go but that did not matter. He picked up the pieces of the pipe and saw Mrs. Hudson at the head of the stairs. The noise of the scuffle had attracted her. Without a word, Mouseknees held out the broken pieces.

"What will the General say now?" Mrs. Hudson asked.

Mouseknees shook his head. Everything he did went wrong. He just stood trembling while Mrs. Hudson went to the front veranda. When she came back, he could tell from her face that the General had not been very pleasant. Then Mouseknees heard Mrs. Hudson say something to him, dreadful words.

Five minutes later he was running away from the hotel, discharged, and murmuring to himself, "Got the sack! Got the sack!"

That night Mouseknees, with Pahdetoo beside him, sat on the wharf. He would not go home until it was the usual time, so as not to arouse any questions from his mother or father. The wharf is at the edge of the one main street, and as Mouseknees sat there he saw an automobile drive by rapidly, with Roderick at the wheel and Mr. Leedon and the General in the rear. The top of the automobile had been lowered. They were going for a drive on this pleasant evening.

Mouseknees wished he had someone to talk to besides the goat, who was a good listener, but very poor at answering. He had looked forward to this day so eagerly; he had seen an important and famous man, but the whole day had been spoiled. He would not let himself think about his dismissal from the hotel. After the General and his wife were gone, he could ask Mrs. Hudson if he could start working again, doing the hardest work in the garden. As for Roderick and the threat of jail, he only had to move faster than Roderick, and he could keep away from him. For a moment he thought of running from Roderick from one end of the island, at Stor Bay, to the other end at Speyside.

"Roderick be awful out of breath," Mouseknees said to himself.

He walked to the end of the wharf and saw a pile of packing

Mouseknees wished he had someone to talk to beside the goat.

boxes, probably unloaded from the ship. He would have passed them by except that he thought he heard them move and he was sure that the boxes would not move themselves. He stood a little way off, watching nervously.

A man's head emerged from the boxes, and in the dim light Mouseknees was sure he recognized it. When he took a step forward the head disappeared.

"Crawfoot! Good night!" That is the Tobago way of saying "good evening."

At that the head appeared again, and Crawfoot said, "You scared me! Is that Roderick St. Giles Buzby around?"

"No, he's drivin' the General."

Crawfoot came out from the boxes and sat down in a shadowy place against the warehouse wall. "Things is different on this island today."

Mouseknees had to smile. That was what he wanted to talk about.

"Yes, sir," Crawfoot said, "just because important people come everybody acts different."

Mouseknees had noticed that, too. "What's wrong with you and Roderick?"

"Him an' me had a busup an' he say he put me in jail." A busup is a quarrel.

"What for?"

"When the boat was comin' in this mawnin', Roderick was actin' important-like an' I get in the way he say," Crawfoot said. "He looked so funny, bein' all puffed up. He say I made people laugh at him. People laugh just lookin' at him."

"Yeah," Mouseknees said. Then he told about his day at the hotel.

"That's bad," Crawfoot said. "Trouble comes on horseback an' goes on foot. Seems like some people is two people. One way sometimes, one way another."

Mouseknees nodded. That was what he had decided.

"People is like that," Crawfoot continued. "You never know who is who when important folk come around. Little whos become big whos, and big whos try to be bigger whos."

"What's important?" Mouseknees asked. "You can't see important."

"Important people don't look no different from other people," Crawfoot explained. "They just is."

"Yeah," Mouseknees said, not understanding.

"Is like monkeys," Crawfoot explained. "Monkeys play on the beach laughin' an' happy. They all look alike, don't they? Then one who can climb good climbs a coconut tree, an' he starts throwin' down coconuts, an' he say I'm importantest of all because I can thrown down coconuts on you. So he's higher up, an' that makes him important, an' that makes other monkeys scared because they afraid he throw coconuts at them."

"Then what?" Mouseknees asked.

"So they all go and start to learn to climb an' they forget how happy they was on the beach. You get high so you throw coconuts, then someone gets higher an' he is importanter than you. It oughtn't to be that way but that's the way it is."

"Yeah," Mouseknees said, trying to imagine the General climbing a coconut tree. "How important is the General?"

"He's way up. Every night in London, I hear, the King say, 'General Kittleton, we're havin' some mighty fine fried plantains for dinner tonight. You come over an' have some.' "

"I'd rather have mangoes," Mouseknees said, listening intently.

"You ain't invited an' when you is, you eat what the King sets in front of you and you say, 'Thank you, King!' "

"Yeah," Mouseknees said.

The sound of a speeding automobile along the road attracted Mouseknees' attention. He recognized the white coat of Roderick at the wheel.

"How you goin' to keep away from Roderick?"

"Don't know," Crawfoot said, but he did not sound worried. "He chase me this mornin', this afternoon twice, so I hide here. Maybe after the General goes, Roderick'll stop being a big who."

Mouseknees nodded. He was trying to imagine Roderick climbing a tree. "How'm I goin' to get my job back?"

"Mouseknees," Crawfoot said solemnly, "there is some things I don't know!"

He woke up the next day, at "day clean," which is the Tobago word for dawn. He started to dress mechanically before he realized that there was no need to hurry. No one would expect him at the hotel. He had no job there. Rather than have to explain that to his parents, he left the house, untied Pahdetoo, and decided to go walking. He went along the same road that he used every morning on the way to the hotel.

Usually the road was deserted at this time of day, but near the hotel he saw a man searching in the bushes at the side of the road. It was Mr. Hudson.

"Mornin', sir," Mouseknees said.

"Good morning." Mr. Hudson kept on searching.

Mouseknees did not want to ask any questions. He could not go on the hotel grounds, so he sat on the beach in front of the hotel where he could see all that went on. Between the beach and the road was a strip of brush. Pahdetoo began to nose around in the brush. After a few minutes he appeared with something in his mouth, a piece of cloth with hair fastened to it.

"Put that down," Mouseknees said, taking it from Pahdetoo and throwing it into the bushes. "That ain't fit breakfast, even for a goat!"

That reminded him that he was hungry. He always had breakfast at the hotel. To go home and get something to eat would mean explanations, and he decided to stay hungry.

For the next two hours he watched everything that went on. He saw the other boys setting the tables and he felt hungrier. He saw Mr. Hudson go hurriedly to the hotel. He saw Mrs. Hudson on the veranda. The first guest appeared. Then Mr. Leedon drove up in his car with Roderick at the wheel. Roderick looked unhappy. Mr. Leedon and Mr. Hudson went to one corner of the veranda and stood there for some time. There was no sign of the General, but after a little while his wife appeared and she joined the two men. Then Mr. Leedon and Mr. Hudson and Roderick came down to the road and Mouseknees had to hide behind the brush to keep from being seen by

Roderick. All three men began to hunt in the bushes, first on one side of the road, then on the other. Mouseknees would have liked to go and help, but he was afraid of Roderick, who seemed the most anxious of the three men.

It was bad enough to be hungry but worse not to know what was going on. That made Mouseknees impatient. Obviously something was happening.

Finally Alfred Yangler, one of the downstairs boys, came down the walk, sweeping at each step. Mouseknees stuck his head out of the brush.

"Hey, Alfred!" That was a loud whisper, and he repeated it.

Alfred jumped and almost dropped the broom. "Mouseknees!"

"What's goin' on?"

"Somethin's terrible wrong," Alfred said. He crossed the road and came into the bushes beside Mouseknees. "They say the General is sick in his room. He won't come out, but he don't sound sick. I heard him shoutin'.."

"What are they searchin' the brush for?"

"Don't know." Then Alfred went hurriedly back to work.

Incomplete news was worse than none, and for an hour Mouseknees had to sit restlessly on the beach, out of sight of Roderick. He saw the three men leave the road and return to the hotel, but he could not understand what they were doing. A little later Porker, one of the upstairs boys, came down to the road, and Mouseknees called to him, "Hey, Porker. What you doin'?"

"Makin' a message for Mis' Hudson." That meant he was going on an errand.

"What's wrong at the hotel?"

"Don't know," Porker said. "I heard the banquet at the Warden's house tonight won't be."

"Why not?"

"The General say he can't go. He's in his room. I heard him shoutin' somethin' fierce."

After the plans for that banquet this would cause excitement.

Then Mr. Hudson and Roderick came down to the roadside

again, and Mouseknees moved through the brush so that he could hear snatches of conversation.

"If you had not been driving so fast," Mr. Hudson said angrily, "it would not have happened."

Roderick said nothing. He moved off alone into the brush.

Mr. Leedon came down and joined Mr. Hudson. "You'd think the old boy would have sense enough to carry two with him," he said. "A frightful nuisance, having to call off the dinner after all the preparations."

"He still won't leave his room?"

"He won't even stick his head out," Mr. Leedon said. "Why don't you call the house boys and have a real search made?"

"He doesn't want it known," Mr. Hudson answered.

"Roderick knows it," Mr. Leedon said. "That will spread the news over the island just a little faster than the wind. But we really are in a hole if we can't find it."

Mouseknees was listening too intently to hear Roderick come up from behind.

"Hey, Mouseknees!"

Mouseknees turned, then wanted to run but he knew the brush would stop him.

267

"I ain't concerned about you," Roderick said and he seemed strangely friendly. "I'm sorry you got the sack."

"Yeah," Mouseknees said.

"Everybody's in trouble," Roderick said sadly. "You see a toupee here in the brush?

"A toupee. It blow off the General's head last night as we was drivin' home."

"What's a toupee?"

"You don't know nothin'," Roderick said. He had never heard the word until last night. "It's what the General wears on his head in place of hair. It's a piece of cloth with hair on it."

"Huh," Mouseknees said, thinking fast. "I'll help look."

He yanked Pahdetoo to his feet. Roderick moved off a few feet, and Mouseknees went to a near-by bush, searched for a moment, and picked up the toupee. "Maybe that's the difference," he said aloud. "The General got no hair!"

Then, smiling happily, as if he had made a satisfactory discovery, he walked toward Mr. Leedon.

An hour later the General, his reddish gray hair in place, was shaking hands with Mouseknees. Mouseknees tried to smile, and he was glad when he could leave.

"Run along and get to your work," Mr. Hudson said and Mrs. Hudson near by smiled pleasantly. "You did an important favor for all of us."

Important!

Mr. Leedon came by, smiling. "That was good work, Mouseknees!"

"Yes, sir," Mouseknees said. "Please, Mr. Leedon, don't let Roderick throw coconuts at Crawfoot."

"What?" Mr. Leedon looked puzzled.

"I mean, don't let Roderick put Crawfoot in jail."

"Jail? Roderick had better try a little harder to stay out himself."

Mouseknees went to the veranda in the rear. "Is important," he said to himself. Then suddenly he smiled, remembering the General's troubles. "Would rather be a monkey playin' on the beach!"

Norma Bicknell Mansfield

CAKE AT MIDNIGHT

ILLUSTRATED BY *Sylvia Haggander*

JUDY awoke the morning of June 21st deeply concerned with her personality. On one's twelfth birthday, Judy thought maturely, one should take stock, and this was her twelfth birthday. It stretched ahead of her, deliciously endless, for this was Alaska. She had heard of Alaskan days; in the summertime they became nights with no one knowing the difference, since the sun continued to shine. Especially on June 21st.

This day—Judy rolled to her stomach and punched her pillow vigorously—was the nicest thing that could have happened. Because—and here Judy scooped up the pillow and flung it joyously away—nobody knew her here in Alaska. She had been in school two weeks, of course, the last two weeks of the semester but, miraculously, nothing had happened to give her away.

"And, anyway," she told herself fiercely, "I'm changed. I really am. Inside I'm sweet, and gentle, and thoughtful. All the things Mom wants me to be."

It was only her outer shell that spoke too loud, and moved too fast, upsetting things, and threw the nearest object when excitement shook her. "And nobody's responsible for his outer shell," Judy told herself. "I didn't *ask* to have freckles and red hair. I don't *like* being skinny." She had complained about these things to Mom.

"What we look like outside," Mom had answered, "doesn't matter half so much as what we feel like inside." Mom wasn't very helpful sometimes. "But I wouldn't complain if I were you," Mom had added. "You look just what you are, a happy, eager, loving child."

"Hey!" Outside Judy's door her brother Bill yelled through the keyhole. "Come on out, dizzy, and get your birthday spanking!"

"Go away," Judy said. "I'm too old for that kid stuff."

"Oh yeah!" The door snapped open, and young Bill streamed in. "OOpsidaisy!" He made a flying tackle and missed the bed, so Judy got the upper hand and sat down on him.

"Oh," Bill said, "tactics, huh?"

He rolled over and got hold of one ankle, and after that it was touch and go to get him flattened to the floor again, but Judy did it.

"Holler enough?" she said, panting. Her hair was in her eyes, one of her fingernails was broken, and there was a three-inch rip in her pajama top. The rip recalled some vague thought she had been pursuing before Bill had barged in.

Abruptly she stood up.

"There I go again," she thought. The new personality had already slipped. "Bill—" Judy reached for her hairbrush and sat down on the bed—"you going to the school picnic tonight?"

"Sure," Bill said, "aren't you?" Perpendicular, he looked a little shorter than he was, being stocky. His black hair stood up in peaks and down in valleys. "Gee, is all that hair yours?"

"I'm letting it grow," Judy said severely. "And that's what I want to talk to you about, Bill. I'm going to change my—my personality." Now it was out she felt sure he would laugh, but he didn't. He hadn't heard.

"Spud broke his arm," he said.

"Spud!"

Spud had burst painfully on Judy the first day she'd been in school up here. He was tall and awfully good-looking and quiet-spoken, but he laughed a lot, and everybody liked him. And Judy had tripped over his feet that very first day. She

270

hadn't thought so much about it at the moment, concerned that she might have hurt him, but later, remembering, she had ached at her own awkwardness. Spud, as a matter of fact, was responsible for her decision to change.

"How'd he do it?"

"Fell off his little brother's tricycle!"

Bill, for no good reason, accompanied the news with a heartless guffaw. Judy smacked him with the hairbrush.

"I hope you break your arm someday," she said, but that, of course, was her outer shell speaking, and she immediately amended. "A finger would be enough," she said. "Get out. I'm busy."

Rascal, her Irish terrier, came bounding in and picked up one of her slippers. She had to dive under the bed to get it away from him.

"Honestly," she said, standing up, "I don't have a chance."

And she wondered how, through all these twelve years of her life, she had kept her sanity. It took a rush and a swish, now, to be dressed in time for breakfast.

Mom was waiting at the foot of the stairs for her. Mom's hair was red too, but it had waves, and her freckles were just sweet, not messy as Judy's were.

"Happy birthday," Mom said, and kissed her. Then Daddy grabbed her and turned her over and spanked her lightly, and Judy had to laugh and hug him.

"Breakfast first," Mom said, "and presents later."

"Aw, mom!"

"And what's more," Mom continued, "you forgot to bring home the eggs yesterday, so you'll have to go to the store to get more to bake your cake. We have just enough for breakfast."

"I want two," Bill yelled.

"Now, don't gobble," Mom said firmly. "And remember, both of you, you're to take naps this afternoon if you're going to stay up all night. It's a queer country that has midnight picnics."

"It's a swell country," Bill said.

"Twenty-four hours of daylight," Judy said, "of sunshine. No wonder people stay up all night to see it happen."

Her heart went down a little when she saw her pile of presents. There were only four boxes. One was little and long, and one was big and flat, and one was messily tied—Bill's—and the other was long and flat.

"Silk stockings?" Judy cried, hoping.

"Open it and see."

There they were, three pairs, long and really silk.

"Oh, mom!" Judy whispered.

"Go on, open mine," Bill urged. "Go on. Here, I'll do it."

Judy slapped his hands, but her own were shaking, and then she was laughing. Bill's present was an alarm clock, with a Dopey face and a peeked hat which stood straight up when the alarm went off.

The big, flat package was a woolly bathrobe, a soft and tender blue.

"Oh, mom," Judy cried and hugged her. "You didn't get brown this time."

But it was the last box that brought tears to her eyes. Marked simply, "Love, Daddy," it held a wrist watch, a dainty little square-faced timekeeper.

Judy stayed in her father's arms a long time, rubbing her eyes surreptitiously on his shoulder.

"And see you use it," Daddy said gruffly. "With Bill's present and mine you'll have lots of time now. No need to be always rushing."

Judy put the wrist watch on at once. It gave her wrist a grown-up look—ladylike, she thought—and suddenly her new resolve was stronger. It wouldn't be hard to be gentle and sweet and quiet, like Mom, with long silk stockings and a wrist watch to help her.

"May I wear it to the store?" She touched the dainty face of the watch.

"It's yours," Daddy told her, so she grabbed the dollar bill he gave her, whistled for Rascal and flung out the door—only to halt on the top step and compose herself for dignified descent. Halfway down she giggled. The Irish terrier was standing at the foot of the steps, head cocked, looking up at her.

The day was clear and blue and sparkling. It was queer, Judy thought, how even the summer days up here could sparkle, how fresh the air could be. Some of it must come straight from the mountains, steady and pure.

"Rascal, to heel!" He had started a fight day before yesterday. Rascal liked Alaska. Dogs everywhere. Spunky, too.

"Rascal!" He came back to heel reluctantly, turning his head to look back around his shoulder, prancing a little, showing off.

Judy tucked the fingers of her left hand into her belt; by a swift little glance she could see the wrist watch any time she cared to look. She almost missed seeing Spud, standing on the corner, arm in thick white bandages from wrist to elbow, on a frame thrust stiffly out from his body. He was talking to another boy, and when they spoke Judy looked up to see they had both been watching her.

273

"Good morning," she said, and went sedately past, stepping around Spud's big dark Airedale. She could feel swift color mounting in her face.

"That your dog?" Spud said.

"Hey, watch out!"

It was the other boy. Judy whirled and looked back. Rascal had encountered the Airedale. He drew back from his first rush and pranced, stiff-legged, asking for trouble. Spud reached down and touched his tense back, and in that second the Airedale leaped. There was a startled "Yi-yip" from Rascal before he gathered his strength and sailed in, battle-minded.

"Rascal!"

Yelling did no good. He didn't hear. The Airedale, bigger, stronger, got on top. He set his teeth in Rascal's neck and shook the terrier.

"*Rascal!*"

Spud couldn't do anything, but he tried, and the other boy got hold of Rascal's leg, but the fight went on. Judy looked around her with a desperate, searching eye. People came out of stores to watch the fight. A man on a crutch limped up.

"Here." Judy grabbed his hand and planted it firmly against a building. "Lean on that." She caught the crutch as it swayed, and advanced, heavy and swinging dangerously, toward the dogs. She was quick of eye and sure of movement—had earned the post of captain on the softball team back home. With both hands clutching the crutch now she brought it down on the Airedale's skull. He staggered, stood a moment, shook his head. Rascal, crouching, leaped, but Judy was impartial. She hit him too.

Spud reached down and got his fingers in the Airedale's collar. Stooping, he looked up at Judy.

"Gosh," he said, "you're as strong as a boy."

Judy said nothing. Gathering Rascal under one arm, still struggling, she returned the crutch to the stranger. And went on up the street, trying to smooth down her flying red hair, trying to still her trembling. While in her mind she heard again his blurted statement, "Strong as a boy."

274

"I'll never get over being myself," she thought miserably. "And it isn't just my outer shell. It's me."

Mom had planned to go calling that morning, to step across the way to Mrs. Beeker's with a few glasses of youngberry jelly. Mrs. Beeker had been ill.

"Please go tomorrow, mom." Judy kept her hand on her mother's arm, holding her urgently. "This cake has to be just perfect. It just *has* to be. It's really my birthday cake. Please stay and help me."

"Why, of course, dear," Mom said promptly, but in the end she stirred up a batch of cookies while Judy made the cake. It was a devil's food, dark and even-textured.

"You've always been a good cakemaker," Mom said with satisfaction, but Judy walked around and around the cake, looking for unsightly air bubbles, for some streak in its rich, dark brown. She mistrusted its perfection.

"Because it has to be just perfect," she repeated.

"It is," Mom said. "Get your frosting started." Judy wanted to tell her why it was so important. She wanted to pour out the troubles in her mind, how hard she was trying to be quiet and gentle, and what an awful time she was having with all the odds stacked against her. But if the cake was good, was perfect, that would be some proof, wouldn't it, that she wasn't really a tomboy? Not exclusively.

The frosting came out exactly so, and Judy worked with swift, anxious fingers, spreading it on. She liked it thick. On top, in the exact center, she made a little swirl. It stood up in a saucy peak. Judy laughed, but sobering instantly, smoothed down the peak and left the surface one smooth gleam of chocolate. She sighed. This personality business seemed to crop up everywhere.

"Mom." At the sink Judy kept her back turned, scrubbing her fingers industriously. "Would it be all right, d'you think, to wear a pair of my new stockings tonight? You know, with my," she swallowed swiftly, "new dress."

She could hear Mom pause behind her, feel her looking.

"What will the other girls be wearing?"

276

"I don't know. Slacks, I suppose. But this is my birthday."

Mom was silent a moment.

"I think you'd have more fun if you were dressed like the other girls," she said firmly. "Just stir that cream sauce for me. It's time for lunch."

And after that it was time to rest; only Judy didn't rest. She spent the time trying on all three pairs of stockings, and doing her hair a different way, and rubbing her nails on a woolen blanket to make them shine. Until she lay down for just a moment to turn things over in her mind, and went sound asleep.

In the end she wore slacks, and brushed her hair hard, and parted it as straight as she could, and made the braids smooth, and found small blue ribbons to tie them. A new mood was possessing her, resigned, unhappy. It lay like a crust on top a bubbling turmoil in her stomach.

"I can't stand being this excited," Judy thought. "I can't stand it. Something will happen."

"Aren't you taking Rascal?" Mom asked when she came downstairs. Just for a moment, seeing Mom's eyes light with pride at sight of her, the whirling agony in her stomach subsided. She did look well in slacks, she knew, and these were white; heavy so they wouldn't show creases the first time she sat down. Her blouse was white too, and the woolly blue sweater Mom had given her at Easter was the sweetest thing she owned. Just for a moment Judy was reassured, and then somebody called out to her from the car at the curb.

"Come *on!* It's a hundred miles."

Miss Hepley, the teacher, was driving the car. There were two girls beside her. In the back two more moved over to make room.

"What about Rascal?" Mom insisted.

"I'm going to leave him home. He always starts a fight." With her foot on the running board, Judy looked back wildly. "My cake! Where's my cake?"

"It's in the car," Mom said. "And here: graham crackers. You'll be starved before you get there."

Graham crackers, Judy thought bitterly. Crumbs all over

everything. One of the girls giggled. Judy took the paper bag, kissed her mother swiftly, and climbed in. They started off.

Judy sat there, holding the bag, looking off through the window, seeing nothing.

"Aren't you going to eat the crackers?"

"You can have them," Judy said stiffly. "I'm not hungry."

It didn't help to hear the others munching. Judy had nothing to say. Up in front the chatter was gay and continuous, but back here the silence grew deeper and deeper.

"They don't like me," Judy thought. She was miserable.

The road was narrow and twisty. From time to time she could see the Alaska Range, poking its serrated ridge above the nearer hills. And over everything at nine o'clock at night the incredible sun still shone, getting pinkish now but still warm and brilliant. Moss clung to everything, like yards of velvet flung down for a carpet.

"Your brother had a ride, didn't he?" Miss Hepley called back across her shoulder.

"Daddy's going to drive him out with some of the other boys," Judy said. She had a guilty twinge. She hadn't thought of Bill since morning.

"I'll give him a big piece of my cake," she thought.

"Do you like Alaska?" one of the girls beside her asked politely.

"It's awfully nice," Judy said carefully, and heard the flat, dead words echo and re-echo in her ears. She thought the car would never stop and let them out, but presently they were up above the timber line, climbing still higher, and then they had arrived.

On the flat table of the summit were picnic groups everywhere you looked, Alaskans enjoying their own peculiar treasure, a nightless day. And close to the horizon, paralleling it, the sun seemed to move around the far rim of the world. Its rays were reddish now, and there was little warmth from them, but the world was daylight bright. And later, Judy knew, the sun would turn again to daytime yellow, and yield new heat.

She stood a moment looking off to the white mountains, so

278

near and so far, serene and ageless. Looking at them Judy felt her problem grow vague and small, while in her all the eagerness she hoped to smother rose unconquerably. She threw out her arms and lifted her head and drew in a deep, full breath.

"Oh, boy!" she said.

"You do like it, don't you?" It was the same girl asking the same question.

"Better than any place I've ever been," Judy blurted out swiftly. To her surprise the girl took her hand.

"Come on," she said. "Let's help spread the food. The boys will get here, and they're always hungry."

It was fun, spreading the food, setting the dishes of potato salad at strategic points, buttering buns, starting a fire for the steaks. Judy wasn't as much at home in this business as the others; she had to remember not to push and jostle, not to run and jump, but it was still fun.

It was fun right up to the minute she took her own cake from the car, but just then Daddy's car rolled up and Bill jumped out of it, and another car came to a stop near by, and Spud got cautiously out—it was fun right up to that moment. At precisely that moment Rascal bounded from Daddy's car. Spud's Airedale leaped out after Spud, and a fight began.

"Oh, Daddy!" Judy wailed.

"Hey, Jinx!" Spud yelled at the Airedale but it did no good. Judy screamed at Rascal, but he didn't hear her. They met right at Spud's feet. They backed him up against the side of the car and swarmed up him and down him. He couldn't move. Judy heard him gasp. Rascal had hit the hurt arm. Then the Airedale was clawing his way up and sliding down.

A long, bloody scratch appeared on Spud's white cheek. He couldn't move.

"*Rascal!*"

Judy forgot her personality. She forgot everything but that savage warfare staged on a helpless battlefield. She started forward at a bounding run, and as she did so she felt the weight in her hand. It was something to throw. She threw it.

There was a startled gasp, a high, pained "Yip!"

279

Rascal drew off, howling, rubbing his nose with a paw. Daddy grabbed him.

Judy couldn't move. She stood, appalled, looking at Spud. At what had been Spud. Just now it was a boy with a chocolate cake head, the cake all broken and smeary, falling away in rich, dark chunks.

Judy wanted to cry. She wanted to run, to hide. She wanted to feel Daddy's arms around her, but Daddy's arms were full of Rascal. So she just stood, aching. And then Daddy spoke to her.

"Good girl!" he said. "That was quick thinking. The rim of that plate hit Rascal square on the nose. Here!" He handed the dog to Bill. "Put him in the car and shut him in. Spud, are you hurt?"

By that time everybody was crowded around the boy. Somebody brought a wet napkin—Miss Hepley. Somebody else brought a knife, and presently Spud's face emerged.

Judy looked away.

She looked away to the mountains, so far off, unseeing, while inside of her the tears swelled up and burst, but they didn't show in her eyes. Her eyes and her mouth were hard and set.

"Yeah," she thought bitterly, "you've changed your personality, you have!"

Behind her there was an abrupt and overpowering silence.

"Where's Judy?" It was Spud.

The next minute he was standing there beside her, his good hand thrust out, a grin on his face.

"You sure do throw like a boy," he was saying. Judy forced her glance to meet his. His eyes were glowing, laughing. "What's wrong with you, anyway? Most of the time you act like a stick of wood. And then all of a sudden you limber up and get human. Hey, you're not crying!"

"Me!" Judy said, and suddenly she was laughing. "Wait till you get to know me."

An Australian picnic.

Faith Baldwin

BOILING THE BILLY

ILLUSTRATED BY *Helen Prickett*

LAST year when Jimmy and Janet Townsend went to Australia they were pretty excited about it. Of course, it was a wrench, leaving their pretty home on Long Island . . . with the woods so near the house that you could look out of the windows and see straight into birds' nests, the picnic oven down by the brook, which meant good times on long summer days, on spring days too when the leaves were just greening and in the autumn when the air was brisk and the smell of wimpies cooking was something to make you go all hollow and happy in the pit of your stomach.

But their father had to go to Australia on business. He'd be gone a long time and hated like the dickens to leave Janet and Jimmy at home—to say nothing of their mother, who had the yellowest hair and the bluest eyes you ever saw and was, most of the time, a great deal of fun.

Janet was like her, round and sunny, and Jimmy was like his father, dark and slender and going to be very tall. They were twins, although they didn't look, or even think, alike. They were going-on thirteen.

"But what about school?" wailed Mrs. Townsend, who often thought of such practical things.

"We'll take their books along," said Mr. Townsend, "and we'll teach 'em. Anyway, travel is very educational."

"Whoops!" said Jimmy when he heard that, and turned a handspring. But Janet just went off quietly and stood on her head in a corner as she always did when anything of great importance occurred.

281

It was hard to say good-bye to the house which had eyebrows over its shining windows. Harder still to say good-bye to Pat and Pete, the cocker spaniel pups, Ginger, the nondescript cat, and even Simple, the canary. It was hard to say good-bye to Melia, the fat, black cook, and to Parsons, who drove the car and did the gardening. And one day before they left home Jimmy and Janet went down to the woods and looked sadly at the picnic oven. Pat and Pete came too, sat down on their golden rear ends, waggled their long curly ears, and cried a little as if they knew that this spring and summer there would be no delectable odd bits of wimpies left over for them.

"I don't suppose they have picnics in Australia," said Jimmy sadly. He had been reading about Australia in his geography. He knew that it was a big place, as big as the place we live in. He knew that it had all sorts of exciting things in it, parrots flying around loose and just as common as sparrows here, and a creature called a platypus which has a furry body and a flat tail like a beaver, a bill like a duck, and webbed feet, an enchanted kind of creature which lays eggs and then nurses its babies and is ever so shy. Jimmy had explained the platypus to Janet, and when she looked at its picture in the geography she said, "I should think it *would* be shy with a face like that!"

Jimmy knew too that kangaroos grow in Australia, and wallabies and emus. He used to think that emus existed only in crossword puzzles. He knew all about the great surfing beaches in summertime and the sharks, and that there were lifeguards up in towers who rang shark bells to warn the swimmers. He knew about the koalas, those furry little animals which people mistakenly call bears. But in all his geography book and even in the encyclopedia there wasn't a word about picnics.

Picnics were awfully important to the Townsends. They had picnics all year round. When it snowed and the trees were bare they picnicked at home round a fire. They had settled all sorts of family disputes and serious problems over picnics. They were the picnickingest people you ever saw.

Well, you can't have everything, as Jimmy and Janet agreed. Platypus instead of picnic, then. They'd have to be content.

It was almost summer at home when they left. The leaves were green, and the tulips danced in the garden. They took a train and went away across the continent, which was fun, though a little confining. And when they reached California they got on board a big white boat and sailed right off for Australia.

The water got bluer and bluer. When they came to the Hawaiian Islands it was deep summer, and when they reached Samoa and Fiji it was even more so. But after that it began to get cool again and when they came to New Zealand it was quite cold. And so was Australia.

That was a funny place, they thought, where it was late autumn in June.

When they got off the boat at Sydney they had quite a roll in their walk after all those days of just deck and water and the boat going up and down. Sometimes it went too much up and down for Janet. But Jimmy scorned the wind and weather, played deck games like mad, and had fun all the time.

They had met a lot of Australian people on the boat and found to their astonishment that they were very like people they knew at home. They talked a little differently perhaps, but they looked the same. And the Australian children played all the same games. Sometimes they said "I say" and "No fear" and sometimes they said "Too right," but mostly they were just like any other children. Jimmy was quietly astonished at this although he didn't tell anyone. He was a little ashamed of thinking that almost everyone in Australia would be an aborigine. You see, in the geography there weren't pictures of the Australian white people, just pictures of aborigines. Of course, *they* were Australian people, as they'd been there first, long before Captain Cook even thought about Australia!

Mr. Townsend's business took him to several big cities, and Jimmy and Janet and their mother went along. Sometimes they went by train, a rather different sort from the ones we have. And sometimes they went by car, well bundled up against the cold. For if they went south it grew much colder, and at one place there was a lot of snow and people skiing; yet if they went north it grew warmer. This fact confused Jimmy and Janet a good deal.

Everything they saw was pretty exciting, the bright-colored parrots flying along the way, the laughing jackass birds that sat on fences and laughed fit to split their sides when they saw the two little American faces peering from the window of the car. Jimmy and Janet had heard about the jackies. They were amazed to find them looking so much like overgrown kingfishers. They had thought they might perhaps resemble little donkeys with wings!

They went to nice parks and saw the platypus and were not

at all disappointed; they saw the koalas and loved them, the furry little things, shaped like bears; and one night on a dark road they saw two kangaroos sitting up and looking solemnly at their approaching headlights. And, of course, they saw lots and lots of sheep.

"Australia," said Jimmy, remembering his geography, "grows a lot of wool. More wool than anyone else, almost." Janet felt the fine softness of her sweater, and looked out the car window at the baby lambs stumbling around their mothers on their thin little legs, and felt very sorry. She felt so sorry that she almost cried. When her mother turned around and saw her eyes, she asked, "For goodness' sake, Janet, what's the matter?"

Janet explained. She'd rather go without a sweater and even freeze a very little bit, she said, than to think that baby lambs must be taken from their mothers and killed in order to provide her with wool.

Jimmy said something superior about, "Well, they just didn't take to lamb chops, did they?" but luckily Janet hadn't thought of that and anyway she was too busy asking her mother, "Do they *pull* it out?"

Her father said: "I tell you what, we'll go visit on a sheep station. I'll have a little free time next week, and that nice man we met on the boat—Mr. Greene, remember him, darling?—asked us to come and visit him when we could arrange it."

So the very next week Janet and Jimmy and their parents drove to a sheep station in New South Wales, which is a state in Australia.

Sheep station sounded a little mysterious, as if it should have been some sort of depot near by. But, their father explained, a station is what we call a ranch out west. And this was a big ranch, thousands and thousands of fenced acres and on top of a hill, near a little town, the long low house which belonged to the Greenes.

The Greenes had lots of children, all ages and sizes. Some of them were away at the university and some in other schools in the big city of Sydney, but four were at home, over the week-end, on the sheep station. There were Ann, who was seven, and Betty, who was eleven, and of all things twins, Dennis and Sylvia, who were just two months older than Jimmy and Janet.

There were big coal and wood fires burning in the fireplaces when they reached the station—most people in Australia do not have furnaces as we do. Jimmy was given a bed on a big enclosed porch, a sort of dormitory in which the Greene boys slept, Janet had a bed in the girls' dormitory, their mother and father had a big room with a fireplace and a big old-fashioned double bed. Every bed in the house had a nice hot-water bottle in it. For it was very nearly winter, you see, and cold when the sun decided to go down.

Of course, before they went to bed they had to have dinner, ever so many of them, around the great table and the fire burning brightly and lots to eat—a regular British-Australian dinner, with a joint of mutton and for dessert something called a trifle, which wasn't a trifle at all. Jimmy had three helpings.

The next day Janet woke up on her porch wondering where she was. She was cuddled to the eyebrows in grand woolly blankets, the sun was shining in, and somewhere near by a jackie was laughing. Ann was asleep and so were Sylvia and Betty, but Janet hopped out of bed and went to the windows to look out. She could see an icing of frost on the ground, she could see the black and white magpies flying in the orchard, she could see the flowers in the garden, for even in winter there were flowers in that part of the world, and she could see the far paddocks and the hills all dotted with the moving white shapes of sheep. And she was much too excited to remember that she hadn't put on her bedroom slippers.

When she went out to breakfast she found that Jimmy and Dennis had been up for hours. They'd been down to the barn where Mr. Greene kept all sorts of things but not cows . . . there aren't barns for cows in Australia, or pens for sheep, not in this part anyway. Jimmy had met some of the sheep dogs and their puppies, and he'd seen a green and red and blue parrot, and Dennis had taken him into the sheds where they shear the sheep and explained to him just how the machines worked.

There was a lot of breakfast, including lamb chops and a

good deal of tea. Jimmy and Janet didn't drink tea at home, they didn't care for it except now and then in the summer, iced; besides, they weren't allowed tea any more than they were allowed coffee. But the Greene children drank tea, with milk in it, even seven-year-old Ann with the black bangs and the blue eyes. And Sylvia explained that the grownups drank morning tea, very early, 'way before breakfast. She and the others, she said, didn't like it much, they'd rather sleep.

Now the sun was up, and the frost had vanished, and you could see all over the little town from this hilltop. And the children went walking in the garden. Red poinsettias grew there, and the golden wattle, and the pink daphne which smells heavenly, and there were late roses climbing over a trellis, not really frost-bitten, just a little chilly looking and pinched.

Out came Mr. Greene, a big man with a jolly laugh. He was asking:

"How'd you like to go out to the paddocks today and take a hamper?"

Since he spoke to Jimmy, Jimmy answered cautiously:

"We'd like to very much, sir—a hamper of what?"

"A cut lunch," explained Mr. Greene, clapped him between the shoulder blades, and went back toward the house. Jimmy looked at Janet with his black eyebrows telegraphing inquiries. What on earth was a cut lunch? he wondered, and didn't like to ask for fear he would be thought very ignorant.

But Janet guessed. Her round and rosy face was radiant, and her yellow curls danced all over her head. And she cried, "Oh, Jimmy, it must mean a *picnic!*"

A picnic in Australia!

Ann was dancing from one foot to the other. She wore a blue serge dress, rather like a sailor suit, and long black stockings on her little legs. And she was saying, "We'll boil the billy!"

Jimmy and Janet looked at each other. They said nothing, politely. But later as they were walking back toward the house where their mother waited with sweaters and directions and all the things mothers always wait with, Janet whispered, a little frightened:

287

"You don't suppose she means a billy *goat?*"

"Of course not, silly," replied Jimmy very superior.

"I'm sure I saw one near the barn," said Janet, and shuddered. "I'd hate to see a billy boiled!"

"Poof!" scoffed Jimmy, but he felt somewhat uneasy. So later he had a word, alone, with his mother. He mentioned, with elaborate carelessness, "One of the girls said something about a billy."

"That's tea," his mother said briskly. "Are you sure you scrubbed those nails?"

"Of course I did. Tea!"

Mrs. Townsend thought he was distressed because he wasn't a tea drinker and did not wish to be impolite, so she said kindly, "Well, as it's a picnic, you and Janet may have some."

Presently they all piled into two cars and off they went: down the private, tree-bordered road which led to the station-house and along a dusty, curving road; when they turned off that, there was a great getting out and opening of gates and then shutting them again, and no more roads, just the bumpy, velvet green paddocks which they rocked over for, it seemed, miles. Then they stopped.

Here, the tall gum trees grew in clumps. They call them eucalyptus, mostly, at home. There was a little gully with a brook and more trees, and the very bright birds were busy flying in and out, flashes of blue and red, yellow and green, dove gray and rose. The magpies sang and quarreled, dressed in their half mourning. The bright nearly winter sun of Australia grew hot and hotter. And the children ran, explored the brook, climbed a tree or two, scared the chattering parrots, and watched the sheep grazing some distance away, because sheep are timid and run when they see you coming. They saw the big old rams with the curly horns, a few snow-white, awkward babies with funny clown faces, and the placid mothers. They saw a sheep dog or two, and the sky overhead was a clear and blazing blue.

And presently they were very hungry—if they had ever *not* been hungry.

288

"Come," shouted big Mr. Greene, "come and help me boil the billy."

Janet had forgotten. Now she was a little frightened again. But Jimmy gave her a poke in the ribs. He said loftily, "It's just the way they make tea!"

Mr. Greene had selected the hollow stump of a gum tree. In that he built his fire. Dennis carried dried twigs, sticks and branches of gumwood. The wind was just right so that the smoke went, blue and gray and brave, right up the little chimney of the stump. And on a tree near by, a soldier bird sat and whistled and watched.

Then came the billy, a tin can. That's what it was, just a quart can with a lid on it. Mr. Greene had a big pail full of fresh spring water. And into the billy went the water. The lid was left off, a twig was laid across the top, and the billy went on the fire.

"Why the twig?" asked Mr. Townsend, who had an inquiring nature. He stood with his hands in his pockets and watched.

"I haven't the least idea," admitted Mr. Greene, "but we always do it. They say it keeps turning and prevents the smoke from going into the water too much."

When the water was boiling like fun Mr. Greene shouted, "Where's the tea?" and Mrs. Greene, who had put blankets down on the ground and was unpacking the lunch with the help of Sylvia and Mrs. Townsend, came running with the tea in a canister. And Mr. Greene didn't bother to measure it. He just threw in a lordly handful and waited for the billy to boil up again. When it had, he took it off the fire, with the tea leaves swirling all around in it, set it on the ground, and beat a jolly tune on its sides with the twig until the leaves had settled.

That was billy tea.

They drank it from tin cups. Janet and Jimmy had milk in theirs, and so did their mother and Ann. The rest didn't. But everyone took sugar. And Jimmy lifted his cup, which was pretty hot, in his hand and took a scalding sip, just to be polite. But his eyes grew wide, and he set the cup down again. He said, "That's the only tea I ever liked."

The cut lunch came out of the hamper, lettuce and tomato and asparagus sandwiches, cold lamb chops and cold legs of chicken, and lots and lots of cakes, some with cream in them and all pretty exciting. And everyone sat down on the blankets or on a tree stump and ate and ate and ate. And were so quiet and happy that the sheep forgot to be afraid and came down from the hill again and went to grazing not too far off. The magpies sat near too and waited to see if there'd be anything left over. Down in the gully a wattle tree in bloom was like spilled sunlight with the birds flying through it, the bright birds, like a patchwork quilt.

And Mrs. Townsend said, "This is the best tea I ever drank."

Mrs. Green nodded her head, which was brown like a thrush's back. "No one knows why. Maybe it's the faint smell and taste of the gum smoke. But it *is* the best tea. . . ."

And Jimmy asked, "Could I have another cup?"

"Please," said his mother.

"Please," said Jimmy.

So he had another cup.

Afterwards with a few little leftover cakes he and Dennis went to sprawl in the sun and talk. Dennis talked about cricket and his kind of football, and Jimmy talked about baseball and his kind of football. Then they talked about swimming and school and vacations. And when Jimmy heard that Dennis had six weeks' holiday at Christmas he almost choked on the last cake. But Dennis straightened him out while kindly thumping his back. Christmastime was summertime in Australia and very hot, he explained, so they had their long vacation then and a shorter one at Easter and at the end of every term.

While the boys were talking Janet and Sylvia, Betty and Ann were down by the brook, not quite getting their feet wet but watching the birds and talking about dolls and books they had read and the radio programs they heard. But, of course, the Greene girls hadn't heard any American programs except now and then on short wave. They talked about dogs, and cats, and what happened in school, and did you ever have a teacher you didn't like at all? You know, that sort of thing.

While this was going on, their elders sat on the blankets and talked too, about the world and about wars that had been and might be again and about people they had known. And the mothers talked about their children and the fathers about business. Just as mothers and fathers always do.

After a while they packed up what was left of the cut lunch—there wasn't much—got back in the cars and bumped out of the paddocks. This time Jimmy got out to open and shut gates. Then they went for a drive on the public road which ran like a brown ribbon through two halves of the property and stopped now and then to watch a bird or a flock of sheep, or to speak to a sheepherder going by or a drover driving his cattle to a far place. And every so often they came upon men along the roadside, half asleep, or just resting or even reading, with their billies boiling brightly beside them.

When it was almost dark they went back to the station-house to hot shower baths and a big dinner, and games afterwards. Then bed for the children because they had to leave ever so early in the morning. And it was hard to go, when morning came. It is always hard to leave your friends.

Sylvia and Janet promised to write each other; Jimmy and Dennis promised they would exchange stamps. And so the visit was ended.

Not long after that they went aboard a white boat again and started sailing toward summer and home. And there was a boy on that boat who was making the round trip. He had had pneumonia and had come away for his health. He was fourteen, skinny, and pretty badly spoiled. Jimmy couldn't stand him because he cheated at quoits. And the boy—his name was Roger—said:

"I'm sure I don't know how you stood Australia for over a month—it's not a bit like home, not nearly so progressive. Why, the houses haven't any heat, and they don't have all the new movies, and they've only one streamlined train and no big highways like ours—"

This made Jimmy mad, and he said, scowling:

"I don't see that it's so different. I like it. They're just like us."

"Really?" said Roger and looked supercilious. That's the way a camel looks. You know. Jimmy knew too. He'd seen camels in Australia, brought over to the coast from the big desert.

"They're swell," said Jimmy; "they like the things we do."

"What, for instance?" inquired Roger, who didn't believe anything he didn't say himself.

"Picnics," answered Jimmy, "and anyone who likes picnics is all right." He looked fiercely at Roger. Then added carelessly:

"I dare say you've never even boiled a billy."

"Done what?" asked Roger, stumped.

"Skip it," said Jimmy briefly, "you wouldn't understand." And he smiled a little, all to himself. When he got home he'd have so much to tell . . . all about koalas and kangaroos, platypuses and parrots. But most of all about picnics and the billy boiling and friends having fun together under the blue sky and the blazing sun.

DOBRY is a boy who lives with his grandfather and his mother, Roda, in Bulgaria, and who wants very much to become an artist. Encouraged by his friend Neda, who is Hristu the shoemaker's daughter, and by the schoolmaster, Semo, Dobry made a Nativity scene of snow for Christmas, which amazed all the village with its beauty. And now it is time for the celebration of the New Year. . . .

Monica Shannon
DOBRY'S NEW YEAR

ILLUSTRATED BY *Rosemary Buehrig*
and Kay Lovelace

BETWEEN Christmas and New Year, Grandfather was busy in a secret way, because Bulgarians give New Year presents instead of Christmas presents. Grandfather was busy especially, because in Bulgaria a peasant gives presents at New Year to those only who are younger than himself, and naturally Grandfather's age made him the busiest and most secretive person in the whole village.

He looked over all his sashes, trying to make up his mind about which one Dobry would like best. At last he decided on a sash wider, longer even than the others, and handwoven in green with a pattern of storks.

"It looks like April," Grandfather told himself.

He sorted out ancient Greek, Macedonian, and Turkish coins their family plow had turned up through the years and made two bracelets out of the coins, one for Roda and the other for Neda. Bracelets as strong as they were beautiful, the coins linked together by wrought iron links Pinu let him make in the blacksmith shop.

Grandfather shut one eye.

Remembering that Hristu had made him a pair of birthday shoes, Grandfather whittled a flute out of river linden and painted it with autumn colors for the shoemaker. And once started on flute making, he made up his mind to give Michael-acky, Semo, and Pinu each a new painted flute. But Grandfather could think of nothing for Asan, and he said to Roda,—

"I can't think of a present for that narrow-faced, half-asleep boy. Nothing! If I could give him a flute now—but he already has the most wonderful flute anybody ever saw."

Roda relieved his mind and his curiosity, too, by showing him a blouse she had woven for Asan and a golden-looking dress she had woven for Neda, because the two of them were without their mothers.

Dobry, too, was busy. He carved out a wooden lamb for Semo's baby, who was able to walk now. For Neda he made two fantastic slender animals out of the very hard wood of their mountain dran bush.

Dobry felt he had to make these animals out of dranwood, because the dran bush always begins its budding under snow in time for New Year's Eve, and a budding dran branch had come to mean New Year itself. First to leaf out under late snow and last to ripen its cranberry-like fruits, early snow often covered the dranka berries so that the dran bush was looked upon as the spirit of the year, alive to each season and friendly with snow.

On New Year's Eve everybody in the village carried dran branches, as a hint to winter that even the heartiest welcome may be worn out. These branches of sheathed buds were the image of spring. And eager for spring itself, the peasants now were expecting spring to come faster than was possible in a high mountain village such as theirs.

Every peasant looked forward now to his bath as well as to spring's coming. The gypsies brought their massaging bear along in early spring, and if the bear would take his bath in the Yantra river then the villagers knew that the water was warm enough for themselves and they could wash and soak in the river without any fear of cramps.

Roda killed the oldest rooster in their courtyard for New Year's Eve. Only the oldest rooster was thought wise enough to predict the details of spring's arrival, and Roda had invited Semo, his peasant wife, and walking baby to a Weather-man Rooster supper.

And for the first time in his life, Dobry felt impatient of holiday ceremony, eager to be off to Neda with his fantastic animals and a story he had made up to go with them, a part of his New Year present to her.

But *Na lay* took possession of him when twilight took possession of the earth. Semo's walking baby came in at twilight, switched everybody with a dran branch, and said as best he could,—

"*Surva, Surva, survaknetca godina,*" or Happy New Year, a greeting all Bulgarians call out to each other. And a Bulgarian is allowed to switch anybody older than himself when he chants the New Year greeting.

Dobry no sooner thought of *Na lay* than he began to sing it at the top of his lungs. Everybody sang the gypsy song with him and when it was done Roda took up a dran branch, a candle, and a little pot of incense. And Semo's baby, being the youngest of them all, followed her on a small pilgrimage about the house while Roda blessed each room in preparation for the New Year.

The others were very quiet at table, waiting. Roda came back, set the candle in the middle of the table, lifted the boy to his stool, and for a moment everybody felt too excited to speak, anticipating the pause and death of one year before another year leaps to take its place.

Grandfather took up a dran branch, held it over the candle, said, "Roda, this is your branch!" And Roda, anxiously watching, knew her luck by the number of leaf buds the flame popped open. There were three buds on Roda's branch, two of them popped, but if only one had opened, Roda would have expected little from this New Year. If no buds at all had opened, Roda would have expected the year ahead to be a waste year.

Grandfather said, "Well, two is fairly good. If three leaf buds had opened, the year would have belonged to you,

Roda. Now you will have to belong a little to this New Year."

He told everybody's fortune by holding a dran branch over the candle and then carved up the weather-wise rooster, saving out the wishbone for himself.

"I keep the weather man for myself," he said. "Why not? I see through him better than any of you do."

And his rooster meat eaten, Grandfather held its wishbone up to the candle flame, shut one eye, peered through the bone.

"Very clear. No snow. No clouds even," he declared. "Perfect! An early spring this year. The earliest spring I ever saw in a weather bone. All of the bone transparent. Perfect! Yes, the gypsy bear will be here before long and we'll take our baths! You'll see me rolling in the river like a buffalo. The water will be high this year, but I'll soak up a lot of river. And how we'll all feel after our baths! Perfect!" Grandfather made a big noise of snorting as if he already felt himself a water buffalo.

Dobry got up to go to Neda, but Semo stopped him. "Wait a minute," Semo begged him. "I have to tell you about your New Year present. It's—well, your Nativity made me think of it, Dobry. I'm going to give you that little north room in the school and let you work there with your clay. An hour out of school time every day. Then—"

Roda interrupted the schoolmaster. "Wait, wait!" she cried to Dobry, gathered up the fortune-telling dran branches, putting them away carefully on a shelf under the jamal's hood to be the family's *survaktcy* for the coming year. The *survaktcy* is used when anybody hesitates about getting up at daybreak. An earlier riser beats a tattoo with dran branch on the lazy one's bed, repeats, "*Surva, surva, survaknetca godina!*" until the laziest person in the world would rather get up than listen to the tiresome racket.

"Come here!" Roda called to Dobry and took out from her pocket a handful of gold coins. "The coins from my wedding dress," she told him. "I saved them for you, all of them. Coins from the head kerchief, coins from all around the hem of the skirt. They're for you—" Roda made her voice steadier. "They're for you so you can go to Sofia and grow to be an artist." Grand-

father shook his head gravely. "You go in the spring, Dobry, after you've had your bath," he said. "I've saved all the money we got from the wood for your art education. That's a New Year present for you, too."

The weather turned clear as the weather-bone had predicted, a blue sky over deathly cold and snow. And on New Year's Day Maestro Kolu surprised Dobry by sending him a cap of white astrakhan.

"I have my cap from Macedonia," Dobry told everybody. "White astrakhan and you see my hair now—very black."

He wore the cap to school and all the peasants understood that it was a cap nobody would wish to take off. But Dobry explained to Semo, "It does something wonderful to me, so I keep my cap on, school or no school."

When Semo dropped into the little north room to talk to him, Dobry was working away at an enormous lump of clay, the astrakhan cap still on his head.

"What are you making?" Semo asked him. "I wished to talk to you before you set to work. I am troubled about you, Dobry. Look, your grandfather and your mother think that a little sum from wood chopped and hauled and a handful of wedding coins will put you through art school in Sofia. They won't. Your mother and your grandfather think that life in Sofia is exactly like life in this village. It isn't."

298

Dobry cocked his white astrakhan cap over one ear and his eyes went brilliant with laughter.

"But what is that to worry about—coins! Every Mama in the village has a wedding dress heavy with coins. If I need more—all right, but don't worry about it. The village is full of coins. Who cares?"

"But—" Semo began earnestly.

Dobry interrupted him, "If I need more coins I'll have them—that's all. A week from today I'll have plenty of coins, anyway. This year I dive for the golden cross on the feast of Saint John the Baptist. In this cold nobody else wishes to take the risk. There's no question about who will bring up the cross this year. I dive by myself. Michaelacky has forbidden his son—the Little Mayor—to dive, and every old Mama in the village is going around saying that if any boy goes down into the ice hole this year, he will come up an icicle. But Grandfather says that if no boy dives for the cross on this feast of Saint John the Baptist, it will be a lasting shame for the village. And its men to come will be unfit masters for our oxen and our water buffaloes. This coldest winter makes the dive more important—that's all." Semo got himself a little bench and sat down.

"On the feast of Saint John the Baptist, I take off my white astrakhan cap, Semo, and you will see me dive into the ice hole. And there'll be so many gold coins tossed into my crucifix basket that I'll be able to take some to your brother's family in Sofia when I go there—a present from the village. Mountain coins on your niece's wedding dress, Semo, and she will bear strong sons. Very strong sons with deep roots." Dobry shook his head. And Semo went back to his teaching, feeling somehow that his brother's family were about to come into their own.

On the seventh of February, the feast of Saint John the Baptist, the village priest bundled himself up and then got into his stiff robes, put on his tall black hat, took his crozier, a golden crucifix, and set off for the Yantra River. Altar boys and a peasants' choir followed him with incense and chants. Ruddy-faced children got in their way, but looked up with eyes bright and trustful enough to avert scoldings.

299

Peasant men, Grandfather at their head, broke a big hole in the river ice with iron poles and stood to look at the water underneath, black, powerful, deep moving. The village priest threw the golden crucifix into the water. Dobry dived in and was out again so quickly with the cross that the crowding peasants had only time to think, as they all did think, "The boy who made our Nativity!" and hold their breath in suspense.

Their tension broke loose in a happy roar that drowned all prayers and chants. And a ceremony that was usually very quiet turned into an uproar. Peasants shouted to each other, "The boy who made our Nativity!" "Nobody else would risk it!" "This cold is like death cold!" "He did it, you saw him?" "Is he all right?" "Fine, fine!" "All of him glows! The skin very red." "Everybody—even the Mayor said it was impossible this year— impossible!" Other peasants roared without words, opened their mouths to let their emotion out.

And the villagers had always singled out the boy who came up with the crucifix as a boy in another country might be singled out for a scholarship. Each winter the villagers put what money they had into the basket holding the wet cross, a lift toward the boy's grown-up life, so that he might buy himself a pig or a cow or even a small field.

Dobry, dry, glowing, got into fleece-lined sheepskins, put on his white astrakhan cap, placed the golden crucifix in its basket.

The basket was immediately filled up with golden coins old Mamas had ripped from their wedding dresses and multiplied by the coins the men brought along in their sashes.

Grandfather, Roda, Semo, Hristu, all tried to embrace Dobry at once, so that Neda could only shiver and call up to him:

"It must have been terrible—that water?"

Dobry looked down into her eyes while the others embraced him, and said to her,—

"But I'm warm now, Neda. *Na lay.* And the dive was more important this year." He disentangled himself from the crowd and ran headlong for home.

And that night everybody in the village danced the *rachanitza.* Old Mamas, grandfathers, children, everybody danced.

300

Dobry and Neda and Roda and Grandfather danced at the mayor's house with a crowd of peasants, Asan playing the music for them on his wonderful flute.

Winter, for all its cold, was shorter than usual, and spring came with a rush of green water and green leaves. An eager spring in the mountains, wild grass pushed up through pine needles, while sunless mountainsides were still patched with snow. The poplar tree in Dobry's courtyard had leaves again, and the leaves were big and mature for their age.

Every peasant had danced himself into perspiration during the wedding months of January and February. And salty wet now behind his plow, the peasant felt that the Gypsy Bear was his most urgent necessity.

Villagers exclaimed, "But the bear should be here! Those gypsies—to the devil with them! Nobody can depend on them. The river might be warm enough now for a bath and a swim."

Yet no peasant took off his winter clothes to soak himself clean in the high, rip-roaring Yantra until the Gypsy Bear came to prove by going in that the water was as warm as it should be and the spring current less powerful than it looked. It was a matter of tradition, custom, and common sense that waited upon the Gypsy Bear.

Bears love to wash up in spring, and the Gypsy Bear was as reliable as a thermometer. Water he found comfortable, un-cramping, and a current that he could master always proved to be equally comfortable, uncramping, and safe for the peasants.

The gypsies followed spring up the mountains, stopping over at every village with their massaging and bath-testing bear. They stayed on at each village, tempted by peasant food, tempted by peasant dancing and the love they had for fiddling out the song everybody sang:

> "Spring is flighty,
> Highty-tighty.
> Love is fresher than the grass,
> Life is lighter, nights are whiter,
> With the sky a petaled mass.

302

"Spring is flighty,
Highty-tighty.
Hills of snow run warm, run free.
Sun is throbbing, quail go bobbing
Under dran bush, under tree.

"Love is flighty,
Highty-tighty,
Sudden as a waterfall.
Bees are fatter. What's the matter?
Clap her now or not at all!"

Dobry waited for the Gypsy Bear with a special kind of excitement, because he was going to leave for Sofia on the morning after his bath. The adventure of uprooting himself from the
village made Dobry feel that all of life was too uncertain for
caution. And, impatient for the swim, he plunged into the
Yantra river when the bear plunged in. Dobry swam with the
bear and loafed with him in the water, content to feel himself
a bear instead of the water buffalo Grandfather liked to imagine
himself when taking his spring bath.

Every villager went into the Yantra for a swim and a scrub
with homemade soap, while gypsies ate, drank, fiddled, and
danced on the river bank. Grandfather said, "It may look like
spring but it never feels like spring until we get into the river."
And he drove Hristu's water buffaloes down to the Yantra to get
their spring baths while other peasants danced the Horo in the
village square.

Woodpeckers, yellow hammers, nightingales, woodcrows, all
of them were back in mountain trees. Only the village storks
had not come, and their absence intensified Dobry's feeling that
all of life was moving in a new direction.

Grandfather was to drive Dobry as far as the mill town in the
morning and see him off for Sofia. And after taking the buffaloes
to the river, Grandfather busied himself in the courtyard, washing down Sari and Pernik before combing them out, polishing
their horns, and greasing their hoofs. Dobry found him at work
there and offered to help. Grandfather looked up from his
scrubbing: "What the devil?" he cried. "You just had your bath

303

and you must keep yourself clean for the trip tomorrow. All the soap in the village is used up, and you and I have to be off before daybreak. And I love it—but love it—to get oxen ready for a journey." He went on, excitedly scrubbing Pernik's flank.

Dobry left him, went into the kitchen, and took a stool. His mother was kneading bread. She kneaded and perspired, kneaded and perspired, her long braids pinned back out of the way. She said to him:

"I'll make an enormous ring of bread. You can carry it on your arm. I'll put the cheese bread in your basket with the other things. I have everything on my mind today. Besides all the special cooking for your baskets, I must get around to washing everything up fresh for your bundles. There's so little time left now. We all stayed too long in the river."

"I'll haul the water," Dobry said and got up.

"You! You must do nothing today except keep yourself clean for the journey," Roda said emphatically and slapped the bread into an enormous circle with her vigorous slaps.

Dobry went out the kitchen door, feeling that he had stopped being Dobry and become only a boy who was leaving the world for a place called Sofia. He felt separated from everything that belonged to his life.

The locust trees were in bloom up and down the village streets. "Locusts in bloom and still no storks!" Dobry thought. He climbed up a steep canyon, hoping to find Asan and the village cows in its top meadow, but instead found a dran bush there, covered with late flowers because of the altitude and crowded around by pine trees. Dobry threw himself on the young wild grass under the dran bush, put his head on its roots, and looked up from its cloud of dran blossoms to a cloud topping a mountain peak.

"Everything is one," he thought. "All the same thing—earth, everything—One. And I'm a part of it all." He thought about *Hadutzi-dare* and said to himself: "Mountains cannot say "No" to me. Rivers stop to let me pass, valleys are my servants. The darkest canyon gives me a present."

He lay there until day, drawing up strength from the earth.

304

A whirring, rattling noise startled him. Dobry jumped up, threw his cap to the sky. All the village storks—the mayor's stork, the blacksmith's storks, the coppersmith's storks, the two storks that belonged in Neda's courtyard, his own storks, circled the forest sky and headed down for the village. Dobry broke off heavy dran branches, ran down the mountain alongside a torrent, and burst into the shoemaker's courtyard.

Neda looked up, startled. She was dressed afresh after her river bath in blue cotton, green aproned. And little wet braids shone on her forehead. She was making cakes for Dobry's journey baskets in the courtyard oven and, in her anxiety for the goodness of the little cakes, had made herself too warm by opening the oven doors oftener than was necessary.

"Look! The dran flowers!" Dobry said to her. "We'll get a whole bucketful of dran berries when we have our Betrothal Feast, instead of the cupful Mother buys from the gypsies every fall. Where's Peter?"

305

Neda took the dran branches and tried to smile up at him.

"Peter?" she asked. "I let him go off to feed with Michael-acky's goats today. All the goats were going to fat grass and I—"

"Never mind," Dobry told her. "I'll see him before I go. It never seemed real to me until today. About going away, I mean. Never!"

Neda closed her eyes and could hardly speak. "But when you come back you'll be a great man—a great artist. Your grandfather says you will be, and Semo tells me that, too."

"Of course," Dobry shook his head. "That's why I'm going. And that's why I'm coming back, too, Neda. Neda!"

THE LITTLE TOY LAND OF THE DUTCH
Author Unknown

Away 'way off 'cross the seas and such
Lies the little flat land of the Dutch, Dutch, Dutch!
Where the green toy meadows stretch off to the sea
With a little canal where a fence ought to be,
Where the windmills' arms go round, round, round,
And sing to the cows with a creaky sound,
Where storks live up in the chimney top,
And wooden shoes pound plop, plop, plop,
Where little toy houses stand in a row,
And dog carts clattering past them go,
Where milk cans shine in the shiniest way,
And the housemaids scrub, scrub, scrub all day,
Where dikes keep out the raging sea,
And shut in the land as cozy as can be,
Oh, that little toy land I like so much,
That prim little, trim little land of the Dutch!

ABDUL AZIZ, an Arab boy living in Tunisia, North Africa, journeyed southward to live with Si Maror, his grandfather, and the Bedouin tribe of his mother Kadijah's people. With the Son of Satan, a funny stray donkey whom Abdul Aziz rescued from starvation on the desert, he began a fascinating new life; riding camels, driving sheep, and making new friends.

Eunice Tietjens

DESERT ADVENTURE

ILLUSTRATED BY *Hazel Frazee*

IT WAS one hot day not so long after this that a new adventure, and a surprising one, befell the boy. Partly, he thought afterwards, it was his own fault. He should not have gone so far away from camp with Youssef's camels. But he was curious to see what lay to the southward, across the silver line of the track of the iron caravan. So when Youssef asked him to pasture his six camels the boy drove them southward across the plain, leaving the city of Kairouan away to the right and behind him. He had chosen to ride the Son of Satan, rather than one of the rocking camels.

The adventure began after he had crossed the tracks and found nothing but the same desert plain, except that he saw ahead a little rise of rougher country. Four Bedouins mounted on tall camels, who were also going southward, came up with him from behind. Abdul Aziz saw them coming, but thought little of it. The country is at peace under the French and travelers, meeting one another on the desert, speak and pass on. But

307

when these men came close to him he did not like their faces. Especially the leader, an unusually tall man even for a Bedouin, with a deep scar across his right cheek, looked at the boy in a most unfriendly way. Nevertheless the boy spoke politely.

"May Allah protect you," he called as they came near.

But the leader did not return the greeting. Instead he gave an order in a low voice to his followers, who presently to Abdul Aziz' dismay spread out and began to urge Youssef's camels forward at a swifter pace. The boy felt a sudden sinking in the pit of his stomach. The men were robbers! He looked quickly about for help, but the great plain was empty as far as his eye could reach. Then his courage returned, his cheeks grew very red, and he spoke bravely, like a man.

"These are the camels of Youssef ben Mohammed," he said. "By Sidi Okbar, you would best leave them alone! The Ouled ben Idress can protect their own!"

But the leader spoke now in a harsh voice. "A fig for the Ouled ben Idress! We need the camels and we shall take them."

"Sons of perdition, may you roast in four fires!" cried the boy. "Wait till my grandfather the sorcerer gets after you!"

But it was no use. The leader only eyed him coldly and drew a French pistol from his robe.

"As for you," he said coldly, "if we leave you here, you will spread the alarm, which would not suit me. I am considering what to do with you." And he balanced the pistol in his hand.

The boy's heart gave a great leap . . . . But then a sort of calm came over him. "Maktoub! What is to be, is written," he thought. "Here I shall die."

But one of the other men spoke up quickly.

"The French are very finicky," he said. "It would go hard with us if they caught us. Let us rather take the boy with us. He is too young to do us harm."

The other men agreed in gutturals. For an instant the leader hesitated; then he put away the pistol.

"So be it!" he said at last. "Go forward with the camels quietly, and all will be well. But make us trouble and—" he tapped the pistol meaningly.

Abdul Aziz' heart began to beat . . . in great throbs that shook him painfully. But he had no choice.

"I will go," was all he said.

The robber Bedouins urged their mounts and the captured camels of Youssef forward at a smart pace towards the southward. With them, since he could not help it, rode Abdul Aziz on the Son of Satan. The boy's heart was like a hot stone in him, and his head buzzed like a whole hive of bees. But he went silently, making no further protest.

Very soon they reached the stretch of higher ground, where the going was more difficult. And here, looking down in front of him, the boy saw a great white glittering plain, with edges like a lake and smooth as a floor. It stretched away to the far horizon.

He was riding near the end of the cavalcade, and the man who had taken his part chanced to be near. The boy dared not speak, but he looked inquiringly at the man, whom the others had called Mahmoud. The robber answered the unspoken question.

"Salt!" he said tersely.

It was indeed the dry bed of a great salt lake from which the fierce sun had sucked up all the water. When they had come down upon it, the boy saw that the white glitter was caused by a thick coating of hard salt. On it the feet of the Son of Satan made a crackling sound. Once, when they had dismounted for a moment, he broke a piece of the crust and found it two or three inches thick.

Over this level ground they made good time and by nightfall had covered many a weary mile. Towards the last the little Son of Satan lagged painfully, in spite of all the boy's urging, and when they finally stopped for the night, still on the featureless salt plain, the boy took his skin bag of water and gave the last drops to the donkey which looked gratefully at him out of tired eyes.

At the place where the robbers had stopped, some dried camels' dung lay on the salty ground. Of this they made a little fire and brewed themselves tea. Mahmoud gave the boy a drink of this and a handful of dates, for Abdul Aziz' lunch had been eaten long ago, and he had no other food. Then they hobbled the camels, tying their feet together as Amor ben Nila had tied the feet of his bubbling camel before the gates of Hammamet, wrapped themselves in their bournouses and lay down to sleep. But before doing so, one of the men bound the boy securely with a rope, fastening his hands behind him and his feet together. Poor Abdul Aziz was almost choking with rage, but he submitted quietly enough. It would have been folly to struggle. He waited till all was still, then tried furiously to free himself. But it was no use. The ropes were too firmly tied. And after a while, overcome by a great weariness, the boy also slept, under the wide and quiet stars that take no count of human good and evil.

The next morning the men waked before dawn and, after eating a few more dates, set off as before. Abdul Aziz, stiff and sore as he was from his bonds, climbed on one of Youssef's camels, knowing his weight too much for the little donkey on such a long journey. And the donkey, free now of his burden, went more easily.

So another day passed, and another night. The second day was as the first, save that in the afternoon they passed the edge of the salt lake and camped more comfortably beside a well, where they all drank their fill. The country here was gently rolling, and once in a while they passed a spot of green where a house stood and a few bushes grew. Here, as in most places in Tunisia, where the soil has water it is fertile enough.

Here too there were roads, and now and again people passed them, Arabs going to market, or moving Bedouins like themselves. Once, too, a swift French motorcar tore past, scattering the camels like scared chickens. The leader shook his closed fist after the car with a curse for the "pigs of infidels." But his captors spoke to no one, and the boy dared not make a sign.

On the second morning the boy saw not far away a huge gaunt structure of gray stone which reared great ruined arches into the cloudless sky. He looked at it in amazement. In this open country it rose almost like a small mountain, a mountain made by man, and long since abandoned. Abdul Aziz had seen near Hammamet small crumbling ruins which his father explained had been left by a race of Roumis—they were really the ancient Romans—who had once ruled this country centuries before. The boy now guessed that here was a greater ruin of the same sort, and he wished to go closer to look at it.

But his captors passed close beside it and went on. Yet for hours as they went, the boy could look back from the tops of little rises and see the gaunt arches against the horizon. He counted it a landmark, and he determined to explore it if ever he could get back.

This day the Bedouins traveled more slowly. Evidently their fear of pursuit had lessened with time. They seemed in a better

HAZEL FRAZEE

humor, and even the fierce leader with the scarred face jested once or twice. The boy gathered from their talk that they were nearing their own tribe after a journey which had taken them far north of where he had met them. He decided that they had only gathered in Youssef's camels by the way.

But now the boy had formed a plan of escape, and towards evening he acted on it. For several hours he complained bitterly of weariness—which he did not really feel—until the leader told him harshly to keep quiet. When they stopped finally beside a trickle of water he slid heavily from his camel, fell in a sprawling heap and lay still, feigning the sleep of utter exhaustion. Mahmoud, who was kinder than the others, shook him gently to give him dates and water, but he made no sign. The robbers then left him and lit their own fire. Before they slept, the leader came to the motionless figure and turned it over roughly with his foot. Still Abdul Aziz did not move; only he gave a deep sigh. One of the men bound him as he had done the two nights before; but this time he was careless, thinking the boy too tired to move.

When all was quiet Abdul Aziz began slowly, moving as quietly as a hunting animal, to free himself from his bonds. It was slow work and painful, for even in his carelessness the robber had made the knots firmly. But this time it was possible. After what seemed to the boy an eternity he got one hand free. The rest was easier, and at last it was accomplished.

Still the boy did not at first rise, but lay taking stock of his position. There was a small moon shining, and by its light he could see objects near him. The Bedouins, sleeping in a little group, lay only a few feet from him. He knew they slept lightly, like all healthy creatures who live close to nature. Further away the camels knelt, all but one which was moving slowly about in its hobbled fashion. Beyond the robbers the little Son of Satan stood, its legs also tied together, its head hanging down, and its eyes closed.

Slowly, very slowly, Abdul Aziz began to crawl along the ground. Once one of the men turned over, and the boy held his breath in fear. But the robber did not wake, and presently the boy started on again. He made no sound on the sandy soil as he circled past the sleeping men and came to the little animal. He knew that he could go further and more surely if he took the camel, but he loved the donkey, and he chose his friend.

When he had come quite close he stood up beside the donkey, laid his hand on the animal's nose, and whispered softly into its long ear. He was in mortal terror lest the Son of Satan should bray, and so lose all. But his fuzzy friend only opened his eyes and looked at him quietly. The boy stooped, and after some difficulty loosened the rope that tied his feet. Then he put his arm around the donkey's neck and began quietly to lead him to safety.

So they stole away. And fate was kind. The cool night covered them, and the robbers slept on. When they were finally out of sight Abdul Aziz mounted the donkey and urged him to a trot. His pet seemed to understand and, tired as it was, it set off smartly towards the north.

After an hour the boy felt that he was safe. He leaned over and spoke to the Son of Satan.

"Now," he said, "we are even. I saved your life, and you are saving mine, for without you I could never reach home. When we get back, I shall buy you five whole kilos of carrots!" Then he added as an afterthought, "And if you really are my protecting djinni, may Allah reward you as a djinni should be rewarded!"

For a while longer they traveled on. But after all they were only a boy and a young donkey, and when the small moon set they were too weary to go further. So the boy chose a little gully where they would not be noticed and dismounted. Here they both fell sound asleep, and when they waked, the sun was already high in the heavens.

The donkey breakfasted on some young cactus that grew beside the way, but Abdul Aziz, who had had no supper the night before, was ravenously hungry. He felt a corner of his bournous where he had tied up a franc before leaving camp, and found to his delight that it was still safe. The robbers had not thought it worth while to search him. But the franc could not be used

HAZEL FRAZEE

today if he was to eat on the white salt lake. So he begged Arab bread and some carobs from an obliging farmer's wife in a place where there was water.

Then they set out on the long way home.

A little after noon the boy saw on the horizon the great ruined building which had made him so curious the day before. "This time I shall look at it," said Abdul Aziz to himself, and steered towards it across the plain.

But it was farther away than it looked, and it kept retreating uncomfortably before them, so that the sun had almost set before they reached it. Seen against the sunset glow, the great gaunt arches, set in a huge oval, seemed to reach into the sky,

314

making the cluster of squat Arab houses around its base look not much higher than toadstools.

The people who lived in the houses must all have been at supper, for the boy saw no one, and he and the Son of Satan trotted up unnoticed to a great hole on one side where the arches are broken down. Here there was a barbed wire, but the two of them slipped under it and went in.

Abdul Aziz looked about him. And suddenly he seemed to himself to shrink; to grow small and most insignificant. The place was so gigantic, and it was so lonely!

In it, when it was new, sixty thousand people could sit on great banks of marble seats, crowned by the gaunt arches, to watch tremendous spectacles in the arena below. Here gladiators fought, and chariot races were run. Here tawny African lions shook their manes. And to this amphitheater, twenty miles from the sea, water was brought by an underground passage to turn the arena into a lake for naval fights and pageants. For this huge coliseum of El Djem was built by the ancient Romans when centuries ago they conquered and ruled all of North Africa. And then it did not stand, as it does today, on an arid empty plain, for this same plain was green with gardens, and cities and villages rose on every side, which centuries ago have been swallowed by the drought and the sand.

All this history Abdul Aziz could not know, but now, crumbling and falling into ruin, in the red light of the sunset glow, the great amphitheater seemed like something more than mortal, as though a race of giants had sported there. And it was lonely with a great loneliness, the loneliness of the dead past as well as of the living present.

The boy's breath came a little short, and he held his head very high as he walked with the Son of Satan into the arena. The donkey's hoofs rang sharp in the stillness, and a flight of bats whirled about them in the twilight.

But the boy was not daunted. He tied the donkey to a stone and set out to explore the ruins. He scrambled over the broken seats and mounted crumbling marble staircases. He went down vaulted hallways, and under the floor of the whole he peered gingerly into dark passageways and little cells which must have been dark even at noonday. Now, in the dusk and the silence, when even the scraping of his own bare feet sounded loud in the stillness, they were doubly strange and eerie. He wondered what the people could have been like who used these passageways; and he shivered a little as the twilight bats whirled out of the darkness and brushed past him.

But in the open space of the arena, where the moon shone and his golden donkey stood waiting, his courage returned.

"Son of Satan," he said, "here we shall pass the night. For if we go into the village, people will ask me questions, and I do not care to see any more strange people just now."

So he looked about for a place to sleep. But, because the floor was uneven and cumbered with broken masonry, he could not at first find a comfortable spot. At last, however, under an archway he found a level space. He hobbled the donkey's feet, wrapped himself in his bournous, and lay down.

But it was long before he slept in his eerie bedroom. The gaunt arches in the moonlight, the tiers on tiers of crumbling seats, and the strange sense of a race of such builders gone like a puff of smoke haunted his imagination. He felt very small and lonely, and wished hard for the shelter of the tent of skins where his mother slept smiling. Even when he fell asleep he was haunted by dreams of a strange people who swarmed over the broken masonry and danced weird dances under the silver moon.

When he wakened, the first gray streak of dawn was showing in the east. He rose stiffly and stretched himself. Then he looked about for the Son of Satan. But the donkey was nowhere to be seen. Abdul Aziz wandered about the ruins, calling. If he had lost his pet so far from camp he would be lost indeed.

Then, from a passageway to the right he heard a thud and a rattle of stones. Quickly he ran in that direction. There in the dusky passage he saw the Son of Satan kicking up his heels in his morning gambol, and out of pure sport trying his hoofs against the piles of rubble on the flooring. As the boy came near, the heels thrashed again, and he heard a sharp crack like

316

that made by breaking pottery. Then the words of his grandfather the sorcerer came to his mind. "When the donkey kicks
in the dawn, look carefully!"

He held his breath with excitement—and looked.

There among the crumbling rubble lay the broken pieces

317

of an ancient pottery jar, and on the ground, in a gleaming shower, lay dozens and dozens of gold pieces, big thick shining gold pieces. And on each of them was the head and super-scription of a Roman emperor gone to dust these many centuries.

Two days later, when the sun was hanging in a golden ball over the sacred city of Kairouan, a boy and a donkey came into the camp of the Ouled ben Idress.

They were tired, but they were happy. The long journey back, over the dried salt lake, had passed without mishap and under his bournous Abdul Aziz was still clutching the cloth—it was part of his shirt—in which he had wrapped the gold pieces.

The camp was quiet when he entered, for the men had not yet returned with the animals. No one saw him coming, and he made straight for the tent of his mother. As he came near, he saw that Kadijah was sitting in the doorway. But she was not working. She sat in a little heap, her face buried in her hands, and his heart beat very quickly, for he knew that she was weeping.

He dismounted—and still she did not raise her head. Then Abdul Aziz ran forward with a glad cry and flung himself upon her. . . .

"Your grandfather told me you were safe. He told me," she said. "But O my son, it was hard to believe!"

A little later, when the camp was alive again, and he was telling for the tenth time the story of the robber Bedouins and of how he had found the gold pieces, he saw his grandfather coming and ran towards him to kiss his robe.

The old man smiled and patted the boy's head. "The djinni told me truth," he said. "The spirit of Moulay ben Idress protected you, and you have done well. But it is not fitting that a small boy should carry with him so much treasure. Give me the gold, and I will sell it for you. In this form we cannot pass it." Then he turned to the other excited Bedouins who stood listening. "And watch your tongues carefully, that no word of this gets to strangers, lest we also meet with robbers."

In the morning the old man went alone to the city. It was late when he returned and sent for Abdul Aziz.

"Son of Kadijah," he said, looking at the boy with his piercing eyes which seemed to look through the boy to something beyond. "You are now the richest among us. Fate was kind and sent a party of tourists from beyond the seas who bought the gold, asking no inconvenient questions. Here is your wealth." And he showed the boy a large package of French banknotes . . . and a saddle of fine embroidered leather, studded with silver. It had a pointed horn in front and a red saddle-cloth to hang over the donkey's rump. "It is a saddle for a blooded mare," he said. "No donkey of the tribe has ever worn one. But the Son of Satan is no ordinary donkey!"

Abdul Aziz was wild with delight and kissed the old man's robe again and again. "May Allah reward you!" he cried with shining eyes.

A Burma adventure definitely
for older readers.

Willis Lindquist

THE CURSE OF KAING

ILLUSTRATED BY *Harry H. A. Burne*

T HE sun rose over the jade-green jungled
hills of Chindwin in Upper Burma, and the day grew warm. But
for Kaya there was no warmth. He shivered as he lay in the dust
of the market place, his hands and feet tied securely with thongs
of bark.

It seemed like a horrible dream from which he must surely
awaken. But the angry, vengeful villagers pressing about the
square, screaming for his death—they were real. And beyond
them lay the desolation and ruin that had once been a village.
That was real, too.

It had been a beautiful little village of *poonghee* houses—
made of bamboo and thatch, and mounted on high stilts—when
Kaya had entered it the night before.

He had meant no harm. He had come with rupees for his
widowed mother, money he had earned as the white master's
servant in the elephant camp. He had known, of course, that
since he bore the curse of kaing it would be unlawful for him
to stay the night. But he had stayed.

He had lived so long with the wise and powerful white
master that he'd lost some of his fear of the strange tribal curse.
The hour had been late. He had not seen his mother since his
father's death, many months ago, and there had been much to
talk about.

She had questioned him about Shwe Kah, the giant bull
elephant his father had ridden. The big tusker had run away
many months ago, he told her. It had killed the *oozies* (elephant

320

riders) sent out to capture it, and now, like a wild beast, it roamed the jungles.

"You could capture him," said his mother. "You are the son of his *oozie*. You played at his feet. It was you who took him to the river for his bath. He would know you and love you as he always did."

"I have tried and failed," Kaya confessed. He had narrowly escaped death on the big tusks by plunging into the river. The rogue elephant hated all men.

Yet, even as Kaya lay tightly bound in the village square, he wondered if Shwe Kah remembered him. Could it be that the elephant had found his scent yesterday, where he'd walked on the road of the bullock carts down through the hills? Had the big beast recognized his smell and trailed him to the village?

It was a possibility, no more. Every now and then wild elephants raided villages to get at the stored rice.

Kaya knew only that Shwe Kah had suddenly come in the night and attacked the village in a frenzy of hate, ramming down the frail *poonghee* houses one after another until he found the rice warehouses and feasted on the new harvest.

Except for an old man and a child, trampled in their sleep, all had escaped to the edge of the river near the pagoda temple and huddled there through the night.

Among the first to search for victims, Kaya had discovered the heap of branches at the edge of a paddy field. He had recognized it at once as a grave made by the elephants and had torn away the branches until he saw that the body within was only that of a pye-dog.

Even in the excitement of raiding a village Shwe Kah had given way to his strong, instinctive urge to cover the dead or helpless. Kaya was not surprised. He himself had been buried alive by a herd of wild elephants in a similar raid sixteen years ago. The witch doctor had said it was a curse upon him and made a prophecy that he was doomed to a life of wretchedness, which could end only when the elephants buried him once again.

It was because of the dreaded curse of kaing that they were

about to try him now as a lowly criminal. The council of elders took seats in a half circle, and the chief elder raised his hand for silence.

"What is the charge against this boy?" he asked.

The *sayah* (witch doctor) stepped forth, dressed in a leopard skin, with a bonnet of horns, and with frog legs and eagle claws tied in his matted hair.

"Oh, noble council of elders, listen well," he began. "This one is possessed of an evil curse. This is he whom the elephants buried when they destroyed our village in the Year of Many Sorrows."

Kaya was jerked to his feet and held between two strong villagers. Somewhere in the pressing throng behind him he could hear the soft wailing of his mother.

"We have a law," continued the sayah, "that forbids those bearing a curse from spending a night in our village. This one slept here last night in the house of his mother. He brought the curse of kaing into this peaceful village. Because of this, noble elders, our beloved Theebaw lies dead, and his child with him. Our village has been destroyed. Our rice crop has been devoured. What further proof of his guilt is needed?"

"Has the prisoner anything to say?" asked the chief elder.

Kaya hung his head. There was nothing he could say. All would believe the sayah, for they feared his mysterious powers.

"He admits his guilt," cried a villager. "Let him die by the spear!"

Cried another, "Tie him to the tree of the biting red ants!"

"Let the crocodiles tear his flesh!"

"Death to him! Death!" chanted the villagers. "He deserves to die."

Kaya sucked in his breath. His heart was hammering. Great beads of perspiration rolled down his slender brown body.

Now the chief elder looked expectantly at the sayah, as if to ask what manner of death would be most fitting.

It was the sayah who would decide his fate. The sayah was the real ruler here, the one feared by all. And suddenly Kaya saw a slender ray of hope.

322

"Noble elders," he said. "It is not in your power to kill me.
The chief blinked at him. "What is this you say?"

"You cannot kill me." Kaya licked the dust from his dry lips.
"Did not the sayah predict that I would be buried again by
elephants? How could the prophecy come to pass if you killed
me now?"

The chief elder squirmed uncomfortably. He had no wish to
offend the powerful man of dark magic. "We have not yet
decided the punishment."

The sayah, too, looked a bit unhappy by the sudden turn of
things. "It was in my mind," he said with great dignity, "that
there are punishments worse than death. Which of you," he
asked the elders, "would not rather choose death than to live
your days under the evil curse of kaing?"

"Truly, the sayah is wise," muttered the chief elder.

"This boy must go free to fulfill his horrible fate. But—" He
paused, dug into his bag of charms and evil magic and came up
with a dried lizard, suspended on the string. This he hung about
the neck of Kaya.

"He shall wear this as a sign of his evil curse, so that all may
avoid him. And I, myself, with a party of villagers, shall lead
him back to the elephant camp and make known the evil he
has brought to us here."

On the following day, far up in the hills above the Valley
of Ten Villages, a strange procession entered the busy elephant

camp. Far behind them, burdened with cooking things, came Kaya's mother.

To all the excited oozies who gathered quickly around them the sayah told what had happened. "This one you call Kaya brings evil among you," he warned. "So long as he lives in this camp there will be much trouble and sickness and death. Even now the evil of his curse spreads over you."

The eyes of the oozies shone whitely as they glanced at each other. "It is even so. He casts an evil spell," said one. "His father died of a mysterious ailment. His father's elephant went mad. Now his home village has been destroyed."

"We shall banish him from the camp," declared another. "Let him wander in the jungle with the mad elephant Shwe Kah. Such as he is not fit to live among men and good elephants."

There were loud and angry rumblings of approval.

Kaya stiffened. These were his people, with whom he had lived and worked. Even though they feared the curse many of them had been kind. But now—now they would have him banished. All his dreams of becoming an oozie, of commanding an elephant and working him in the teak forest—all this would be denied him.

Tears stung his eyes as they caught him roughly and took him to the hut of the white master. The lean Englishman met them at the doorway, and as he listened to their demands his sandy brows came down in a scowl.

"I'll see the boy in my office," he said, holding the door for Kaya.

Once the door had closed behind them the Englishman's scowl vanished. "Looks like you've got yourself into a peck of trouble, young man."

He cut the bonds from Kaya's arms and rubbed the circulation back into them. Then he ordered food. Kaya ate out of politeness, for his hunger had left him.

"I once told your father I'd keep an eye on you. But this curse business—" The white master lifted his hands and let them fall again. "Tell me, how did it begin?"

Kaya swallowed. "I was but a few months old. A wild elephant herd raided our village. Our house fell. I rolled in the street before them, and they covered me with sticks and branches, as they cover the dead. The sayah said I was cursed from that day."

"Oh, he did!" The Englishman's scowl was back again. "There's nothing very remarkable about you being buried by the elephants. It's like a fever with some of them. Shwe Kah had it bad. It seems to me he was always covering something or other."

Kaya smiled faintly, remembering the strange urge that made Shwe Kah forget everything else when he came upon a dead or helpless animal in the jungle. "Once he covered a wounded samba deer. I could not stop him."

"All this rubbish about a curse!" snorted the Englishman. "It was all invented in the mean little mind of that rascal out there who calls himself a witch doctor."

The Englishman had said such things before, but now, somehow, it disturbed Kaya to hear it. "Perhaps there really is no curse, but thakin (white master) does not understand the strange power of the sayah. If he says there is a curse it is enough. The people believe and tremble."

"I don't question that." The Englishman lit his pipe. "It's all superstitious nonsense, nonetheless. He holds you all in his power. He didn't come up here now to protect these people from you. He came to frighten them into buying his dirty little charms for all the money he can squeeze out of them."

Kaya began to have hope. "Is there something we can do, thakin?"

The Englishman shook his head. "I'm afraid not. I'm sorry, Kaya. The oozies are frightened. They fear that crow-bait witch doctor and his curses more than they do me. If I refuse to send you away they'll take their families and move out. Where would I be then? I can't say I blame them much. They have their families to—"

There was a cry at the door. The head oozie burst into the hut. "Thakin, come!" he cried breathlessly. "The mad bull Shwe Kah! He is down by the tamarinds. He came after me, and it was only by a miracle that I escaped."

"That settles it!" The Englishman strode to the wall and took down his rifle. "Since we can't capture him, there's only one thing to do."

"No!" Suddenly Kaya stood between him and the door. "Do not shoot him, thakin. He was my father's elephant."

"There is no other way."

"If I capture him."

"Don't be foolish!" snapped the white master.

"But there is a way! There is a way!" Kaya cried. Quickly, he told how it could be done.

For an instant the Englishman's face froze in horror. "You don't know what you're saying. That's—that's suicide. Do you think I'd allow—"

Kaya made a dash for the door. "I go, thakin. Of what value is my life to anyone?"

"Stop him!" shouted the white master. "Stop that boy!"

But Kaya had already slipped around the hut and entered the jungle. For a time he ran swiftly along the high ridge, leaping over the stumps and teak logs with joyous bounds.

The whirling white madness within him gave him wings. He was the wind in the treetops, a cloud before a storm, the swirling white waters under the falls of Chit See. Nothing could stop

him now. He would serve the only two friends he had ever known—the white master and mighty elephant Shwe Kah.

He came to the smooth towing path used by the elephants for dragging the logs to the river. Parakeets rose up before him in noisy, green-swirling flocks.

He took the good free air deeply into his lungs and plunged down a slope into green jungle twilight. Somewhere a samba deer belled to its mate. Monkeys raced high overhead in the leafy crowns of the jungle roof. Life was sweet. It was good, and Shwe Kah would live to enjoy it for many years.

Presently, Kaya paused to listen. Then he heard it again, the flopping of elephant ears, and the tearing and breaking and blowing sounds of a feeding elephant. Cutting over a nullah, he circled to windward so Shwe Kah could smell him. He began shouting to attract the beast.

Three twangy reports rang through the jungle. Shwe Kah was pounding his trunk on the ground as a warning.

Kaya's heart beat faster. He kept going ahead, kept calling until the great beast, with a squeal of rage, came crashing toward him through thickets of bamboo.

Suddenly the magnificent animal came into sight. It burst through the green jungle wall of vines and creepers and bamboo and stood for a moment, ears forward, mighty tusks gleaming in naked splendor.

Then it saw Kaya. Up came the great trunk in the coiled position of attack, and the beast charged.

For an instant Kaya stood rooted, sudden terror gripping him. This time there was no river into which he could plunge. There could be no thought of escaping. Did he have the courage?

He turned and ran. Toward the nullah he fled, running with every ounce of his strength.

Behind him the crashing sounds grew louder. The elephant would soon overtake him, he knew. There was so little time.

He reached the small clearing he had spotted earlier, the end of the trail, the place for an elephant grave.

He stumbled, fell heavily to the ground. He made no effort to rise.

Shwe Kah came on like an avalanche, closer and closer, until the sounds of the savage charge became a thunder in Kaya's ears. He closed his eyes tighter.

Panic beat wildly in his chest. His body quivered. He caught in a breath of air, like a great sob, and held it.

For a horrible, nightmarish instant, the earth quaked beneath him with furious impact.

Then the sounds faded. Kaya let out his breath. The elephant had charged right over his body.

With a bellow of rage it wheeled, came rushing back. Once again the earth quaked. A giant pad smashed down inches from his nose. Earth exploded in his face, choked him.

Again and again the big tusker charged, trumpeting, stamping furiously. But Kaya had seen such savage elephant dances before. He moved not a muscle, for he knew that any attempt to escape would bring instant death under the big pads. All his hopes rested on one fact—that he had never known an elephant to trample or harm a motionless thing.

After an eternity the attacks ceased and Shwe Kah, true to his instincts, began building an elephant grave.

The weight of branches over the boy grew. Kaya kept his eyes expectantly on the edge of the clearing. As the elephant went farther in search of branches the oozies slipped out from the brush and spread snares on the ground about the grave, working quickly and quietly.

Almost at once, it seemed to Kaya, it happened. The jungle erupted with screams of a terrified elephant. Shwe Kah was frantic. His hind legs had been securely snared by a steel rope. And as he turned and struggled one of his front legs was caught, too.

Down he went. Oozies came swarming out of the jungle, casting more snares until the big bull was completely helpless.

"Are you all right, boy?" the Englishman asked anxiously as he helped Kaya out of the grave. "Thank heaven! You gave me a bad turn, boy."

"Look, thakin," Kaya pointed to a group coming from the camp. "There comes that rascal witch doctor." He raised his voice. "Hail to the great sayah whose prophecies always come true! He foretold how my curse would not die till I was buried again in an elephant grave. Now it has come to pass!"

He tore the ugly black lizard from his neck and held it high. "The curse is dead as the sayah foretold. I am free! Hail to the great sayah!"

The sayah looked as though he were about to choke. But the people about him were shouting and hailing him joyously. The curse was dead. They had nothing to fear, and that was reason enough for rejoicing.

The white master caught Kaya's urgent glance and he seemed to know exactly what had to be said.

"After this who can doubt the sayah's power of prophecy?" he declared loudly. "His fame, from this day, will surely spread to far villages."

Dark displeasure faded from the sayah's wrinkled face. He drew himself up just a little taller and accepted the lizard from Kaya's hand with great dignity.

"It was this very elephant grave that I saw clearly in a vision many years ago when I made the prophecy," he announced solemnly.

Later, the white master chuckled over it as he took Kaya back to camp. "The old rascal knows the value of his new fame. He'll make a pretty penny on it. You had it all figured out, didn't you?"

"No, thakin. I was only thinking of Shwe Kah. But in the elephant grave I remembered that the prophecy was fulfilled. My fear was that the sayah might deny it, so I gave him the hail."

The Englishman laughed until his face grew red.

"Now I am free," said Kaya, choking with new-found happiness. "No more curses. I must find my mother and tell her this."

Phillis Garrard

THE FERN TIKI

ILLUSTRATED BY *Gladys Peck*
and Eleanor Osborne Eadie

UR-UR-UMPH! Wass today?" groaned Hilda, slowly waking. "Wassmatter with today? Oh, not arithmetic test! It's *not!*"

But of course it was. And there was a steady rain falling, too. So the only reason Hilda didn't roll disgustedly out of bed on the wrong side was that her bed was against the window and she couldn't without landing on a very thorny rosebush. But the effects were there just the same. Such as:

Pyjamas, wrenched off savagely, went flying over the foot of the bed. A sock with a huge hole in the heel arrived disgraced in a far corner. A comb caught in short red-gold locks, then bounced away in terror and slithered under the dressing table to hide until the storm blew over—which it didn't, for from the bathroom issued no cheerful morning whistle, but only snorts and grunts, mingled with outrageous splashing.

At the breakfast table matters failed to improve, in spite of eggs and bacon, golden toast and marmalade, and the serene presence of Mrs. Luke, the housekeeper, who took the place of the mother that Hilda couldn't remember.

"Where's Dad?" mumbled Hilda, spearing bacon with a spiteful fork.

332

"Your father went with Ernest over to the far paddock to look at the yearling lambs. He thinks feed's getting a bit short there. But this rain will do good."

"Good?" snorted Hilda. "And here's me, got to wear my oilskins to go to school in, and it's so darned muggy and hot I'll be boiled alive."

Mrs. Luke, steering the marmalade in Hilda's direction, made sympathetic sounds that probably meant "You poor lamb!"

"And they never caught Roger for me before they went, did they? No, of course they didn't."

Mrs. Luke, looking as if she wished she could serve up Roger, ready saddled and bridled, along with the breakfast, made still more sympathetic noises.

Hilda jabbed a piece of bacon. "And I'll just bet you twenty million pounds he's at the farthest, farthest end of the paddock taking a mud bath."

She glared from bacon to Lukey. The latter said, "My *poor* lamb!" and hurriedly pushed the toast, the mustard, the bacon dish, the butter, the flower vase, and the pepper towards the cranky thirteen-year-old, who certainly was not requiring any pepper *this* morning.

In awful silence Hilda finished breakfast. Grimly she arrayed herself in the hated oilskins, sou'wester and gum-boots. Stonily she took her waterproof schoolbag, stuffed with books and sandwiches, from the kind hands of Mrs. Luke. Patiently she accepted her parting kiss. "Take care of yourself, pet."

It was gloomily gratifying to find that her horse Roger the Red really was away down by the creek and that his chestnut coat showed he had indeed been rolling in the mud. He followed Hilda to the stable meekly as she strode sternly ahead. She brushed him vigorously and pulled his girths up so sharply that he bunted a twitching nose against her elbow.

But he was a good-natured horse and covered the three and a quarter miles of New Zealand bush roads from the sheep farm to the district public school in the little township at quick, steady trot and easy canter. Hilda left him to himself, for weighty matters oppressed her. This arithmetic test!

333

Well, no one could say Mac, their classmaster, hadn't warned them. Why, he'd been hurling the miserable thing at their heads for about three weeks. Yet naturally one hadn't bothered. There had been swimming, gardening, tennis, and riding picnics on Saturdays since the warm weather came. Now it was the horrid day. And what did Hilda know about sums, proportion, decimalization of money, and measures of area and volume?

Almost nothing. And what had Mac sternly said regarding those who should fail to get at least fifty per cent of marks?

Plenty, for a man sparing of his words. And what would be her probable marks?

About thirty-seven with luck. Well, what could one do?

One could and did snap at one's best chum, black-haired Mary, who had arrived at the school paddock before her, and was just giving her big pony Sambo a parting smack as he moved off, grazing.

"Why the dickens didn't you wait for me at the crossroads this morning?"

"Why, Hilda, you know we always said if either of us started late we should go straight on 'cos the other'd be ahead, and our clock said—"

"Don't care what your clock said."

"Oh, all right, crank!"

"I'm *not* cranky!" Hilda tramped into the saddle shed. "Alec, *must* you put your saddle on my peg?"

"I must," said innocent-eyed Alec solemnly.

"I'd just like to know why."

"Just to see your little face all aglow with smiles." He dodged with a snort of laughter as his saddle came hurtling down off its peg, barely missing his fair head. Hilda followed up its dislodgment with a kick, and began hoisting her own gear in its place.

Alec, on vengeance bent, came softly behind her and suddenly seized her wrist, twisting her arm back with a jerk. The scuffle that followed was hardly the best preparation for a demure entrance to Mr. Macdonald's classroom, nor for a quiet and studious frame of mind.

334

The arithmetic test was certainly horrid. "Simplify the fractions . . ." "Reduce to a decimal . . ." "Find the value of . . ." And more. And worse. Hilda counted on her fingers, mopped her brow, tugged her short curls, and made faces at Mac, who looked quite pleased with himself (or so she fancied). She closed her woeful attempts at answers by drawing a row of cats with dismal faces and drooping whiskers across the bottom of her paper. Then she surveyed her classmates gloomily. How wretchedly busy they were! Rows of girls' bobs and wavy locks and plaits, and the rough thatches of the boys, all fervently bent to their work.

At ten o'clock Mac said cheerfully: "Dick and Helen, collect the papers, please. I'll correct them as soon as I can and let you know your marks before school closes this afternoon." He smiled blandly, having just caught sight of Hilda's dismal cats as Dick, with monitorial zeal, popped an untidy sheaf of foolscap down before him. "Hullo, whose paper is that? Hilda's? Why the decorations? This wasn't a drawing test, you know."

"I know that, sir," said the artist grumpily.

"I suppose the questions weren't difficult enough to take all your energies?" suggested Mr. Macdonald, and the class grinned. Hilda did not.

Nor did she at a quarter to three that afternoon, when the marks were read out. Mac said briefly that a person who only made 32½ per cent (the lowest of the class) in an easy arithmetic test was obviously in need of special coaching. He wasn't keen on giving up time to her, but saw nothing for it but half an hour after school for a few days.

So she and Mac did not part company until 3:35 that afternoon. Then Hilda, sizzling with resentment, strode off to find Roger, and Mac betook himself to tennis. "And I hope he muffs every ball," was the muttered benediction of his victim.

The rain had stopped long ago, and the sun was out. Once in the saddle, Hilda did not feel like going straight home, especially as Mary had not been able to wait for her. So she turned into the road that led down to the gorge of the Rangitiki and soon heard the river leaping boulders and pouring its hurried waters between the wooded cliffs that towered densely green on either side. There was a bridge here, but the ford a hundred yards or so below it was Hilda's favorite crossing-place.

Roger, after pausing for a drink, splashed carefully across the river. The swift water was running high, due to heavy spring rains upcountry. Hilda had to draw her knees up as he waded through one of the eddying, rock-bordered pools. They gained the opposite bank, where there was a little stony beach. Hilda slipped down, hung the reins to a tree's projecting root, and started off on a fossil hunt.

The Rangitiki was a grand place for fossils, and many had she found among the stones of its banks and beaches. The smooth black imprints of fishlike skeletons or of fluted, petrified shells on stones and pebbles fascinated her. She had a small boxful at home. She walked slowly along the beach, turning up likely-looking stones and kicking slabs of broken rock.

A stout, short-legged pony, ridden by a small boy and a smaller girl, trotted down to the ford and began crossing. Hilda scowled. Johnny and Janie Higgins were nice enough kids, though plain and awkward, and were inclined to be admirers of herself in their silly little way. This should have endeared them to her, of course, but it didn't always. They were rather nuisances sometimes.

Just now she felt annoyed with them. Their pony wasn't really big enough to ford the river; they had disturbed her solitude, which, being in sulks, she was cherishing; they would be sure to stay and chatter.

No, pony didn't much like the ford. He shook his head, stepped gingerly, blew and snorted as the current whirled under his nose and around his riders' bare legs.

"Why don't you kids cross by the bridge?" Hilda asked crossly, as the pony clambered up the stony beach at last.

Janie for the moment was tongue-tied. Johnny spoke up with a self-conscious giggle. "Well, *you* came over by the ford, didn't you?"

"That's different. My horse is bigger than your pony. And why do what I do?"

"We don't!" they cried together.

Hilda turned her back on them. "You'd better hurry and go home. It's getting late," she flung over her shoulder.

"Weren't you kept in this afternoon, Hilda?" asked tactless Janie. "I saw you and that awful Mr. Macdonald coming out of school after we'd been to the grocer's. It's too bad. He's always keeping you in."

Hilda relieved her feelings by pitching a big stone into the river. "It's nothing to do with you. Anyway, he *isn't* always keeping me in. 'Bye, kids. Trot along home!"

"Well, I think he's mean. What are you looking for, Hilda? Can't we help?"

"No, you can't. Good-bye," said the ungracious one decidedly.

They trailed off, turning reproachful eyes in her direction, but she did not look round until the rattle of their pony's hooves on the pebbles had changed to die-away thuddings on the road above. "Why, they'd have messed around forever if I'd let 'em. And it's so nice here alone."

Truly there was plenty of room to be alone. High above her head the dark native bush climbed the gorge, tall spires of trees, creepers twining thickly, tree-ferns throwing out huge fronds as they had done in dim, prehistoric forests. No sound but the rushing river and one bellbird chiming somewhere.

But Hilda's temper was not cured yet, which accounted for her seizing a hefty stone and smashing it down upon a greenish-gray boulder that lay in her path. The boulder split into several pieces, and she stared in astonishment. Were her eyes playing tricks? Or did one of the broken pieces of rock hold the perfect black silhouette of a fern leaf, even to a short bit of stalk?

Here at her feet was the most beautiful, the most rare fossil she had ever seen. Magic! Ferns—all kinds—all sizes—everywhere in the bush, and now a fern deep within the rock, too! And how long had it been there? Through how many springs?

That evening her father was very interested in her find. "That must be marlstone," he said. "I've heard of fossil ferns being found near the mouth of the Waikato River, but I didn't know our good old Rangitiki produced them. Going to present it to a museum, Tuppence?"

"No, *sir!*" said Hilda, shaking her short curls. "I'll keep it for luck."

"That little fern left a good impression of itself, didn't it?" mused Daddy, gazing at the smooth black tracery embedded in the stone he held. "It grew beautiful and straight and never guessed that anyone would be looking at it thousands or perhaps millions of years afterwards. What ages since it uncurled its fronds in the damp, jungly, primeval forest. You'd better take it to school to show Mr. Macdonald tomorrow, Miss Geologist."

"I might throw it at his head if I did," giggled Hilda, for she didn't feel like showing it to anyone just yet.

She awoke next morning with her father's sentence repeating itself in her head. *That little fern left a good impression of itself.* Such a lovely day! Sunshine, sweet breeze, deep blue sky. She whistled shrilly in her bath; was all smiles at breakfast; cheerfully ate a second helping of porridge. Roger, when

338

she went to catch him, was in frisky mood. He kicked up his heels and galloped around the paddock. Hilda laughed, munching an apple, and waited patiently until he tired of the fun and let her slip a rope on his neck. "Here's half an apple for you, circus horse!"

Mary was at the crossroads, mounted on fat Sambo. "Nice of you to wait, Mary. Are we late? Mac'll be boiling."

"If he's boiling, we may get scalded," was her chum's dry remark.

"Say, Mary, what a bonzer, splendiferous day! I feel just great." She tweaked Roger's mane. Aha! Mary didn't know about the magic fossil fern.

When Hilda, lugging her saddle, entered the sadd̲l̲e̲ there was Master Alec ahead of her again. putting his gear on her peg, he must needs batics, put himself there too, and was sittin̲ at her. "Peg engaged, Hilda."

She heaved a resigned sigh, finger on t

"Mary, why is it that yonder grinning youth reminds me strangely of an extremely foolish hen?"

The bystanders giggled and gave it up. "Because," said Hilda solemnly, "a silly hen sits on addled eggs and Alec sits on saddle pegs."

That fixed Alec. He had to laugh and leave his perch.

Second lesson was composition, and—oh, shocks and shivers! —Hilda had clean forgotten to write her homework essay. Too much fern excitement last night, of course. "No, sir, I didn't write it. I forgot."

"You must stay after school and do it then," said Mac, looking stern.

Hilda grinned. "I'm staying in already. For arithmetic, you know, sir." Then—what was it that got into her? what grown-up, detached sort of feeling that made her add, "Are the sentences to run con-concurrently?"

Those of the class who understood, giggled. Those who didn't, gaped. If that wasn't enough to make Mac rummage for his seldom-used "tawse" as he called the school strap, what was? Hilda remained calm, however.

Mr. Macdonald himself had a rather interested look on his brown, straight features as he studied his saucy pupil. "More or less. We'll see," he said, and smiled.

Hilda was elated. In some funny way she felt as if she had been one grownup speaking to another. That fossil fern must really be bringing her good luck.

After school Mac was very good. He yarned away about words, their origins, their history, their true meanings. Hilda was astonished to learn that even the word "cat" was about two thousand years old. He didn't make her do any work and dismissed her after only twenty minutes. Marvellous!

Hilda again started for the Rangitiki ford, in the hope of finding more magic fossils there. In high spirits she cantered along, murmuring, "So saying, with a haughty gesture Sir Bedivere hurled defiance at the uncouth rabble and put his trusty war horse to the gallop."

Hardly had she crossed when she heard a pony's footfalls,

340

and there were those plaguey Higgins kids once again, preparing to follow. "Oh, gollywogs!" said Hilda, and urged Roger up the bank. She would keep ahead of them, make a roundabout turn through the bush by a track she knew, and return to the river. But the little bothers were actually daring to yell at her.

"Hil-da! Hil-da! Come ba-a-ack!"

"Well, I'll be jiggered!" said the superior one. She intended to take no notice and to canter on. As she had felt yesterday, she certainly would have done so, but instead something made her look back. What she saw made her swing Roger round sharply.

The children's pony was floundering in midstream. He had come down on his knees and was trying to rise. Johnny was pulling the reins frantically, and Janie, clinging behind him, was screaming. As Roger and Hilda slithered down the bank again, the pony, struggling to regain his feet in the racing current, sank lower. Hilda urged Roger into the river.

Now the pony was almost under—only his head and neck were showing—he must be lying down. The children were off his back. Johnny, standing, still hung on to reins and mane to steady himself and had an arm around Janie, who was clutching him and half floating. The water would be above her head—it was almost up to Johnny's neck. Suppose Janie got carried down the river?

"All right! I'm coming! Hang on!" shouted Hilda. Her mind was racing. What was best to do? Would Roger behave well and help her? She was sure neither of the youngsters could swim, and there were deep pools just below the ford. The river was really dangerously high.

"Go on, Roger. That's right!" she muttered, as the water swirled over her legs. He splashed sturdily on, snorting his uneasiness as he neared the pony. Hilda leant forward and grasped the pony's reins, trying to lift him. No use—she nearly overbalanced. With hand, foot, and voice she guided Roger closer and, leaning down, managed to put her arm round the little girl.

341

"Janie! Let go of Johnny, and I'll lift you on to my saddle in front."

Janie turned a white, scared face to her, but clung the harder to her brother, who in turn clung desperately to the pony's mane.

"Hurry! You may be drowned if you don't!" yelled Hilda, trying hard to keep Roger in position. She exerted all her strength and pulled the child up until she was seated before her on the saddle. Then Roger plunged away.

What about Johnny? Could he manage to get up behind her if she could make Roger close in again? Or could he wade ashore? He was so small, and the water was up to his shoulders. He seemed unwilling to let go his hold of the now quiet pony.

Hilda at last made Roger turn back again. She leant down to the boy and kicked one foot out of the stirrup. "Here, get your toes in this stirrup and climb behind me. I'll help you."

Johnny turned and tried. But he couldn't do it. The current scared him, Roger wouldn't stand still enough, and the stirrup iron was high. He didn't seem able to haul himself up and stood grasping Hilda's foot and looking miserably like a little drowned rat in the water.

"Janie, you hold on tight. I'm going to get off," Hilda said. With the reins over her arm, she slid carefully down, while Johnny seized the stirrup iron as a sort of lifeline and looked fearfully at the pony, which had begun to struggle again.

Somehow it was managed. Hilda encouraged and boosted, Roger stood better, and Johnny at last scrambled up behind his little sister. Then the big horse, with Hilda, in water above her waist, holding his stirrup, bore his dripping burdens safely to the shore. Janie was howling, Johnny was snuffling, and Hilda was shaking a little with the tension of the last few minutes.

The pony meanwhile had solved his own problem by making fresh efforts to rise, and finally succeeding, he splashed ashore after Roger.

An hour and a half past Hilda's usual time, she arrived home, soaking wet and tired. The bedraggled children had needed to be soothed, lectured, and despatched homeward with directions

to hurry. Hilda had rather enjoyed herself here.

"And what did I tell you yesterday?" she had asked with
awful sternness. "I told you the water was too high for your
pony. It's a wonder his knees aren't cut to pieces."

The two culprits had been quite humble and thankful for
her help—not such bad kids after all. She would buy them some
lollies tomorrow—they were poor and seldom had sweets.

Well, she had managed all right and without any grownup's
help. It was fun to pull a thing off by yourself. "The bold Sir

343

Bedivere had plunged right nobly through the raging stream to the rescue." Thanks to Roger, of course. That gallant steed had stood by like a trump.

Later, after telling her adventure to her father, she remembered the fossil fern. "I bet it *is* lucky, Dad. I've had such a good day today. A million times better than yesterday."

She jumped up and skipped madly about the room, bare brown legs twinkling. She twirled on her toes, lurched dizzily, and almost bumped into the wall. Laughing, she noticed the Poets' tear-off calendar, which she had knocked askew. "Hullo, I never read what the frenzied poet said today. Oh, Longfellow!

> "For the structure that we raise,
>   Time is with materials filled;
> Our todays and yesterdays
>   Are the blocks with which we build."

"Well!" she breathed, struck. "Did you hear that, Dad?"

"I did. What about it?"

"Well, it's funny, you know." She came and plumped down on the arm of his chair. "I was just talking about *my* today and yesterday—one rotten, the other good. I hope this fossil fern really is a *tiki,* as the Maoris say—a sort of charm. Then it will always give me good todays."

Her father laughed, pinching her knee. "I think perhaps it's yourself that gives you those—or doesn't. We build for ourselves to a great extent."

"I s'pose so," said Hilda, her blue eyes upon the beautiful black silhouette of the fossil fern on the mantelpiece. "It would be nice to make and leave as good an impression as that fern did, wouldn't it?"

"All your todays turning into really magnificent, worth-while yesterdays—safe and lovely memories?" suggested Daddy, smiling. "Yes, that would be a real *tiki* indeed. A fern secure for ever within the rock, that nothing could change."

"So the bold Sir Bedivere respectfully harkened to his sire's admonitions and preserved the magic fern *tiki* all the days of his life," murmured Hilda, tweaking her father's ear.

344

Armstrong Sperry

THE FORBIDDEN ISLAND

ILLUSTRATED BY
THE AUTHOR

MAFATU and his dog Uri run away from their home in Hikueru in the South Seas. Mafatu has been accused of being a coward and decides to prove that he is not one. His canoe goes through a big storm, then crashes, throwing him in the boiling surf. He finally swims to safety on an island where he sees an idol and bones and fears cannibals are near.

THE very next morning Mafatu set about building his canoe. He had banked his fire the night before in the natural shelter of a cave, and he resolved never to let the sparks die out. For it was altogether too difficult to make fire with the firestick, and it required too much time. In Hikueru, for that reason, the fires were always kept burning, and it was the special charge of the younger members of a family to see that fuel was ever at hand. Woe unto the small boy who let the family fires go out!

While his breakfast roasted in the coals, the boy cleared the brush away from the base of the great tamanu. There was no wood better for canoe building than this. It was tough, durable, yet buoyant in the water. Mafatu could fell his tree by fire and burn it out, too. Later he would grind an adze out of basalt for the finished work. The adze would take a long time, but he had made them often in Hikueru and he knew just how to go about it. The boy was beginning to realize that the hours he had spent fashioning utensils were to stand him now in good stead. Nets and knives and sharkline, implements, and shell fishhooks—he knew how to make them all. How he had hated those tasks in Hikueru! He was quick and clever with his hands, and now he was grateful for the skill which was his.

The fire crackled and snapped about the base of the tamanu

345

tree. When at length it had eaten well into the trunk, Mafatu climbed aloft and crept cautiously out upon a large branch that overhung the beach. Then taking firm hold of the branches above his head, he began to jump up and down. As the fire ate deeper into the trunk, the tree began to lean under the boy's weight. With a snap and a crash it fell across the sand. As it fell, Mafatu leaped free of the branches, as nimbly as a cat.

"That's enough for today, Uri," he decided. "Tomorrow we'll build our fires down the trunk and start burning it out. When the eaters-of-men come, we will be ready!"

In the meantime there were many other things to do: a fish trap of bamboo, a net of sennit, a fishhook, too, if only he could find some bone. And while the canoe was building, how could Mafatu get out to the distant reef to set his trap, unless first he made a raft of bamboo?

The boy decided that the raft was of first importance. He chose a score or more of fine bamboos as large around as his arm, felling them by fire; then he lashed them together with strips of *purau* bark, making a sturdy raft of two thicknesses. It would serve him well until his canoe should be finished.

As he worked, his mind returned again and again to the wild pig he was determined to kill. How could he go back to Hikueru without a boar's-tooth necklace? Why, that necklace was almost as important as a canoe! For by that token men would know his strength and courage. When the day came that he should leave this high island, he would sail to the north and east. Somewhere in that quarter lay the Cloud of Islands; the great Tuamotu Archipelago which extends across a thousand miles of ocean and ten degrees of latitude. Within those reef-spiked channels floated Hikueru, his homeland. . . . There was no doubt in his mind that he would find it; for Maui, who had led him safe to this shore, would someday guide him home again. But first, Mafatu knew, he must prove himself worthy. Men should never again call him Mafatu, the Boy Who Was Afraid. And Tavana Nui should say with pride: "Here is my son, come home from the sea."

Kivi, the albatross, came and went on his mysterious errands, emerging out of blue space, vanishing into it again. At sundown, regularly, the white bird came wheeling and circling, to alight clumsily on the beach almost at Mafatu's side, while Uri pranced about and greeted his friend after his own fashion. As for Uri, he was having the time of his life; for there were countless sea birds nesting along the shore to be chased and put to rout; and wild goats and pigs in the mountains to make life exciting enough for any dog.

Mafatu had discovered a mulberry tree. He stripped off the bark and removed the inner white lining. Then he wet the fiber and laid it upon a flat stone and set about beating it with a stick of wood. The fiber spread and grew thinner under the persistent beating. The boy added another strip, wet it, and beat it into the first one; then another and another. Soon he had a yard of "cloth" to serve as a *pareu*. It was soft and white, and now at last he was clothed.

"Before I go home I will make a dye of *ava* and paint a fine design on my *pareu*," the boy promised himself. "I must not go back ill-clothed and empty-handed. Men must know that I have conquered the sea and made the land serve me as well."

The days passed in a multitude of tasks that kept Mafatu busy from dawn till dark. His lean-to grew into a three-sided house with bamboo walls and a thatch of palm leaves. The fourth wall was open to the breezes of the lagoon. It was a trim little house, and he was proud of it. A roll of woven mats lay on the floor; there was a shelf in the wall with three bowls cut from coconut shells; bone fishhooks dangled from a peg; there was a coil of tough sennit, many feet long; an extra *pareu* of tapa waterproofed with gum of the *artu* tree, for wet weather. All day long the wind played through the openings in the bamboo walls, and at night lizards scurried through the thatch with soft rustlings.

One morning, wandering far down the beach, Mafatu came upon a sheltered cove. His heart gave a leap of joy; for there, white-gleaming in the sun, was all that remained of the skeleton of a whale. It might not have meant very much to you or to me; but to Mafatu it meant knives and fishhooks galore, splin-

347

tered bone for darts and spears, a shoulder blade for an ax. It was a veritable treasure trove. The boy leaped up and down in his excitement. "Uri!" he shouted. "We're rich! Come—help me drag these bones home!"

His hands seemed all thumbs in his eagerness; he tied as many bones as he could manage into two bundles. One bundle he shouldered himself. The other Uri dragged behind him. And thus they returned to the camp site, weary, but filled with elation. Even the dog seemed to have some understanding of what this discovery meant; or if not, he was at least infected with his master's high spirits. He leaped about like a sportive puppy, yapping until he was hoarse.

Now began the long process of grinding the knife and the ax. Hour after long hour, squatting before a slab of basalt, Mafatu worked and worked, until his hands were raw and blistered and the sweat ran down into his eyes. The knife emerged first, since that was the most imperative. Its blade was ten inches long, its handle a knob of joint. It was sharp enough to cut the fronds of coconut trees, to slice off the end of a green nut. *Ai*, but it was a splendid knife! All Mafatu's skill went into it. It would be a fine weapon as well, the boy thought grimly, as he ground it down to a sharp point. Some sea robber had been breaking into his bamboo trap, and he was going to find out who the culprit was! Probably that old hammerhead shark who was always cruising around. . . . Just as if he owned the lagoon!

Fishing with a line took too long when you were working against time. Mafatu could not afford to have his trap robbed. Twice it had been broken into, the stout bamboos crushed, and the contents eaten. It was the work either of a shark or of an octopus. That was certain. No other fish was strong enough to snap the tough bamboo.

Mafatu's mouth was set in a grim line as he worked away on his knife. That old hammerhead—undoubtedly *he* was the thief! Mafatu had come to recognize him; for every day when the boy went out with his trap, that shark, larger than all the others, was circling around, wary and watchful. The other

348

sharks seemed to treat the hammerhead with deference.

Hunger alone drove Mafatu out to the reef to set his trap. He knew that if he was to maintain strength to accomplish all that lay ahead he must have fish to add to his diet of fruit. But often, as he set his trap far out by the barrier-reef, the hammerhead would approach, roll over slightly in passing, and the cold gleam of its eye filled Mafatu with dread and anger.

"Wait, you!" the boy threatened darkly, shaking his fist at the *ma'o*. "Wait until I have my knife! You will not be so brave then, Ma'o. You will run away when you see it flash."

But the morning that the knife was finished, Mafatu did not feel so brave as he would have liked. He hoped he would never see the hammerhead again. Paddling out to the distant reef, he glanced down from time to time at the long-bladed knife where it hung about his neck by a cord of sennit. It wasn't, after all, such a formidable weapon. It was only a knife made by a boy from a whale's rib.

Uri sat on the edge of the raft, sniffing at the wind. Mafatu always took his dog along, for Uri howled unmercifully if he were left behind. And Mafatu had come to rely upon the companionship of the little yellow dog. The boy talked with the animal as if he were another person, consulting with him, arguing, playing when there was time for play. They were very close, these two.

This morning as they approached the spot where the fish trap was anchored, Mafatu saw the polished dorsal of the hated hammerhead circling slowly in the water. It was like a triangle of black basalt, making a little furrow in the water as it passed.

"*Aiá*, Ma'o!" the boy shouted roughly, trying to bolster up his courage. "I have my knife today, see! Coward who robs traps—catch your own fish!"

The hammerhead approached the raft in leisurely fashion; it rolled over slightly, and its gaping jaws seemed to curve in a yawning grin. Uri ran to the edge of the raft, barking furiously; the hair on the dog's neck stood up in a bristling ridge. The shark, unconcerned, moved away. Then with a whip of its powerful tail it rushed at the bamboo fish trap and seized it in its jaws. Mafatu was struck dumb. The hammerhead shook the trap as a terrier might shake a rat. The boy watched, fascinated, unable to make a move. He saw the muscles work in the fish's neck as the great tail thrashed the water to fury. The trap splintered into bits, while the fish within escaped only to vanish into the shark's mouth. Mafatu was filled with impotent rage. The hours he had spent making that trap—But all he could do was shout threats at his enemy.

Uri was running from one side of the raft to the other, furious with excitement. A large wave sheeted across the reef. At that second the dog's shift in weight tipped the raft at a perilous angle. With a helpless yelp, Uri slid off into the water. Mafatu sprang to catch him, but he was too late.

Instantly the hammerhead whipped about. The wave slewed the raft away. Uri, swimming frantically, tried to regain it. There was desperation in the brown eyes—the puzzled eyes so faithful and true. Mafatu strained forward. His dog. His companion. . . The hammerhead was moving in slowly. A mighty rage stormed through the boy. He gripped his knife. Then he was over the side in a clean-curving dive.

Mafatu came up under his enemy. The shark spun about. Its rough hide scraped the flesh from the boy's shoulder. In that instant Mafatu stabbed. Deep, deep into the white belly. There was a terrific impact. Water lashed to foam. Stunned, gasping, the boy fought for life and air.

It seemed that he would never reach the surface. *Aué*, his lungs would burst! . . . At last his head broke water. Putting his face to the surface, he saw the great shark turn over, fathoms deep. Blood flowed from the wound in its belly. Instantly gray shapes rushed in—other sharks, tearing the wounded hammerhead to pieces.

Uri—where was he? Mafatu saw his dog then. Uri was trying to pull himself up on the raft. Mafatu seized him by the scruff and dragged him up to safety. Then he caught his dog to him and hugged him close, talking to him foolishly. Uri yelped for joy and licked his master's cheek.

It wasn't until Mafatu reached shore that he realized what he had done. He had killed the *ma'o* with his own hand, with naught but a bone knife. He could never have done it for himself. Fear would have robbed his arm of all strength. He had done it for Uri, his dog. And he felt suddenly humble, with gratitude.

Now the adze was completed. Thus the canoe, too, was beginning to take finished shape. It was fifteen feet long, three feet deep, and scarcely a foot wide. Often as he worked, the boy would pause to stand off and admire his craft. It was a beautiful canoe! How proud his father would be. . . . Alas that it was such slow work.

When the hull had been hollowed out, it must be smoothed off with the adze and caulked with *artu* gum. Then a mast must be made of pukatea, straight and true; a sail woven from pandanus. And there was rigging to be made of sennit, tough and strong as wire. The craft would have been finished sooner if only there were not so many things to interfere. Every day, for example, Mafatu climbed the plateau to his lookout. He had not missed one day since he arrived at the island. He knew that when the eaters-of-men came they would sail by day; they would have to beat against the prevailing wind. It would take them many hours to come from Smoking Island. Mafatu would be able to see them from his lookout long before they arrived. If only he could be ready before they came! He must, he must! But that trip up the mountain every day took so much precious time. His canoe would have been finished days ago, but for that.

"Today I will not go," the boy thought, as his adze whirred and chipped. "It takes too long."

Then he sighed and laid down the adze. Caution was the better part of wisdom. He picked up his shining spear with its new shaft and turned toward the trail that led to the high plateau. Uri leaped ahead, his nose keen-pointed to the ground.

This day as Mafatu climbed the rough trail through the jungle, he was preoccupied, lost in his thoughts. His mind was not in this business at all: he was thinking about the rigging of his canoe, planning how he could strengthen it here, tighten it

351

there. Some instinct of danger must have made him pause, warning him to beware. There it was—just a rustle in the undergrowth. Scarcely louder than an insect's hum. The boy drew up tense and listening. Uri had dashed off on some wild-goose chase of his own. The boy stood rooted, alert. He saw it then: a wild boar with lowered head. Eyes red with hate. The flash of its wicked tusks.

The animal pawed the ground suddenly. Its grunting snort broke the stillness. Mafatu knew a blind impulse to turn and run. Then he drew a deep breath and shouted out a challenge:

"*Puaa viri!* Wild pig! I, Mafatu, have come to kill you!"

The boar charged. Over the ground it tore. Foam flew back from its tusks. The boy braced himself. He met the charge with a perfectly timed thrust of the spear. The boar impaled itself, shoulder-deep, upon the spearhead.

Mafatu was thrown off balance, sent spinning headlong. Over and over he rolled. He leaped to his feet in a panic, defenseless. But the boar toppled, gave a convulsive shudder, lay still.

Mafatu was struck dumb. He had killed a wild pig! For a second he could not grasp the wonderful truth of it. Then he leaped wildly into the air, shouting: "*Aué te aué!* I have killed the *puaa!* Do you hear me, Tavana Nui? I, your son, have killed a boar! Ho! Ha!"

Uri came leaping out of the jungle and barked himself hoarse at sight of the pig.

"A fine one you are!" Mafatu joked at his dog. "Where were you when I needed you? Off chasing butterflies, that's you! Was it for this I saved you from the teeth of the *ma'o?* I've a mind not to give you one mouthful of *puaa.*"

Uri hung his head and dropped his tail, then brightened as Mafatu laughed joyously. "Foolish one! Here—drag your share."

The boy made a rude sled of bamboo and loaded the heavy animal onto it. Then he hitched a stout liana about Uri's neck, and the dog threw his weight into the task. The two started home in triumph with their burden, Mafatu singing at the top of his lungs a lusty song of blood and battle. He was all Polynesian now, charged with the ancient fierceness of his race.

Victory coursed through his veins. There was nothing he would not have dared! Nothing he feared! *Aiá,* but life was good!

When they reached the camp site, Mafatu built up a roaring fire and set a pile of stones to heat. While the stones were heating, the boy cleaned the pig at the water's edge, then stuffed its empty belly with succulent *ti* leaves and red bananas. When at last the oven stones were white and smoking, Mafatu dragged the pig back to the fire and rolled it upon the hot *umu.* Then he covered it with layer upon layer of plantain leaves—dozens of them—to hold in the steam and to allow the pork to cook through slowly. Uri leaped about, sniffing at the delicious odors, barking his delight. *Pork!* After weeks of fish and fish and fish, how good it would taste! Besides, fish was not good for dogs. Too many bones. Kivi, no meat eater, looked on calmly, wondering what all this disturbance was about; the bird was content with a coconut that Mafatu split open for him, that he might join in the feast.

Mafatu's mouth fairly watered in anticipation. But even as he settled back to await the feast, his hands were busy: the sun gleamed brightly on the curving tusks that already he was making into a necklace. They formed almost a complete circle and were as white as bleached coral. *Aué!* How men's tongues would chatter when they saw this fine necklace! Even Grandfather's had been no finer.

A strange picture on that lonely beach under the palms: a pig roasting on a fire; a boy lean and brown and whip-strong, making a boar's-tooth necklace; a prancing yellow dog; a calm, wide-winged albatross pecking at a coconut.

Mafatu slipped the necklace about his throat, and he could fairly feel its magic charging him with strength! He pulled the oven stones away from the *umu,* and there lay the pig, golden, glowing, done to a turn. Rich juices ran in little rivulets down its sides. And as Mafatu ate, one thought alone filled his mind, overshadowing even his enjoyment of this rare feast: soon, soon now he would be ready. He had killed the *ma'o.* The *puaa,* too. His canoe would soon be completed. And then—then he would return to Hikueru!

354

The canoe was finished.

Mafatu lashed the tough *purau* outrigger into place with hands that trembled. The woven sail was complete and ready; the rigging strong as wire. There—it was all over! The boy could hardly wait to get his craft into water.

Placing logs under the curving stem, he gave a shove and a push. The canoe stirred, moved forward, quick with life. Another shove and the craft slid into the lagoon. And there it floated lightly, easily as a gull poised for flight. Mafatu stood back and surveyed it with shining eyes. He could hardly believe that all these weeks of labor were at an end. Suddenly he was quiet. With lifted head he offered up the prayer with which all ships were launched at Hikueru:

> "Taaroa, Mighty One!
> My thanks to you
> In this task completed.
> Guide it on your back
> To safe harbor.
> Taaroa, *e!*"

The boy leaped into the stern, picked up the paddle, and ran up the sail. Uri sprang into the bow, yelping for very joy. Kivi sailed far overhead on widespread wings. The breeze caught the sail, swelled it to a golden curve. The outrigger leaned at a sharp angle and sped ahead toward the distant reef. Spray flew back from the prow, and Mafatu's heart beat high. He let out the sheet, wrapped the sennit rope around his foot, and gripped the steering paddle with both hands. He was filled with pride in his canoe. Never had he been as happy as in this moment.

Out toward the black reef, closer and closer the canoe skimmed on a wide arc of speed. It was late afternoon and the sun was setting in a blaze of glory, but the boy was reluctant to turn back. He knew that he should have climbed to the lookout that morning. This was the first day he had neglected that duty. But the temptation to complete his canoe had been too great. Tomorrow at daybreak he would climb the plateau for the last time. And then—and then Hikueru!

As the little craft skimmed out toward the barrier-reef, the thunder of the surf increased in volume to an overwhelming sound. Waves, born far south in the Antarctic ice fields—the home of all waves—broke their backs upon this coral rampart. Gathering far out, they charged the reef: sea horses with flinging manes of foam. The surf shot skyward, and above its mist sea gulls swooped and darted. The reef thunder no longer filled Mafatu with unease. He had lived too close to it these past weeks. Out here, half a mile from shore, detached from all security of the land, he had come to believe that at last he had established a truce with Moana, the Sea God. His skill against the ocean's might.

The boy skirted along the edge of the reef, lowered his sail, and dropped overboard the lump of coral which served as anchor. Then he took out his fishline and baited the hook with a piece of crab meat. He wanted to enjoy to the full this new sensation of confidence in himself, this freedom from the sea's threat. He looked back at the land fondly, but without longing. The high peak, purple in the waning light, stood somber against the sky. The valleys were shadowed with mystery. All these weeks he had lived close to this island and been grateful for its bounty. But he had been born on an atoll—a low island—and all his life had been spent in the spaciousness of open sea and wind-swept palms. There was something gloomy and oppressive in this high island. The reef—this was a part of his heritage. The sea, at last, was as much his element as the land.

The realization flooded through him in a warm tide of content. He lowered his fishline, fastened it to the mid-thwart, and looked deep down into the clear water. He saw a scarlet rock-cod materialize, hang in the shadow of the canoe, motionless save for the slight movement of its gills. With a sudden flip of the tail it vanished.

How fantastic was that undersea world! The boy saw branching staghorn corals, as large as trees, through which jellyfishes floated like a film of fog. He saw shoals of tiny mullet, miniature arrowheads—the whole school scarcely larger than a child's hand. A conger eel drew its ugly head back within a shadowy cavern.

356

Here beside the wall of reef Mafatu's bamboo fish trap hung suspended; before he returned to shore he would empty the trap. It had been undisturbed since the hammerhead was killed, and each day had yielded up a good supply of mullet or cray-fish or lobsters. Here the wall of living coral descended to the lagoon floor. Its sides were pierced with caves of darkness whose mystery the boy felt no desire to explore. Far below, perhaps forty feet, the sandy floor of the lagoon was clear and green in the dappled light. A parrot fish emerged from the gloom, nibbled at Mafatu's bait, then vanished.

"*Aué!* These fish must be well fed. My piece of crab meat does not tempt them."

The boy decided to give it up and content himself with the fish in the bamboo trap. He leaned over the gunwale and pulled it up out of water. Through the openings in the cage he could see three lobsters, blue-green and fat.What luck! But as he dragged the heavy, wet trap over the gunwale, the fiber cord that fastened his knife about his neck caught on an end of bamboo. The trap slipped. The cord snapped. The knife fell into the water.

With dismay the boy watched it descend. It spiraled rapidly, catching the sunlight as it dropped down, down to the sandy bottom. And there it lay, just under the edge of a branching staghorn. Mafatu eyed it uncertainly. His knife—the knife he had labored so hard to shape. . . He knew what he ought to do: he should dive and retrieve it. To make another knife so fine would take days. Without it he was seriously handicapped. He *must* get his knife! But . . .

The reef-wall looked dark and forbidding in the fading light. Its black holes were the home of the giant *feké*—the octopus. . . . The boy drew back in sudden panic. He had never dived as deep as this. It might be even deeper than he thought, for the clarity of the water confused all scale of distance. The knife looked so very near, and yet . . . There it lay, gleaming palely.

The boy gazed down at it with longing. He remembered the morning he had found the whale's skeleton; the first one he had ever seen. Surely Maui, God of the Fishermen, had sent the whale there to die for Mafatu's use! The long hours that had gone into the making of the knife. . . It had saved Uri's life, too. And now Uri, in the bow of the canoe, was looking at his master with eyes so puzzled and true.

Mafatu drew a deep breath. How could he abandon his knife? Would Maui (the thought chilled him) think him a coward? Was he still Mafatu, the Boy Who Was Afraid?

He leaped to his feet, gave a brave hitch to his *pareu*. Then he was overside in the water. He clung for a moment to the gunwale, breathing deeply. Inhaling, then releasing the air in a long-drawn whistle, he prepared his lungs for the pressure of the depths. Many times he had seen the pearl divers do it. In the canoe lay a coral weight fastened to a length of sennit. Mafatu took this weight and held the cord in his toes. With a final deep breath he descended feet-first, allowing the weight to pull him downward. At about twenty feet he released the weight, turned over, and swam for the bottom.

Here the water was cool and green. The sunlight filtered from above in long, oblique bands. Painted fishes fled before him. He saw a giant *pahua,* a clam shell, five feet across and taller than he: its open lips waiting to snap shut upon fish or man. Green fronds waved gently as if in some submarine wind. A shadow moved above the boy's head, and he glanced upward in alarm: only a sand shark cruising harmlessly. . . . An eel, like a cold waving ribbon, touched his leg and was gone.

The knife—there it lay. How sharp and bright it looked. Now the boy's hands were upon it. He seized it and sprang upward toward the light.

In that second a whiplash shot out from a cavern at his back: a lash like a length of rubber hose. The boy caught the flash of vacuum cups that lined its under surface. Panic stabbed him. The *feké*—the octopus! Another lash whipped forth and encircled his waist. It drew taut. Then the octopus came forth from its den to face and kill its prey.

Mafatu saw a purplish globe of body, eyes baleful and fixed as fate; a parrot-mouth, cruel and beaked, that worked and wabbled. . . . Another whiplash encircled the boy's leg. The

In that instant Mafatu stabbed.

knife— Desperately Mafatu stabbed for one of the eyes. Then darkness clouded the water as the octopus siphoned out his venom. There in submarine gloom a boy fought for his life with the most dreaded monster of the deep. He could feel the sucking pressure of those terrible tentacles. . . . His wind was almost gone.

Blindly Mafatu stabbed again, this time for the other eye. The blow, so wildly driven, went true. The terrible grip relaxed, slacked. The tentacles grew limp. Then Mafatu was springing upward, upward, drawn up toward light and air and life.

When he reached the canoe he had hardly enough strength to cling to the gunwale. But cling he did, his breath coming in tearing gasps. Uri, beside himself, dashed from one end of the canoe to the other, crying piteously. Slowly strength returned to the boy's limbs, warmth to his chilled soul. He dragged himself into the canoe and collapsed on the floor. He lay there, as in a trance, for what seemed an eternity.

The sun had set. Dusk was rising from the surface of the sea. Mafatu struggled upright and peered cautiously over the side of the canoe. The inky water had cleared. Down there, forty feet below, the octopus lay like a broken shadow. The white cups of its tentacles gleamed dully in the watery gloom. With sharkline and hook the boy fished up the *feké's* body. As he dragged it into the canoe one of the tentacles brushed his ankle. Its touch was clammy and of a deathly chill. Mafatu shuddered and shrank away. He had eaten squid and small octopi ever since he was born, but he knew that he could not have touched a mouthful of this monster. He raised his spear and plunged it again and again into the body of his foe, shouting aloud a savage paean of triumph. A thousand years of warrior-heritage sounded in his cry.

Once more Maui had protected him! What to do with the *feké?* The boy decided that he would cut off the tentacles; they would dry and shrink, but they would be still of prodigious size, and the people of Hikueru would say: "See, Mafatu killed the *feké* single-handed. *Aué te aué!*"

Dusk, almost in an instant, deepened into night. As Mafatu

turned the nose of his canoe toward shore, the first stars were appearing, bright and close and friendly. There was the Southern Cross, pointing toward the end of the world. . . . The lagoon was a black mirror dusted with star-shine. Far below in the dark waters, illuminated fishes moved and had their being: meteors, galaxies, constellations under the sea. The boy saw a line of light, narrow as a blade, as the rare *pala* flashed away in its everlasting quest. A sand shark, phosphorescent ghost, darted after the *pala*—seized it in a swirl of luminous mist. The mist faded slowly. It was blood. Mysterious life forces were completing their cycle in those dark depths, even as on the earth and in the air above. This sea—no more to be feared than earth or air: only another element for man to conquer. And he, Mafatu, had killed the *feké. Aué te aué!*

As he dipped his paddle with a swinging rhythm, the rhythm of his thought swung in unison: "Tomorrow I shall start home! Tomorrow, tomorrow! *Aiá!*"

The very thought of it set him aquiver. "Tomorrow, tomorrow!" he had been here so long. . . .

He dragged the canoe up on the beach, placed the logs under

the curving stem so that he might launch it easily on the morrow. He would never need to climb the high plateau to the lookout again. Let the eaters-of-men come!

As Mafatu waited for his supper to cook, he set about preparing for his homeward journey; he would start at daybreak with the ebbing tide. He would be ready. He filled bamboo containers with fresh water, sealed them with leaves that were gummed into place, watertight and secure. Then he stored them carefully in the canoe. He prepared a *poi* of bananas and sealed it, likewise, into containers; there it would ferment and sour and become delicious to the taste. Then he picked a score or more of green drinking nuts and flung them into the canoe. And as he trotted back and forth across the beach and his supper steamed on the fire, one thought alone, like an insistent drum beat, echoed in the boy's heart: "Tomorrow I shall start home! Tomorrow, tomorrow!"

Never again need he hang his head before his people. He had fought the sea for life and won. He had sustained himself by his own wits and skill. He had faced loneliness and danger and death, if not without flinching, at least with courage. He had been, sometimes, deeply afraid, but he had faced fear and faced it down. Surely that could be called courage.

When he lay down to sleep that night there was a profound thankfulness in his heart. "Tavana Nui," he whispered, "my father—I want you to be proud of me." . . .

He fell into a heavy, dreamless sleep.

Before dawn he was awakened by a sound of measured booming, like the beating of a supernatural drum. Thump-thump THUMP! Thump-thump THUMP! It rose above the thunder of the reef, solemn and majestic, filling the night with thunder.

Instantly awake, listening with every sense, Mafatu sat upright on the mats. Far out on the reef the seas burst and shot upward like sheeted ghosts in the moonlight. There it came again: Thump-thump THUMP! Thump-thump THUMP! Steady as a pulse, beating in the heart of darkness. . . .

And then Mafatu knew. The eaters-of-men had come.

A chill sweat broke out over Mafatu's body. He crouched there listening, unable for the moment to make a single movement. The rhythmic message that boomed across the mountain brought him a message of doom. Thump-thump THUMP! It shivered along his nerves, setting his hair on edge.

Warily, moving with utmost caution, Mafatu crept out of the house. The beach was softly brilliant in the light of the waning moon. Any figure moving along the sand he could have seen instantly. He stopped, every nerve strung like a wire: the beach was deserted, the jungle silent and black with mystery. The boy rose to his feet. Swift as a shadow he turned into the undergrowth where the trail led to the high plateau. The jungle had never seemed so dark, so ominous with peril. The tormented roots of the *mapé* trees clutched at him. Lianas tripped him. Tree-ferns, ghostly in the half-light, rustled about him as he passed, their muted hush seeming to say: "Not yet, Mafatu, not yet." . . .

By the time he reached the plateau he was breathless and panting. He dropped to his knees and crawled forward, an inch or two at a time. One false move might spell destruction. But he had to know, he *had* to know. . . .

Thump-thump THUMP!

The measured booming grew louder with every inch that he advanced. Now it pounded in his ears, reverberated through his body, thrummed his nerves. Somewhere below in darkness, black hands drew forth from hollowed logs a rhythm that was a summation of life, a testament of death. Uri crept close to his master's side, the hair ridging on his neck, his growl drowned in the thunder.

Now the boy could see into the cleared circle of the Sacred Place. Leaping fires lighted a scene that burned itself forever into his memory. Fires blazed against the basalt cliffs, spurts of flame that leaped and danced, showers of sparks borne off on the back of the night wind. Now a deep wild chanting rose above the booming of the drums. From his vantage point Mafatu saw six war canoes drawn up on the beach. Mighty canoes they were, with high-curving stems and decorations of white shell that caught the firelight in savage patterns. But what held the boy's eyes in awful trance were the figures, springing and leaping about the flames: figures as black as night's own face, darting, shifting, bounding toward the sky. The eaters-of-men. . . Firelight glistened on their oiled bodies, on flashing spears and bristling decorations. High above the drums' tattoo rose the mournful note of the conch shells, an eerie wailing, like the voices of souls lost in interstellar space.

Mafatu saw that the savages were armed with ironwood war clubs—clubs studded with sharks' teeth or barbed with the sting-ray's spike. Zigzags of paint streaked their bodies. And towering above all, the great stone idol looked down with sightless eyes, just as it had looked for untold centuries.

Mafatu, lying there on the ledge of basalt, watched the strange scene, powerless to move, and he felt Doom itself breathing chill upon his neck. He drew back from the edge of the cliff. He must flee! In that very instant he heard a crashing in the undergrowth, not twenty yards away. A guttural shout ripped the darkness. The boy flung a desperate glance over his shoulder. Four black figures were tearing toward him through the jungle; he could see them now.

He turned and ran blindly down the trail whence he had come. Slipping, sliding, stumbling, his breath all but choking in his throat. He felt like a man drowning in ice-cold water. He felt as he had sometimes felt in dreams, fleeing on legs that were weighted. Only one thought gave him courage as he ran: his canoe, ready and waiting. His canoe. If only he could reach it, shove it into the water before the savages overtook him. Then he would be safe. . . .

He knew this trail as he knew the back of his hand. That knowledge gave him an advantage. He could hear his pursuers, slipping, stumbling through the brush, shouting threats in a language strange to his ears. But there was no mistaking the meaning of their words.

On the boy dashed, fleet as an animal. Thorns and vines clutched at him. Once he tripped and sprawled headlong. But he was up and away in an instant. Through the trees he caught a glimpse of white beach, and his heart surged. Then he was speeding across the sand, Uri at his heels.

The canoe was at the lagoon's edge. The boy fell upon the thwart, shoved the craft into the water. The logs under the stem rolled easily. In that second, the black men, yelling wildly, broke from the jungle and dashed across the beach. Mafatu was not a minute too soon. He leaped aboard and ran up the sail. The savages rushed after him into the shallows. A gust of wind filled the sail. It drew smartly. Now the men were swimming. One of them, in the lead, reached to lay hold of the outrigger. His black hand clutched the *purau* pole. The canoe slacked. Mafatu could see the gleam of bared teeth. The boy lifted the paddle and cracked it down. . . . With a groan the man dropped back into the water. The canoe, freed, skimmed out toward the barrier-reef.

The savages stopped, turned back toward shore. Then they were running back to the trail that led across the island, shouting to their fellows as they ran. Mafatu knew that it was only a question of minutes until the whole pack would be aroused and in pursuit. But he had the advantage of a head start and a light craft, while their canoes would have to beat around the southern point of the island before they could catch up with him. If only the breeze held. . . Mafatu remembered then that the canoes he had seen drawn up on the beach had not been sailing canoes. There were strong arms to propel those black canoes, to overtake him if they could.

Mafatu's canoe, so slim and light, sped like a zephyr across the lagoon. The tide was on the ebb, churning in its race through the passage into the outer ocean. The boy gripped the steering paddle and offered up a prayer. Then he was caught in the rip-tide. The outrigger dashed through the passage, a chip on a torrent. The wind of the open sea rushed to greet it. The sail filled; the outrigger heeled over. Mafatu scrambled to windward to lend his weight for ballast. He was off! Homeward, homeward. . .

Soon, rising above the reef thunder, the boy could hear a measured sound of savage chanting. They were after him!

364

Looking back over his shoulder, he could see the dark shapes of the canoes rounding the southern headland. Moonlight shone on half a hundred wet paddles as they dipped and rose to the rhythm of the chant. It was too dark to see the eaters-of-men themselves, but their wild song grew ever more savage as they advanced.

The breeze was almost dead aft. The crab-claw sail swelled smooth and taut, rigid as a block of silver against the sky. The little canoe, so artfully built, ran with swell and favoring wind, laying knots behind her. She was as fleet and gracile as the following gulls. But the eaters-of-men were strong paddlers with death in their hearts. Their *motu tabu* had been profaned by a stranger. Vengeance powered their muscles. They were tireless. On they came.

The wind dropped. Imperceptibly at first. Sensing it, Mafatu whistled desperately for Maui. "Maui *é!* Do not desert me," he prayed. "This last time—lend me your help."

Soon the black canoes were so close that the boy could see the shine of dark bodies, the glint of teeth, and flash of ornament. If the wind died, he was lost. . . . Closer, closer the canoes advanced. There were six of them, filled each with ten warriors. Some of them leaped to their feet, brandished their clubs, shouted at the boy across the water. They were a sight to quake the stoutest heart. With every second they were cutting down the distance which separated their canoes from Mafatu's.

Then the wind freshened. Just a puff, but enough. Under its impetus the little canoe skimmed ahead while the boy's heart gave an upward surge of thanks. Maui had heard his prayer and answered.

Day broke over the wide Pacific.

There were the six black canoes, paddles flashing, now gaining, now losing. The boy was employing every art and wile of sailing that he knew. As long as the wind held he was safe. He managed his little craft to perfection, drawing from it every grace of speed in flight.

He knew that with coming night the wind might drop, and then— He forced the thought from his mind. If the wind deserted him it would mean that Maui had deserted him, too. But the savages would never get him! It would be Moana, the Sea God's turn. The boy looked down into the blue depths overside, and his smile was grim: "Not yet, Moana," he muttered fiercely. "You haven't won. Not yet."

But with falling night the wind still held. Darkness rose up from the sea, enveloping the world. The stars came out clear and bright. The boy searched among them for some familiar constellation to steer by. Should it be *Mata Iki*—Little Eyes? Would *Mata Iki* lead him back safe to Hikueru? And then he saw, and knew: there, blazing bravely, were the three stars of the Fishhook of Maui. Maui—his sign. Those were his stars to steer by. They would lead him home. In that moment he was aware that the chanting of his pursuers had become fainter, steadily diminishing. At first he could not believe it. He listened intently. Yes—there was no doubt about it: as the breeze freshened, the sound grew fainter each passing moment.

The boy quenched his thirst, ate a scrap of *poi*, fought against sleep as the night waxed and waned.

By daybreak the chanting had ceased altogether. There was no sign of the canoes upon the broad expanse of the sea. The sunburst marched across the swinging waters. Far off an albatross caught the light of gold on its wings. Was it Kivi? Mafatu could not tell. The wind held fresh and fair. The high island had vanished over the curve of the sea, and the eaters-of-men had vanished with it. But now the great ocean current that had carried Mafatu so willingly away from Hikueru was set dead against him.

He put his little craft first on one tack, then on another. As the long hours passed, it seemed as if he were making no headway at all, even though the canoe still cut smartly through the water. There was a drift and pull that appeared to make a forward gain impossible. Was it Moana, the implacable one, trying to prevent Mafatu from returning to his homeland?

"Perhaps," the boy thought wearily, "Maui is not yet ready for me to return. Is there still a shadow of fear in my heart? Is that it?" He was tired now in every nerve and sinew, tired in

the marrow of his bones, tired of struggle.

The long hours passed slowly while the sun climbed. Mafatu lashed the steering paddle and slept fitfully. Uri lay in the shadow of the sail. The sun sank in a conflagration like the death of a world. Night came and fled. Dawn rose in a burst of flame, and still Mafatu's canoe skimmed across the sea currents, now on this tack, now on that.

He was to learn in the hours to come that all days, all time, would be like that: hours of blasting heat, of shattering sunlight; nights of fitful respite and uneasy sleep. Only the sea and the sky, the sea and the sky. A bird now and then, a fish leaping from the sea, a boy in a frail canoe. That was all.

As one day dragged into another, Mafatu scanned the heavens for some hint of rain. Storm, anything would have been a welcome relief to this blasting monotony, to this limitless circle of sea. His store of *poi* vanished. The coconuts likewise. His water was being guarded, drop by drop. But there would come a moment when the last drop must be taken, and then. . .

The season of storm was long past. The days, as they came,

were cloudless and untroubled. Each day broke like a clap of
thunder and night fell softly as a footfall. The sea was sparkling
and benign. The sun's rays were unbroken in their violence. At
night the Fishhook of Maui twinkled down like friendly eyes,
luring Mafatu on; and torch-fishes darted up from the lower
depths while the black waters gleamed with strange lights.
Then gradually as the canoe entered some other current of the
sea, the wind slackened and diminished, this wind that had
blown for him so long. Now the sail began to slat and bang in
the dead air. The canoe drifted on the slow, majestic tide. The
ceaseless heave and surge of the sea's dark breast lulled the boy
to half-sleeping rest; the murmur of the waters playing about
the prow sounded like his mother's reassuring voice.

Each sun as it rose seemed hotter than that of the preceding
day. Now the face of the ocean was a disk of blazing copper.
Masses of seaweed, heavy with the eggs of fishes, floated on the
sluggish tide, seeming to clutch at the canoe, to hold it back
from its destination. Hikueru, the Cloud of Islands—did they
really exist? Were they not, like the chambered nautilus, only
an iridescence dreamed by the sea? Sharks were beginning to
appear—as they did always about a craft becalmed. One dorsal
fin, larger than the others, followed the canoe in leisurely paral-
lel; just far enough distant so that Mafatu could not see the
body that supported it. But he knew from the size of the dorsal
that it must be a tiger-shark. . . . It began at length to play upon
his nerves and set him jumpy. He scarcely dared now, at night,
to lash his steering paddle and sleep.

The sail slatted and banged. The boy paddled through the
long hours, paddled until the muscles of his arms and shoulders
ached in agony and every sinew cried in protest. And at night,
when darkness brought blessed release from the sun, there was
always the Fishhook of Maui leading him on. But now when
the boy looked up at the ancient constellation, doubt lay heavy
on his heart. Hikueru—where was it? Where was it? The sea
gave back no answer.

"Maui," the boy whispered, "have you deserted me? Have
you looked into my heart and found me wanting?"

And suddenly, like the snapping of a string, he was overwhelmed with despair. Maui *had* deserted him. It was Moana, the Sea God's turn. The sea looked dark and cool and inviting. Little wavelets lapped and chuckled about the hull like beckoning hands. He looked overside. Deep down in those cool depths it seemed to him that he could see faces . . . his mother's, perhaps. . . . He dashed his hand across his eyes. Had the sun stricken him daft? Had he been touched by moon-madness? Then a wave of overpowering anger brought him to his knees: anger at this dark element, this sea, which would destroy him if it could. His voice was thick and hoarse, his throat bursting with rage.

"Moana, you Sea God!" he shouted violently. "*You!* You destroyed my mother. Always you have tried to destroy me. Fear of you has haunted my sleep. Fear of you turned my people against me. But now"—he choked; his hands gripped his throat to stop its hot burning—"now I no longer fear you, Sea!" His voice rose to a wild note. He sprang to his feet, flung back his head, spread wide his arms in defiance. "Do you hear me, Moana? I am not afraid of you! Destroy me—but I laugh at you. Do you hear? *I laugh!*"

His voice, cracked but triumphant, shattered the dead air. He sank back on his haunches, shaking with spasms of ragged laughter. It racked his body, left him spent and gasping on the floor of the canoe. Uri, whimpering softly, crept to his master's side.

Off to the northeast a haze of light glowed up from the sea. Sometimes the lagoon of an atoll throws up just such a glow. It is the reflection of the lagoon upon the lower sky. Lifting his head, the boy watched it with dulled eyes, uncomprehending at first.

"*Te mori,*" he whispered at last, his voice a thread of awe. "The lagoon-fire."

There came a whir and fury in the sky above, a beat of mighty wings: an albatross, edged with light, circled above the canoe. It swooped low, its gentle, questing eyes turned upon the boy and his dog. Then the bird lifted in its effortless flight,

flew straight ahead and vanished into the lagoon-fire. And then Mafatu knew. Hikueru, his homeland, lay ahead. Kivi. . .

A strangled cry broke from the boy. He shut his eyes tight, and there was a taste of salt, wet upon his lips.

The crowd assembled upon the beach watched the small canoe slip through the reef-passage. It was a fine canoe, artfully built. The people thought at first that it was empty. Silence gripped them, and a chill of awe touched them like a cold hand. Then they saw a head lift above the gunwale, a thin body struggle to sit upright, clinging to the mid-thwart.

"*Aué te aué!*" The cry went up from the people in a vast sigh. So they might speak if the sea should give up its dead.

But the boy who dropped overside into the shallows and staggered up the beach was flesh and blood, albeit wasted and thin. They saw that a necklace of boar's teeth shone upon his chest; a splendid spear flashed in his hand. Tavana Nui, the Great Chief of Hikueru, went forward to greet the stranger. The brave young figure halted, drew itself upright.

"My father," Mafatu cried thickly, "I have come home."

The Great Chief's face was transformed with joy. This brave figure, so thin and straight, with the fine necklace and the flashing spear and courage blazing from his eyes—his son? The man could only stand and stare and stare, as if he could not believe his senses. And then a small yellow dog pulled himself over the gunwale of the canoe, fell at his master's feet. Uri. . . Far overhead an albatross caught a light of gold on its wings. Then Tavana Nui turned to his people and cried: "Here is my son come home from the sea. Mafatu, Stout Heart. A brave name for a brave boy!"

Mafatu swayed where he stood. "My father, I . . ."

Tavana Nui caught his son as he fell.

It happened many years ago, before the traders and missionaries first came into the South Seas, while the Polynesians were still great in numbers and fierce of heart. But even today the people of Hikueru sing this story in their chants and tell it over the evening fires.

Index